PENGUIN BOOKS

THE PENGUIN BOOK OF SCOTTISH FOLKTALES

Neil Philip was born in York in 1955. He now lives in Oxfordshire, where he divides his time between writing and research and his work as editorial director of a small publishing company. His consuming interest is folk narrative, but he has also written on children's literature and on English social history. His essays and reviews have appeared in numerous journals, including *The Times*, *The Times Educational Supplement*, *The Times Literary Supplement* and *Folklore*, of which he is a former reviews editor. Among his other books are *A Fine Anger: A Critical Introduction to the Work of Alan Garner* (1981), winner of the ChLA Literary Criticism Book Award; a country anthology, *Between Earth and Sky* (Penguin, 1984); *The Tale of Sir Gawain* (1987), shortlisted for the Emil/Kurt Maschler Award; and *The Cinderella Story* (Penguin, 1989). He has also edited *English Folktales*, published by Penguin. His *A New Treasury of Poetry* (1990), illustrated by John Lawrence, was hailed by *The Times* as 'among the great anthologies for the young'. He is currently editing *The New Oxford Book of Children's Verse*.

THE PENGUIN BOOK OF
SCOTTISH FOLKTALES

❄

EDITED BY NEIL PHILIP

PENGUIN BOOKS

PENGUIN BOOKS

Published by the Penguin Group
Penguin Books Ltd, 27 Wrights Lane, London w8 5tz, England
Penguin Books USA Inc., 375 Hudson Street, New York, New York 10014, USA
Penguin Books Australia Ltd, Ringwood, Victoria, Australia
Penguin Books Canada Ltd, 10 Alcorn Avenue, Toronto, Ontario, Canada m4v 3b2
Penguin Books (NZ) Ltd, 182–190 Wairau Road, Auckland 10, New Zealand

Penguin Books Ltd, Registered Offices: Harmondsworth, Middlesex, England

First published 1995
1 3 5 7 9 10 8 6 4 2

The acknowledgements on p. xiii constitute an extension of this copyright page

The moral right of the editor has been asserted

Typeset by Datix International Ltd, Bungay, Suffolk

Printed in England by Clays Ltd, St Ives plc
Set in 10.5/12pt Monophoto Garamond

For Donald McFarlan

CONTENTS

CONTENTS

3: HISTORICAL TRADITIONS

4: JESTS AND ANECDOTES

5: TALES OF THE SUPERNATURAL

6: THE SECRET COMMONWEALTH

CONTENTS

ACKNOWLEDGEMENTS

The editor and publishers are grateful to the following for permission to reproduce copyright material.

The Duke of Argyll, for 'The Appin Murder'

The Duke of Atholl, for 'Lasair Gheug, the King of Ireland's Daughter' and 'Go Boldly, Lady, and Don't go Boldly, Lady'

Catherine Clark, for 'The Three Feathers' and 'Johnnie in the Cradle'

Maurice Fleming, for 'The Ghost of Gairnside'

Mrs Kenneth H. Jackson, for 'Four Local Anecdotes from Harris'

D. A. MacDonald, for 'The Three Shirts of Bog Cotton'

John MacInnes, for 'The Tale of Michael Scot'

Alasdair Stewart, for 'The Maraiche Mairneal'

Bryce White, for 'The Black Laird' and 'The Man in the Boat'

Duncan Williamson, for 'Daft Sandy and the Mare's Egg'

Every effort has been made to contact or trace copyright holders. The publishers will be glad to make good in future editions any errors or omissions.

INTRODUCTION

In his autobiographical *My Schools and Schoolmasters* (1854), the journeyman mason turned geologist and man of letters Hugh Miller recalls evenings in a mason's barrack in the 1820s. The general gossip and talk would sometimes give way to song or story, and among all the company 'there was in especial one story-teller whose powers of commanding attention were very great'. This man, who would be utterly lost to human recall were it not that one of his companions nurtured literary ambitions, can stand for many whose storytelling gift has left no trace in any written record:

> He was a middle-aged Highlander, not very skilful as a workman, and but indifferently provided with English; and as there usually attaches a nickname to persons in the humbler walk that are marked by any eccentricity of character, he was better known among his brother workmen as Jock Mo-ghoal, i.e. John my Darling, than by his proper name. Of all Jock Mo-ghoal's stories Jock Mo-ghoal was himself the hero; and certainly most wonderful was the invention of the man. As recorded in his narratives, his life was one long epic poem, filled with strange and startling adventure, and furnished with an extraordinary machinery of the wild and supernatural; and though all knew that Jock made imagination supply, in his histories, the place of memory, not even Ulysses or Aeneas – men who, unless very much indebted to their poets, must have been of a similar turn – could have attracted more notice at the courts of Alcinous or Dido, than Jock in the barrack. The workmen used, on the mornings after his great narratives, to look one another full in the face, and ask, with a smile rather incipient than fully manifest, whether 'Jock was na perfectly wonderfu' last nicht?'

Jock's tales, marvellous adventures full of extravagant improvisation, represent a kind of folktale which has rarely been adequately recorded. Miller tells us that 'getting into conversation with individuals of the more thoroughly lapsed classes of our larger towns, I have found that a faculty of extemporary fabrication was almost the only one which I could calculate on finding among them in a state of vigorous activity': but such stories, among the least respectable and least classifiable of all oral narratives, have had no books devoted to them, no assiduous researchers to trace their formal characteristics or their inter-related motifs.

The folktale, being an oral form, is essentially a performance art. Only in the nineteenth century did scholars begin to take it seriously enough to try to collect tales, and strive to preserve the very words of the narrators. Only in this century, with tape recorders and video film, has it become possible to consider intonation, pace, gesture. No one has found a way to record atmosphere, or the collective feeling of storyteller and audience. And, of course, no one has found a way of preventing the act of recording a story, whether on tape or film or by laborious dictation, from distorting it.

These comments – obvious enough, perhaps – are nevertheless worth making. To the literate mind, it is fatally easy to assume that the record we happen to have of a particular narration is either the 'correct' version or, even more mistakenly, a debased or corrupted version of some original ideal. It is not. The tale is made afresh each time it is told. Each telling is a new creation, an exchange of energies between storyteller and story, creativity and tradition. In the endless rehearsal and reappraisal of tradi-tional themes, each telling is as valid as the last, or the next.

I have chosen in this book stories which appealed to me as stories, with a bias towards those in which individual characteris-tics of the narrator have been preserved. But in almost every case there are several, sometimes many, Scottish variants or analogues which another editor might have chosen instead.

For each tale I have given my source, the narrator if known, and, where relevant, a tale-type number. There is nothing forbid-ding or mysterious about these numbers. They are a tool of classification by plot structure, developed by the Finn, Antti Aarne, and refined by the American, Stith Thompson. By using them, one may trace comparative versions and variations of a traditional tale throughout the world. My numbers refer to two books: *The Types of the Folktale*, by Aarne and Thompson, and *The Migratory Legends*, by Reidar Christiansen. Thus 'The Milk-White Doo', which is a version of the international tale-type best-known to us through the Grimms' 'Juniper Tree', can be cited as AT720 'My Mother Slew Me, My Father Ate Me'. A legend from the same source, 'Short-Hoggers of Whittinghame', can be cited as ML4025 'The Child Without a Name'. The ML numbers of *The Migratory Legends* are continuous with the AT numbers of *The Types of the Folktale*.

The plot content and structure of a folk narrative are by no means the only important things about it; nor can all oral tales be adequately categorized by type numbers. Nevertheless, the numbers offer a marvellous short-cut to the wealth of comparative material. Unfortunately there is no separate Scottish index, and Ernest Baughman's *Type and Motif Index of the Folktales of England and North America* covers Scotland very patchily. But many tradition areas do have their own indexes: of particular interest in this context is Seán Ó Súilleabháin and Reidar Christiansen, *The Types of the Irish Folktale*. In addition to the standard indexes, many modern folktale collections, such as Katharine Briggs, *A Dictionary of British Folk-Tales in the English Language*, are also indexed by tale-type.

But if the folktale is an international art, it is also a national, a local, and a personal one. The aims and artistry of the storyteller, the social setting and function of the storytelling, the imaginative impact of the story, are all defined by unique pressures. While the dynamics of Scottish storytelling are far too complex to clarify in a short introduction, it is nevertheless worth while sketching in some of the background to the texts that follow.

The first thing to say is that Scotland has two distinct storytelling traditions, in Gaelic and in Scots. The Gaelic, Highland, tradition has many affinities with Irish storytelling, although there is a much greater emphasis on historical narratives and clan traditions. Individuals prized for their repertoire and narrative skill formed a focus for community life. Storytelling sessions were relatively formal affairs, and the 'rhetoric' of storytelling was shaped by the storyteller's confidence in the patient, close attention of the audience. Convoluted plots are conveyed in heightened language which has many formalized features, such as the poetic passages known as 'runs', which act as markers in a story and seem to perform something of the function of a scene-change at the theatre. The Scots, Lowland tradition, while obviously influenced by Gaelic storytelling, is much closer to the English model. Texts are briefer, the language is more direct, storytelling itself played a more improvised, perhaps more domestic, role in social life.

The greater social importance of the folktale in Highland tradition, with a high status accorded both the story and the storyteller, gave it a greater chance of surviving social change, in however modified a form. The mainstream Scots tradition, on the other hand, dwindled in much the same manner as the English one, and the records we have of Lowland storytelling are dwarfed by the great mass of published and unpublished material recorded in the Highlands. As with the comparable English material, the Lowland stories which were recorded seem to have been 'saved' almost at random, with a high preponderance of tales recollected from the childhood narration of nursemaids.

Indeed, as far as *märchen* or wonder tales are concerned, there is one overriding source. Robert Chambers published his *Popular Rhymes of Scotland* in 1826, and added to succeeding editions a long chapter of 'Fireside Nursery Stories'. Without it, anyone attempting to assess this aspect of Lowland storytelling would be stumbling in the dark. Chambers combines a wide familiarity with storytelling with a real sympathy for the artistry of the oral tale, supplying texts which, while not verbatim, convey much of the vigour and idiosyncrasy of the spoken story. This sensitivity to idiom and atmosphere is crucial. Unfortunately a comparable haul of Lowland wonder tales, collected by Peter Buchan and his blind assistant Jamie Rankine between 1827 and 1830, survives only in a pallid Englished version. Chambers was familiar with Buchan's 'curious manuscript collection', and printed 'The Red Etin' (p. 23) from it. This version is in good Scots, and in the opinion of some, notably the scholar and collector Hamish Henderson, was 'scoticized' by Chambers; but it is just as likely that Chambers, who had access to the tales through Charles Kirkpatrick Sharpe, was using the 'rough sketch' of the tales which Buchan sent to Sharpe on 3 December 1830, rather than the anglicized texts of the surviving manuscript. This manuscript – almost certainly the interleaved volume which Buchan first sent to Sharpe on 4 February 1829 – was eventually published as *Ancient Scottish Tales* in 1908. Its fourteen stories, including 'Green Sleeves' (p. 28) and 'The Princess of the Blue Mountains' (p. 38), are immensely important as historical texts, but grievously depleted as vital stories.

Buchan's stories are generally versions of the great international folktales – AT400 'The Man on a Quest for His Lost Wife', AT313 'The Girl as Helper in the Hero's Flight', AT851 'The Princess Who Cannot Solve a Riddle', etc. – and such distinctive Scots characteristics as they may have originally displayed are ironed out in the published texts, which are essentially English plot summaries. In the case of 'The Red Etin', while it can be categorized as a version of AT303 'The Twins or Blood-Brothers', the case is different. This is a tale with a long oral history in Scotland. It is among the stories whose titles are listed in *The Complaynte of Scotland* in 1549; Sir David Lindsay used to entertain his young pupil King James V with 'tales of the Red Etin'. Though the interspersed verses may betray some literary influence, they also represent a characteristic *cante-fable* form, which is one of a number of similarities between this text and that of 'Childe Rowland' in Jamieson's *Illustrations of Northern Antiquities* (1814). The repetition of phrase and incident in 'The Red Etin', which I follow Chambers in abbreviating for the reader, is one of the means by which storytellers structure, and audiences absorb, folktales. Such repetition is one of the most striking differences between the oral and the literary tale.

Another key feature of such oral tales is the formulaic openings and closures which ease us into and out of the fairytale world. In 'The Red Etin' these approximate to the now standard formulae of 'Once upon a time' and 'They lived happily ever after'. The story opens 'There were ance . . .' and ends '. . . so they a' lived happily a' the rest o' their days'. Chambers' collection contains many variations on these themes: 'And they lived happy and (died) happy/ And never drank oot o' a dry cappy'; 'and they lived happy a' their days, and had a heap o' bonny wee bairns'; 'and they were married, and he and she are living happily till this day, for aught I ken'. There are also ingenious disclaimers – 'If a' tales be true, that's nae lee' – and, most interestingly of all, a formula – 'Sae ye see, bairns, &c' – which suggests that even wonder tales were habitually used in Knox's Scotland to point a moral rather than simply to delight. At the end of an Ayrshire version of 'The Wee Bunnock' (AT2925 'The Pancake'), for instance, Chambers' source remembers his grandmother's words, 'Now, weans, an ye live to grow muckle, be na owre lifted up about onything, nor owre sair cuisten down; for ye see the folk were a' cheated, and the puir tod got the bunnock.'

A Dumfriesshire variant of this tale, also in Chambers, gives an opening formula familiar in many forms throughout England:

> When cockle shells turned music bells,
> And turkeys chewed tobacco,
> And birds biggit their nests in auld men's
> beards, as hereafter they may do in mine . . .

Such nonsense formulae exist in all languages; the Gaelic ones are particularly rich and inventive. In the resonant, idiomatic translation of J. F. Campbell, a story might start,

> There was a king and a knight, as there was and will be, and as grows the fir tree, some of it crooked and some of it straight . . .

and end,

> John married the daughter of the king of the Green Isle, and they made a great rich wedding that lasted seven days and seven years, and thou couldst but hear leeg, leeg, and beeg, beeg, solid sound and peg drawing. Gold a-crushing from the soles of their feet to the tips of their fingers, the length of seven years and seven days.

Chambers and Buchan are not, of course, the only witnesses to the Scots tradition. Local collectors such as Walter Gregor recorded much in the nineteenth century, and their work has been carried on to the present day. There is also much valuable narrative material hidden in the byways of Scottish literature and social history – not to mention the works of Sir Walter Scott, whose massive contribution to our knowledge of Lowland folklore must be recognized. Two good anthologies which draw on these various sources are Hannah Aitken, *A Forgotten Heritage* (1973), and David Buchan, *Scottish Tradition* (1984).

But recently our appreciation of Lowland storytelling has been transformed – and perhaps slightly unbalanced – by the revelation of a vigorous living narrative tradition among Scottish travellers, or 'tinkler-gypsies'. Alan Bruford has made an excellent selection of traveller stories in *The Green Man of Knowledge* (1982); in his introduction he claims with some justice that 'both in range and style this is the richest repertoire of these international folktales yet found in any variant of the English language'. Sheila Douglas's *The King o the Black Art* (1987) contains stories collected from the Stewart family; the traveller storyteller Duncan Williamson has with his folklorist wife Linda published a number of collections from a seemingly inexhaustible repertoire, including *A Thorn in the King's Foot* (1987); another exceptional storyteller, Betsy Whyte, has drawn an unforgettable picture of traveller life in her autobiography *The Yellow on the Broom* (1979). Traveller storytelling is represented in this volume by 'The Three Feathers' (p. 60), 'The Black Laird' (p. 52), 'The Man in the Boat' (p. 55) and 'Daft Sandy and the Mare's Egg' (p. 345).

The paucity of Lowland material is matched by a superfluity of Gaelic folktales. Some of the great collections of Gaelic stories, such as that of John Dewar, remain mostly in manuscript; even the most famous collection of all, that superintended by J. F. Campbell of Islay, has never been fully published. Add to this the inordinate length of many Gaelic narratives, which might take several nights to complete, and it is clear that a book such as this can only offer a sample of the available material.

As Alan Bruford and D. A. MacDonald's magnificent anthology *Scottish Traditional Tales* (1994) shows, storytelling in Scotland is by no means a dead or archaic art. The stream of tradition, even when driven underground, still nourishes the land. Today there is a strong revival of interest in all aspects of traditional culture: tradition-bearers are still coming forward to share their stories and songs, while a new generation is seeking contemporary relevance in the folktale form, taking to heart the advice of the Inuit storyteller Apákag, who admonished the anthropologist Knud Rasmussen, 'You ruin our stories entirely if you are determined to stiffen them out on paper. Learn them yourself and let them spring from your mouth as living words.' Tradition can never be static. But while change is not the same as decay, it is clear that, for instance, the storytelling tradition of the Western Highlands recorded in the last century by J. F. Campbell has dwindled. D. A. MacDonald, writing in *Scottish Studies* of the death in 1965 of the storyteller Neil Gillies of Barra, sounds a familiar note: 'Niall Mhìcheil Nill was one of the last of his kind – an exponent of a narrative tradition which, at its best, is now on the point of extinction.'

One of J. F. Campbell's most assiduous and trustworthy collectors, Hector Urquhart, a gamekeeper at Ardkinglas, wrote to Campbell about the storytelling tradition of his native village, Pool-Ewe in Ross-shire:

When I was a boy, it was the custom for the young to assemble together on the long winter nights to hear the old people recite the tales or sgeulachd, which they learned from their fathers before them. In these days tailors and shoemakers went from house to house, making our clothes and shoes. When one of them came to the village we were greatly delighted, whilst getting new kilts at the same time. I knew an old tailor who used to tell a new tale every night during his stay in the village; and another, an old shoemaker, who, with his large stock of stories about ghosts and fairies, used to frighten us so much that we scarcely dared pass the neighbouring churchyard on our way home. It was also the custom when an *aiodh*, or stranger, celebrated for his store of tales, came on a visit to the village, for us, young and old, to make a rush to the house where he passed the night, and choose our seats, some on beds, some on forms, and others on three-legged stools, etc., and listen in silence to the new tales . . . The goodman of the house usually opened with the tale of *Famhair Mor* (great giant) or some other favourite tale, and then the stranger carried on after that. It was a common saying, 'The first tale by the goodman, and tales to daylight by the *aiodh*.'

Such scenes could be duplicated across Scotland (in the Lowlands, in the less formal gathering known as the 'Forenicht'), as could their grim sequel: 'The minister came to the village in 1830, and the schoolmaster soon followed, who put a stop in our village to such gatherings.' Alexander Carmichael, in the preface to his great collection of Gaelic prayers *Carmina Gadelica* (*Ortha nan Gaidheal*), documents this wanton destruction of Gaelic popular culture by narrow-minded ministers. To set against this, several of the most sensitive and successful nineteenth-century collectors of Scottish folklore were ministers, such as Father Allan McDonald of Eriskay, the Rev. Donald MacInnes and the Rev. James MacDougall. Without the aid of tape recorders, these men painstakingly transcribed and preserved much valuable material, and, following J. F. Campbell's lead, gave the credit for the stories where it belonged, to the storytellers themselves. MacDougall, for instance, published in his *Folk and Hero Tales* (1891) an entire book of stories from a single narrator, Alexander Cameron, the roadman between Duror and Ballachulish.

The problems involved for such collectors were immense. To take an extreme example, the *Sgeulachd Cois' O'Cein*, the longest and most testing of all Gaelic tales, was intended for narration over twenty-four consecutive evenings. The version in this volume, collected by Donald MacInnes from the Oban shoemaker Archibald MacTavish (p. 137), is by no means the longest. The Gaelic text printed from J. F. Campbell's manuscripts occupies eighty-six close-printed pages of the *Transactions of the Gaelic Society of Inverness*, vol. 25. It was collected for Campbell by Hector Maclean from the Islay shoemaker Lachlan MacNeill, who, in the words of J. H. Delargy, 'in his day must have been one of the best storytellers in Western Christendom'. It took storyteller and scribe a week to complete; no wonder the photograph taken of them with Campbell on 17 August 1870, at the close of this mammoth task, shows them 'rather "screwed"'.

The feats of memory of storytellers such as Lachlan MacNeill may seem extraordinary, but they are common to all orally based

cultures. The modern folklorist Alan Bruford suggests in his
Gaelic Folk-Tales and Mediaeval Romances (1969) that

> It seems likely that the average storyteller who does not memorize
> a whole story word for word remembers much of it in the form
> of a series of tableaux, possibly actually visualized, which he
> then describes in his own words; it may even be the normal way
> of learning stories for all storytellers.

In an interview with folklorist D. A. MacDonald, the storyteller
Donald Alasdair Johnson described how he visualized his stories
'like a film passing in front of you'. On the other hand, Alan
Bruford in a companion essay on the narrative style of Duncan
MacDonald stresses the storyteller's verbal conservatism. While
the contribution of the storyteller to the tale varies greatly, in
general folktale narrators intend to pass on a tale as they heard
it, rather than using it as a peg for their own creativity. Dialogue
in particular is often memorized word for word.

The Gaelic folktale is intensely visual: typically, the succession
of events in the story is subordinate to the succession of images.
If one can make such a wide generalization, it seems to me that
the key element in the Gaelic wonder tale is transformation:
nothing and nobody stays in the same shape all the way through
a story if there is any possibility of turning into something else.
In contrast the overriding theme of the Lowland tale is education:
not in a moralistic sense, but seeing life as a journey from
innocence through experience to maturity. The Highland tales
explore states of being; the Lowland ones, ways of living.

Of course there is considerable interchange between the two
traditions. 'Mally Whuppie' (p. 74) is a Scots version of a
characteristically Gaelic tale, represented here by 'Maol a
Chliobain' (p. 81); 'Go Boldly, Lady, and Don't Go Boldly,
Lady' (p. 171) reproduces many features of English 'Robber
Bridegroom' tales, of which one, 'The History of Mr Greenwood', is in Peter Buchan's collection.

I hope I have gathered in this book enough from both
traditions to enable readers to appreciate some of their characteristic qualities, and the extraordinary storytellers who have
sustained them. These narrators, so rich in imagination, have

generally come from the poorest edge of society, with little or no formal education, and no reward for storytelling other than the enjoyment and appreciation of their audience and the satisfaction of exercising and refining their own artistry. J. F. Campbell of Islay's *Popular Tales of the West Highlands* come from fishermen, crofters, farm servants, from 'James Wilson, blind fiddler', 'James MacLachlan, servant', '"Old Woman", pauper'. Yet they were most of them fine storytellers, and some indisputable masters of the craft. Campbell writes, 'I found them to be men with clear heads and wonderful memories, generally very poor and old, living in remote corners of remote islands, and speaking only Gaelic'. His four volumes include many vivid pictures of storytellers, for instance Donald MacPhie of South Uist, from whom Campbell personally collected nine stories during two visits in 1859 and 1860:

He lives at the north end of South Uist, where the road ends at a sound, which has to be forded at the ebb to get to Benbecula. The house is built of a double wall of loose boulders, with a layer of peat three feet thick between the walls. The ends are round, and the roof rests on the inner wall, leaving room for a crop of yellow gowans. A man might walk round the roof on the top of the wall. There is but one room, with two low doors, one on each side of the house. The fire is on the floor; the chimney is a hole above it; and the rafters are hung with pendants and festoons of shining black peat reek. They are of birch from the mainland, American drift wood, or broken wreck. They support a covering of turf and straw, and stones, and heather ropes, which keep out the rain well enough.

The house stands on a green bank, with grey rocks protruding through the turf; and the whole neighbourhood is pervaded by cockle shells, which indicate the food of the people and their fishing pursuits. In a neighbouring kiln there were many cart-loads about to be burned, to make that lime which is so durable in the old castles. The owner of the house, whom I visited twice, is seventy-nine. He told me nine stories, and like all the others, declared that there was no man in the islands who knew them so well. 'He could not say how many he knew;' he seemed to know versions of nearly everything I had got; and he told me plainly that my versions were good for nothing. 'Huch! Thou hast not got them right at all.' 'They came into his mind,' he said, 'sometimes at night when he could not sleep – old tales that he had not heard for threescore years.'

He had the manner of a practised narrator, and it is quite evident he is one; he chuckled at the interesting parts, and laid his withered finger on my knee as he gave out the terrible bits with due solemnity. A small boy in a kilt, with large round glittering eyes, was standing mute at his knee, gazing at his wrinkled face, and devouring every word. The boy's mother first boiled, and then mashed, potatoes; and his father, a well grown man in tartan breeks, ate them. Ducks and ducklings, a cat and a kitten, some hens and a baby, all tumbled about on the clay floor together, and expressed their delight at the savoury prospect, each in his own fashion; and three wayfarers dropped in and listened for a spell, and passed their remarks till the ford was shallow. The light came streaming down the chimney, and through a single pane of glass, lighting up a tract in the blue mist of the peat smoke, and fell on the white hair and brown withered face of the old man, as he sat on a low stool with his feet to the fire; and the rest of the dwelling, with all its plenishing of boxes and box-beds, dishes and dresser, and gear of all sorts, faded away through shades of deepening brown, to the black darkness of the smoked roof and the 'peat corner'. There we sat, and smoked and talked for hours, till the tide ebbed; and then I crossed the ford by wading up to the waist, and dried my clothes in the wind in Benbecula.

Campbell of Islay and his co-workers, Hector Urquhart, Hector Maclean, John Dewar and others, collected most of their material from men such as this – men whose type survived in storytellers such as Donald Alasdair Johnson, narrator of 'The Three Shirts of Bog Cotton' (p. 180). A few of Campbell's stories, notably the Cymbeline tale 'The Chest' (p. 92) and 'Maol a Chliobain' (p. 81), were collected from women, but they are very much in the minority. Campbell himself notes that the further east he went, the more likely storytellers were to be female; it does seem that in the Western Highlands the highly regarded storytellers were predominantly male – or at least that the male collectors found it easier to find male storytellers and coax tales from them. Conversely, when Lady Evelyn Stewart-

Murray collected in Atholl in the 1890s she gathered her stories, such as 'Lasair Gheug, the King of Ireland's Daughter' (p. 162), from female informants. One of the best Gaelic storytellers to survive into the age of the tape-recorder was a woman, Seonaidh Caimbeul.

In the Lowlands, the indications are that a large proportion of the surviving tales were taken down from women. Several of Chambers' 'fireside' tales are explicitly attributed to women, notably Charles Kirkpatrick Sharpe's 'Nurse Jenny', narrator of 'Whuppity Stoorie' (p. 3) and 'The Changeling' (p. 440), while all fourteen stories in Peter Buchan's collection are claimed to be 'from the recitation of the aged sybyls in the north countrie'. One of Sir Walter Scott's chief informants was Mrs Murray Keith, who claimed authorship of various items in his work with the cry, 'd'ye think I dinna ken my ain groats among other folk's kail?' Among the travellers, storytelling does not seem to recognize barriers of gender, though clearly the sex of the narrator may affect the content or slant of a story. In 'The Man in the Boat' (p. 55), for instance, Betsy Whyte brings a female consciousness to bear on a Gaelic tale-type which has usually been recorded from men.

Individual taste seems to have been a more important factor than gender in deciding what sort of stories a narrator would tell. To quote Campbell of Islay again:

> Each branch of popular lore has its own special votaries, as branches of literature have amongst the learned; that one man is the peasant historian and tells of the battles of the clans; another, a walking peerage, who knows the descent of most of the families in Scotland, and all about his neighbours and their origin; others are romancers, and tell about the giants; others are moralists, and prefer the sagacious prose tales, which have a meaning, and might have a moral; a few know the history of the Feni, and are antiquarians. Many despise the whole as frivolities; they are practical moderns, and answer to practical men in other ranks of society.

There are endless ways of classifying these different types of folk narrative. I have for convenience divided the stories in this book into six sections: Wonder Tales of the Lowlands, Wonder

Tales of the Highlands, Historical Traditions, Jests and Anecdotes, Tales of the Supernatural and The Secret Commonwealth.
Every reader will see that these categories are not the only
possible ones, nor are they discrete from each other. Beliefs
about the dead blend with beliefs about the fairies. The same
tale-type (AT1791 'The Sexton Carries the Parson') is told as a
simple joke, 'Highland Thieves' (p. 366), and as light-hearted
history, 'Lochbuie's Two Herdsmen' (p. 251). Elements from the
longest of Scottish tales, 'Koisha Kayn' (p. 137), and from the
Fenian hero tale 'How Finn Kept His Children for the Big Young
Hero of the Ship' (p. 190), reappear in the fairy legend 'Macphie's
Black Dog' (p. 468).

In choosing the stories to fill these sections, I have had to
discard a mass of material I would have liked to print. Rather
than offering a little bit of everything, I have tried so far as
possible to include enough from each source to give the authentic
flavour of the individual mediators of tradition, whether they be
collectors such as Robert Chambers, Peter Buchan and J. F. Campbell, or storytellers such as Archibald MacTavish (pp. 108–61) or
James Mackenzie (pp. 284–304).

Most of all, I hope this book will stand as a tribute to those
storytellers and collectors on whose work it draws; and will act,
too, as an encouragement to their successors.

NEIL PHILIP

I: WONDER TALES OF THE LOWLANDS

WHUPPITY STOORIE

Source: Robert Chambers, *Popular Rhymes of Scotland*
Narrator: Written down by Charles K. Sharpe as narrated by his Nurse Jenny
at Hoddam Castle, near Dumfries, about 1784
Type: AT 500 'The Name of the Helper'

I ken ye're fond o' clashes aboot fairies, bairns; and a story anent a fairy and the goodwife o' Kittlerumpit has joost come into my mind; but I canna very weel tell ye noo whereabouts Kittlerumpit lies. I think it's somewhere in amang the Debateable Grund; onygate I'se no pretend to mair than I ken, like a'body noo-a-days. I wuss they wad mind the ballant we used to lilt lang syne:

> Mony ane sings the gerse, the gerse,
> And mony ane sings the corn;
> And mony ane clatters o' bold Robin Hood,
> Ne'er kent where he was born.

But hoosover, about Kittlerumpit: the goodman was a vaguing sort o' a body; and he gaed to a fair ae day, and not only never came hame again, but never mair was heard o'. Some said he listed, and ither some that the wearifu' pressgang cleekit him up, though he was clothed wi' a wife and a wean forbye. Hech-how! that dulefu' pressgang! they gaed aboot the kintra like roaring lions, seeking whom they micht devoor. I mind weel, my auldest brither Sandy was a' but smoored in the meal ark hiding frae thae limmers. After they war gane, we pu'd him oot frae amang the meal, pechin' and greetin', and as white as ony corp. My mither had to pike the meal oot o' his mooth wi' the shank o' a horn spoon.

Aweel, when the goodman o' Kittlerumpit was gane, the goodwife was left wi' a sma' fendin. Little gear had she, and a sookin' lad bairn. A'body said they war sorry for her; but

3

naebody helpit her, whilk's a common case, sirs. Howsomever, the goodwife had a soo, and that was her only consolation: for the soo was soon to farra, and she hopit for a good bairn-time.

But we a' weel ken hope's fallacious. Ae day the wife gaes to the sty to fill the soo's trough; and what does she find but the soo lying on her back, grunting and graning, and ready to gie up the ghost.

I trow this was a new stoond to the goodwife's heart; sae she sat doon on the knockin'-stane, wi' her bairn on her knee, and grat sairer than ever she did for the loss o' her ain goodman.

Noo, I premeese that the cot-hoose o' Kittlerumpit was biggit on a brae, wi' a muckle fir-wood behint it, o' whilk ye may hear mair or lang gae. So the goodwife, when she was dichtin' her een, chances to look down the brae, and what does she see but an auld woman, amaist like a leddy, coming slowly up the gaet. She was buskit in green, a' but a white short apron, and a black velvet hood, and a steeple-crowned beaver hat on her head. She had a lang walking-staff, as lang as hersel', in her hand – the sort of staff that auld men and auld women helpit themselves wi' lang syne; I see nae sic staffs noo, sirs.

Aweel, when the goodwife saw the green gentlewoman near her, she rase and made a curchie; and 'Madam,' quo' she, greetin', 'I'm ane of the maist misfortunate women alive.'

'I dinna wish to hear pipers' news and fiddlers' tales, good-wife,' quo' the green woman. 'I ken ye've tint your goodman – we had waur losses at the Shirra Muir; and I ken that your soo's unco sick. Noo, what will ye gie me gin I cure her?'

'Onything your leddyship's madam likes,' quo' the witless goodwife, never guessin' wha she had to deal wi'.

'Let's wat thooms on that bargain,' quo' the green woman: sae thooms war wat, I'se warrant ye; and into the sty madam marches.

She looks at the soo wi' a lang glowr, and syne began to mutter to hersel' what the goodwife couldna weel understand; but she said it soundit like:

> Pitter patter,
> Haly water.

Syne she took oot o' her pouch a wee bottle, wi' something

like oil in't, and rubs the soo wi't abune the snoot, ahint the lugs, and on the tip o' the tail. 'Get up, beast,' quo' the green woman. Nae sooner said nor done – up bangs the soo wi' a grunt, and awa' to her trough for her breakfast.

The goodwife o' Kittlerumpit was a joyfu' goodwife noo, and wad hae kissed the very hem o' the green madam's gown-tail, but she wadna let her. 'I'm no sae fond o' fashions,' quo' she; 'but noo that I hae richtit your sick beast, let us end our sicker bargain. Ye'll no find me an unreasonable greedy body – I like aye to do a good turn for a sma' reward – a' I ask, and *wull* hae, is that lad bairn in your bosom.'

The goodwife o' Kittlerumpit, wha noo kent her customer, ga'e a skirl like a stickit gryse. The green woman was a fairy, nae doubt; sae she prays, and greets, and begs, and flytes; but a' wadna do. 'Ye may spare your din,' quo' the fairy, 'skirling as if I was as deaf as a door nail; but this I'll let ye to wut – I canna, by *the law we leeve on*, take your bairn till the third day after this day; and no then, if ye can tell me my right name.' Sae madam gaes awa' round the swine's-sty end, and the goodwife fa's doon in a swerf behint the knockin'-stane.

Aweel, the goodwife o' Kittlerumpit could sleep nane that nicht for greetin', and a' the next day the same, cuddlin' her bairn till she near squeezed its breath out; but the second day she thinks o' taking a walk in the wood I tell't ye o'; and sae, wi' the bairn in her arms, she sets out, and gaes far in amang the trees, where was an old quarry-hole, grown owre wi' gerse, and a bonny spring well in the middle o't. Before she came very nigh, she hears the birring o' a lint-wheel, and a voice lilting a sang; sae the wife creeps quietly amang the bushes, and keeks owre the broo o' the quarry, and what does she see but the green fairy kemping at her wheel, and singing like ony precentor:

> 'Little kens our guid dame at hame
> That Whuppity Stoorie is my name!'

'Ah, ha!' thinks the wife, 'I've gotten the mason's word at last: the deil gie them joy that tell't it!' Sae she gaed hame far lichter than she came out, as ye may weel guess, lauchin' like a madcap wi' the thought o' begunkin' the auld green fairy.

Aweel, ye maun ken that this goodwife was a jokus woman, and aye merry when her heart wasna unco sair owreladen. Sae she thinks to hae some sport wi' the fairy; and at the appointit time she puts the bairn behint the knockin'-stane, and sits down on't hersel'. Syne she pu's her mutch ajee owre her left lug, crooks her mou on the tither side, as gin she war greetin', and a filthy face she made, ye may be sure. She hadna lang to wait, for up the brae mounts the green fairy, nowther lame nor lazy; and lang or she gat near the knockin'-stane, she skirls out: 'Goodwife o' Kittlerumpit, ye weel ken what I come for – stand and deliver!' The wife pretends to greet sairer than before, and wrings her nieves, and fa's on her knees, wi': 'Och, sweet madam mistress, spare my only bairn, and take the weary soo!'

'The deil take the soo for my share,' quo' the fairy; 'I come na here for swine's flesh. Dinna be contramawcious, hizzie, but gie me the gett instantly!'

'Ochon, dear leddy mine,' quo' the greetin' goodwife; 'forbear my poor bairn, and take mysel'!'

'The deil's in the daft jad,' quo' the fairy, looking like the far end o' a fiddle; 'I'll wad she's clean dementit. Wha in a' the earthly warld, wi' half an ee in their head, wad ever meddle wi' the likes o' thee?'

I trow this set up the wife o' Kittlerumpit's birse; for though she had twa bleert een, and a lang red neb forbye, she thought hersel' as bonny as the best o' them. Sae she bangs aff her knees, sets up her mutch-croon, and wi' her twa hands faulded afore her, she maks a curchie down to the grund, and, 'In troth, fair madam,' quo' she, 'I might hae had the wit to ken that the likes o' me is na fit to tie the warst shoestrings o' the heich and mighty princess, *Whuppity Stoorie*!' Gin a fluff o' gunpowder had come out o' the grund, it couldna hae gart the fairy loup heicher nor she did; syne down she came again, dump on her shoe-heels, and whurlin' round, she ran down the brae, scraichin' for rage, like a houlet chased wi' the witches.

The goodwife o' Kittlerumpit leugh till she was like to ryve; syne she taks up her bairn, and gaes into her hoose, singin' till 't a' the gaet:

'A goo and a gitty, my bonny wee tyke,
Ye'se noo hae your four-oories;
Sin' we've gien Nick a bane to pyke,
Wi' his wheels and his Whuppity Stoories.'

THE PADDO

Source: Robert Chambers, *Popular Rhymes of Scotland*
Narrator: Written down by Charles K. Sharpe from the remembered narration
of his Nurse Jenny, about 1784
Type: AT440 'The Frog King'

Note: The discreet 'Here let us abridge a little' indicates not so much an omission
as a bowdlerization, disguising the fact that it is the lassie's bed to which the frog
(paddo) is led. Once there, he probably asked her to 'cuddle my back' or some
similar euphemism

A poor widow was one day baking bannocks, and sent her
dochter wi' a dish to the well to bring water. The dochter
gaed, and better gaed, till she came to the well, but it was dry.
Now, what to do she didna ken, for she couldna gang back to
her mother without water; sae she sat down by the side o' the
well, and fell a-greeting. A Paddo then came loup-loup-louping
out o' the well, and asked the lassie what she was greeting for;
and she said she was greeting because there was nae water in the
well. 'But,' says the Paddo, 'an ye'll be my wife, I'll gie ye plenty
o' water.' And the lassie, no thinking that the poor beast could
mean anything serious, said she wad be his wife, for the sake
o' getting the water. So she got the water into her dish, and gaed
away hame to her mother, and thought nae mair about the
Paddo, till that night, when, just as she and her mother were
about to go to their beds, something came to the door, and
when they listened, they heard this sang:

> 'O open the door, my hinnie, my heart,
> O open the door, my ain true love;
> Remember the promise that you and I made,
> Down i' the meadow, where we twa met.'

Says the mother to the dochter: 'What noise is that at the door?'
'Hout,' says the dochter, 'it's naething but a filthy Paddo.' 'Open
the door,' says the mother, 'to the poor Paddo.' So the lassie

opened the door, and the Paddo came loup-loup-louping in, and sat down by the ingle-side. Then he sings:

> 'O gie me my supper, my hinnie, my heart,
> O gie me my supper, my ain true love;
> Remember the promise that you and I made,
> Down i' the meadow, where we twa met.'

'Hout,' quo' the dochter, 'wad I gie a filthy Paddo his supper?' 'O ay,' said the mother, 'e'en gie the poor Paddo his supper.' So the Paddo got his supper; and after that he sings again:

> 'O put me to bed, my hinnie, my heart,
> O put me to bed, my ain true love;
> Remember the promise that you and I made,
> Down i' the meadow, where we twa met.'

'Hout,' quo' the dochter, 'wad I put a filthy Paddo to bed?' 'O ay,' says the mother, 'put the poor Paddo to bed.' And so she put the Paddo to his bed. [Here let us abridge a little.] Then the Paddo sang again:

> 'Now fetch me an axe, my hinnie, my heart,
> Now fetch me an axe, my ain true love;
> Remember the promise that you and I made,
> Down i' the meadow, where we twa met.'

The lassie wasna lang o' fetching the axe; and then the Paddo sang:

> 'Now chap aff my head, my hinnie, my heart,
> Now chap aff my head, my ain true love;
> Remember the promise that you and I made,
> Down i' the meadow, where we twa met.'

Well, the lassie chappit aff his head; and no sooner was that done, than he started up the bonniest young prince that ever was seen. And the twa lived happy a' the rest o' their days.

THE MILK-WHITE DOO

❈

Source: Robert Chambers, *Popular Rhymes of Scotland*
Narrator: Unknown
Type: AT720 'My Mother Slew Me, My Father Ate Me'

There was once a man that wrought in the fields, and had a wife, and a son, and a dochter. One day he caught a hare, and took it hame to his wife, and bade her make it ready for his dinner. While it was on the fire, the goodwife aye tasted and tasted at it, till she had tasted it a' away, and then she didna ken what to do for her goodman's dinner. So she cried in Johnie her son to come and get his head kaimed; and when she was kaiming his head, she slew him, and put him into the pat. Well, the goodman cam hame to his dinner, and his wife set down Johnie well boiled to him; and when he was eating, he takes up a fit, and says: 'That's surely my Johnie's fit.'

'Sic nonsense! It's ane o' the hare's,' says the goodwife.

Syne he took up a hand, and says: 'That's surely my Johnie's hand.'

'Ye're havering, goodman; it's anither o' the hare's feet.'

So when the goodman had eaten his dinner, little Katy, Johnie's sister, gathered a' the banes, and put them in below a stane at the cheek o' the door:

> Where they grew, and they grew,
> To a milk-white doo,
> That took to its wings,
> And away it flew.

And it flew till it cam to where twa women were washing claes, and it sat down on a stane, and cried:

> 'Pew, pew,
> My minny me slew,

My daddy me chew,
My sister gathered my banes,
And put them between twa milk-white stanes;
And I grew, and I grew,
To a milk-white doo,
And I took to my wings, and away I flew.'

'Say that owre again, my bonny bird, and we'll gie ye a' thir claes,' says the women.

'Pew, pew,
My minny me slew,' &c.

And it got the claes; and then flew till it cam to a man counting a great heap o' siller, and it sat down and cried:

'Pew, pew,
My minny me slew,' &c.

'Say that again, my bonny bird, and I'll gie ye a' this siller,' says the man.

'Pew, pew,
My minny me slew,' &c.

And it got a' the siller; and syne it flew till it cam to twa millers grinding corn, and it cried:

'Pew, pew,
My minny me slew,' &c.

'Say that again, my bonny bird, and I'll gie ye this millstane,' says the miller.

'Pew, pew,
My minny me slew,' &c.

And it gat the millstane; and syne it flew till it lighted on its father's house-top. It threw sma' stanes down the lum, and Katy cam out to see what was the matter; and the doo threw a' the claes to her. Syne the father cam out, and the doo threw a' the siller to him. And syne the mother cam out, and the doo threw

down the millstane upon her and killed her. And at last it flew
away; and the goodman and his dochter after that

> Lived happy, and died happy,
> And never drank out of a dry cappy.

THE RED CALF

Source: Walter Gregor, 'Three Folk-Tales from Old Meldrum, Aberdeenshire', *Folk-Lore Journal*, vol. 2, 1884
Narrator: Mrs Muir, mother of Mr Muir, Rector of the Grammar School, Aberdeen
Type: AT510b 'The Dress of Gold, of Silver and of Stars'

Ance a long time ago there was a gentleman had two lassies. The oldest was ugly and ill-natured, but the youngest was a bonnie lassie and good; but the ugly one was the favourite with her father and mother. So they ill-used the youngest in every way, and they sent her into the woods to herd cattle, and all the food she got was a little porridge and whey.

Well, amongst the cattle was a red calf, and one day it said to the lassie, 'Gee that porridge and whey to the doggie, and come wi' me.'

So the lassie followed the calf through the wood, and they came to a bonnie hoosie, where there was a nice dinner ready for them, and after they had feasted on everything nice they went back to the herding.

Every day the calf took the lassie away, and feasted her on dainties, and every day she grew bonnier. This disappointed the father and mother and the ugly sister. They expected that the rough usage she was getting would take away her beauty; and they watched and watched until they saw the calf take the lassie away to the feast. So they resolved to kill the calf; and not only that, but the lassie was to be compelled to kill him with an axe. Her ugly sister was to hold his head, and the lassie who loved him had to give the blow and kill him. She could do nothing but greet; but the calf told her not to greet, but to do as he bade her; and his plan was that instead of coming down on his head she was to come down on the lassie's head who was holding him, and then she was to jump on his back and they would run off.

Well, the day came for the calf to be killed, and everything was ready – the ugly lassie holding his head, and the bonnie lassie armed with the axe. So she raised the axe, and came down on the ugly sister's head, and in the confusion that took place she got on the calf's back and they ran away, and they ran and better nor ran till they came to a meadow where grew a great lot of rashes; and, as the lassie had not on many clothes, they pu'ed rashes, and made a coatie for her, and they set off again and travelled, and travelled, till they came to the king's house. They went in, and asked if they wanted a servant. The mistress said she wanted a kitchen lassie, and she would take Rashin-coatie. So Rashin-coatie said she would stop, if they keepit the calf too. They were willing to do that. So the lassie and the calf stoppit in the king's house, and everybody was well pleased with her; and when Yule came, they said she was to stop at home and make the dinner, while all the rest went to the kirk. After they were away the calf asked if she would like to go. She said she would, but she had no clothes, and she could not leave the dinner. The calf said he would give her clothes, and make the dinner too. He went out, and came back with a grand dress all silk and satin, and such a nice pair of slippers. The lassie put on the dress, and before she left she said:

> 'Ilka peat gar anither burn,
> An ilka spit gar anither turn,
> An ilka pot gar anither play,
> Till I come frae the kirk on gude Yule day.'

So she went to the kirk, and nobody kent it was Rashin-coatie. They wondered who the bonnie lady could be; and, as soon as the young prince saw her, he fell in love with her, and resolved he would find out who she was, before she got home; but Rashin-coatie left before the rest, so that she might get home in time to take off her dress, and look after the dinner.

When the prince saw her leaving, he made for the door to stop her; but she jumped past him, and in the hurry lost one of her shoes. The prince kept the shoe, and Rashin-coatie got home all right, and the folk said the dinner was very nice.

Now the prince was resolved to find out who the bonnie lady

was, and he sent a servant through all the land with the shoe. Every lady was to try it on, and the prince promised to marry the one it would fit. That servant went to a great many houses, but could not find a lady that the shoe would go on, it was so little and neat. At last he came to a henwife's house, and her daughter had little feet. At first the shoe would not go on, but she paret her feet, and clippit her toes, until the shoe went on. Now the prince was very angry. He knew it was not the lady that he wanted; but, because he had promised to marry whoever the shoe fitted, he had to keep his promise.

The marriage day came, and, as they were all riding to the kirk, a little bird flew through the air, and it sang:

> 'Clippit feet an paret taes is on the saidle set;
> But bonnie feet an braw feet sits in the kitchen neuk.'

'What's that ye say?' said the prince. 'Oh,' says the henwife, 'would ye mind what a feel bird says?' But the prince said, 'Sing that again, bonnie birdie.' So the bird sings:

> 'Clippit feet an paret taes is on the saidle set;
> But bonnie feet an braw feet sits in the kitchen neuk.'

The prince turned his horse and rode home, and went straight to his father's kitchen, and there sat Rashin-coatie. He kent her at once, she was so bonnie; and when she tried on the shoe it fitted her, and so the prince married Rashin-coatie, and they lived happy and built a house for the red calf, who had been so kind to her.

THE BLACK BULL OF NORROWAY

Source: Robert Chambers, *Popular Rhymes of Scotland*
Narrator: Unknown
Type: AT425 'The Search for the Lost Husband'

In Norroway, langsyne, there lived a certain lady, and she had three dochters. The auldest o' them said to her mither: 'Mither, bake me a bannock, and roast me a collop, for I'm gaun awa' to spotch my fortune.' Her mither did sae; and the dochter gaed awa' to an auld witch washerwife and telled her purpose. The auld wife bade her stay that day, and gang and look out o' her back door, and see what she could see. She saw nocht the first day. The second day she did the same, and saw nocht. On the third day she looked again, and saw a coach-and-six coming alang the road. She ran in and telled the auld wife what she saw. 'Aweel,' quo' the auld wife, 'yon's for you.' Sae they took her into the coach, and galloped aff.

The second dochter next says to her mither: 'Mither, bake me a bannock, and roast me a collop, for I'm gaun awa' to spotch my fortune.' Her mither did sae; and awa' she gaed to the auld wife, as her sister had dune. On the third day she looked out o' the back door, and saw a coach-and-four coming alang the road. 'Aweel,' quo' the auld wife, 'yon's for you.' Sae they took her in, and aff they set.

The third dochter says to her mither: 'Mither, bake me a bannock, and roast me a collop, for I'm gaun awa' to spotch my fortune.' Her mither did sae; and awa' she gaed to the auld witch wife. She bade her look out o' her back door, and see what she could see. She did sae; and when she came back, said she saw nocht. The second day she did the same, and saw nocht. The third day she looked again, and on coming back, said to the auld wife she saw nocht but a muckle Black Bull coming crooning alang the road. 'Aweel,' quo' the auld wife, 'yon's for you.' On hearing this she was next to distracted wi' grief and terror; but she was lifted up and set on his back, and awa' they went.

Aye they travelled, and on they travelled, till the lady grew faint wi' hunger. 'Eat out o' my right lug,' says the Black Bull, 'and drink out o' my left lug, and set by your leavings.' Sae she did as he said, and was wonderfully refreshed. And lang they gaed, and sair they rade, till they came in sight o' a very big and bonny castle. 'Yonder we maun be this night,' quo' the bull, 'for my auld brither lives yonder;' and presently they were at the place. They lifted her aff his back, and took her in, and sent him away to a park for the night. In the morning, when they brought the bull hame, they took the lady into a fine shining parlour, and gave her a beautiful apple, telling her no to break it till she was in the greatest strait ever mortal was in in the world, and that wad bring her out o't. Again she was lifted on the bull's back, and after she had ridden far, and far'er than I can tell, they came in sight o' a far bonnier castle, and far farther awa' than the last. Says the bull till her: 'Yonder we maun be the night, for my second brither lives yonder;' and they were at the place directly. They lifted her down and took her in, and sent the bull to the field for the night. In the morning they took the lady into a fine and rich room, and gave her the finest pear she had ever seen, bidding her no to break it till she was in the greatest strait ever mortal could be in, and that wad get her out o't. Again she was lifted and set on his back, and awa' they went. And lang they rade, and sair they rade, till they came in sight o' the far biggest castle, and far farthest aff, they had yet seen. 'We maun be yonder the night,' says the bull, 'for my young brither lives yonder;' and they were there directly. They lifted her down, took her in, and sent the bull to the field for the night. In the morning they took her into a room, the finest of a', and gied her a plum, telling her no to break it till she was in the greatest strait mortal could be in, and that wad get her out o't. Presently they brought hame the bull, set the lady on his back, and awa' they went.

And aye they rade, and on they rade, till they came to a dark and ugsome glen, where they stopped, and the lady lighted down. Says the bull to her: 'Here ye maun stay till I gang and fight the deil. Ye maun seat yoursel' on that stane, and move neither hand nor fit till I come back, else I'll never find ye again. And if everything round about ye turns blue, I hae beaten the deil; but should a' things turn red, he'll hae conquered me.' She set hersel' down on the stane, and by and by a' round her turned blue. O'ercome wi' joy, she lifted the ae fit and crossed it owre the ither, sae glad was she that her companion was victorious. The bull returned and sought for, but never could find her.

Lang she sat, and aye she grat, till she wearied. At last she rase and gaed awa', she kendna whaur till. On she wandered, till she came to a great hill o' glass, that she tried a' she could to climb, but wasna able. Round the bottom o' the hill she gaed, sabbing and seeking a passage owre, till at last she came to a smith's house; and the smith promised, if she wad serve him seven years, he wad make her airn shoon, wherewi' she could climb owre the glassy hill. At seven years' end she got her airn shoon, clamb the glassy hill, and chanced to come to the auld washerwife's habitation. There she was telled of a gallant young knight that had given in some bluidy sarks to wash, and whaever washed thae sarks was to be his wife. The auld wife had washed till she was tired, and then she set to her dochter, and baith washed, and they washed, and they better washed, in hopes of getting the young knight; but a' they could do, they couldna bring out a stain. At length they set the stranger damosel to wark; and whenever she began, the stains came out pure and clean, and the auld wife made the knight believe it was her dochter had washed the sarks. So the knight and the eldest dochter were to be married, and the stranger damosel was distracted at the thought of it, for she was deeply in love wi' him. So she bethought her of her apple, and breaking it, found it filled with gold and precious jewellery, the richest she had ever seen. 'All these,' she said to the eldest dochter, 'I will give you, on condition that you put off your marriage for ae day, and allow me to go into his room alone at night.' So the lady consented; but meanwhile the auld wife had prepared a sleeping drink, and given it to the knight, wha drank it, and never wakened till next morning. The lee-lang night the damosel sabbed and sang:

> 'Seven lang years I served for thee,
> The glassy hill I clamb for thee,
> The bluidy shirt I wrang for thee;
> And wilt thou no wauken and turn to me?'

Next day she kentna what to do for grief. She then brak the pear, and fan't filled wi' jewellery far richer than the contents o' the apple. Wi' thae jewels she bargained for permission to be a second night in the young knight's chamber; but the auld wife gied him anither sleeping drink, and he again sleepit till morning. A' night she kept sighing and singing as before:

> 'Seven lang years I served for thee,' &c.

Still he sleepit, and she nearly lost hope a'thegither. But that day, when he was out at the hunting, somebody asked him what noise and moaning was yon they heard all last night in his bedchamber. He said he heardna ony noise. But they assured him there was sae; and he resolved to keep waking that night to try what he could hear. That being the third night, and the damosel being between hope and despair, she brak her plum, and it held far the richest jewellery of the three. She bargained as before; and the auld wife, as before, took in the sleeping drink to the young knight's chamber; but he telled her he couldna drink it that night without sweetening. And when she gaed awa' for some honey to sweeten it wi', he poured out the drink, and sae made the auld wife think he had drunk it. They a' went to bed again, and the damosel began, as before, singing:

> 'Seven lang years I served for thee,
> The glassy hill I clamb for thee,
> The bluidy shirt I wrang for thee;
> And wilt thou no wauken and turn to me?'

He heard, and turned to her. And she telled him a' that had befa'en her, and he telled her a' that had happened to him. And he caused the auld washerwife and her dochter to be burnt. And they were married, and he and she are living happy till this day, for aught I ken.

THE WAL AT THE WARLD'S END

Source: Robert Chambers, *Popular Rhymes of Scotland*
Narrator: Unknown (Fife)
Type: AT480 'The Spinning-Women by the Spring'

There was a king and a queen, and the king had a dochter, and the queen had a dochter. And the king's dochter was bonnie and guid-natured, and a'body liket her; and the queen's dochter was ugly and ill-natured, and naebody liket her. And the queen didna like the king's dochter, and she wanted her awa'. Sae she sent her to the wal at the warld's end, to get a bottle o' water, thinking she would never come back. Weel, she took her bottle, and she gaed and gaed or she cam to a pownie that was tethered, and the pownie said to her:

> 'Flit me, flit me, my bonnie May,
> For I haena been flitted this seven year and a day.'

And the king's dochter said: 'Ay will I, my bonnie pownie, I'll flit ye.' Sae the pownie ga'e her a ride owre the muir o' hecklepins.

Weel, she gaed far and far and farer nor I can tell, or she cam to the wal at the warld's end; and when she cam to the wal, it was awfu' deep, and she couldna get her bottle dippit. And as she was lookin' doon, thinkin' hoo to do, there lookit up to her three scaud men's heads, and they said to her:

> 'Wash me, wash me, my bonnie May,
> And dry me wi' yer clean linen apron.'

And she said: 'Ay will I; I'll wash ye.' Sae she washed the three scaud men's heads, and dried them wi' her clean linen apron; and syne they took and dippit her bottle for her.

And the scaud men's heads said the tane to the tither:

> 'Weird, brother, weird, what'll ye weird?'

And the first ane said: 'I weird that if she was bonnie afore, she'll be ten times bonnier.' And the second ane said: 'I weird that ilka time she speaks, there'll a diamond and a ruby and a pearl drap oot o' her mouth.' And the third ane said: 'I weird that ilka time she kaims her head, she'll get a peck o' gould and a peck o' siller oot o' it.'

Weel, she cam hame to the king's coort again, and if she was bonnie afore, she was ten times bonnier; and ilka time she opened her lips to speak, there was a diamond and a ruby and a pearl drappit oot o' her mouth; and ilka time she kaimed her head, she gat a peck o' gould and a peck o' silver oot o't. And the queen was that vext, she didna ken what to do, but she thocht she wad send her ain dochter to see if she could fa' in wi' the same luck. Sae she ga'e her a bottle, and tell't her to gang awa' to the wal at the warld's end, and get a bottle o' water.

Weel, the queen's dochter gaed and gaed or she cam to the pownie, an' the pownie said:

> 'Flit me, flit me, my bonnie May,
> For I haena been flitted this seven year and a day.'

And the queen's dochter said: 'Ou ye nasty beast, do ye think I'll flit ye? Do ye ken wha ye're speakin' till? I'm a queen's dochter.' Sae she wadna flit the pownie, and the pownie wadna gie her a ride owre the muir o' hecklepins. And she had to gang on her bare feet, and the hecklepins cuttit a' her feet, and she could hardly gang ava.

Weel, she gaed far and far and farer nor I can tell, or she cam to the wal at the warld's end. And the wal was deep, and she couldna get her bottle dippit; and as she was lookin' doon, thinkin' hoo to do, there lookit up to her three scaud men's heads, and they said till her:

> 'Wash me, wash me, my bonnie May,
> And dry me wi' yer clean linen apron.'

And she said: 'Ou ye nasty dirty beasts, div ye think I'm gaunie wash ye? Div ye ken wha ye're speakin' till? I'm a queen's dochter.' Sae she wadna wash them, and they wadna dip her bottle for her.

And the scaud men's heads said the tane to the tither:

'Weird, brother, weird, what'll ye weird?'

And the first ane said: 'I weird that if she was ugly afore, she'll be ten times uglier.' And the second said: 'I weird that ilka time she speaks, there'll a puddock and a taid loup oot o' her mouth.' And the third ane said: 'And I weird that ilka time she kaims her head, she'll get a peck o' lice and a peck o' flechs oot o't.' Sae she gaed awa' hame again, and if she was ugly afore, she was ten times uglier; and ilka time, &c. Sae they had to send her awa' fra the king's coort. And there was a bonnie young prince cam and married the king's dochter; and the queen's dochter had to put up wi' an auld cobbler, and he lickit her ilka day wi' a leather strap. Sae ye see, bairns, &c.

THE RED ETIN

Source: Robert Chambers, *Popular Rhymes of Scotland*
Narrator: Unknown, from the manuscript collection of Peter Buchan,
made between 1827 and 1830
Type: AT303 'The Twins or Blood-Brothers'

There were ance twa widows that lived ilk ane on a small bit o' ground, which they rented from a farmer. Ane of them had twa sons, and the other had ane; and by and by it was time for the wife that had twa sons to send them away to spouss their fortune. So she told her eldest son ae day to take a can and bring her water from the well, that she might bake a cake for him; and however much or however little water he might bring, the cake would be great or sma' accordingly; and that cake was to be a' that she could gie him when he went on his travels.

The lad gaed away wi' the can to the well, and filled it wi' water, and then came away hame again; but the can being broken, the maist part o' the water had run out before he got back. So his cake was very sma'; yet sma' as it was, his mother asked if he was willing to take the half of it with her blessing, telling him that, if he chose rather to have the hale, he would only get it wi' her curse. The young man, thinking he might hae to travel a far way, and not knowing when or how he might get other provisions, said he would like to hae the hale cake, come of his mother's malison what like; so she gave him the hale cake, and her malison alang wi't. Then he took his brither aside, and gave him a knife to keep till he should come back, desiring him to look at it every morning, and as lang as it continued to be clear, then he might be sure that the owner of it was well; but if it grew dim and rusty, then for certain some ill had befallen him.

So the young man set out to spouss his fortune. And he gaed a' that day, and a' the next day; and on the third day, in the afternoon, he came up to where a shepherd was sitting with a

flock o' sheep. And he gaed up to the shepherd and asked him
wha the sheep belanged to; and the man answered:

> 'The Red Etin of Ireland
>   Ance lived in Bellygan,
> And stole King Malcolm's daughter,
>   The king of fair Scotland.
> He beats her, he binds her,
>   He lays her on a band;
> And every day he dings her
>   With a bright silver wand.
> Like Julian the Roman,
> He's one that fears no man.
>
> It's said there's ane predestinate
>   To be his mortal foe;
> But that man is yet unborn,
>   And lang may it be so.'

The young man then went on his journey; and he had not gone
far, when he espied an old man with white locks herding a flock
of swine; and he gaed up to him and asked whose swine these
were, when the man answered:

> 'The Red Etin of Ireland', &c.

Then the young man gaed on a bit farther, and came to another
very old man herding goats; and when he asked whose goats
they were, the answer was:

> 'The Red Etin of Ireland', &c.

This old man also told him to beware o' the next beasts that he
should meet, for they were of a very different kind from any he
had yet seen.

So the young man went on, and by and by he saw a multitude
of very dreadfu' beasts, ilk ane o' them wi' twa heads, and on
every head four horns. And he was sore frightened, and ran
away from them as fast as he could; and glad was he when he
came to a castle that stood on a hillock, wi' the door standing
wide to the wa'. And he gaed into the castle for shelter, and
there he saw an auld wife sitting beside the kitchen fire. He
asked the wife if he might stay there for the night, as he was

tired wi' a lang journey; and the wife said he might, but it was not a good place for him to be in, as it belanged to the Red Etin, who was a very terrible beast, wi' three heads, that spared no living man he could get hold of. The young man would have gone away, but he was afraid of the beasts on the outside of the castle; so he beseeched the old woman to conceal him as well as she could, and not tell the Etin that he was there. He thought, if he could put over the night, he might get away in the morning, without meeting wi' the beasts, and so escape. But he had not been long in his hidy-hole before the awful Etin came in; and nae sooner was he in, than he was heard crying:

> 'Snouk but and snouk ben,
> I find the smell of an earthly man;
> Be he living, or be he dead,
> His heart this night shall kitchen my bread.'

The monster soon found the poor young man, and pulled him from his hole. And when he had got him out, he told him that, if he could answer him three questions, his life should be spared. The first was, whether Ireland or Scotland was first inhabited? The second was, whether man was made for woman, or woman for man? The third was, whether men or brutes were made first? The lad not being able to answer one of these questions, the Red Etin took a mell and knocked him on the head, and turned him into a pillar of stone.

On the morning after this happened, the younger brither took out the knife to look at it, and he was grieved to find it a' brown wi' rust. He told his mother that the time was now come for him to go away upon his travels also; so she requested him to take the can to the well for water, that she might bake a cake for him. The can being broken, he brought hame as little water as the other had done, and the cake was as little. She asked whether he would have the hale cake wi' her malison, or the half wi' her blessing; and, like his brither, he thought it best to have the hale cake, come o' the malison what might. So he gaed away; and he came to the shepherd that sat wi' his flock o' sheep, and asked him whose sheep these were. [*Repeat the whole of the above series of incidents.*]

The other widow and her son heard of a' that had happened frae a fairy, and the young man determined that he would also go upon his travels, and see if he could do anything to relieve his twa friends. So his mother gave him a can to go to the well and bring home water, that she might bake him a cake for his journey. And he gaed, and as he was bringing hame the water, a raven owre abune his head cried to him to look, and he would see that the water was running out. And he was a young man of sense, and seeing the water running out, he took some clay and patched up the holes, so that he brought home enough of water to bake a large cake. When his mother put it to him to take the half cake wi' her blessing, he took it in preference to having the hale wi' her malison; and yet the half was bigger than what the other lads had got a'thegither.

So he gaed away on his journey; and after he had travelled a far way, he met wi' an auld woman, that asked him if he would give her a bit of his bannock. And he said he would gladly do that, and so he gave her a piece of the bannock; and for that she gied him a magical wand, that she said might yet be of service to him, if he took care to use it rightly. Then the auld woman, wha was a fairy, told him a great deal that would happen to him, and what he ought to do in a' circumstances; and after that she vanished in an instant out o' his sight. He gaed on a great way farther, and then he came up to the old man herding the sheep; and when he asked whose sheep these were, the answer was:

'The Red Etin of Ireland
    Ance lived in Bellygan,
And stole King Malcolm's daughter,
    The king of fair Scotland.
He beats her, he binds her,
    He lays her on a band;
And every day he dings her
    With a bright silver wand.
Like Julian the Roman,
He's one that fears no man.

But now I fear his end is near,
    And destiny at hand;

And you're to be, I plainly see,
The heir of all his land.'

[*Repeat the same inquiries to the man attending the swine and the man attending the goats, with the same answer in each case.*]

When he came to the place where the monstrous beasts were standing, he did not stop nor run away, but went boldly through amongst them. One came up roaring with open mouth to devour him, when he struck it with his wand, and laid it in an instant dead at his feet. He soon came to the Etin's castle, where he knocked, and was admitted. The auld woman that sat by the fire warned him of the terrible Etin, and what had been the fate of the twa brithers; but he was not to be daunted. The monster soon came in, saying:

'Snouk but and snouk ben,
I find the smell of an earthly man;
Be he living, or be he dead,
His heart shall be kitchen to my bread.'

He quickly espied the young man, and bade him come forth on the floor. And then he put the three questions to him; but the young man had been told everything by the good fairy, so he was able to answer all the questions. When the Etin found this, he knew that his power was gone. The young man then took up an axe and hewed aff the monster's three heads. He next asked the old woman to shew him where the king's daughter lay; and the old woman took him upstairs, and opened a great many doors, and out of every door came a beautiful lady who had been imprisoned there by the Etin; and ane o' the ladies was the king's daughter. She also took him down into a low room, and there stood two stone pillars that he had only to touch wi' his wand, when his twa friends and neighbours started into life. And the hale o' the prisoners were overjoyed at their deliverance, which they all acknowledged to be owing to the prudent young man. Next day they a' set out for the king's court, and a gallant company they made. And the king married his daughter to the young man that had delivered her, and gave a noble's daughter to ilk ane o' the other young men; and so they a' lived happily a' the rest o' their days.

GREEN SLEEVES

Source: Peter Buchan, 'Ancient Scottish Tales'
Narrator: Unknown
Type: AT313C 'The Girl as Helper in the Hero's Flight', followed by
'The Forgotten Fiancée'

There was a king dwelt in Scotland who had a son that delighted much in gambling, and his chief amusement was that of skittles. Having practised it much he became so dexterous a player that no one could be found to contend with him. One day, however, as he went out alone, regretting the want of a partner, an old man appeared, and offered to play with him on the following terms: that, whoever won the game should have it in his power to ask of the other what he pleased, and the loser to be strictly bound to the observance of the same, under pain of death. This being mutually agreed to, they began, when the old man was more successful than the prince, and won the game. The prince was at this a good deal disconcerted, and said he was the first person in Scotland who had ever beat him. The terms of the game, as before explained, were to the loser to do whatever was asked by the gainer. The old man then commanded him to tell him his name and place of abode before that day twelve months, or to suffer death.

The prince upon hearing these hard requests, went home and went to bed, but would tell no one the cause of his anguish, although often interrogated by his nearest relations. At length the king, his father, would needs know the nature of his complaint, and commanded him to inform him forthwith, which he did as already related, viz., that an old man with whom he had played a game at skittles, had commanded him to be able to tell him his name and the place of his abode, before the end of the year, being the terms on which they had played. The king then said it would be much better to go in pursuit of these particulars than lie desponding on a bed of sickness. According to his father's advice, he arose next morning, and travelled the longest summer day in June, till he came to a cottage, at the end of which, on a turf seat, sat an old man, who addressed the prince familiarly saying, 'Well, my prince, you are come seeking that rogue Green Sleeves; but although I am upwards of two hundred years old, I never saw him but twice, and a little ago he passed this house; I cannot, however, tell you where he dwells; but my brother who stays about two hundred miles farther off, and is four hundred years older than I am, perhaps can tell you, and if you will stay all night at my house, I will put you on a plan to go to him quickly.' The prince took lodging accordingly, and was well entertained.

Tomorrow he was led to an adjoining house, and given by the cottager a round ball, with a pair of slippers. The ball he was to roll before him, and the slippers would follow. But on arriving at his brother's cottage, he was to give the slippers and ball a kick, when they would return again to their rightful owner. The prince accordingly went as directed, and found the second old man sitting by his own door, who said: 'Well, prince, I see you have found me, and I know whom you seek; it is that scoundrel Green Sleeves. You have been at my brother's, but I cannot tell you where he stays more than he does; but I shall give you another pair of slippers and a ball which will take you to another brother that lives about eight hundred miles off, and about a thousand years older; he will likely be able to tell you where he dwells.' He, as formerly, goes again on his adventure, and found the old man, who seemed rather sulky, saying, he knew what he wanted, and if he would stay with him till tomorrow, he would endeavour to put him upon a plan to find him out. Tomorrow comes, when the prince was taken to a different apartment of the house where he had slept, and addressed by the old man thus: 'As there are three of Green Sleeves' daughters come to the river Ugie to bathe under the disguise of swans' feathers, you will get behind a hedge of the black sloe-berry tree, and there you will be able to observe all their motions without being seen. As soon as they have stript themselves of their swan-skins and laid them down, there is one with a blue wing, which you will immediately take up and retain.

The prince went as directed, and hid himself behind the sloe-thorn hedge, when he saw three of the most beautiful swans come and hover over the river for a little time, at length alight and throw off their swan-skins, when he snatched up the one with the blue wing. After they had continued for some time in the water, they prepared to proceed directly home; but as the one who had the skin with the blue wing could not find hers, she was at a loss what to do, more particularly as the other two told her they would not wait, but go home without her. On looking wistfully around her, she spied the prince, whom she knew, and asked him if he had her swan-skin. He acknowledged the theft, and said, if she would tell him where Green Sleeves stayed, he would deliver unto her the skin. This she said she durst not venture to do, but upon his immediately giving it up, she would teach him how to discover the place of his retreat if he would follow her directions. He then gave her the skin, and she directed him as follows: 'First you will come to a river which you will easily cross, but the second will appear more difficult, as it will be raging and foaming up from the bottom; this you must not heed, but venture in, when I will stand by you, and cause a wind to blow upon your clothes which will immediately dry them.'

He found the waters as described, but got more easily over them than he imagined, as he was attended by the lady, who whistled him over, and dried his clothes agreeably to the contract. On his arriving at the opposite shore, he spied a castle, which he took to be the residence of Green Sleeves. This castle he walked round and round, but could find no entrance; at one of the corners he discovered a little bell which he rang, and which brought to his view the porter, who surlily asked what he wanted. The prince replied that it was Green Sleeves. Green Sleeves next made his appearance, and said, 'Well, my prince, you have at length found me out.' On being invited into the castle, he espied an old woman sitting among the ashes, whom Green Sleeves commanded for an old hag to rise up immediately and let the prince sit down. She did as required, but the dust that flew from her clothes was likely to smother him. He next commanded her to go and give the prince some meat, when she brought him a few fish-skins and old moulded bread, which he said his delicate stomach could not use. Green Sleeves replied, there was no matter, he could go to bed supperless, as he had to rise in the morning and do a job for him. On going to bed, it was composed of pieces of broken glass, such as bottles and the like, which prevented him from lying down, as the more he attempted to clear away the rubbish, it accumulated the more; but on looking around him he spied Blue Wing through a small aperture in the door, who bade him cheer up and not be afraid, as she would be his friend and assist him in the time of need; and, as a proof of the reality of her promise, she immediately transformed his apartment into one of the finest rooms imaginable, with a soft and easy bed for his accommodation.

In the morning when he arose, everything appeared as it was before, so that, when Green Sleeves appeared, and asked him how he had slept, he was told that it was impossible for anyone to have slept on such a bed, and he considered his treatment very harsh, adding at the same time that if he (the prince) had gained the game, he would not have used him so cruelly. Green Sleeves, however, persisted in giving him another task to perform, which he thought would not be in the power of man to accomplish, and that was to build a house about a thousand miles long, as many broad, and as many high, to be covered over with feathers of every kind of bird that flew; and to have a stone in it out of every quarry in the world, and to be ready before twelve o'clock next day; or it was to cost him his life. On hearing of this, he was sadly distressed, and knew not what to do, when Blue Wing appeared and requested him not to do anything towards the rearing of it, as it was impossible for him to accomplish it alone. She then opened a box, out of which started some thousands of fairies, who immediately commenced working, and had the house all finished against the time appointed by Green Sleeves, who appeared and remarked, that he had finished his task as commanded; he would therefore go home to his supper and bed, as he had another task for him to perform on tomorrow. His supper and bed were composed of the same substance as they were before, when Blue Wing appeared and changed both into what were more suitable and agreeable for a princely stomach and constitution.

On the morning when he arose, Green Sleeves said he had a cask of lintseed to sow which he must sow, reap, and have the seed in the cask in the same condition as that which he gave him out, before tomorrow night. Blue Wing then came in as before, and again set her little fairy emissaries to work, part of them cultivating the ground, part sowing the seed, part reaping, and so on, till the whole were finished by the evening. Thus being done, he waited in the fields till Green Sleeves appeared; who, when he had observed that the work was finished, he ordered him home to his supper and bed, which was as usual, but Blue Wing still continued his friend, and gave him a comfortable supper and bed as before.

In the morning, Green Sleeves had another task for him to perform, which, if he accomplished aright, it was to be the last. He was then put to clean the stable where there had stood for two hundred years, two hundred horses, and to find among the dung a gold needle which had been lost by his grandmother, about a thousand years before. The task, like all the former ones which had been imposed upon him, was impossible for him to accomplish alone; but Blue Wing coming in at the time, again set all her little family to work, and cleaned the stable of its rubbish, found the long lost needle, and gave it to the prince, with an injunction not to let her father know that she assisted him in any manner of way, should he put such a question to him, or even insinuate as much. The whole being now finished, Green Sleeves came in, and on receiving the golden needle said he supposed his daughter Blue Wing had greatly assisted him in all his tasks, or he never would have got them accomplished. But the prince, as desired, denied it. Blue Wing also informed the prince that her father would offer one of his daughters to him in marriage, but to be sure to accept of none of them, for if he did, they would immediately murder him; but as it would be somewhat difficult for him to know them, as he would only see them through a small hole in a door, she would tie a blue thread around her finger, and hold it out, so that he might take hold of it, and cause her father to open the door, as he wanted her in marriage; for, if he once let go the finger she was lost to him for ever. All as Blue Wing foretold him came to pass, for Green Sleeves caused first the one daughter and then the second pass before him; but he would accept of none of them till Blue Wing came, who held out her finger, when he seized it, and commanded the door to be opened. Her father taunted him a good deal about his foolish choice, saying the other two were more handsome and wise women, and that he had made choice of the worst of the three; but being determined to stick to his agreement, he retained her.

Next morning the wedding was to be solemnized, but Blue Wing had previously taught the prince not to drink any of the wine at the marriage feast, as it would be poisoned, but to have a horn prepared by their sides, into which they were to pour the wine. This being done, Blue Wing baked three magical cakes with the wine, and hung one to each of the bed posts in which they were to sleep that night, which would make answer to any question put to them. The prince and Blue Wing, instead of going to bed as anticipated by Green Sleeves, mounted two of the best horses in the stable, and with all haste rode off. Green Sleeves, imagining that the prince and Blue Wing would be now asleep in bed, as he had determined to murder them, went to the bedside and asked if they were asleep, when one of the cakes replied they were not, and seemed very much displeased at their untimely visit. A little time after he went a second time, and received the same repulse, and so on a third time, when the cake in the back of the bed informed him his daughter and the prince were gone off long ago, and were now many hundred miles distant. This enraged him greatly, and so violent was his passion that he determined to devour the old woman, as he said she was art and part in the knowledge of their flight.

He then put on his boots of seven leagues, and followed them with all speed. On their observing him coming up so fast, they were afraid that they would now be murdered, but Blue Wing said to the prince, put your hand into one of the horses' ears and he would find a small piece of wood, which, on throwing over his left shoulder, would immediately turn into a great wood. This having the desired effect, Green Sleeves had to return and call all his hewers of wood to cut it down. The field was no sooner cleared of the wood than he pursued them again with all vigour. On his coming up with them a second time, the prince became fearful; but to allay his fears, the now princess (Blue Wing) desired him to put his hand into the horse's other ear where he would find a small stone, which, when taken out and thrown over his left shoulder, as he had done the piece of wood, there would arise a very great rock. This also being done, Green Sleeves had a second time to return back and call all his quarriers to cut away the rock. He then pursued as formerly; but when he was nearly up with the prince and princess, there being a drop of water at the horse's nose, it was thrown as the others had been, over the prince's left shoulder, when instantly there appeared a great river, which made him return a third time for all his ship carpenters to build him a ship for to sail over it. He again mastered this difficulty, and got over the river, pursuing with all his might the fugitive prince and princess. The prince now became more fearful than ever, thinking all their means and sources of escape had been exhausted, and nothing but inevitable death awaited them. The princess still informed him there was a way left them for deliverance, and desired him to go to the top of a high hill as fast as possible, and there he would find an egg in a certain bird's nest, which he would take out, and if he struck her father on a particular part of his breast, he would fall immediately; but if he chanced to miss that spot, they were both gone. The prince, as good fortune still attended him, found the egg, which had the desired effect, for he had no sooner thrown it than Green Sleeves fell, which rid them of a very troublesome enemy.

They now pursued their journey in peace, till within a few miles of his father's kingdom, when she requested him to pursue his route alone, but to inform his parents on his first arrival at the court the good services she had performed for him, then would they call her with great honour and respect; but if she were to go with him immediately they would conceive her to be some lightsome leman. She also warned him to beware of allowing anyone to kiss him; for if he did, he would then think no more of her, but forget all that she had done for him. This he determined to keep in mind; but unluckily a little lap-dog in the height of his kindness kissed the prince, which had the effect as foretold by the princess, of making him forget his princess, Blue Wing. The princess having continued for a long time in the place where she had been left, went up into a tree near a goldsmith's house, from whence came the housemaid with a pitcher to draw water from a well beneath the tree; but seeing the shadow of the princess in the water, and thinking it to be her own, she got quite vain, broke the pitcher, and said it was a shame for such a beauty to act in the capacity of a servant to such a mean man. She therefore went away to seek a better fortune, and not returning, the housekeeper came to the well next, when being puffed up with the same vain and false delusions, went also away to another place. The goldsmith now wondering much at their long stay, went himself to the well, where seeing the likeness of a female in the water, suspected the cause of their disappearance, and remarked to himself that if he had not known himself to be a man, he also would have been deceived; so looking up to the tree, he saw the princess, whom he charged with being the cause of his servants absenting themselves from his service. She replied that she could not help their indulging in such foolish notions; but if he would take her home to his dwelling, she would endeavour to make up for his loss by her steady perseverance in the way to please him. He accordingly agreed, and home they went together.

She continued in his service till it happened on a day that the young prince, her husband, was going to be married, he sent his groom to the goldsmith to get ready gold mounting for the horses; but he, seeing the princess in the capacity of a menial, was so taken with her beauty that he made love to her, and offered her a considerable sum of money if she would consent to lie with him all that night. This she agreed to, but upon conditions that she was to undress and go first to bed. This being done, she said she had forgot to set down some water by her master's bedside, and must needs to rise and do it; but to prevent her from rising up, he went to do it, which was no sooner done than she commanded him to stand still in the posture he went, and to continue that way all night. He endeavoured with all his might to set himself at liberty, but could not succeed. He then offered her all the money they had agreed upon for the bedding, to set him free, and he would never make such another proposal to her. Upon these terms she liberated him, refusing his money, but requesting him to publish her beauty and powers wherever he went, and whenever he had an opportunity, particularly before all the noblemen in the court.

As soon as at liberty, he did as he had promised, when the Duke of Marlborough went to find her out, which was easily done. He, like the groom, bargained with her for a very large sum of money to have the pleasure of sleeping with her that night. However, as on the former occasion, she went first to bed, and observed to the duke that she had forgot to cover up the fire for fear of danger; but he agreed to do it to prevent her from rising from her bed. He had no sooner taken the shovel in his hand to perform the work than she commanded him to work in that manner all the night, or till she released him. He soon saw he was duped, and begged her to free him from such an ignominious task, and she should have all the money agreed for, and not be subject to lie with him as proposed. She refused the money, and set him at liberty upon conditions of his taking her as his partner to a splendid ball which was to take place at court shortly afterwards. This he promised faithfully to perform, and when the ball commenced, the duke had one of the most handsome and beautifully dressed partners in all the hall. After they had danced till all parties were wearied, it was proposed that they should sing a song, or tell a tale about for their future amusement. Everyone having sung a song, or told a tale, it came to the princess's turn, when she was reminded of her duty, but instead of singing, or telling a tale herself, she put down on the floor a golden cock and hen, with a few particles of bere and oats. The hen began to abuse the cock thus: 'You are now like some other people in this world, you soon begin in the time of your prosperity to forget what I have done for you in the time of your adversity; how I built a house for you, sowed the lintseed, and cleaned the stable, and found the golden needle.' These put the prince in remembrance of everything that had taken place regarding himself, and that the lady was no other than his favourite Blue Wing, to whom he had formerly been married. The other lady was set at liberty, and the princess, Blue Wing, reinstated, with all the honours and joys that love and gratitude could devise. They lived together many years happy, and saw a thriving and beautiful generation rise up in their place, who did honour to their education and talents.

THE PRINCESS OF THE
BLUE MOUNTAINS

Source: Peter Buchan, 'Ancient Scottish Tales'
Narrator: Unknown
Type: AT400 'The Man on a Quest for His Lost Wife'

A poor widow, who had but an only son, indulged him so much that he grew lazy, and at length would not so much as obey her in anything so that she was forced to drive him through violence from her solitary habitation. Having now nowhere to fly for shelter when the merciless storms approached, he thought it better to take heart and pursue his fortune in a strange land. He began his journey early one morning in May when trees were budded, and fields looked green, and continued till he reached the side of a rapid river where he sat down; at times he rose to make a desperate plunge, but as oft his heart recoiled from the apparent danger he had to undergo. In this dilemma, a lady on the opposite bank had observed all his motions, and knew his fear, and made a sign to him to venture in, which he did, and safely reached the opposite shore. The lady now took him under her protection, gave him meat and comfortable clothes, and bade him be easy as to his future journey. She then requested of him to go into a beautiful garden, and pull and bring unto her the fairest flower; but after having searched it all over, he returned, and said that she was the most beautiful flower in all the garden. On hearing this she asked of him if he would accept of her for his wife, with which he most readily answered, yes! She then said that if he knew but half of the dangers that he would have to encounter for her sake, he never would have made such a choice. 'However,' says she, 'I will do the best to preserve you, at least I will give you such armour that, if rightly used, no one will be able to overcome you. Know

38

then,' adds she, 'that I am the Princess of the nine runners of the Blue Mountains that was stolen away from my father's court by Grimaldin the demon; and with his legions you will have to fight before you can set me free. This night you will be attacked by three legions of his demons; but here are three black sticks, and an unction. Each stick will beat off a legion of the demons, and the unction, if you chance to receive any hurt, as soon as applied, will make you whole again. Use these things well, for now I must leave you.'

She had no sooner fled from his presence than the demons made their appearance, and asked his business there, which he answered not at all out of countenance, for he had great faith in the armour with which the lady had chosen to invest him. They then thinking to beat his brains out lifted up their clubs, but the young man parried their blows so artfully that he got no hurt. He then fell to beating them with his black sticks, which had the desired effect of obtaining a complete victory, as the lady had foretold. Next morning the princess paid a visit to our young hero, and remarked that he was the first that had had the courage to withstand the sight of so many fierce cannibals, and hoped he would be able to encounter as many more next night; and with that she gave him other six sticks, one for each legion, and an additional supply of the unction, in case he were wounded. The lady visited him as on the former occasion, in the morning after the engagement, and expressed her joy at seeing him well. She however told him, that that night he had twelve legions of demons to fight, with the tyrant Grimaldin at their head. He replied that he found himself twelve times stronger than at first, and was nowise afraid to meet with them all. She then gave him as before a black stick for every legion, with more of the unction in case he should be by any means hurt, as Grimaldin was more cunning than any of the others which had come before him. She then took her departure, and he to prepare anew for the re-encounter with the demons. They then began to assemble in battle array, when their captain asked him what was his business there. He told him he had come to rescue a princess from his horrid thraldom and slavery, and that he would do or die in the manly attempt. 'Then you shall die,' said Grimaldin. 'Not yet,'

Will said, 'I have more good to perform first.' Grimaldin then caused his demons to strike; but Will having had the charmed sticks, beat them all off. Grimaldin now began to fume and rage, and with a bold stroke made at Will brought him to the ground, but he, immediately applying the ointment, became as whole as ever, and rose more strengthened than before, and beat off Grimaldin also.

Next morning, as she was wont to do, the lady appeared, and seeing him safe from harm, told him he had now no more dangers to fear, all were past and gone, provided he would abide by her counsel. She then gave him a book, wherein was written the lives of all the chiefs of her nation, and requested him to keep reading the same, and upon no account to take his eyes off it; for, if he did, it would cause him much sorrow. She also told him that by due attention to the reading of that book, he would soon become one of her father's favourites, and be transported to the country where she was going, which was a great way off. He had no sooner began to read than he heard many voices calling him all sorts of opprobrious and bad names to attempt him to look off his book; but he withstood all their temptations. Unluckily, however, one person called out 'Who will buy apples?', which he hearing, and being exceedingly fond of that fruit, he chanced to gaze around him, and was immediately thrown with considerable violence against an old woman's basket.

For some time he knew not where he was, so much was he stunned with the suddenness of the shock. On recovering himself a little, he saw an old man resting on a seat in the shade of his cottage to whom he applied for information of the kingdom of the nine runners of the Blue Mountains. The old man said that he did not know, but he would call an assembly of the fishes of the sea, and ask of them. He did so, but none could answer him. He then told him that perhaps his brother could assist to find it, as he was five hundred years older than he, who himself was only two; but the place of his residence was four hundred miles further off; however, that could be easily overcome, as he would give him a pair of swift slippers, and a ball to roll before him, which would bring him safely and shortly to the place. He did as desired, and found himself at the second old man's door. He soon after made his appearance; Will then asked him as he had done his brother, but he could not inform him without calling a council of the birds. Which he shortly after having done, they all appeared at his call unless one very old eagle; but none of them knew. At length the eagle arrived, who excused himself by saying that he had been long away, as he was engaged carrying a witch away to a far distant place of the world. The eagle was then questioned as to his knowledge of this kingdom, who replied that he knew it well, and had orders to carry Will on his back to it, with a good supply of oxen and other provisions. They then mounted, and the eagle flew off.

When they arrived at the kingdom, they alighted, and Will dismounted. He had not travelled long till he reached a house hung around with black, where Will asked for lodgings, but was refused upon the account that the proprietor of the house was that day to suffer death, having been selected for that purpose by a giant, which had come from an unknown country, and had made their nation to pay a human victim to him daily as a sacrifice for his table, and that the king's daughter was offered in marriage to anyone who would deliver their country from this terrible cannibal. She had once been delivered from the oppression of Grimaldin by a Scottish chieftain, but had lost him on her return to her father, which she regretted mightily. Will, hearing these things, again dressed himself in armour, went out next morning, and after a hard struggle slew the giant. He was then recognized by the princess who told her father, who at once consented to their union, and at his death bestowed on him his kingdom. Will then sent for his mother, and they lived all together, long and happy.

THE WIDOW'S SON AND KING'S DAUGHTER

Source: Peter Buchan, 'Ancient Scottish Tales'
Narrator: Unknown
Type: AT300 'The Dragon-Slayer'

There was a widow woman who had only one son whom she indulged in every habit of laziness, never putting him to do any kind of work for fear of offending him. At length her finances became exhausted, and she was under the necessity of asking some meal on credit; but having applied to a neighbour, she was refused with the sarcastic remark that she should put her son to work for her, and then she would not be under obligations to anyone. Having returned empty-handed, and want staring them in the face, for the first time she now told her son he must do something for a living to himself, as she could support him now no longer. He took the hint, and next morning arose by break of day, packed up his little wardrobe, tied it on his back, and in this manner took his departure. After having travelled the greater part of a long summer day, he stopt at a house near a wood, where he asked lodgings for the night as he was faint for want of meat, and weary with travel. His request was granted, and some meat set before him, of which he ate greedily. The goodman of the house said that he should be working, and not going about idle. The young man replied that he would most cheerfully, if anyone would employ him. The farmer then sent him to the field to herd cattle, but strictly enjoined him not to go near a certain field, where a giant lived, for if he did he would undoubtedly be devoured, and the cattle sacrificed to the hungry maw of the greedy giant.

He had not long herded the cattle when, espying the tempting fruit that hung upon some trees in the forbidden garden of the giant's, he longed to taste it, and rather than not satisfy his longing appetite, he would run the risk of his life. Jack then went up into one of the finest trees and began to pluck and eat of the choicest of the fruit, when an old woman chanced to pass, and did ask of him some of the fruit, which was readily granted to her; when she in return gave him three black rods, with a sword, that whomsoever he chanced to strike with the sword, they would immediately drop down dead. Shortly after the disappearance of the old woman, out came one of the giants, for there were three of them, and demanded of him his authority for destroying of the fruit; and, at the same time said, that if he did not come down from the tree immediately, he would eat him up alive. This did not daunt the spirit of Jack, who had great faith in the magical sword; so on the giant tearing the tree up by the root in order to throw Jack down, he was struck with the sword and laid senseless at the feet of his young master. On the morrow, Jack went again to the fruit field, and behold, another giant came running up to him in great fury, who also demanded his business in that place; but Jack killed him also. The third day, Jack went to pluck of the fruit, when the third giant made his appearance, and requested to know to whom the cattle belonged, as he must have some of them to supper; but Jack, who by this time had concealed himself in the hollow of a tree, cried from thence, 'Ask my leave first.' On hearing this the giant turned round with an angry countenance, and says, 'O, you pigmy. Is it you have killed my two brothers? I shall be revenged of you before long.'

Jack, however, killed him as he had done the two former giants, then went to their castle, which was not far off but kept by a blackamoor. This blackamoor Jack soon made deliver up the keys of all the treasures in the castle, and to be at all times at his command. He now left this part of the country and returned home, where he found the people weeping. Having asked the cause, he was told that a dragon had come and imposed upon them a serious task, which was a young lady as a sacrifice to him every day, and tomorrow the princess was to become a victim to his rage unless anyone should step forward in her defence, and rid the country of this monster. Jack, having heard the terms, immediately ordered his man to saddle and bring to him one of the best of his horses, with the white armour. Having all things in readiness, he went to the princess, whom he found bound to a stake, and told her the cause of his coming, that it was in her defence; and, if that she would marry him, he would save her life, or die in the attempt. To this she consented, and he laid his head on her knee, and was lulled asleep. During the time he lay asleep, she wove in his hair a ringlet with white stones, very precious, and beautiful to behold.

She had no sooner accomplished the charm in his hair than she saw the dragon coming to devour her, when she awoke him out of his pleasant slumber. On approaching the princess, Jack drew his sword, and stood between her and the danger to which she was exposed. He made several brave and well-aimed thrusts at the dragon, but owing to the fire which it vomited up, he never prevailed, nor could the dragon succeed in destroying the lady, but was obliged to flee to save its life, for it was becoming much exhausted. Next day the dragon returned, and so did Jack clothed in red armour, but neither was more successful than on the preceding day, for the dragon still kept Jack at bay by vomiting fire, which was likely to burn him up. However, Jack again beat it off, and caused it to take wing and fly away. On the third day Jack chose a camel, and caused it to swallow a great quantity of water, and therewith went a third time to the fight. The dragon again appeared in quest of the princess, but Jack being now his match, having caused the camel to lay in a plentiful supply of water, he dared him to the fight. The dragon, as on the two former occasions, began to spout fire upon Jack, but the camel in return spouted water, so as to quench the dragon's fire, so that, in a little time, it became worsted, when Jack laid so well about him as to deprive it of life.

Having now overcome this monster in single combat, he cut off its head, and carried it along with him. The princess now became his betrothed wife, when he again went away in search of new adventures, till at the end of nine months the princess bore an heir, but she nor her father knew to whom, for Jack had not made himself known unto her nor her father, previous to his going away. The old king was now much vexed at his daughter not knowing the father of her child, and upbraided her unmercifully, as being a prostitute, and a disgrace to the royal name. This made her one day go with her father to ask counsel of a fairy, who told them that the father of the child, and none else, would be able to take the lemon from the child which it then held in its hand. On their return from the abode of the fairy, the king caused a meeting of all the lords, squires, bishops, lairds, farmers, and afterwards their servants, to take place at the king's palace on a certain day which was then named, and try to take the lemon from the child's hand; but it baffled the power and skill of the whole multitude then assembled.

At length Jack made his appearance, and had no sooner touched the child's hand than the lemon left it. The king then, surprised, commanded that both should be put into a bottomless boat and be sent to a distant island. They had not been long in the boat when a lady appeared, and told them that she was the fairy who had given him the sword that killed the giants, and defended the princess from the fury of the dragon; and that she would still be their friend; and as a proof of this, she touched the boat, when it became whole, and their clothes that were ragged became very fine. They then returned to the harbour, dressed in all the splendour of royalty, in which they appeared at court.

Great honours were then paid them, and a rich feast prepared for their entertainment, of which they partook most readily. After dinner, the best wine was set before them, and they were invited to drink freely, but in a short space the king missed his gold cup, which only made its appearance at table on particular occasions. Jack had pocketed it for the purpose of observing the king's countenance on the discovery. The king wondered much where it could be found, when Jack says, he thought that kings wondered continually, for he was the same when his daughter was likely to be devoured by the dragon. He then threw down the cup, and with it the dragon's head, saying, 'In me behold the cause of all your wonder, for it was I who stole your cup, and it was I who saved your daughter from becoming a victim to the fury of the monstrous dragon.' 'And, as a further proof of his statement,' added the princess, 'behold in his hair the identical ringlet which I wove with white stones the first day he attacked the dragon.' The king then caused them to be publicly married, attended with rejoicing and feasting, which lasted many days. Jack afterwards sent for his mother and treated her with great kindness, while he inherited the crown on the old king's death.

THE WIDOW'S SON AND OLD MAN

Source: Peter Buchan, 'Ancient Scottish Tales'
Narrator: Unknown
Type: AT302 'The Ogre's Heart in the Egg'

There was a poor widow who had a number of children, and to whom she could not get sufficient meat nor clothes. One night, in order to still their clamorous tongues, and to get them quietly to bed, she put into the pot a stone, making them believe at the time it was meat, and before they were awakened it would be ready. A little after there came in a stranger, who asked lodgings, but as there was no meat in the house to give him she told him that he could not lodge there that night, as she had nothing for supper. On seeing the pot on the fire, he asked of her what it contained, when she told him. He then replied that it was a leg of excellent mutton which he would show her, and taking it out of the pot convinced her of its reality. He next requested her to go to the other end of the house where she would find in a chest plenty of bread, and other provisions. She found the bread as he had said, and awakened her children to partake of the same.

After having eaten heartily the oldest boy begged the stranger next to tell them some amusing little tale, with which he readily complied. The tale being told as requested, he asked payment from the boy, who said he had nothing to give. The stranger then took him with him to a riverside where he threw him in, and turned him into a fish, and bade him tell at the end of seven days what he could give; but when the time limited was expired, he asked the boy the same question as he had done before, and received the same answer. He then turned him into a serpent which twisted itself around a large tree, and at the end of seven days asked the former question, and received the former answer.

47

Next he turned him into a magpie, and at the end of seven days asked the former question, but now received a different answer. The magpie prayed heaven to bless him for so good a story. The stranger then replied, 'If you had said this at first, you would have saved yourself and me both unnecessary trouble. Go now to yon old castle which is enchanted, and kept by a giant, not far off; the guards in it will all be fast asleep. After having gone through many rooms, you will find the King of Scotland's daughter sleeping on a marble table. Touch the talisman above her head, and she will awake and teach you what is best to be done for her recovery, and those in the other apartments of the castle.' Saying this, he left him.

The young man went, and found everything as the stranger had told; so that when the princess awoke, she asked him how he had got through the guards, which he answered, with many other questions. She then told him that the giant's life lay in an egg, which if destroyed, he would immediately die. She also told him that it was kept by an old woman, who if he could dispose of her in any manner of way, he would find the egg, which he could easily break, and when broken they would be safe. She then directed him to the abode of the old witch, which he found, and bidding her good morrow said, 'You are not well, I see.' 'No,' says she, 'but if you would take me to the air I would be better.' He then took her upon his back and threw her into a large fire, when she went out of the chimney with a noise resembling thunder. He next found the egg, which he destroyed also, when the giant fell with a tremendous crash a lifeless corpse on the ground before the castle. Then all the prisoners who slept awoke, and testified their joy, and gave him thanks for their deliverance.

Each went their own way, and he went home with Malcolm's daughter, and received her in marriage from the old king, as a testimony of his gratitude for her deliverance. The king also conferred on him some of the courtly honours, and it is said to be from him that the whole dukes of Buccleuch have descended. They were afterwards blessed with a numerous and happy family.

KATE CRACKERNUTS

Source: Katharine Briggs, *A Dictionary of British Folk-Tales*
Narrator: Unknown; collected by D. J. Robinson
Type: AT711 'The Beautiful and the Ugly Twin'

Once upon a time there was a king and a queen, as in many lands have been. The king had a dochter, Kate, and the queen had one. The queen was jealous of the king's dochter being bonnier than her own, and cast about to spoil her beauty. So she took counsel of the henwife, who told her to send the lassie to her next morning fasting. The queen did so, but the lassie found means to get a piece before going out. When she came to the henwife's she asked for eggs, as she had been told to do; the henwife desired her to 'lift the lid off that pot there' and see. The lassie did so, but naething happened. 'Gae hame to your minnie, and tell her to keep the press door better steekit,' said the henwife. The queen knew from this that the lassie had had something to eat, so watched the next morning, and sent her away fasting; but the princess saw some country folk picking peas by the roadside, and being very affable she spoke to them and took a handful of the peas, which she ate by the way.

In consequence, the answer at the henwife's house was the same as on the preceding day.

The third day the queen goes along with the girl to the henwife. Now, when the lid is lifted off the pot, off jumps the princess's ain bonny head, and on jumps a sheep's head.

The queen, now quite satisfied, returns home.

Her own daughter, however, took a fine linen cloth and wrapped it round her sister's head and took her by the hand and gaed out to seek their fortin. They gaed and they gaed far, and far'er than I can tell, till they cam to a king's castle. Kate chappit at the door and sought a night's lodging for hersel' and a sick sister. This is granted on condition that Kate sits up all night to watch the king's sick son, which she is quite willing to do. She is also promised a 'pock o' siller, if a's right'. Till midnight all goes well. As twelve o'clock rings, however, the sick prince rises, dresses himself, and slips downstairs, followed by Kate unnoticed. The prince went to the stable, saddled his horse, called his hound, jumped into the saddle, Kate leaping lightly up behind him. Away rode the prince and Kate through the greenwood, Kate, as they pass, plucking nuts from the trees and filling her apron with them. They rode on and on till they came to a green hill. The prince here drew bridle and spoke, 'Open, open, green hill, an' let the young prince in with his horse and his hound;' 'and,' added Kate, 'his lady him behind.'

Immediately the green hill opened and they passed in. A magnificent hall is entered brightly lighted up, and many beautiful ladies surround the prince and lead him off to the dance, while Kate, unperceived, seats herself by the door. Here she sees a bairnie playing with a wand, and overhears one of the fairies say, 'Three strakes o' that wand would mak' Kate's sick sister as bonnie as ever she was.' So Kate rowed nuts to the bairnie, and rowed nuts till the bairnie let fall the wand, and Kate took it up and put it in her apron.

Then the cock crew, and the prince made all haste to get on horseback, Kate jumping up behind, and home they rode, and Kate sat down by the fire, and cracked her nuts, and ate them. When the morning came Kate said the prince had a good night, and she was willing to sit up another night, for which she was to get a 'pock o' gowd'. The second night passed as the first had done. The third night Kate consented to watch only if she should marry the sick prince. This time the bairnie was playing with a birdie; Kate heard one of the fairies say, 'Three bites of that birdie would mak' the sick prince as weel as ever he was.' Kate rowed nuts to the bairnie till the birdie was dropped, and Kate put it in her apron.

At cockcrow they set off again, but instead of cracking her nuts as she used to do, Kate plucked the feathers off, and cooked the birdie. Soon there arose a very savoury smell. 'Oh!' said the sick prince, 'I wish I had a bite o' that birdie.' So Kate gave him a bit o' the birdie, and he rose up on his elbow. By and by he cried out again, 'Oh, if I had anither bite o' that birdie!' So Kate gave him another bit, and he sat up on his bed. Then he said again, 'Oh! if I had a third bite o' that birdie!' So Kate gave him a third bit, and he rose quite well, dressed himself, and sat down by the fire, and when the folk came i' the mornin' they found Kate and the young prince cracking nuts th'gether. So the sick son married the weel sister, and the weel son married the sick sister, and they all lived happy and dee'd happy, and never drank out o' a dry cappy.

THE BLACK LAIRD

Source: *Tocher* 17
Narrator: Betsy Whyte; recorded by Peter Cooke and Linda Headlee
(Linda Williamson) in February 1975. The story was learned from her grandmother
Type: AT325 'The Magician and His Pupil'

Well, this one is an auld man and woman at the seaside, ye see, an they had a son, but he wisnae much good for anything. But he used to sit an watch the boats comin in an the ships an that, and jist sit an look. But one day one o the captains o the boats came and asked if he would take him to sea for a year and a day, an he says, 'I can guarantee that he'll be a much better man when he comes back.'

So they said och, they'd just le him go. So away he goes now, this man – but he wis a Black Laird, ye see, although he wis a sea captain: but he also had places on the land, ye see, that he came back tae. So he took this laddie away, an he taught him an taught him the Black Art, ye see, as well as his work, an he taught him an taught him, because he was gettin aald himsel an he wanted somebody . . .

So he taught this boy and he came back at the end o the year an the day as good as his word, and he said to the aald man an woman, 'I'd really like him for another year and a day, if yeze dinnae mind, and A'll give yeze another five gold sovereigns.' So they were quite happy wi this, ye see, and away they went again. And as good as his word he wis back the next year and a day.

He says, 'Now, he can come back,' he says, 'but,' he says, 'I don't know,' he says. 'I'd like him to come up and see me' – because he had taught him too well, ye see, an Jack wis as good as his learnin master.

So up he goes and they were havin games and one was testin the other out on this an that an the next thing, but this Black

52

Laird jist saw that the laddie was jist a bittie too much for him. So he says, 'Ah na, A cannae hae this no as long as A'm livin.' So he changed him intae a horse in his stables – ye see, he hed this big farm on land as well as the boats at sea: he could dae whit he liked. An he changed this laddie intae a horse, an he said tae the servants, 'Now don't let him go or give him nothing,' he says; 'ye can feed him, but don't take the bit oot o his mooth or let him go.'

So this servant lassie she did that, but when she was goin aboot her workin ... he could speak, ye see, he says, 'Oh, ye might,' he says, 'take me oot for one drink o water,' he says. 'A'm dyin for a drink o water.'

She says, 'Well, don't tell him.'

He says, 'A'll no tell him,' he says. 'Jist take me oot.' So she took the horse oot for a drink o water tae this little stream. And he says, 'A cannae drink wi this bit in ma mooth.' He says, 'It's no like A wis a real horse an used wi a bit in ma mooth,' he says; 'wid ye take it oot jist for one minute?'

So she took pity on him and she took the bit oot o his mooth. Now he immediately changed intae a fish intae the water, an he's away doon the water. But this Black Laird, he wisnae lang in gettin wind o this, ye see, he knew whit was whit; so he changed intae an otter an he's after this fish. But right further doon when the stream went intae the river, an the river was flowin past the houses, there wis a lady sittin, and she had her hand in the water like this, ye see. So Jack, he changed himsel intae a ring on her finger, and the Black Laird, he changed back intae a man again. Now this lady went home an she says, 'Where did I get this?' she says. 'That is ma most beautiful ring, but I can't remember gettin it.' Ye know? So he jist stayed there.

But the Black Laird, he came up tae the hoose, up tae her hisband's hoose, an he dressed himself up as a workman, ye see, and he said tae her husband, 'Are ye want' any work done about the estate?' he says. 'There's some parts in a lot o disrepair an that that I could fix up fir ye, very cheaply.'

An he says, 'Ah, yeze aa say that but yeze never make a good job and dae it cheap.'

He says, 'I promise I will, A'll make the best job ye've ever saw an the cheapest job ye've ever saw.' He says, 'All roond aboot this part here,' he says, 'I could face all that up fir ye an make it really nice, an sort that gable-end,' and so on and so forth.

So he says, 'Well, all right, but,' he says, 'not a penny if the job's not as good as ye say.' So – but he just wanted to be near Jack, ye see. So he worked an worked and he did the job an even built a big new wing ontae the place an made everything lovely.

And . . . Jack wis beginnin to get a bit worried, ye see? So there was one night he changed back into himself, when the lady was on her own. She got an awfae fright. She says, 'Ma goodness, who are you and where did ye come from?'

'Well,' he says, 'ye'll maybe no believe me,' he says, 'but I'm the little ring you've hid on your finger for this past weeks.' And she looked, and she says, 'A ring?' He says, 'Yes.' 'Well,' she says, 'and what do you want?' she says.

'Well,' he says, 'I've been enchanted, an,' he says, 'A'm bein hunted,' he says, 'wi that man that's doin your husband's work fir ye. An,' he says, 'A want you to try an help me,' he says, 'because he means tae kill me.'

She says, 'Well, whit can I do?'

He says, 'Well, A'll tell ye,' he says. 'The job's finished now, and,' he says, 'you tell your husband you want tae celebrate for gettin all this work done an everything, an tell him you want a big bonfire on the grounds o the estate made, an,' he says, 'A want you tae scatter peas an barley all round about the bonfire, but no too close,' he says. 'Will ye dae that?'

She says, 'I will.' So the followin night they had this big bonfire put up, an they lit it up and they're all making merry roond aboot it and, eh, Jack, he changed himself intae one o these seeds o barley, ye see, that was roond aboot the bonfire. But this Black Laird, he knew aboot that. So he changed himself intae a big cockerel, and he started peckin at the peas an barley.

But Jack immediately turned intae a fox and got him by the neck and killed him. And that was the end o the story!

THE MAN IN THE BOAT

Source: Previously unpublished
Narrator: Betsy Whyte; recorded by Linda Williamson on 16 April 1987 at
Collessie, Fife. Betsy learned it from her mother. A video-recording of her telling
The Man in the Boat was made at the School of Scottish Studies in 1978.
Type: Classified in Ó Súilleabháin and Christiansen, *The Types of the Irish Folktale*,
as 2412b 'The Man Who Had No Story'

Long ago near Rannoch Moor there lived a laird and he owned a lot o' land, had lots of farm houses, cotter houses an gamekeepers' houses on this land. And every year this laird used to give a big ceilidh for all the district, people came from far and near tae attend.

Many o' them looked forward tae it for months and practised what they were goin to do at the ceilidh. Now this laird, un'nounced to anybody, he dabbled a wee bit in the Black Art, in mesmerism. But he never used it for any wickedness, only for playin tricks on some o' his friends. And he also had a cattleman called Sandy. Now Sandy was a simple man. He was good with the animals, at feeding them and looking after them, but he was quite a simple man otherwise. He always looked forward to this ceilidhs, but he would never do anything.

So this year the laird said, 'Now, there's new rules, everybody must take their turn and do something. And the rules are this, that ye tell a story, sing a sang, show yer bum or oot ye gang!' So at this ceilidh it wasna only singin, dancin, storytellin and music, there was all sorts o' tricks and games an feats o' strength and things like that that the country folk were so fond o' doin. And one o' the events was tae see who could tell the biggest lie. The winner of every event got a golden guinea – which was an awfae lot o' money at that time.

Now the thing went round and round – singin, dancin an everything else. And every time it came Sandy's turn he would say, 'No, no, Laird, ye ken fine I cannae dae nothin! I cannae, no, no!'

So the laird just let him sit there a while, until it came to an event in which everybody had to try and see who could tell the biggest lie. And when it came Sandy's turn the laird says, 'Come on, Sandy, here's yer chance! I'm sure ye could tell a lee!'

'No, no!' Sandy says. 'Ye ken fine, Laird, I cannae tell a lee! I cannae think o' a lee tae tell.'

'Come on, Sandy!' the laird says. 'This is yer last chance.'

'No, I just cannae,' Sandy said.

'Well,' the laird said, 'that's it. If ye cannae dae anything here, ye'll go oot, ye can go and make yersel useful some other way. I'll tell ye what ye can dae. Go down to the water and clean my boat, and bail the water oot o' it. Because I'll be usin it soon.'

So Sandy's away oot – wi his tail between his legs sort o' thing, his heid hangin doon – and he tramps away doon. He was really low because he didna get leave to stay at the ceilidh, he enjoyed it so much. But he got to the boat. And he scraped all the green mossy algae off it. And then he bailed oot the water, but he had tae step into the boat to get the water at the bottom. And when he stepped into the boat this boat took off wi him – like a swift it went across the water! And Sandy couldna swim. But even if he could have swum there was no way that he could hae got back, this boat were goin so swiftly across the water. And he sat there, his simple mind just completely confounded – in a daze because he couldna understand what was happenin.

But after a while he gave himsel a shake and cam tae himsel again. And when he looked doon at himsel, there on his feet were beautiful green satin slippers, beautiful silk stockins an a taffeta dress! He felt hissel all up; he was dumbfoonded before – but he was a thousand times mair dumbfoonded then! He didna ken what was happenin tae himsel, he felt this golden ringlets an this lovely smooth skin o' his face. He looked ower the side o' the boat into the water, and there was as bonny a lassie as ever yer eyes beheld – gazin up at him. And he got still mair dumbfoonded. He just sat there, and he didna come tae himsel till he felt the boat scrape the bottom at the other side of the water.

Then she, because he was a she now, stood up and looked at this wee bit o' water between the boat and the land, wonderin how she would get there without wettin her lovely green satin slippers. And just then who should come along the bank o' the water but a young man! He looked down and saw this beautiful lassie in distress. So he ran down the bank, lifted her oot o' the boat and set her on the ground.

And he said, 'Where's yer oars?'

'Ah, I don't know,' she said, in a beautiful lady's voice.

He says, 'Well, you must have had a paddle or an oar before you could get here.'

She says, 'Well, I just don't know, I can't remember what happened to them.'

And he said, 'Well, where did you come from?'

She says, 'I came from the other side of the water.'

He said, 'I know you came from the other side of the water, but what's the name o' the place or the farm that ye come from?'

'Ah . . . I-I really can't remember,' she said. She didna want to say.

And then he said, 'Can you remember where you're goin?'

'No,' she said, 'I can't.'

'Can you remember your name then? What is your name?'

Now he didna want to say, I'm Sandy the cattleman from such-an-such a farm. So she just says, 'I can't remember.'

'I know what's happened,' this young man said. 'Ye've probably lost yer oar, and tryin tae get it you've bumped yer head on the boat and now ye've lost yer memory. But dinna worry, it'll come back again in a day or two. But I think ye should come home wi me to my mother and she'll look after ye till yer memory comes back.'

So he took her home to his mother and the mother liked her, and she helped the mother roond the hoose. But weeks and weeks went past and there was no sign o' her memory comin back. And eventually this young man and her fell in love. They got married and had two o' the bonniest bairns that you could see in a month's walk.

Every Sunday they went oot for a walk with the bairns when

he wasna workin. But this particular Sunday she said, 'I would like to go doon the waterside today.'

'Oh, that's fine,' he said.

'Yes,' she says, 'we haven't been down there for a long long time.'

So away they went down the waterside with the two bairns. And suddenly she cried out, 'Oh look! There's the little boat that I came in. Oh look, it's half sunk wi water! And look at all that moss – I must go and clean it.' So she ran doon the bank. And she scraped the moss off the boat. Then she started to bail oot the water. She had to step into the boat to reach the water at the bottom, and the boat takes off with her again!

Before the young man ran doon the bank and put the bairns down, the boat was right away oot almost in the middle o' the water. And she started tae howl an scream, 'Take me back, take me back, take me back tae ma man and ma bairns! Take me back!'

But of course the boat never let on it heard her. It just kept goin. And she howled and gret and howled and gret for her man and her bairns. And she covered her face wi her hands. She sat there just the tears runnin doon between her fingers.

Then she took her hands away, and when she looked down at hersel, there on her feet was this old tackety boots and this auld mole-skinned trousers and them aa covered with coo's shearn, and this auld sleive waistcoat. And he felt himsel up, he felt the stubbles; he looked ower the side o' the boat. There was Sandy, the auld cattleman! And he gave a howl that would have waukened the dead! And started tae scream, 'No, no, no, I want back tae ma man and ma bairns. No, no!' But he just kept howlin, he couldna stop. He was really upset.

And then he felt the boat scrape the bottom right back where it had started. He jumped oot o' the boat and ran up towards the farm. He had to pass this great big barn where they held the ceilidhs, and there was a ceilidh goin on. He went and peeped in the door.

The laird saw him and the laird says, 'Ay, Sandy!'

And Sandy says, 'Dinna speak tae me!'

He says, 'What's the matter wi ye, man?'

Sandy says, 'Dinna speak tae me! It's ma man and ma bairns, ma man and ma bairns!' And he went to run away.

'Come back, Sandy! Come on and tell us aboot it.'

So Sandy came in and he sat doon beside the laird.

He said, 'That's a good laddie. Stop greetin now. Sit doon and tell us aa aboot it.'

So Sandy sat and he told them what had happened.

And Sandy had really only been away for twenty minutes! Because the laird had mesmerized him, and the event was still goin on – tae see who could tell the biggest lie in fact. So the laird turned roond and he said, 'Well, Sandy, that is definitely the biggest lie we've heard the nicht! You've won the golden guinea!' And that is the end o' that story.

THE THREE FEATHERS, OR,
SILLY JACK,
THE WATER-CARRIER

❧

Source: *Tocher* 14, School of Scottish Studies tape SA 1956/128/B2
Narrator: Andra Stewart, Blairgowrie, Perthshire; recorded by Hamish Henderson
in Glasgow in 1956. Andra learned the story from his father, John Stewart
Type: AT402 'The Mouse (Cat, Frog, etc.) as Bride'

Well, oncet upon a time there was a king and this king wis gettin up in years, he wid be away nearly the borders o eighty year auld, ye see, and he took very ill, an he wis in bed. So his doctor come tae see him and . . . he soundit oot the old king lyin in bed, an everything – he come doon, he's asked for the oldest brother tae come, ye see, so he spoke tae the oldest brother, and he says tae the oldest brother, he says: 'Yer father hasnae very long tae live,' he says, 'the best o his days is bye, an,' he says, 'Ah wouldn't be a bit surprised,' says the doctor, 'if ye come up some mornin an find him lyin dead in his bed,' ye see?

So, of coorse, it wid come as a blow tae the oldest brother, and here, the oldest brother sent for the other two brothers, ye see, sent for Jeck and the other two brothers, see? So when the two brothers come up, there wis one o this brothers like, ye understand, they cried him 'Silly Jeck', he wis awfae saft an silly, ye know, he widnae dae nothing. He wis a humbug tae the castle; he'd done nothin for the father – in fact he wasnae on the list o gettin onything left when the father died at aw. That wis jist the way o't, ye see. He wis a bad laddie. So anyway, here the three sons is stan'in, the oldest brother tellt them that the father wis goin tae die and something wid have tae be done, and 'at he was goin to be king, ye see. So the good adviser said: 'Well,' he says, 'before the father dies,' he says, 'he told me that the one that would get the best table-cover, the best an the dearest table-cover that could be found in the country, would get the castle and be king,' ye see?

'Well,' says the oldest brother, he says, 'what are we goin to do,' he says, 'have we tae go an push wir fortune?'

'No,' says the good adviser, he says, 'your father gave us three feathers,' he says, 'here they're here,' he says, 'out of an eagle's wing,' an he says, 'each o yese got tae take a feather each an go to the top tower o the castle, and throw yer feather up in the air,' he says, 'an whatever way the feather went, flutter't, that wis the way ye had tae go an push yer fortune for the table-cover.'

So right enough they aa agreed, ye see, an Jeck wi his guttery boots an everything on – the other yins wis dressed in gaads, ye know, and swords at their side, an Jeck jist ploo'ed the fields an scraped the pots doon in the kitchen an everything, cleaned the pots, but Jack wis up wi his guttery boots along wi the rest o the brothers, ye see, an they threw the feathers up, ye see, the two brothers, an one o the feathers went away be the north, the oldest brother's. 'Well,' he says, 'brothers,' he says, 'see the way my feather went,' he says, 'away be the north,' he says, 'Ah suppose that'll have to be the way Ah'll have to go an look for the table-cover.' The other second oldest brother threw the feather up, and hit went away be the south. 'Ah well,' he says, 'Ah think,' he says, 'Ah'll have tae go be the south.' So poor Jeck, they looked at Jeck, an they werena gaen tae pey any attention tae Jeck, ye see, but Jeck threw his feather up an it swirl't roon aboot an it went doon at the back o the castle, in the back-yaird o the castle, ye see? Aw the brothers starit laughin at him: 'Ha! ha! ha! ha!' They were makin a fool of Jack, ye see, because his feather went doon at the back o the castle. So Jack gien his shooders a shrug like that an he walks doon the stairs, intae the kitchen.

Noo the two brothers, they got a year an a day to get a good table-cover. So Jack never bothered goin to see aboot his table-cover or nothing, ye see, aboot his feather, rather, or nothing, ye see, so he'd jist aboot a couple o days tae go when the year an the day wis up and Jack's up one day lyin in his bed and he says:

'Ma God!' he says, 'Ah should go an hae a look at ma feather tae,' he says, 'Ah've never seen where it wis gettin.' It wis a warm kind o afternoon. He says: 'Ah'll go for the fun o the thing,' he says, 'an see where ma feather went.' So for curiosity Jeck went roon the back o the castle, an went roond the back o the castle, an he wydit through nettles an thistles an he hears a thing goin: 'Hoo-ho, o-ho-ho-ho,' greetin. Jack looks doon at his feet an here there wis a big green frog sittin, a green puddick, sittin on top o a flagstane, an the tears wis comin out o its een. An Jack looks doon an says: 'Whit's wrang wi ye, frog?'

'Oh Jeck, ye didnae gie us much time tae go on tae get ye a table-cover, did ye? Ye should hae been here long ago. You were supposed tae follow yer feather the same as ony ither body.'

But Jeck says: 'I didnae ken,' he says, 'I thocht . . . when the feather went doon at the back o the castle Ah jist had tae stay at the castle.'

'Oh well, ye cannae help it noo,' said the frog, he says, 'ye'd better come away doon. Luft that flagstane,' he says. There wis a ring, an iron ring in the flagstane. (Ye know whit a flagstane is? It's a square big stone that's in the ground an ye can lift it up, ye see.) An this big iron ring wis in this flagstane, an Jack wis a big strong lump o a fella, he lifts the stane up aboot half a turn aff the grun, ye see, an there wis trap stairs goin doon. Jack went doon the trap stairs, an the puddick hopped doon the stairs like 'at, an tellt Jack tae mind his feet.

Jeck went in. He says: 'Well, Ah never seen frogs,' he says, 'haen a place like this before.' A big long passage an 'lectric lights burnin an everything an frogs goin past him, hoppin past him, an the smell o them eatin, nice smell o restaurant an everything was something terrible, ye see. Took Jack into a lovely place like a parlour, an here when Jack went in he sut doon on this stool, an the frogs aw speakin speakin tae him, ye see, an one frog jumpit on tap o Jack's knee, an Jack's clappin the wee frog like this, an it's lookin up wi its wee golden eyes, up at Jack's face, an Jack's clappin the wee frog, pattin him on top o the back, an it's lookin up at him an laughin at him in his face.

'Well, Jack,' he says, 'you better go now,' he says, 'ye havenae much time, yer brothers'll be comin home tomorrow,' he says, 'we'll hae tae get ye a table-cover.' So Jack thocht tae hissel, where wis a ... puddicks goin tae get him a table-cover, frogs, ye see, goin tae get a table-cover tae him. But anyway, they come wi a broon paper.

'Now,' he says, 'Jack,' he says, 'there is a broon paper parcel,' he says, 'an there's a cover in there,' he says. 'Right enough,' he says, 'yer brothers will have good table-covers, but,' he says, 'the like o this,' he says, 'is no in the country.' He says, 'Don't open it up,' he says, 'till you throw it on your father's bed, an when you throw it on your father's bed,' he says, 'jist tell him tae have a look at that.' See?

Jack said, 'Aa right.'

'Haste up noo, Jack.'

He could hae done wi lookin at the table-cover, but he stuck it 'neath his airm an he bid the wee frogs farewell, an he come up, pit the flagstane doon, an back intae the kitchen. So one o the maids says tae him, 'What hae ye got 'neath yer airm, Jeck?' Jack's pitten it up on a shelf, ye see, oot the road.

'Och,' he says, 'it's ma table-cover,' and aw the weemen start laughin, 'Ha-ha-ha-ha-ha, silly Jeck gettin a table-cover in his father's castle. You've some hopes o bein king, Jack.' An they never peyed nae attention tae Jack, ye see, so Jack jist never heedit, he's suppin soup wi a spoon, liftin the ladle an suppin, drinkin a ladle oot at a pot, drinkin the soup an everything, ye see.

When he looks up the road, up the great drive, an here comin down is the two brothers comin gallopin their brae steeds, an the medals on their breist an the golden swords, they were glutterin, an here they're comin at an awful speed down the drive, ye see. 'Here's ma two brothers comin,' an he ran oot the door an he welcomed his two brothers, ye see, an they widnae heed Jack.

'Get oot o ma road,' one o them said. 'Get oot o ma road, eediot,' he says, 'you get oot o the road.' An they stepped up, ye see, an opened the door an went up tae see their father. So the father said, 'There no time the now, sons' – they were greedy, they wantit tae get made king, ye see . . . 'Wait,' he says, 'until yese get yer dinner, boys,' he says, 'an then come up an . . . Ah'll see yer table-covers. Ah'll have tae get the good advisers in, ye see.' (The good advisers was men. There wis three o them an they pickit whatever wan wis the best, ye see, same as solicitors an things in this days nowadays, ye see.)

So anyway, the two brothers efter they got their feast an everything, their dinner, an come right up, ye see, an here the good advisers – rung the bells, an here the good advisers come up, red coats on them an they're stan'in beside them. Well, the father, the two sons felt awfy sorry for the old king because he wis gettin very weak an forlorn lookin. He wis ready for tae die any time. 'Well, sons,' he says, 'Well, sons, did yese get the table-covers?'

'Yes,' says the oldest son, 'father,' he says, 'have a look at this table-cover.' And he throwed it ower on the bed an they all came an liftit the table-cover, an he examined the table-cover an it was a lovely, definitely, a lovely silk that ye never seen the like o this table-cover, heavy. Ah couldnae explain whit kind o table-cover this wis.

'Yes,' he says, 'son,' he says, 'it definitely is a good table-cover,' he says, 'an it'll take a bit o beatin. Have you got a table-cover?' he says tae the second youngest son.

'Well,' he says, 'father, there's a table-cover,' he says, 'Ah don't know if it's as good as ma brother's or no,' he says, 'but have a look at that table-cover.' An they looked at the table-cover. Well, the one wis as good as the other. The good advisers couldnae guess which o them wis the best.

'Aw but,' says, 'hold on,' says one – there wis wan o the good advisers likit Jack, ye see. He says, 'Hold on,' he says, 'where's Jack?'

'Aw,' says the other good advisers, 'what dae we want with Jack?' he says.

'Aw, but he's supposed tae be here,' he says, 'and see if he's got a table-cover,' the oldest yin said . . . tae the other good advisers. He says, 'Ye're supposed tae be here,' ye see?

So anyway, here now . . . they shouts for Jack an Jack come up the stairs, in his guttery boots as usual, an he's got the broon parcel 'neath his airm. So the two brothers looked at Jeck wi the green [sic] parcel 'neath his airm, ye see, an he says, 'Have you got a table-cover,' he says, 'son?' the old king said.

'Yes, father,' he said, 'did ma brothers get the table-covers?'

'Aye,' he said, 'there they're there.'

'Well,' says Jack, he says, he says, 'they're definitely nice table-covers, but,' he says, 'if Ah couldnae get a better table-cover,' he says, 'than what ma two brothers got,' he says, 'in yer ain castle, father,' he says, 'Ah wadnae go searchin, Ah widnae go,' he says, 'seekin ma fortune,' he says, 'the distance they've went,' he says, 'tae look for table-covers,' he says.

So the men start laughin at Jack as usual: 'Ha-ha-ha-ha! Nonsense, Jack.' An the old king says, 'Ah told ye not tae send for him, he's daft,' ye see.

'Well,' he says, 'have a look at that table-cover, father.' So here the father took the scissors and opened the string, an took out . . . Well, what met their eyes was something terrible. It wis lined with diamonds and rubies, this table-cover. One diamond alone would a' ha' bought the two table-covers that the brothers had, ye see?

'Aye, aye,' says the good adviser, he says, 'that is a table-cover an a table-covers in time,' he says. 'Where did ye get it, son? Did ye steal it from some great castle?'

'No, father,' he says, 'I got this,' he says, 'in yer own castle.'

'It can't be true,' says the king, he says, 'I've never had a table-cover like that in ma life.'

But tae make a long story short, the two brothers wouldnae agree. They said, 'Naw, naw, naw, father,' he says, 'that's not fair,' he says. 'We'll have tae . . . have another chance,' ye see. 'We'll have tae have another chance.' An here they wouldn't let Jack be king. 'Aw right,' says Jack, he says, 'it's all the same tae me,' he says, 'if yese want a chance,' he says, 'again,' he says, 'very good,' he says, 'it's aa the same tae me.'

So the father says, 'Well, if yese want anither chance,' he says, 'Ah tell ye what Ah want yese tae bring back this time,' he says, 'an Ah'll give the three of yese a year an a day again,' he says, 'seein that Ah'm keepin up in health,' he says, 'Ah'll give yese another chance. Them 'at'll go an bring back the best ring,' he says, ''ll get my whole kingdom,' he says, ye see, 'when Ah die.'

Well, fair enough. The three brothers went an got their feathers again and went tae the top of the tower. The oldest brother threw his feather up an it went away be the east. 'Aw well,' he says, 'it'll have tae be me away for east.' The other brother threw a feather up – the secondest youngest brother – an it went away be the south. 'Aw well,' says the other brother, he says, 'Ah'll go away be the south.' Jack threw his feather up, but they didnae lauch this time. It swirl't roon aboot like that an it went doon the back o the castle in amongst the nettles an the thistles. So they looked, the two brothers looked at each other, but they never said a word. They jist went doon the stair an Jack follae't them the big tower, ye see, doon the steps. (Stone steps in them days in the old castles.) And the two brothers bid farewell, mountit their horses and they're away for all they can gallop in each direction, waved tae each other wi their hands an away they went. Ye could see them goin ower the horizon, see?

Jack never bother't, ye see. He went down an he's two or three month in the hoose an oot he went roon. An he seen the same thing happen't again, he went roond the back o the castle an here's the frog sittin on tap o the flagstane. 'Aye,' he says, 'Jack, ye're back quicker this time,' he says. 'What did ye think of the table-cover?'

'Och,' he says, 'it wid hae bought ma faither's castle althegither, right oot be the root.'

'Aye,' he says, 'Ah tellt it wis a good table-cover,' he says. 'Now,' he says, 'Ah'll have tae get ye a ring,' says the frog. 'Ye better come away doon an see the rest o the family,' ye see? Lifts the flagstane up an Jeck went doon the steps, ye see, an intae this big parlour place an he's sittin down, the 'lectric light is burnin, an this wee frog jumped on tap o his knee an he's aye clappin this wee frog, ye see, on tap o his knee, clappin the wee frog, an it's croakin up in his face wi its wee golden eyes, ye see. Well, when the time come when Jack got – they gien him a good meat, ye know, no frogs' meat or onythin like that, it wis good meat they gien him on dishes, this frogs hoppin aboot the place an gien him a nice feed, ye see, an they gies him this wee box – it wis a velvet box, black, did ye ever see wee black velvet boxes? He says, 'There it is, Jack,' he says, 'an the like of that ring,' he says, 'is not in the country,' he says. 'Take it tae yer father an let him see that.'

So Jack stuck it in his waistcoat pocket – an auld waistcoat he had on, ye see, an he's oot, an he's cleanin – but he wis forgettin aboot the year an the day – it passed quicker, ye see. Here's the two brothers comin doon the avenue on their great horses, galloping. Jumped aff an said, 'Did ye get . . .' They wantit tae ken if Jack got a ring.

Jack says, 'Look,' he says, 'dinnae bother me,' says Jack, he says. 'Go up an see the aul man,' he says, 'instead o goin lookin for rings,' he said. 'Ah've never seen as much nonsense as this in ma life.' He says, 'Why can they no let you be king,' he says, 'onywey, ye're the oldest,' he says, ''stead o cairryin on like this.'

'Oh,' he says, 'what's tae be done is tae be done, Jack.' So away they went, up tae see their father. The good advisers wis there. And they showed the rings tae their father, an the father's lookin at the two rings, an judgin the rings, oh, they were lovely rings, no mistake about it, they were lovely rings, ye see, diamonds an everything on them. Here they come – Jack come up the stair again an he wabbles in an he's lookin at them arguin aboot the rings and Jack says, 'Look, father,' he says, 'have a look at that ring.' Jack never seen the ring, and the father opened the wee box and what met his eyes, it hurtit the good advisers' an the old king's eyes, it hurted them. There wis a stone, a diamond stone, sittin in it would have bought the whole castle an the land right about it, ye see?

So anyway, here the brothers widnae be pleased at this. 'Naw, naw, naw, this is nae use, father,' he says, 'give us another chance,' he says. 'The third time's a charm,' he says, 'give us another chance.'

'But,' says the father, he says, 'Jack won twice,' he says, 'it's no fair.' An this good adviser, the old man 'at liked Jack said, 'No, no, Jack'll have to be king; he won twice.'

'No, no, father, gie us another chance,' he says, so the brothers says, 'Ah'll tell ye, father, let us get a good wife,' he says, 'tae fit the ring an them that gets the nicest bride tae fit the ring'll get the king's castle. How will that do, Jack?'

Jack says, 'Fair enough tae me.' But Jack got feart noo

because he mindit it was puddicks he wis amongst. Where would he get a wife from amongst a lot o wee puddicks, frogs an things, ye see. Same thing again, up tae the tap o the tower an threw off their feathers, and one feather went away one road and the other feather went away the other road, but Jack's feather went roon tae the back o the castle. 'Aw,' says Jack, 'Ah'm no goin back. That's it finished now, Jack.' Jack says, 'Ah'm lowsed.' He says, 'Ah'm no goin tae tak nae wee frog for a wife,' ye see?

So anyway, Jack waited tae the year wis up, an jist for the fun o the thing, he says, 'Ah'll go roond the back o the castle,' he says, 'an see what's goin 'ae happen.' Roon he went tae the back o the castle and here's three or four frogs sittin greetin, and the wee frog that sut on his knee, hit wis greetin, the tears runnin out o its een, an it wis jist like a man playin pibroch, 'Hee-haw, hee-haw'. An aa the frogs is greetin, ye see, an here all danced wi glee, and this wee frog come an met him an looked up in his face and climbed up his leg, this wee tottie frog, an he lifted the flagstane an they hoppit doon, ye see.

'Well, Jack,' he says, the old frog says to Jack, he says, 'Ah wis thinkin,' he says, 'Jack, ye widnae come,' he says. 'Ye were frightened,' he says, 'we couldnae get ye a wife, didn't ye, Jack?'

'Yes,' says Jack, 'tae be truthful wi ye,' he says, 'I thought,' he says, 'a frog,' he says, 'widnae do me for a wife.'

'Well,' says the old man, efter they gied him somethin tae eat, he says, 'how wid ye like Susan for a wife?' An this wis the wee frog that wis on his knee, an he wis clappin it.

Jack says, 'That wee frog,' he says, 'how could that make a wife tae me?'

'Yes, Jack,' he says, 'that is yer wife,' he says, 'an a woman,' he says, 'a wife,' he says, 'yer brothers,' he says, 'will have pretty women back wi them,' he says, 'but nothing like Susan.'

So anyway, here, they says, 'Go out,' to Jack, 'go out for an hour,' he says, 'round the back,' he says, 'an intae the kitchen,' he says, 'and take a cup o tea an come back out again,' he says; 'we'll have everything ready for ye.' Jack went roond noo an he's feared, he didn't know what wis gonnae tae happen, an he's taken a cup o tea, but he's back roond.

Here when he come roon at the back o the castle beside the trees, there wis a great big cab sittin, lined wi gold, an the wee frog, it wis the frog, was the loveliest princess ever ye seen in yer life. She wis dressed in silk, ye could see through the silk that wis on her – she wis jist a walkin spirit, a lovely angel she looked like, an when Jack seen her, he says, wi his guttery boots an everything, he wouldn't go near her. So this old king, it wis an old king, a fat frog wi a big belly, green, an he says, 'There is yer bride, there's Susan,' he says. 'How dae ye like the look o her, Jack?'

Jack rubbed his eyes like that . . . He says, 'Look,' he says, 'I couldnae take a lady like that,' he says, he says, 'it's impossible . . . Look at the mess Ah'm in.'

'Oh but,' says the puddicks, they says, 'we'll soon pit that right,' says the old frog, and he says, 'jist turn three times roon aboot.' An Jeck turned three times: an as he's turnin roon aboot his claes wis changin, an there he's turned the beautifullest king ye ever seen in yer life – a prince, medals an a gold sword – ye never seen the like o it in yer life, an this cab wi six grey horses in it and footmen an everything on the back o the cab, an here when she seen Jack she come an put her airms roon Jack's neck, an Jack kissed her, ye see, an they went intae the cab.

Now they drove oot – this wis the year an a day up now, ye see, this was the term's day – but when they come roon here they're comin drivin up the road, but the two brothers wis up before Jack, an . . . they sees the cab comin up the drive, an the two brothers looked oot the windae, an 'Aw, call out the guard,' they said, an here's the guard out and the old king got up oot o his bed, he's lookin through the windae, opened the big sash curtains back, an he says, 'Ah told ye,' he says, 'Jack stole the ring an stole the table-cover. This is the king come,' he says, 'tae . . . claim his goods,' he says, 'that Jack stole.'

Well anyway, here, what happens but the two brothers cam oot an they says, 'Oh,' they says, 'Ah told ye, father, not tae take Jack.' But here when Jack stepped oot o the cab an they seen Jack, Jack waved up tae the windae, his father. 'Hi, Dad!' he says, an he shouts tae his father. The father looked doon an he rubbed his een an he says, 'Is that you, Jack?'

Jack says, 'Yes, father, it's me,' he says, 'an here is ma wife. Ah'm comin up tae see ye.'

Well, when the two brothers seen Jack's wife they went an took their two wifes an they pit them intae the lavatories an locked the door. Haud them oot o the road, intae the lavatories they pit them. 'Get away oot o here, shoo, get oot o here, get oot o here! Oh, Jack's wife,' he says, 'we wouldn't be shamed wi youse women!' An the two lassies that the two oldest brothers had started tae cry ye see, they shoved them intae the lavatories. 'Go in there,' he says, 'oot o the road,' he says, 'until I get ye a horse,' he says, 'that ye can gallop away.'

An when Jack come up an . . . when the father an the good advisers seen this lovely princess, the like wis never in the country, they made Jack king, and the bells were ringin for the feast an Jack was the king; an he wis good to aw the poor folk aw roon the country, folk 'at the owld king used tae be good to, Jack wis three times better tae them an they loved Jack for ever after, an Jack lived happy, an he's king noo on the tap o Keelymabrook, away up in the hills. That's the end o ma story.

THE HUMPH AT THE FUIT
O' THE GLEN AND THE HUMPH
AT THE HEID O' THE GLEN

❀

Source: *Scottish Studies*, vol. 10, 1966
Narrator: Mrs Bella Higgins, Blairgowrie, Perthshire; recorded July 1955
by Hamish Henderson
Type: AT503 'The Gifts of the Little People'

Well, this is the story o' the Humph at the fuit o' the glen, an' the Humph at the heid o' the glen, this wis two men, an' they were very good friends. But the wan at the fuit o' the glen, he wis very humphy, he wis near doublet in two wi' the humph that wis on his back. The other one at the top o' the glen, he wisnae jist quite sae big in the humph, but he wis pretty bad too.

Well, Sunday about they cam' to visit one another, wan would travel up aboot three mile up to the top o' the glen, to spend the day wi' his friend, the Humph at the heid o' the glen. An' then the Humph at the heid o' the glen next Sunday would come down to the Humph at the fuit o' the glen an' spend the day.

So anyway, it wis the wan at the fuit o' the glen, he had to go to see the Humph at the heid o' the glen, it wis his Sunday to walk up to the heid o' the glen to see his friend. Well, he had a wee bit o' a plantin' to pass, an' when he wis comin' past this plantin', he hears a lot o' singin' goin' on. He says: 'Wheesht!' – an' a' the sang they had wis:

> 'Saturday, Sunday,
> Saturday, Sunday,
> Saturday, Sunday'

an' that's a' the length they could get.

'Gosh!' he says, 'I could pit a bit tae that song.' An' he goes:

'Saturday, Sunday,
Monday, Tyoooosday!'

O, an' he heard the laughs an' the clappin' o' the hands.

'God bliss me,' he says, 'what can that be?'

But this wis three kind o' fairies that wis in the wood. An' the wan says to the other:

'Brither, what dae ye wish that man,' he says, 'for that nice part that he put tae our song?'

'Well,' he says, 'I wish him that the humph will drop an' melt off his back,' he says, 'that he'll be as straight as a rush. An' whit dae you wish him?'

'Well,' he says, 'I wish him to have the best of health,' he says, 'an' happiness. An' whit dae you wish him, brither?'

'Well,' he says, 'I wish him full an' plenty, that he'll always have plenty, tae he goes tae his grave.'

'Very good!'

Och, this man wis walkin' up the glen, an' he feels hisself gettin lighter an' lighter, an' he straightens hissel' up, an' he's wonderin' what's come owre him. He didnae think it was hisself at all, that he could jist march up, like a soldier, up this glen.

So he raps at the door when he came tae his friend, the Humph at the heid o' the glen, an' when he cam' out, they askt him whit he wantet, they didnae know him.

'Oh,' he says, 'I want to see So-an'-So, my friend.'

'But who are you?'

'Och,' he says, 'ye know,' he says, 'the humphy man that lives at the fuit o' the glen,' he says, 'I'm his friend, ye know me.' An' told his name.

'Oh my!' he says, 'whit whit whit happent tae ye, whit come owre ye?'

'Oh wheesht,' he says, 'if you come down,' he says, 'wi' me, or when ye're comin' down next Sunday, listen,' he says, 'at the wee plantin' as ye're goin' doon the road, an' ye'll hear singin'.' An' he told him that they only had 'Saturday, Sunday, Saturday, Sunday,' but he says, 'I pit a bit tae their song; I says "Saturday, Sunday, Monday, Tyoooosday", an' I felt mysel' – everything

72

disappearin' from me.' An' he says, 'If you come down, you'll be made as straight as whit I am.'

Anyway, this man's aye wishin' it wis next Sunday, an' he's comin' – when Sunday come – he's comin' marchin' down the road, an' jist at the wee plantin' he hears them a' singin', this song, the bit that the ither humph pit oot tae it, ye know. They're goin':

> 'Saturday, Sunday,
>   Monday, Tyoooosday!'

'Wheesht,' he says, 'I'll pit a bit tae that.' He goes:

> 'Saturday, Sunday,
> Monday, Tuesday,
> Wednesday, Thursday,
> Friday, Saturday,'

an' then he waitet. Ah, an' he got no clap.

He says, 'Whit dae ye wish him, brither?' he says, 'that man, for destroyin' our lovely song?'

He says, 'I wish him that if his humph wis big, that it'll be a thousand times bigger: an' whit dae you wish him?'

'I wish him,' he says, 'to be the ugliest man that ever wis on the face o' the earth, that nobody can look at him: an' whit dae you wish him?'

'I wish him,' he says, 'to be in torture an' punishment tae he goes tae his grave.'

Well, he grew, an' he grew tae he wis the size o' Bennachie – a mountain! An' he could hardly walk up, an' when he come tae his house, he couldnae get in no way or another. Well, he had to lie outside, an' it would have ta'en seventeen pair o' blankets to cover him, to cover him up. An' he's lyin' out winter an' summer till he died an' it ta'en twenty-four coffins to hold him. So he's buried at the top o' the glen.

MALLY WHUPPIE

Source: Walter Gregor, 'Three Folk-Tales from Old Meldrum, Aberdeenshire',
Folk-Lore Journal, vol. 2, 1884
Narrator: Mrs Muir, mother of Mr Muir, Rector of the Grammar School,
Aberdeen
Type: AT328 'The Boy Steals the Giant's Treasure', AT1119 'The Ogre Kills
His Own Children'

Ance upon a time there was a man and a wife had too many children, and they could not get meat for them, so they took the three youngest and left them in a wood. They travelled and travelled and could see never a house. It began to be dark, and they were hungry. At last they saw a light and made for it; it turned out to be a house. They knocked at the door, and a woman came to it, who asked what they wanted. They said if she would let them in and gee them a piece. The woman said she could not do that, as her man was a giant, and he would fell them if he came home. They priggit that she would let them stop for a little whilie, and they would go away before he came. So she took them in, and set them doon afore the fire, and gave them milk and bread; but just as they had begun to eat a great knock came to the door, and a dreadful voice said:

> 'Fee, fie, fo, fum,
> I smell the blood of some earthly one.

Who have you there, wife?' 'Eh,' said the wife, 'it's three peer lassies caul' an hungry, an they will go away. Ye winna touch them, man.' He said nothing, but ate up a great big supper, and ordered them to stay all night.

Now he had three lassies of his own, and they were to sleep in the same bed with the three strangers. The youngest of the three strange lassies was called Mally Whuppie, and she was very clever. She noticed that before they went to bed the giant put straw rapes round her neck and her sisters', and round his ain lassies' necks he put gold chains. So Mally took care and did not fall asleep, but waited till she was sure everyone was sleeping sound. Then she slippit out of the bed, and took the straw rapes off her own and her sisters' necks, and took the gold chains off the giant's lassies. She then put the straw rapes on the giant's lassies and the gold on herself and her sisters, and lay down. And in the middle of the night up rose the giant, armed with a great club, and felt for the necks with the straw. It was dark. He took his own lassies out on the floor, and laid upon them until they were dead, and then lay down again, thinking he had managed fine.

Mally thought it time she and her sisters were out of that, so she wakened them and told them to be quiet, and they slippit out of the house. They all got out safe, and they ran and ran, and never stoppit until morning, when they saw a grand house before them. It turned out to be the king's house; so Mally went in, and told her story to the king. He said, 'Well, Mally, you are a clever cutty, and you have managed well; but, if you would manage better, and go back, and steal the giant's sword that hangs on the back of his bed, I would give your eldest sister my eldest son to marry.' Mally said she would try. So she went back, and managed to slip into the giant's house, and crept in below the bed. The giant came home, and ate up a great supper, and went to bed. Mally waited until he was snoring, and she crept out, and raxed in ower the giant and got doon the sword; but just as she got it oot ower the bed it gave a rattle, and up jumped the giant, and Mally oot at the door and the sword with her; and she ran, and he ran, till they cam to the 'Brig o' ae hair'; and she wan ower, but he cuddna, and he says, 'Wae worth ye, Mally Whuppie! lat ye never come again.' And she says, 'Twice yet, carle,' quo she, 'I'll come to Spain.' So Mally took the sword to the king, and her sister was married to his son.

'Well,' the king he says, 'ye've managed well, Mally; but if ye would manage better, and steal the purse that lies below the giant's pillow, I would marry your second sister to my second son.' And Mally said she would try. So she set out for the giant's house, and slippit in, and hid again below the bed, and waited till the giant had eaten his supper, and was snoring sound asleep.

She slippit out, and slippit her hand below the pillow, and got out the purse, but just as she was going out the giant wakened, and after her; and she ran, and he ran, till they came to the 'Brig o' ae hair', and she wan ower, but he cuddna, and he said, 'Wae worth you, Mally Whuppie! lat you never come again.' 'Ance yet, carle,' quo she, 'I'll come to Spain.' So Mally took the purse to the king, and her second sister was married to the king's second son.

After that the king says to Mally, 'Mally, you are a clever cutty, but if you would dee better yet, and steal the giant's ring that he wears on his finger, I will give you my youngest son to yoursel.' Mally said she would try. So back she goes to the giant's house, and hides herself below the bed. The giant wizna lang ere he came hame, and, after he had eaten a great big supper, he went to his bed and shortly was snoring loud. Mally crept out, and raxed in ower the bed, and got hold of the giant's hand, and she pirlt and pirlt until she got off the ring; but just as she got it off the giant got up, and grippit her by the hand, and he says, 'Now I hae catcht you, Mally Whuppie, and, if I had deen as muckle ill to you as ye hae deen to me, what wad ye dee to me?'

Mally considered what plan she would fall upon to escape, and she says, 'I wad pit you into a pyock, and I wad pit the cat inside wi' you and the dog aside you, and a needle and thread and a shears, and I wad hang you up upon the wa', and I wad gang to the wood, and wile the thickest stick I could get, and I would come hame, and take you down, and lay upon you till you were dead.'

'Well, Mally,' says the giant, 'I'll just do that to you.'

So he gets a pyock, and puts Mally into it, and the cat and the dog beside her, and a needle and thread and shears, and hings her up upon the wa', and goes to the wood to choose a stick.

Mally she sings, 'Oh, gin ye saw faht I see.'

'Oh,' says the giant's wife, 'faht divv ye see, Mally?'

But Mally never said a word but, 'Oh, gin ye saw faht I see!' The giant's wife pleaded that Mally would take her up into the pyock till she would see what Mally saw. So Mally took the shears and cut a hole in the pyock, and took out the needle and thread with her, and jumpt down, and helpit the giant's wife up into the pyock, and sewed up the hole.

The giant's wife saw nothing, and began to ask to get down again; but Mally never minded, but hid herself at the back of the door. Home came the giant, and a great big tree in his hand, and he took down the pyock, and began to lay upon it. His wife cried, 'It's me, man;' but the dog barkit and the cat mewt, and he did not know his wife's voice. But Mally did not want her to be killed, so she came out from the back of the door, and the giant saw her, and he after her; and he ran, and she ran, till they came to the 'Brig o' ae hair', and she wan ower, but he cuddna; and he said, 'Wae worth you, Mally Whuppie! lat you never come again.' 'Never mair, carle,' quo she, 'will I come again to Spain.'

So Mally took the ring to the king, and she was married to his youngest son, and she never saw the giant again.

2: WONDER TALES OF THE HIGHLANDS AND ISLANDS

MAOL A CHLIOBAIN

Source: J. F. Campbell, *Popular Tales of the West Highlands*
Narrator: Ann MacGilvray, Kilmeny, Islay, April 1859; collected by
Hector MacLean. Passages in brackets are interpolated by Campbell from three
further versions discussed in his notes to the tale
Type: AT328 'The Boy Steals the Giant's Treasure', AT1119 'The Ogre Kills
His Own Children'

There was a widow ere now, and she had three daughters;
and they said to her that they would go to seek their
fortune. She baked three bannocks. She said to the big one,
'Whether dost thou like best the little half and my blessing, or the
big half and my curse?' 'I like best,' said she, 'the big half and thy
curse.' She said to the middle one, 'Whether dost thou like best
the big half and my curse, or the little half and my blessing?' 'I
like best,' said she, 'the big half and thy curse.' She said to the
little one, 'Whether dost thou like best the big half and my
curse, or the little half and my blessing?' 'I like best the little half
and thy blessing.' This pleased her mother, and she gave her the
two other halves also. They went away, but the two eldest did
not want the youngest to be with them, and they tied her to a
rock of stone. They went on; but her mother's blessing came
and freed her. And when they looked behind them, whom did
they see but her with the rock on top of her. They let her alone a
turn of a while, till they reached a peat stack, and they tied her
to the peat stack. They went on a bit (but her mother's blessing
came and freed her), and they looked behind them, and whom
did they see but her coming, and the peat stack on the top of
her. They let her alone a turn of a while, till they reached a tree,
and they tied her to the tree. They went on a bit (but her
mother's blessing came and freed her), and when they looked
behind them, whom did they see but her, and the tree on top of
her.

They saw it was no good to be at her; they loosed her, and let

81

her come with them. They were going till night came on them. They saw a light a long way from them; and though a long way from them, it was not long that they were in reaching it. They went in. What was this but a giant's house! They asked to stop the night. They got that, and they were put to bed with the three daughters of the giant. (The giant came home, and he said, 'The smell of the foreign girls is within.') There were twists of amber knobs about the necks of the giant's daughters, and strings of horse hair about their necks. They all slept, but Maol a Chliobain did not sleep. Through the night a thirst came on the giant. He called to his bald, rough-skinned gillie to bring him water. The rough-skinned gillie said that there was not a drop within. 'Kill,' said he, 'one of the strange girls, and bring to me her blood.' 'How will I know them?' said the bald, rough-skinned gillie. 'There are twists of knobs of amber about the necks of my daughters, and twists of horse hair about the necks of the rest.'

Maol a Chliobain heard the giant, and as quick as she could she put the strings of horse hair that were about her own neck and about the necks of her sisters about the necks of the giant's daughters; and the knobs that were about the necks of the giant's daughters about her own neck and about the necks of her sisters; and she laid down *so* quietly. The bald, rough-skinned gillie came, and he killed one of the daughters of the giant, and he took the blood to him. He asked for MORE to be brought him. He killed the next. He asked for MORE; and he killed the third one.

Maol a Chliobain awoke her sisters, and she took them with her on top of her, and she took to going. (She took with her a golden cloth that was on the bed, and it called out.)

The giant perceived her, and he followed her. The sparks of fire that she was putting out of the stones with her heels, they were striking the giant on the chin; and the sparks of fire that the giant was bringing out of the stones with the points of his feet, they were striking Maol a Chliobain in the back of the head. It is this was their going till they reached a river. (She plucked a hair out of her head and made a bridge of it, and she run over the river, and the giant could not follow her.) Maol a Chliobain leaped the river, but the river the giant could not leap.

'Thou art over there, Maol a Chliobain.' 'I am, though it is hard for thee.' 'Thou killedst my three bald brown daughters.' 'I killed them, though it is hard for thee.' 'And when wilt thou come again?' 'I will come when my business brings me.'

They went on forward till they reached the house of a farmer. The farmer had three sons. They told how it happened to them. Said the farmer to Maol a Chliobain, 'I will give my eldest son to thy eldest sister, and get for me the fine comb of gold, and the coarse comb of silver that the giant has.' 'It will cost thee no more,' said Maol a Chliobain.

She went away; she reached the house of the giant; she got in unknown; she took with her the combs, and out she went. The giant perceived her, and after her he was till they reached the river. She leaped the river, but the river the giant could not leap. 'Thou art over there, Maol a Chliobain.' 'I am, though it is hard for thee.' 'Thou killedst my three bald brown daughters.' 'I killed them, though it is hard for thee.' 'Thou stolest my fine comb of gold, and my coarse comb of silver.' 'I stole them, though it is hard for thee.' 'When wilt thou come again?' 'I will come when my business brings me.'

She gave the combs to the farmer, and her big sister and the farmer's big son married. 'I will give my middle son to thy middle sister, and get me the giant's glave of light.' 'It will cost thee no more,' said Maol a Chliobain. She went away, and she reached the giant's house; she went up to the top of a tree that was above the giant's well. In the night came the bald, rough-skinned gillie with the sword of light to fetch water. When he bent to raise the water, Maol a Chliobain came down and she pushed him down in the well and she drowned him, and she took with her the glave of light.

The giant followed her till she reached the river; she leaped the river, and the giant could not follow her. 'Thou art over there, Maol a Chliobain.' 'I am, if it is hard for thee.' 'Thou killedst my three bald brown daughters.' 'I killed, though it is hard for thee.' 'Thou stolest my fine comb of gold, and my coarse comb of silver.' 'I stole, though it is hard for thee.' 'Thou killedst my bald, rough-skinned gillie.' 'I killed, though it is hard for thee.' 'Thou stolest my glave of light.' 'I stole, though it is hard for thee.' 'When wilt thou come again?' 'I will come when my business brings me.'

She reached the house of the farmer with the glave of light; and her middle sister and the middle son of the farmer married. 'I will give thyself my youngest son,' said the farmer, 'and bring me a buck that the giant has.' 'It will cost thee no more,' said Maol a Chliobain. She went away, and she reached the house of the giant; but when she had hold of the buck, the giant caught her. 'What,' said the giant, 'wouldst thou do to me: if I had done as much harm to thee as thou hast done to me, I would make thee burst thyself with milk porridge; I would then put thee in a pock! I would hang thee to the roof-tree; I would set fire under thee; and I would set on thee with clubs till thou shouldst fall as a faggot of withered sticks on the floor.' The giant made milk porridge, and he made her drink it. She put the milk porridge about her mouth and face, and she laid over as if she were dead. The giant put her in a pock, and he hung her to the roof-tree; and he went away, himself and his men, to get wood to the forest. The giant's mother was within.

When the giant was gone, Maol a Chliobain began, "'Tis I am in the light! 'Tis I am in the city of gold!' 'Wilt thou let me in?' said the carlin. 'I will not let thee in.' At last she let down the pock. She put in the carlin, cat, and calf, and cream-dish. She took with her the buck and she went away. When the giant came with his men, himself and his men began at the bag with the clubs. The carlin was calling, "'Tis myself that's in it.' 'I know that thyself is in it,' would the giant say, as he laid on to the pock. The pock came down as a faggot of sticks, and what was in it but his mother.

When the giant saw how it was, he took after Maol a Chliobain; he followed her till she reached the river. Maol a Chliobain leaped the river, and the giant could not leap it. 'Thou art over there, Maol a Chliobain.' 'I am, though it is hard for thee.' 'Thou killedst my three bald brown daughters.' 'I killed, though it is hard for thee.' 'Thou stolest my golden comb, and my silver comb.' 'I stole, though it is hard for thee.' 'Thou killedst my bald, rough-skinned gillie.' 'I killed, though it is hard for thee.' 'Thou stolest my glave of light.' 'I stole, though it is hard for thee.' 'Thou killedst my mother.' 'I killed, though it is hard for thee.' 'Thou stolest my buck.' 'I stole, though it is hard for thee.' 'When wilt thou come again?' 'I will come when my business brings me.' 'If thou wert over here, and I yonder,' said the giant, 'what wouldst thou do to follow me?' 'I would stick myself down, and I would drink till I should dry the river.'

The giant stuck himself down, and he drank till he burst. Maol a Chliobain and the farmer's youngest son married.

THE BROWN BEAR OF THE
GREEN GLEN

❊

Source: J. F. Campbell, *Popular Tales of the West Highlands*
Narrator: John MacDonald, a travelling tinker, May 1859; collected by
Hector Urquhart. 'It should be much longer, but the wandering spirit of the man
would not let him rest to dictate his story. They had to move to an outhouse
and let him roam about amongst the shavings, and swing his arms, before this
much was got out of him'
Type: AT551 'The Sons on a Quest for a Wonderful Remedy for Their Father'

There was a king in Erin once, who had a leash of sons. John was the name of the youngest one, and it was said that he was not wise enough; and this good worldly king lost the sight of his eyes, and the strength of his feet. The two eldest brothers said that they would go seek three bottles of the water of the Green Isle that was about the heaps of the deep. And so it was that these two brothers went away.

Now the fool said that he would not believe but that he himself would go also. And the first big town he reached in his father's kingdom, there he sees his two brothers there, the blackguards! 'Oh! my boys,' says the young one, 'it is thus you are?' 'With swiftness of foot,' said they, 'take thyself home, or we will have thy life.' 'Don't be afraid, lads. It is nothing to me to stay with you.' Now John went away on his journey till he came to a great desert of a wood. 'Hoo, hoo!' says John to himself. 'It is not canny for me to walk this wood alone.' The night was coming now, and growing pretty dark. John ties the cripple white horse that was under him to the root of a tree, and he went up in the top himself. He was but a very short time in the top, when he saw a bear coming with a fiery cinder in his mouth. 'Come down, son of the king of Erin,' says he. 'Indeed, I won't come. I am thinking I am safer where I am.' 'But if thou wilt not come down, I will go up,' said the bear. 'Art thou, too, taking me for a fool?' says John. 'A shaggy, shambling creature like thee, climbing a tree!' 'But if thou wilt not come down, I will go up,' says the bear, as he fell out of hand to climb the tree. 'Lord! thou canst do that same?' said John. 'Keep back from the root of the tree, then, and I will go down to talk to thee.' And when the son of Erin's king drew down, they came to chatting. The bear asked him if he was hungry. 'Weel! by your leave,' said John, 'I am a little at this very same time.' The bear took that wonderful watchful turn and he catches a roebuck. 'Now, son of Erin's king,' says the bear, 'whether wouldst thou like thy share of the buck boiled or raw?' 'The sort of meat I used to get would be kind of plotted boiled,' says John; and thus it fell out. John got his share roasted. 'Now,' said the bear, 'lie down between my paws, and thou hast no cause to fear cold or hunger till morning.'

Early in the morning the Mathon [bear] asked, 'Art thou asleep, son of Erin's king?' 'I am not very heavily,' said he. 'It is time for thee to be on thy soles then. Thy journey is long – two hundred miles; but art thou a good horseman, John?' 'There are worse than me at times,' said he. 'Thou hadst best get on top of me, then.' He did this, and at the first leap John was to earth. 'Foil! foil!' says John. 'What! thou art not bad at the trade thyself. Thou hadst best come back till we try thee again.' And with nails and teeth he fastened on the Mathon, till they reached the end of the two hundred miles and a giant's house. 'Now, John,' said the Mathon, 'thou shalt go to pass the night in this giant's house; thou wilt find him pretty grumpy, but say thou that it was the brown bear of the green glen that set thee here for a night's share, and don't thou be afraid that thou wilt not get share and comfort.' And he left the bear to go to the giant's house.

'Son of Ireland's king,' says the giant, 'thy coming was in the prophecy; but if I did not get thy father, I have got his son. I don't know whether I will put thee in the earth with my feet, or in the sky with my breath.' 'Thou wilt do neither of either,' said John, 'for it is the brown bear of the green glen that set me here.' 'Come in, son of Erin's king,' said he, 'and thou shalt be well taken to this night.' And as he said, it was true. John got meat and drink without stint.

But to make a long tale short, the bear took John day after day to the third giant. 'Now,' says the bear, 'I have not much acquaintance with this giant, but thou wilt not be long in his house when thou must wrestle with him. And if he is too hard on thy back, say thou, "If I had the brown bear of the green glen here, that was thy master."' As soon as John went in – 'Ai! ai!! or ee! ee!!' says the giant, 'if I did not get thy father, I have got his son;' and to grips they go. They would make the boggy bog of the rocky rock. In the hardest place they would sink to the knee; in the softest, up to the thighs; and they would bring wells of spring water from the face of every rock. The giant gave John a sore wrench or two. 'Foil! foil!' says he, 'if I had here the brown bear of the green glen, thy leap would not be so hearty.' And no sooner spoke he the word than the worthy bear was at his side. 'Yes! yes!' says the giant, 'son of Erin's king, now I know thy matter better than thou dost thyself.' So it was that the giant ordered his shepherd to bring home the best wether he had in the hill, and to throw his carcass before the great door.

'Now, John,' says the giant, 'an eagle will come and she will settle on the carcass of this wether, and there is a wart on the ear of this eagle which thou must cut off her with this sword, but a drop of blood thou must not draw.' The eagle came, but she was not long eating when John drew close to her, and with one stroke he cut the wart off her without drawing one drop of blood. ('*Och! is not that a fearful lie?*') 'Now,' said the eagle, 'come on the root of my two wings, for I know thy matter better than thou dost thyself.' He did this; and they were now on sea, and now on land, and now on the wing, till they reached the Green Isle. 'Now, John,' says she, 'be quick, and fill thy three bottles; remember that the black dogs are away just now.' ('*What dogs?*' '*Black dogs; dost thou not know that they always had black dogs chasing the Gregorach!*')

When he filled the bottles with the water out of the well, he sees a little house beside him. John said to himself that he would go in, and that he would see what was in it. And the first chamber he opened, he saw a full bottle. ('*And what was in it?*' '*What should be in it but whisky.*') He filled a glass out of it, and he drank it; and when he was going, he gave a glance, and the bottle was as full as it was before. 'I will have this bottle along with the bottles of water,' says he. Then he went into another chamber, and he saw a loaf; he took a slice out of it, but the loaf was as whole as it was before. 'Ye gods! I won't leave thee,' says John. He went on thus till he came to another chamber. He saw a great cheese; he took a slice off the cheese, but it was as whole as ever. 'I will have this along with the rest,' says he. Then he went to another chamber, and he saw laid there the very prettiest little jewel of a woman he ever saw. 'It were a great pity not to kiss thy lips, my love,' says John.

Soon after, John jumped on top of the eagle, and she took him on the selfsame steps till they reached the house of the big giant, and they were paying rent to the giant, and there was the sight of tenants and giants and meat and drink. 'Well! John,' says the giant, 'didst thou see such drink as this in thy father's house in Erin?' 'Pooh,' says John, 'Hoo! my hero; thou other man, I have a drink that *is* unlike it.' He gave the giant a glass out of the bottle, but the bottle was as full as it was before. 'Well!' said the giant, 'I will give thee myself two hundred notes, a bridle and a saddle for the bottle.' 'It is a bargain, then,' says John, 'but that the first sweetheart I ever had must get it if she comes the way.' 'She will get that,' says the giant; but, to make the long story short, he left each loaf and cheese with the two other giants, with the same covenant that the first sweetheart he ever had should get them if she came the way.

Now John reached his father's big town in Erin, and he sees his two brothers as he left them – the 'blackguardan'! 'You had best come with me, lads,' says he, 'and you will get a dress of cloth, and a horse and a saddle and bridle each.' And so they did; but when they were near to their father's house, the brothers thought that they had better kill him, and so it was that they set on him. And when they thought he was dead, they threw him behind a dike; and they took from him the three bottles of water, and they went home. John was not too long here, when his father's smith came the way with a cart-load of rusty iron. John called out, 'Whoever the Christian is that is there, oh! that he should help me.' The smith caught him, and he threw John amongst the iron; and because the iron was so rusty, it went into each wound and sore that John had; and so it was, that John became rough-skinned and bald.

Here we will leave John, and we will go back to the pretty little jewel that John left in the Green Isle. She became pale and heavy; and at the end of three quarters, she had a fine lad son. 'Oh! in all the great world,' says she, 'how did I find this?' 'Foil! foil!' says the henwife, 'don't let that set thee thinking. Here's for thee a bird, and as soon as he sees the father of thy son, he will hop on the top of his head.' The Green Isle was gathered from end to end, and the people were put in at the back door and out at the front door; but the bird did not stir, and the babe's father was not found. Now here, she said she would go through the world altogether till she should find the father of the babe. Then she came to the house of the big giant and sees the bottle. 'Ai! ai!!' said she, 'who gave thee this bottle?' Said the giant, 'It was young John, son of Erin's king, that left it.' 'Well, then, the bottle is mine,' said she.

But to make the long story short, she came to the house of each giant, and she took with her each bottle, and each loaf, and each cheese, till at length and at last she came to the house of the king of Erin. Then the five fifths of Erin were gathered, and the bridge of nobles of the people; they were put in at the back door and out at the front door, but the bird did not stir. Then she asked if there was one other or anyone else at all in Erin, that had not been here. 'I have a bald rough-skinned gillie in the smithy,' said the smith, 'but –' 'Rough on or off, send him here,' says she. No sooner did the bird see the head of the bald rough-skinned gillie, than he took a flight and settles on the bald top of the rough-skinned lad. She caught him and kissed him. 'Thou art the father of my babe.'

'But, John,' says the great king of Erin, 'it is thou that gottest the bottles of water for me.' 'Indeed, 'twas I,' says John. 'Weel, then, what art thou willing to do to thy two brothers?' 'The very thing they wished to do to me, do for them;' and that same was done. John married the daughter of the king of the Green Isle, and they made a great rich wedding that lasted seven days and seven years, and thou couldst but hear leeg, leeg, and beeg,

beeg, solid sound and peg drawing. Gold a-crushing from the soles of their feet to the tips of their fingers, the length of seven years and seven days.

THE CHEST

Source: J. F. Campbell, *Popular Tales of the West Highlands*
Narrator: Catherine Milloy, wife of Angus MacGeachy, farmer, Kilmeny, Islay;
April 1859; collected by Hector MacLean. Mrs MacGeachy came from Cowal,
and learned the story there from Robert MacColl
Type: AT882 'The Wager on the Wife's Chastity'

Before this there was a king, and he wished to see his son
with a wife before he should depart. His son said he had
better go for a wife; and he gave him half a hundred pounds to
get her. He went forward into a hostelry to stay in it. He went
down to a chamber with a good fire in front of him; and when
he had gotten meat, the man of the house went down to talk to
him. He told the man of the house the journey on which he was.
The man of the house told him he need not go further; that
there was a little house opposite to his sleeping chamber; that
the man of the house had three fine daughters; and if he would
stand in the window of his chamber in the morning, that he
would see one after another coming to dress herself; that they
were all like each other, and that he could not distinguish one
from the other, but that the eldest had a mole; that many were
going to ask for them, but that none got them, because whoever
wished for one, must tell whether the one he liked best was
younger or older; and if he made her out, that she would cost
him a hundred pounds. 'I have but half a hundred,' said the
king's son. 'I will give thee another half hundred,' said the man
of the house, 'if thou wilt pay me at the end of a day and a year;
and if thou dost not pay me, a strip of skin shall come from the
top of thy head to the sole of thy foot.'

On the morrow when he rose he went to the window; he saw
the girls coming to dress themselves; and after meat in the
morning, he went over to the house of their father. When he
went in he was taken down to a chamber, and the man of the

house went down to talk to him. He told the journey on which he was, and he said to him, 'They tell me that thou hast three fine daughters.' 'I have that same, but I am afraid that it is not thou who wilt buy them.' 'I will give them a trial, at all events,' said he. The three were sent down before him, and it was said to him, whether she, the one he liked best, was the elder or younger. He thought he would take the one with the mole, because he knew she was the eldest. She then was much pleased that it was she herself he was for. He asked her father how much she would be, and her father said she would be a hundred pounds. He bought her, and he took her to the house of his father, and they married. Shortly after they married his father departed.

A day or two after the death of the old king, the young king was out hunting; he saw a great ship coming in to the strand; he went down to ask the captain what he had on board. The captain said that he had a cargo of silk. 'Thou must,' said he, 'give me a gown of the best silk thou hast for my wife.' 'Indeed!' said the captain, 'thou must have an exceedingly good wife when thou must have a gown of the best silk I have on board.' 'I have that,' said the king, 'a wife many of whose equals are not to be got.' 'Wilt thou lay a wager,' said the captain, 'that with all her goodness I will not get leave to enter thy chamber?' 'I will lay a wager, anything thou desiredst, that thou wilt not.' 'What wager wilt thou lay?' said the captain. 'I will put the heirship in pledge,' said the king. Said the captain: 'I will put all the silk in the ship in pledge to thee that I will.' The captain came on shore and the king went on board.

The captain went where the henwife was, to try if she could make any way to get into the king's chamber that night. The henwife thought a while, and she said that she did not think that there was any way that would succeed. The captain rose here, and he was going. 'Stop thou!' said she, 'I have thought on a way: her maid servant and I are well with each other; I will say to her that I have got word from a sister of mine that I will scarce find her alive; I will say to the king's wife that I must go to see my sister; that I have a big kist, of good worth, and I should like if she would oblige me and let it into her own sleeping chamber till I come back.' She went where the queen was, she asked her this, and she got leave. Here the captain was put into the kist, and the king's gillies were gathered, and the kist put in the chamber. The king's wife was within by herself wearying, for the king was not coming home. At last she went to bed; when she was going to bed she put a gold ring that was on her finger, and a gold chain that was about her neck, on a board that was opposite to the bed.

When the man who was in the kist thought that she had time to be asleep, he rose and he took with him the chain and the ring, and he went into the kist again. At the mouth of day came the henwife to ask for the kist; the gillies were gathered, and the kist was taken down. When everyone went from the house, as soon as he could, the captain rose and he went down to the ship; he shook the chain and the ring at the king. Then the king thought that the captain had been with his wife, or that he could not have the chain and ring. He said to the captain, would he put him over to the other side of the loch. The captain said that he would. When the captain got him over he returned himself, and he went to dwell in the king's house. Then the king's wife did not know what to do with herself, for that the king had not come home.

She went that day and she dressed herself in man's clothes, and she went down to the strand; she met with a boat, and she said to them, would they put her over on the other side. They put her over, and she went on forward till she reached the house of a gentleman; she struck in the door, and the maid servant came down. She said to her, did she know if her master wanted a stable gillie. The maid servant said that she did not know, but that she would ask. The maid servant went and she asked her master if he wanted a stable gillie. He said he did; and he asked that he should come in; he engaged her, and she stayed working about the stable. There was a herd of wild beasts coming every night, and going into an empty barn that the gentleman had; a wild man after them, and his face covered with beard. She kept asking her master to send a man with her, and that they would catch him. Her master said that he would not; that they had no business with them; and that he had not done any harm to them.

She went out one night by herself, and she stole with her the key of the barn door; she lay hid in a hole till the wild man and the beasts went in; she took with her the gillies, and they caught the wild man. They brought him in and they took off his beard; when the beard came off him she knew him, but she took no notice; and he did not know her. On the morrow he was about to go, but she spoke to her master to keep him; that the work was too heavy on her, and that she needed help. Her master ordered her to keep him. She kept him with her, and he himself and she were cleaning the stable.

A short time after this she spoke to her master for leave to go home on a trip to see her friends. Her master gave her leave. She said she would like well to have her gillie with her, and the two best horses that were in the stable.

When they went, she was questioning him by the way what had made him go with these wild beasts; or what he was at before the day. He would not tell her anything. They went on forward till they came to the hostelry where he had got the half hundred pounds. When she set her face down to the house, he refused to go into it. She said to him, did he do anything wrong, as he was refusing to go into it. He said that he had got half a hundred pounds from the man of the house. She said to him, had he paid them; and he said that he had not paid, and that a strip of skin was to come from the top of his head to the sole of his foot, if it was not paid at the end of a day and a year. She said it would be well deserved; but that she was going to stay the night in the hostelry, and that she must go down. She asked him to put the horses into the stable, and they went into the hostelry. He was standing in the door of the stable, and his head was bent. The man of the house came out, and he saw him. 'My big gillie, I have thee here,' said the man of the house; 'art thou going to pay me today?' 'I am not,' said he. Then he went in, and they were going to begin to cut the strip of skin. She heard the noise, and she asked what they were going to do to her gillie. They said they were going to cut a strip of skin off him from his crown to his sole. If that was to be done, said she, he was not to lose a drop of blood: 'Send up here a web of linen, let him stand on it, and if a drop of blood comes out of him, another strip of skin shall come off thee.' Here there was nothing for it but to let him go; they could not make anything of it.

Early on the morrow she took him over with her to the house of her father. If he was against going to the hostelry the night before, he was seven times as much when going to her father's house. 'Didst thou do harm here too, as thou art against going in?' 'I got a wife here such a time since.' 'What came of her?' 'I don't know.' 'No wonder whatever happens to thee, thou hast only to put up with all that comes thy way.' When her father saw him, he said, 'I have thee here! Where is thy wife?' 'I don't know where she is.' 'What didst thou to her?' said her father. He could not tell what he had done to her. Now there was nothing to be done but to hang him to a tree. There was to be a great day about the hanging, and a great many gentlemen were to come to see it. She asked her father what they were going to do to her gillie. Her father said that they were going to hang him: 'He bought a wife from me, and he does not know what has happened to her.' She went out to see the gentles coming into the town; she asked of the one of the finest horse, what was his worth. 'Five score,' said he. 'Though he were five hundreds, he's mine,' said she. She told her servant to put a shot in the horse. She asked her father if he had paid for his wife. He said he had paid. 'If he paid,' said she, 'thou hast no business with him, he might do what he liked with her; I bought the finest horse that came into the town today; I made my gillie put a shot in him, and who dares to say that it is ill.' Here there was nothing to be done but to let him loose. They could do nothing to him because he had bought her.

Here she went into her father's house, and she told one of her sisters to give her a gown. 'What art thou going to do with a gown?' said she. 'Never mind, if I spoil it I'll pay for it.' When she put on the gown her father and sisters knew her. Her father and sisters told him that it was she was with him, and he did not believe them. She put off the woman's clothes and put on the man's clothes again. They went, herself and he; they went on forward till they were near his own old house. 'Now,' said she, 'we will stay here tonight; do thou sit at the top of the stair, and thou shalt set down all the talk that I and the man of the house will have.' When they went in and sat, she and the man of the house began to talk together. 'I thought,' said she to the captain, 'that a king was dwelling here; how didst thou get it?' 'He was that who was here before; but I am thinking, as thou art a stranger, that I may tell thee how I got it.' 'Thou mayest,' said she, 'I will not make a tale of thee, the matter does not touch me.' He told her every turn, how the henwife had put him in the kist, and the rest of the matter, to the going of the king on the morrow.

Very early on the morrow the man of the house was going to court; he said to her that if she was not in a hurry to go away, that she might go with him to listen to the court. She said she would be willing, and she would like well that her gillie should be with her. She went in the coach with the captain, and her gillie rode after her. When the court was over she said that she had got a word or two to say, if it were their pleasure to let her speak. They said to her to let them hear what she had to say. She said to her gillie, 'Rise up and give them the paper thou wrotest last night.' When they read the paper, she said, 'What should be done to that man?' 'Hang him, if he were here,' said they.

'There you have him,' said she, 'do with him what you will.' Herself and the king got back to their own house, and they were as they were before.

MACIAIN DIREACH

Source: J. F. Campbell, *Popular Tales of the West Highlands*
Narrator: Angus Campbell, quarryman, Knockderry, Roseneath, April 1860;
collected by John Dewar
Type: AT550 'The Bird, the Horse and the Princess'

At some time there was a king and a queen, and they had one son; but the queen died, and the king married another wife. The name of the son that the first queen had, was Iain Direach. He was a handsome lad; he was a hunter, and there was no bird at which he would cast his arrow, that he would not fell; and he would kill the deer and the roes at a great distance from him; there was no day that he would go out with his bow and his quiver, that he would not bring venison home.

He was one day in the hunting-hill hunting, and he got no venison at all; but there came a blue falcon past him, and he let an arrow at her, but he did but drive a feather from her wing. He raised the feather and he put it into his hunting bag, and he took it home; and when he came home his muime said to him, 'Where is thy game today?' and he put his hand into the hunting bag, and he took out the feather and he gave it to her. And his muime took the feather in her hand, and she said, 'I am setting it as crosses, and as spells, and as the decay of the year on thee; that thou be not without a pool in thy shoe, and that thou be wet, cold, and soiled, until thou gettest for me the bird from which that feather came.'

And he said to his muime, 'I am setting it as crosses and as spells, and as the decay of the year on thee; that thou be standing with the one foot on the great house, and the other foot on the castle; and that thy face be to the tempest whatever wind blows, until I return back.'

And MacIain Direach went away as fast as he could to seek the bird from which the feather came, and his muime was standing with the one foot on the castle, and the other on the great house, till he should come back; and her front was to the face of the tempest, however long he might be without coming.

MacIain Direach was gone, travelling the waste to see if he could see the falcon, but the falcon he could not see; and much less than that, he could not get her; and he was going by himself through the waste, and it was coming near to the night. The little fluttering birds were going from the bush tops, from tuft to tuft, and to the briar roots, going to rest; and though they were, he was not going there, till the night came blind and dark; and he went and crouched at the root of a briar; and who came the way but an Gille Mairtean, the fox; and he said to him, 'Thou'rt down in the mouth a Mhic Iain Direach; thou camest on a bad night; I have myself but one wether's trotter and a sheep's cheek, but needs must do with it.'

They kindled a fire, and they roasted flesh, and they ate the wether's trotter and the sheep's cheek; and in the morning Gille Mairtean said to the king's son, 'Oh son of Iain Direach, the falcon thou seekest is by the Great Giant of the Five Heads, and the Five Humps, and the Five Throttles, and I will shew thee where his house is; and it is my advice to thee to go to be as his servant, and that thou be nimble and ready to do each thing that is asked of thee, and each thing that is trusted thee; and be very good to his birds, and it well may be that he will trust thee with the falcon to feed; and when thou gettest the falcon to feed be right good to her, till thou gettest a chance; at the time when the giant is not at home run away with her, but take care that so much as one feather of her does not touch any one thing that is within the house, or if it touches, it will not go well with thee.'

MacIain Direach said that he would take care of that; and he went to the giant's house; he arrived; he struck at the door.

The giant shouted, 'Who is there?'

'It is me,' said MacIain Direach, 'one coming to see if thou hast need of a lad.'

'What work canst thou do?' said the giant.

'It is this,' said MacIain Direach. 'I can feed birds and swine, and feed and milk a cow, or goats or sheep.'

'It is the like of thee that I want,' said the giant.

The giant came out and he settled wages on MacIain Direach; and he was taking right good care of everything that the giant had, and he was very kind to the hens and to the ducks; and the giant took notice how well he was doing; and he said that his table was so good since MacIain Direach had come, by what it was before; that he had rather one hen of those which he got now, than two of those he used to get before. 'My lad is so good that I begin to think I may trust him the falcon to feed;' and the giant gave the falcon to MacIain Direach to feed, and he took exceeding care of the falcon; and when the giant saw how well MacIain Direach was taking care of the falcon, he thought that he might trust her to him when he was away from the house; and the giant gave him the falcon to keep, and he was taking exceeding care of the falcon.

The giant thought each thing was going right, and he went from the house one day; and MacIain Direach thought that was the time to run away with the falcon, and he seized the falcon to go away with her; and when he opened the door and the falcon saw the light, she spread her wings to spring, and the point of one of the feathers of one of her wings touched one of the posts of the door, and the doorpost let out a screech. The giant came home running, and he caught MacIain Direach, and he took the falcon from him; and he said to him, 'I would not give thee my falcon, unless thou shouldst get for me the White Glave of Light that the Big Women of Dhiurradh have;' and the giant sent MacIain away.

MacIain Direach went out again and through the waste, and the Gille Mairtean met with him, and he said, 'Thou art down in the mouth MacIain Direach; thou didst not, and thou wilt not do as I tell thee; bad is the night on which thou hast come; I have but one wether's trotter and one sheep's cheek, but needs must do with that.'

They roused a fire, and they made ready the wether's trotter and the sheep's cheek, and they took their meat and sleep; and on the next day the Gille Mairtean said, 'We will go to the side of the ocean.'

They went and they reached the side of the ocean, and the Gille Mairtean said, 'I will grow into a boat, and go thou on board of her, and I will take thee over to Dhiurradh; and go to the seven great women of Dhiurradh and ask service, that thou be a servant with them; and when they ask thee what thou canst do, say to them that thou art good at brightening iron and steel, gold and silver, and that thou canst make them bright, clear, and shiny; and take exceeding care that thou dost each thing right, till they trust thee the White Glave of Light; and when thou gettest a chance run away with it, but take care that the sheath does not touch a thing on the inner side of the house, or it will make a screech, and thy matter will not go with thee.'

The Gille Mairtean grew into a boat, and MacIain Direach went on board of her, and he came on shore, at Creagan nan deargan, on the northern side of Dhiurradh, and MacIain Direach leaped on shore, and he went to take service with the Seven Big Women of Dhiurradh. He reached, and he struck at the door; the Seven Big Women came out, and they asked what he was seeking. He said he could brighten, or make clear, white and shiny, gold and silver, or iron or steel. They said, 'We have need of thy like,' and set wages on him. And he was right diligent for six weeks, and put everything in exceeding order; and the Big Women noticed it; and they kept saying to each other, 'This is the best lad we have ever had; we may trust him the White Glave of Light.'

They gave him the White Glave of Light to keep in order; and he was taking exceeding care of the White Glave of Light, till one day that the Big Women were not at the house, he thought that was the time for him to run away with the White Glave of Light. He put it into the sheath, and he raised it on his shoulder; but when he was going out at the door the point of the sheath touched the lintel, and the lintel made a screech; and the Big Women ran home, and took the sword from him; and they said to him, 'We would not give thee our White Glave of Light, unless thou shouldst get for us the Yellow Bay Filly of the King of Eirinn.'

MacIain Direach went to the side of the ocean and the Gille Mairtean met him, and he said to him, 'Thou'rt down in the mouth, MacIain Direach; thou didst not, and thou wilt not do as

I ask thee; I have tonight but one wether's trotter and one sheep's cheek, but needs must do with it.'

They kindled a fire, and they roasted flesh, and they were satisfied. On the next day the Gille Mairtean said to MacIain Direach, 'I will grow into a barque, and go thou on board of her, and I will go to Eirinn with thee; and when we reach Eirinn go thou to the house of the king, and ask service to be a stable lad with him; and when thou gettest that, be nimble and ready to do each thing that is to be done, and keep the horses and the harness in right good order, till the king trusts the Yellow Bay Filly to thee; and when thou gettest a chance run away with her; but take care when thou art taking her out that no bit of her touches anything that is on the inner side of the gate, except the soles of her feet; or else thy matter will not prosper with thee.'

And then the Gille Mairtean put himself into the form of a barque, MacIain Direach went on board, and the barque sailed with him to Eirinn. When they reached the shore of Eirinn, MacIain Direach leaped on land, and he went to the house of the king; and when he reached the gate, the gate-keeper asked where he was going; and he said that he was going to see if the king had need of a stable lad; and the gate-keeper let him past, and he reached the king's house; he struck at the door and the king came out; and the king said, 'What art thou seeking here?'

Said he, 'With your leave, I came to see if you had need of a stable lad.'

The king asked, 'What canst thou do?'

Said he, 'I can clean and feed the horses, and clean the silver work, and the steel work, and make them shiny.'

The king settled wages on him, and he went to the stable; and he put each thing in good order; he took good care of the horses, he fed them well, and he kept them clean, and their skin was looking sliom, sleek; and the silver work and the steel work shiny to look at; and the king never saw them so well in order before. And he said, 'This is the best stable lad I have ever had, I may trust the Yellow Bay Filly to him.'

The king gave the Yellow Bay Filly to MacIain Direach to keep; and MacIain Direach took very great care of the Yellow Bay Filly; and he kept her clean, till her skin was so sleek and slippery, and she so swift, that she would leave the one wind and catch the other. The king never saw her so good.

The king went one day to the hunting-hill, and MacIain Direach thought that was the time to run away with the Yellow Bay Filly; and he set her in what belonged to her, with a bridle and saddle; and when he took her out of the stable, he was taking her through the gate, she gave a switch, sguaise, with her tail, and the point of her tail touched the post of the gate, and it let out a screech.

The king came running and he took the filly from MacIain Direach; and he said to him, 'I would not give thee the Yellow Bay Filly, unless thou shouldst get for me the daughter of the king of the Frainge.'

And MacIain Direach needs must go; and when he was within a little of the side of the sea the Gille Mairtean met him; and he said to him, 'Thou art down in the mouth, oh son of Iain Direach; thou didst not, and thou wilt not do as I ask thee; we must now go to France, I will make myself a ship, and go thou on board, and I will not be long till I take thee to France.'

The Gille Mairtean put himself in the shape of a ship, and MacIain Direach went on board of her, and the Gille Mairtean sailed to France with him, and he ran himself on high up the face of a rock, on dry land; and he said to MacIain Direach to go up to the king's house and to ask help, and to say that his skipper had been lost, and his ship thrown on shore.

MacIain Direach went to the king's house, and he struck at the door; one came out to see who was there; he told his tale and he was taken into the fort. The king asked him whence he was, and what he was doing here.

He told them the tale of misery; that a great storm had come on him, and the skipper he had was lost; and the ship he had thrown on dry land, and she was there, driven up on the face of a rock by the waves, and that he did not know how he should get her out.

The king and the queen, and the family together, went to the shore to see the ship; and when they were looking at the ship, exceeding sweet music began on board; and the King of France's daughter went on board to see the musical instrument, together with MacIain Direach; and when they were in one chamber, the music would be in another chamber; but at last they heard the music on the upper deck of the ship, and they went above on the upper deck of the ship, and so it was that the ship was out on the ocean, and out of sight of land.

And the King of France's daughter said, 'Bad is the trick thou hast done to me. Where art thou for going with me?'

'I am,' said MacIain Direach, 'going with thee to Eirinn, to give thee as a wife to the King of Eirinn, so that I may get from him his Yellow Bay Filly, to give her to the Big Women of Dhiurradh, that I may get from them their White Glave of Light, to give it to the Great Giant of the Five Heads, and Five Humps, and Five Throttles, that I may get from him his Blue Falcon, to take her home to my muime, that I may be free from my crosses, and from my spells, and from the bad diseases of the year.'

And the King of France's daughter said, 'I had rather be as a wife to thyself.'

And when they came to shore in Eirinn, the Gille Mairtean put himself in the shape of a fine woman, and he said to MacIain Direach, 'Leave thou the King of France's daughter here till we return, and I will go with thee to the King of Eirinn; I will give him enough of a wife.'

MacIain Direach went with the Gille Mairtean in the form of a fine maiden, with his hand in the oxter of MacIain Direach. When the King of Eirinn saw them coming he came to meet them; he took out the Yellow Bay Filly and a golden saddle on her back, and a silver bridle in her head.

MacIain Direach went with the filly where the King of France's daughter was. The King of Eirinn was right well pleased with the young wife he had got; but little did the King of Eirinn know that he had got Gille Mairtean; and they had not long been gone to rest when the Gille Mairtean sprung on the king, and he did not leave a morsel of flesh between the back of his neck and his haunch that he did not take off him. And the Gille Mairtean left the King of Eirinn a pitiful wounded cripple; and he went running where MacIain Direach was, and the King of France's daughter, and the Yellow Bay Filly.

Said the Gille Mairtean, 'I will go into the form of a ship, and go you on board of her, and I will take you to Dhiurradh.' He grew into the form of a ship; and MacIain Direach put in the Yellow Bay Filly first, and he himself and the King of France's daughter went in after her; and the Gille Mairtean sailed with them to Dhiurradh, and they went on shore at Creagan nan deargan, at Cilla-mhoire, at the northern end of Dhiurradh; and when they went on shore, the Gille Mairtean said, 'Leave thou the Yellow Bay Filly here, and the king's daughter, till thou return; and I will go in the form of a filly, and I will go with thee to the Big Women of Dhiurradh, and I will give them enough of filly-ing.'

The Gille Mairtean went into the form of a filly, MacIain Direach put the golden saddle on his back, and the silver bridle in his head, and he went to the Seven Big Women of Dhiurradh with him. When the Seven Big Women saw him coming, they came to meet him with the White Glave of Light, and they gave it to him. MacIain Direach took the golden saddle off the back of the Gille Mairtean, and the silver bridle out of his head, and he left him with them. And he went away himself with the White Glave of Light, and he went where he left the King of France's daughter, and the Yellow Bay Filly which he got from the King of Eirinn; and the Big Women of Dhiurradh thought that it was the Yellow Bay Filly of the King of Eirinn that they had got, and they were in great haste to ride. They put a saddle on her back, and they bridled her head, and one of them went up on her back to ride her, another went up at the back of that one, and another at the back of that one, and there was always room for another one there, till one after one, the Seven Big Women went up on the back of the Gille Mairtean, thinking that they had got the Yellow Bay Filly.

One of them gave a blow of a rod to the Gille Mairtean; and if she gave, he ran, and he raced backwards and forwards with them through the mountain moors; and at last he went bounding on high to the top of the Monadh mountain of Dhiurradh, and he reached the top of the face of the great crag that is there, and he moved his front to the crag, and he put his two fore-feet to the front of the crag, and he threw his aftermost end on high, and he threw the Seven Big Women over the crag, and he went away laughing; and he reached where were MacIain Direach and the King of France's daughter, with the Yellow Bay Filly, and the White Glave of Light.

Said the Gille Mairtean, 'I will put myself in the form of a boat, and go thyself, and the daughter of the King of France on board, and take with you the Yellow Bay Filly and the White Glave of Light, and I will take you to the mainland.'

The Gille Mairtean put himself in the shape of a boat; MacIain Direach put the White Glave of Light and the Yellow Bay Filly on board, and he went himself, and the King of France's daughter, in on board after them; and the Gille Mairtean went with them to the mainland. When they reached shore, the Gille Mairtean put himself into his own shape, and he said to MacIain Direach, 'Leave thou the King of France's daughter, the Yellow Bay Filly from the King of Eirinn, and the White Glave of Light there, and I will go into the shape of a White Glave of Light; and take thou me to the giant and give thou me to him for the falcon, and I will give him enough of swords.'

The Gille Mairtean put himself into the form of a sword, and MacIain Direach took him to the giant; and when the giant saw him coming he put the Blue Falcon into a muirlag, and he gave it to MacIain Direach, and he went away with it to where he had left the King of France's daughter, the Yellow Bay Filly, and the White Glave of Light.

The giant went in with the Gille Mairtean in his hand, himself thinking that it was the White Glave of Light of the Big Women of Dhiurradh that he had, and he began at fencing, and at slashing with it; but at last the Gille Mairtean bent himself, and he swept the five heads off the giant, and he went where MacIain Direach was, and he said to him, 'Son of John the Upright, put the saddle of gold on the filly, and the silver bridle in her head, and go thyself riding her, and take the King of France's daughter at thy back, and the White Glave of Light with its back against thy nose; or else if thou be not so, when thy muime sees thee, she has a glance that is so deadly that she will bewitch thee, and thou wilt fall a faggot of firewood; but if the back of the sword is against thy nose, and its edge to her, when she tries to bewitch thee, she will fall down herself as a faggot of sticks.'

MacIain Direach did as the Gille Mairtean asked him; and when he came in sight of the house, and his muime looked at him with a deadly bewitching eye, she fell as a faggot of sticks, and MacIain Direach set fire to her, and then he was free from fear; and he had got the best wife in Albainn; and the Yellow Bay Filly was so swift that she could leave the one wind and she would catch the other wind, and the Blue Falcon would keep him in plenty of game, and the White Glave of Light would keep off each foe; and MacIain Direach was steadily, luckily off.

Said MacIain Direach to the Gille Mairtean, 'Thou art welcome, thou Lad of March, to go through my ground, and to take any beast thou dost desire thyself to take with thee; and I will give word to my servants that they do not let an arrow at thee, and that they do not kill thee, nor any of thy race, whatever one of the flock thou takest with thee.'

Said the Gille Mairtean, 'Keep thou thy herds to thyself; there is many a one who has wethers and sheep as well as thou hast, and I will get plenty of flesh in another place without coming to put trouble on thee;' and the fox gave a blessing to the son of Upright John, and he went away; and the tale was spent.

THE SON OF THE KING
OF EIRIN

Source: D. MacInnes, *Folk and Hero Tales*

Narrator: Archibald MacTavish, shoemaker, Oban; Duncan MacInnes recorded
this tale and the three following ones from him in 1881–2. The storyteller, then in
his seventies, was originally from Laggan, Lochbuie, Mull, where he learned his
stories from the tailor, Hugh MacLachlann

Type: AT313c 'The Girl as Helper in the Hero's Flight', 'The Forgotten Fiancée'

The King of Eirin had an only son who was very fond of
hunting. He was one day hunting, and killed a big black
raven. He took the raven up in his hand, and looked at it. The
blood was coming from its head where the lead had entered it;
and he said to himself, 'I will never marry any woman except
one whose hair will be as black as the raven's feathers, and
whose cheek will be as red as the raven's blood.'

When he went home in the evening his father said to him,
'Had you good sport today?'

The lad said to him, 'I had not; I killed only one raven. I said
to myself that I would not marry any woman except one whose
hair would be as black as the raven's feathers, and whose cheek
would be as red as the raven's blood.'

His father said to him, 'It is not so easy to find the like of
her.'

The lad said, 'I will travel through all places to try if I can see
the like of her.'

His father said, 'It is foolish of you to do such a thing.'

His son said, 'Be that as it will, I will go, at any rate.'

He then bade his father goodbye, and went away. As he was
going on, and making inquiry, he was informed where the like
of her was to be found. He was told that the youngest of the
three daughters of the King of the Great World was such a
person. He went on his way, and arrived at a smithy in which a

smith was working, and knocked at the door. The smith opened the door, and said to him, 'Oh! come in; you will be a lucky man.'

The lad said, 'Really I do not know. How do you know that I shall be lucky?'

'I will tell you that,' said the smith. 'I am working here at a big needle; and it defied me to put the eye in it till you knocked at the door; but when you knocked I managed to form the eye. Be seated, and tell me your news. Whence have you come, and to whom do you belong?'

The lad said to him, 'I am a son of the King of Eirin.'

The smith said to him, 'Where are you going?'

The lad said to him, 'I will tell you that. I have heard of the daughter of the King of the Great World, and I am going in quest of her that I may get a sight of her, and that I may speak to her father to see if he will give her to me in marriage.'

'Oo!' said the smith; 'everyone knows that the son of the King of Eirin would get the daughter of the King of the Great World. I have told you already that you will be lucky. The needle at which I am working is for the King of the Great World; and you will get across tomorrow with his people. I myself will ask them to ferry you. Remain with me tonight, and you shall not lack either food or bed.'

He spent that night cheerily and comfortably with the smith. On the morrow the King of the Great World's boat came for the needle; and the smith asked those in charge to take the young man across. They said that they would. 'We are very much pleased,' said they, 'that the needle was ready when we came, and that we did not require to wait for it.'

They then returned home to the house of the King of the Great World, and gave him the needle. When the king saw the son of the King of Eirin, he knew that he did not belong to the place, and he asked him what he wanted. The lad said to him that he came to ask one of his daughters in marriage.

The king said to him, 'To whom do you belong, and whence have you come? You must be of nobler rank than I suppose, when you have come to ask my daughter.'

The lad said, 'I am the son of the King of Eirin.'

The King of the Great World said, 'I thought that you were nobly come when you took upon you to ask my daughter. You shall get my daughter, but you have three things to do before you get her.'

The son of the King of Eirin said, 'I will do these things if I can;' and he asked him what they were.

The King of the World said, 'I have a big byre in which there are seven couples; and you must put out today all the filth that is in it; and it must be so clean that a gold ball will run from end to end of it.'

The king brought him to the byre and showed it to him. He then began to clean it out, but twice as much would come in as he would put out. He kept working at it, and was distressed with the toil; but he could not clean the byre; and he said to himself, 'I wish that I had never come to ask the daughter of the King of the Great World.'

About twelve o'clock in the day the king's three daughters came the way to take a walk; and the eldest of them said to him, 'You are harassed, son of the King of Eirin.'

'Yes,' said he.

'If I thought,' said she, 'that it was for me that you came, I would clean the byre for you.'

The middle one said the same; but the young one said, 'Whether it was for me that you came or not I will clean the byre, son of the King of Eirin.' She then said, 'Clean, clean, crooked graip, put out shovel.' The byre was cleaned so thoroughly that a gold ball would run from end to end of it. The king's three daughters returned home, and left the son of the King of Eirin at the byre.

That same day the king came to the byre, and said, 'Son of the King of Eirin, is the byre clean?'

'Oo yes!' said the son of the King of Eirin.

'I am very much pleased with you for making it so clean,' said the king.

The son of the King of Eirin then said, 'Shall I get your daughter now?'

The King of the Great World said, 'You have more to do tomorrow. You have to thatch the byre tomorrow with birds' feathers. The stem of each feather shall be inwards, and its point shall be outwards. A slender silk thread shall be keeping the covering on the roof of the house.'

The son of the King of Eirin said, 'Will you give me the feathers?'

'No,' said the king, 'you must gather them yourself wherever you can find them.'

On the morrow he began to gather the feathers in the shore. When he would gather a handful, and put it on the byre, a breeze of wind would come and sweep it away. He said to himself, 'I wish I had never come to ask the daughter of the King of the World.'

About twelve o'clock in the day the three daughters of the King of the World came his way to take a walk. The eldest of them said, 'Son of the King of Eirin, you are harassing yourself thatching the byre. If I thought that it was for me that you came, I would thatch the byre for you.' The middle one said the same. The young one said, 'Whether it was for me that you came or not, son of the King of Eirin, I will thatch the byre for you.' She put her hand in her pocket, and took out a whistle, and blew it; and the birds came and shook themselves over the byre; and it was thatched with the birds' feathers. The stem of each feather was inwards and its tip was outwards. A slender silk thread was keeping the covering on the roof.

The king's children returned home, and left him at the byre. That same day the king came where he was, and said to him, 'Son of the King of Eirin, I see that you have thatched the byre. I am much obliged to you; but I am not pleased with your teacher.'

The son of the King of Eirin said to the king, 'Will you give me your daughter now?'

'You shall not get her today yet,' said the king; 'you have more to do tomorrow.' The king then returned home.

On the morrow the son of the King of Eirin saw the King of the World, who said to him, 'I have five swans, and you shall go to keep them; if you let them away you shall be hanged, but if you keep them you shall get my daughter.'

He went to herd the swans, but it defied him to keep them;

they ran off from him. In his plight he sat down, saying to himself, 'It is a pity that I left my father's house to seek the woman. Everything has prospered with me till now; but this thing has gone against me.'

About twelve o'clock in the day the king's three daughters came his way to take a walk; and the eldest of them said, 'The swans have run away from you, son of the King of Eirin.'

'Yes,' said he, 'and I cannot find them; they have gone out on the sea in spite of me.'

She then said to him, 'Well, son of the King of Eirin, if I thought that it was for me that you came, I would find the swans for you.' The middle one said the same. The young one said, 'Whether it was for me that you came or not, I will find the swans for you.' With this she blew her whistle; and the swans returned home.

As the King of Eirin's son was keeping them the King of the World came to him in the course of the day, and said to him, 'I see that you have managed to keep the swans, son of the King of Eirin.'

'Oo! yes,' said he. 'Shall I get your daughter now?'

'No,' said the king; 'you have a small thing to do yet; and when you do it you shall get her.'

They then returned home to the palace. The King of the World said to the son of the King of Eirin, 'I am going to fish tomorrow, and you must clean and boil for me the fish that I catch.'

On the morrow the king caught a fish, and gave it to the son of the King of Eirin to clean and boil. 'I am going to sleep for a while,' said the King of the World, 'and you must have the fish boiled when I waken.'

He began to clean the fish; and as the scales came off it twice as many went on it: and he was beat. Then the eldest of the daughters came, and said to him, 'If I thought that it was for me that you came, I would clean the fish for you;' and the middle one said the same. The young one said, 'Whether it was for me that you came or not I will clean the fish for you.'

She cleaned the fish, and it was put on the fire. She then took the king's son aside, and said to him, 'You and I must take to flight together before my father wakens.' A steed each was got for them from the king's stable: and they fled together. The young daughter said to the son of the King of Eirin that her father would kill them both as soon as he would waken.

When the king awoke, he asked where the son of the King of Eirin and his daughter were. He was told that they had fled together. They went on as fast as their steeds' legs would carry them. The king went after them to see if he could overtake them. Hearing a great noise behind them, the king's daughter said to the son of the King of Eirin, 'Look if you can see anything in the steed's ear.'

He said, 'I see in it a little bit of thorn.'

'Throw it behind you,' said she. He did so: and the little bit of thorn formed a great wood seven miles long and three miles wide. The son of the King of Eirin was on the one side of it, and the King of the World was on the other. The wood was so thick that the king could not get through it. He had to return home to get an axe to cut a path through it. He succeeded in making a path with the axe. The son of the King of Eirin and the young daughter perceived the king pursuing them again. Being tired, they had rested for a while; and thus the king had the more time to overtake them. When they noticed him coming they set off. When he was drawing pretty near them the daughter said to the son of the King of Eirin, 'Try what you can find in the steed's ear.'

'I see a small stone in it,' said he.

'Throw it behind you,' said she. He did so: and the stone became a big high rock seven miles long and a mile high. The king was at the foot of the rock, and they were on the top of it. They looked over the edge of the rock to see how it would fare with him. He looked up; and when he saw that he could make nothing of it he returned home. They pursued their journey back to Eirin. When they got across to Eirin, and were but a short distance from the palace of the King of Eirin, the king's daughter said, 'I will not go to the house for a while. When you go home the dog will be leaping up to your breast with joy. Try to keep it off you, for if it touch your face you will forget that you ever saw me.'

They then bade each other goodbye: and she went to reside with a smith that was in the place. Having bought men's clothes and put them on, she went to the smith, and asked him if he was in want of a servant. The smith said that he was, the servant that he had having left him on the previous day. The new servant then began to learn the smith trade, and made excellent progress, and everyone remarked how fine-looking he was. He was working with the smith for a year. The smith never had a servant so apt at learning, and so good in every way.

Word came that the son of the King of Eirin was going to marry the daughter of the King of Farafohuinn. Among those invited to the wedding was the smith, and he insisted on his servant accompanying him. The servant said to the smith, 'I have something to make in the smithy that I wish to have with me when I go. Will you give me the smithy tonight?' The smith consented; and the servant made a gold hen and a silver cock. On the day of the wedding the smith and he went to the wedding. Before going he put grains of wheat in his pocket. When they arrived at the wedding-house, the king's palace, there was a roomful of people before them. Many of them knew the smith, and welcomed him. They asked him if he could make sport to pass the time. 'I cannot,' said he; 'but perhaps my servant here will afford us diversion for a while.'

They asked him if he could do so; and he said that he would try. He then put out on the floor the gold hen and the silver cock, and threw three grains of wheat to them. The cock picked up two of them, and the hen got but one. The hen said, 'Gok! gok!' and the cock said, 'What is the matter with you?'

The hen said to the cock, 'Do you remember the day when I cleaned the big byre for you?'

The company began to laugh and make fun. The smith's servant threw out other three grains. The cock picked up two of them, and the hen got but one. 'Gok! gok!' said the hen. 'What is the matter with you?' said the cock.

The hen said to the cock, 'If you remembered the day when I thatched the byre for you with birds' feathers, the stem of each feather being inwards and its tip outwards, and a slender silk thread keeping the cover on the roof, you would not eat two grains while I had but one.'

The king's son looked at the smith's servant, and said to him, 'Try if you have more to throw to them.' He recollected at once how it fared with him when he went to ask the king's daughter, and he said to himself, 'If I get another proof of the matter I shall be more assured.' The servant then threw out more grains; and the cock picked up two of them, and the hen got but one. The hen said, 'Gok! gok!' and the cock said, 'What is the matter with you?'

The hen said, 'Do you remember the day when I found the swans for you? If you did you would not eat two grains while I had but one.'

The king's son perceiving how the matter stood, went over, and put his two hands round the smith's servant, and said, 'Dearest of women, it is you;' and he opened the breast of the smith's servant in presence of the company, and showed them that it was a woman. Without further delay she was taken to another room, and had a woman's dress put on her. A gold chain was put about her neck, a gold ring was put on her finger, and a gold watch was given her.

He said to the woman that he was going to marry, 'This is the woman that I went in quest of; and I will take none but her, because I passed through many trials on her account. If you choose to stay you may, and you will participate in the wedding amusements; but if you do not so choose you may go, for you have no hold on me.' She whom he was going to marry first, taking the treatment that she received as an affront, was deeply offended, and went away. The son of the King of Eirin and the daughter of the King of the World were married on that day by the minister that was in the house.

THE KINGDOM OF THE GREEN
MOUNTAINS

Source: D. MacInnes, *Folk and Hero Tales*
Narrator: Archibald MacTavish, shoemaker, Oban, 1881–2
Type: AT400 'The Man on a Quest for his Lost Wife'

There were three soldiers who arranged with each other that they would desert, and who said to each other, 'We three will not set off in company at all; each of us shall take a separate road.' The three then said, 'Perhaps we shall meet sometime.' One of them was a sergeant, another a corporal, and another a private. The friends separated; and each took his own way.

On the evening of the second day after this the sergeant came walking to a big and splendid palace; and he was tired and hungry. He asked at the outer door if he would be allowed to remain. A young lady came out, and spoke to him, and said that he would, 'because,' said she, 'it is said that soldiers and sailors have many stories.' She brought him in, and said to him, 'Your dinner will be down in a short time. I know that you are very needful of food and drink.'

Night came, and dinner came down, and was placed on the table for him, every kind of food that he could think of; and she said to him, 'You will not take it amiss that we have no light at our meals here, and you will mark the dish that is most acceptable to you.'

'Hoo,' said he, 'if that is the custom of the place, I will do as you bid.'

She then extinguished the candle, and he set to work on the dish that he saw proper to select. She struck her foot on the floor, and called down two officers, and said, 'Seize this rascal, and put him in prison.' The officers took him away, and put him in prison; and he was fed there on bread and water.

On the following evening the corporal came to the same

house, and asked if he would be allowed to remain for the night. The lady came out, and said that he would. 'I understand,' said she, 'that you are a soldier, and a soldier and a sailor have often had a story.' She brought him in, and requested him to sit on a chair, and said to him, 'I know that you are needful of food and drink; your dinner will be down in a short time.'

Night came, and he was wearying that dinner was not coming, for he was hungry. At last dinner came, and was placed on the table; and the lady came down with a light, and said to him, 'The custom of this place is not to have light at meals, and you will mark the dish that is most acceptable to you.' He then set to work on the dish; and she extinguished the candle, struck her foot on the floor, called down two officers, and bade them put that rascal in prison. The officers took him away and put him in prison; and his fare there was bread and water.

On the following evening the private came to the house. He was pretty far gone through lack of food, and asked if he would be allowed to remain for the night. The lady came out, and said to him that he would. 'I understand,' said she, 'that you are a soldier, and a soldier and a sailor have often had a story.' She then took him in, made him sit on a chair, and said to him, 'Dinner will come to you in a short time.'

Night came on him, and he was wearying that dinner was not coming. At last it came, and the lady came where he was, and said, 'The custom of this place is not to have light at meals, and you will mark the dish that is most acceptable to you, and set to work on it.' She then went and extinguished the light.

Upon this he rose, and put his two hands round her, and kissed her, and said, 'The food is good, but I prefer yourself to it.'

She then struck her foot on the floor, and called for a light. The man-servant came with a light; and she and the soldier sat down, and had dinner together. They spent the night in conversation and in telling stories to each other. She asked him if he had any education; and he said that he had. She requested him to show her his handwriting; and he did so. At last she came round him artfully, till she said to him, 'Will you marry me?'

'That I will,' said he.

'Well!' said she, 'I am the daughter of the King of the Green Mountains, and have had no desire to marry a king or a knight, but a comely, common lad. I have a large estate and plenty of gold and silver.' They then appointed a day for their marriage.

When bedtime came she brought him to a room, and bade him good-night; and he went to bed. She came in in the morning when it was time for him to rise, and requested him to rise and dress himself for breakfast. When breakfast was on the table they sat down, and had it together. When it was over she took a gold purse out of her pocket, and gave him money to get a suit of clothes for himself, and sent him to a tailor with whom she was acquainted to make the suit. He went to the tailor, and requested him to make the suit, and to make it well, and said to him that he was to wait till he should have it with him. The tailor began, and made the suit; and it was a good fit. The soldier then set off to return home; and the tailor's mother said, 'Go a part of the way with him. He will be seized with thirst. Give him this apple, and he will fall asleep.'

The lady was to go to meet him with a coach on the day on which she expected him. He and the tailor set off, and they sat down to rest; and the soldier said, 'I am thirsty.' The tailor said, 'I think that I have an apple in my pocket, which I will give you.'

When the soldier ate the apple he fell asleep. The lady then arrived with the coach, and said to the tailor, 'Is that fellow asleep? If so, waken him.'

The tailor began to waken him, and shake him from side to side, but he could not be wakened. The lady took a gold ring out of her pocket, and gave it to the tailor, and requested him to give it to the sleeper, and to tell him that she would meet him next day. 'He shall return with yourself tonight,' said she.

She then went away and returned home; and they returned to the tailor's house. He spent that night with the tailor. When he was going to set off after breakfast on the morrow the tailor took the gold ring out of his pocket, and said, 'Here is a gold ring that the lady left with me to give to you.'

When they were setting off the tailor's mother said, 'I am sure that it will be of no use to give him an apple today; but here is a pear that you shall give him when he is seized with thirst. Perhaps the daughter of the King of the Green Mountains will fall to your own lot.'

The soldier and the tailor set out on their journey. They sat down to rest; and the soldier said, 'I am thirsty today again.'

'Well!' said the tailor, 'I have a pear here that is good for quenching thirst.'

'Well!' said the soldier, 'I got an apple from you yesterday; and it set me asleep; and I am afraid to take the pear.'

'Toch! you gomeril,' said the tailor, 'you need not think that.'

The tailor gave him the pear; and he ate it, and fell asleep. The lady then arrived with the coach, and said to the tailor, 'Surely that fellow is not asleep today!' The tailor said, 'He is asleep;' and she said, 'Try if you can waken him.'

The tailor began to waken him, but he could not be wakened. The lady took a penknife out of her pocket, and gave it to the tailor, and said, 'You shall give him this, and say to him that I will meet him here tomorrow; and he shall return home with yourself tonight.'

After she went away the soldier wakened and asked if the lady had arrived.

'She has,' said the tailor, 'but it defied us to waken you. Here is a penknife that she left with me to give to you; and she said that she would meet you here tomorrow.' He and the tailor then returned home, and they spent the night together.

After breakfast next day, when they were going away, the old woman said, 'It will be of no use to give him an apple or a pear today; but when you arrive at the place where you used to rest you shall put this pin in the back of his coat; and if he was sleepy before he will be seven times sleepier this time.'

They set off, and reached the place where they used to rest; and the tailor put the pin in the back of his coat; and he fell asleep. The lady then arrived with two men to raise him into the coach; and she said to the tailor, 'Is he asleep today?'

'He is,' said the tailor.

'Waken him,' said she, 'if he can be wakened.'

The tailor began to waken him, but he could not be wakened. She then sent out the two men that she had in the coach, but the three of them could not lift him. She went, and gave the tailor a gold pin, and said, 'Give him this. I will not come to meet him any more.'

When she went away the tailor took the pin out of the soldier's coat; and he wakened. The soldier asked if the lady had arrived; and the tailor told him that she had, and had gone away, and said, 'There is a pin that she left as a remembrance. You are not likely to see her more. You will return home with me to-night yet.'

'Indeed I will not,' said the soldier. 'I wish that I had not returned so often with you. I will be setting off to push my own way. Goodbye.' They then parted.

He was going on, and inquiring for the road to the kingdom of the Green Mountains. He was told by those of whom he made inquiry that they had never heard of such a kingdom. He was travelling from place to place, but was getting no information about the kingdom. He was ridiculed for speaking at all of such a place. He came one day to houses, and saw an old man putting divots on a house, and said to him, 'Ah! how old you are! and yet you are putting divots on the house.'

The old man said, 'I am old; but my father is older than I.'

'Ah!' said the soldier, 'is your father alive?'

'He is,' said the old man. 'Where are you going?'

'I am going,' said the soldier, 'to the kingdom of the Green Mountains.'

'Well,' said the old man, 'I am old, but I have never heard of that kingdom. Perhaps my father knows about it.'

'Where is your father?' said the soldier.

'He is conveying the divots to me,' said the old man, 'and will be here in a short time, when you may speak to him about that kingdom.'

The man who was conveying the divots arrived; and the soldier said to him, 'Ah! man, how old you are!'

'By Mary, I am old; but my father is older than I,' said the old man.

'Is your father still alive?' said the soldier.

'He is,' said the old man.

'Where is he?' said the soldier.

'He is cutting the divots,' said the old man.

They then went to the man who was cutting the divots; and the soldier said, 'Ah! man, how old you are! and yet you are cutting the divots.'

The old man said, 'I am old; but my father is older than I.'

'Ah!' said the soldier, 'is your father, I wonder, still alive?'

'He is,' said he.

'Where is he?' said the soldier.

'He is hunting birds in the hill,' said the old man.

The soldier said to him, 'Have you ever heard of the kingdom of the Green Mountains?'

'I have not,' said he; 'but perhaps my father has; and when he comes home tonight you may ask him.'

He remained with the old man till evening, when the fowler came home. When the fowler came home the soldier said to him, 'Ah! man, how old you are!'

'I am old,' said he; 'but my father is older than I.'

'Ah!' said the soldier, 'is your father, I wonder, still alive?'

'By Mary! he is,' said the fowler.

'Where is he?' said the soldier.

'He is in the house,' said the fowler.

The soldier said to him, 'Have you ever heard of the kingdom of the Green Mountains?'

'I have not,' said he; 'but perhaps my father has.'

They went down to the house; and when they went in the old man was being rocked in a cradle. The soldier said to him, 'Ah! man, what a great age has been granted to you!'

'Well! yes, a very great age,' said he.

The soldier said to him, 'Have you ever heard of the kingdom of the Green Mountains?'

'Really,' said the old man, 'I have never heard of that kingdom.'

The fowler then said to the soldier, 'I am going to the hill tomorrow; and when I blow a whistle that I have there is not a kingdom in the world from which birds will not come to me; so that I shall know if there be such a kingdom.'

The soldier spent that night with the old men. After breakfast next day he went away with the fowler to the hill. When they arrived the fowler blew his whistle; and the birds gathered to him from every quarter; but there was a large eagle which was much later of coming than the other birds. The fowler said to her, 'You nasty baggage! what has kept you so far behind the others?'

'Really,' said the eagle, 'I had a much greater distance to accomplish than they.'

'Whence have you come?' said the fowler.

'I have come this very day from the kingdom of the Green Mountains,' said she.

'Well!' said the fowler, 'there is a man here whom you must carry on your back tomorrow to the kingdom of the Green Mountains.'

'I will do so,' said she, 'if I get enough of food.'

'You shall get that,' said he; 'you shall get a good quarter of meat.' They then returned home; and the eagle remained with them that night.

After breakfast next day the fowler, the soldier, and the eagle set off, and went to the hill; and they had with them a quarter of meat for the eagle and a quarter for the soldier. The soldier then went on the eagle's back, and bade the fowler goodbye; and the eagle spread her wings, and went away. On the way she ate the quarter of meat, and she said to the soldier, 'I am hungry, and must let you go.'

'Ah! don't,' said he. 'I have a little of my own share; and you shall get it.'

'Bring it over, then,' said she. He gave it to her; and she ate it, and went a good distance on it. 'Ah!' said she, 'I am hungry again, and must let you go.'

'Ah! don't,' said he. 'Bring me, at any rate, safely to the kingdom of the Green Mountains.'

'Look,' said she, 'if you have a bit left of the meat.'

'Ah! no,' said he.

'You have a good thigh,' said she; 'bring it over here.'

He held his thigh to her till she ate what was on the outer side of it. 'I am the better of that,' said she; 'that is the sweetest meat that I have yet eaten;' and she went a great distance on it. She became hungry again. 'Ah!' said she, 'I must let you go now at any rate, I have become weak; but turn over to me the other thigh, that the two thighs may be alike.' Hard though it was, he had to turn over his thigh to her. She ate it, and said, 'Ah! I am doubly stronger. I think that I can now manage to reach the kingdom of the Green Mountains.'

She did manage to reach it, and she left him on dry ground there. There was a dead horse there which had just been flayed. The eagle requested the soldier to cut a quarter off it, and lay it on her back. He did so; and she returned home. He was in a wretched plight, and could not walk on account of the condition of his thighs, but he struggled on till he reached the house of the gardener of the King of the Green Mountains. The gardener's wife was very good to him, and he stayed with her till she cured him. When he was cured he went to work with the gardener.

Intelligence came that the daughter of the King of the Green Mountains was going to be married. 'Ah!' said he to the gardener's wife, 'what a pity that I could not get a sight of her!'

'You shall get that,' said the gardener's wife. 'I will devise a plan for your seeing her.' She dressed him in fine clothes, and sent him off with a basket of apples, and said to him, 'Remember that you deliver them into no one's hands but her own.'

He went off, and reached the king's house, and said that he had a basket of apples from the gardener for the daughter of the King of the Green Mountains. The servants were going to take the basket from him, but he would not give it to them, and asked to be allowed to see herself. The king's daughter then sent word to him to come in to see her. He went in, and gave her the basket of apples; and she took hold of a bottle, and filled a glass with wine for him. 'Excuse me,' said he, 'it is the fashion of the country whence I have come for those giving the drink to taste it first.' Whereupon she drank to him first, and then filled the glass for him. He went and took the gold ring that she gave him, and returned it to her in the glass. She took hold of it, looked at it, and saw her own name on it, and said to him, 'Where did you find this ring?'

He said, 'Do you remember the soldier whom you sent to a tailor for a suit of clothes?'

'I think that I do,' said she. 'Have you further proof of that?'

'I have,' said he; and he took out the penknife, and handed it to her.

'Have you another proof of it?' said she.

'I have,' said he; and he gave her the gold pin.

'I see now,' said she, 'that the thing is true;' and she put her two hands round him, and rejoiced greatly over him. They fixed a day for their marriage; and she discarded the man whom she was going to marry.

He returned to the gardener's wife, and told her that he was going to marry the daughter of the King of the Green Mountains. 'Be not concerned lest I do not prove a good backing to you and your husband.' They then married.

After their marriage she took him to see the prisoners that she had; and when he saw them he recognized his companions, and felt great compassion for them. He requested that they should be set at liberty, and handed them a good sum of money to take them away.

THE SHIP THAT WENT TO
AMERICA

Source: D. MacInnes, *Folk and Hero Tales*
Narrator: Archibald MacTavish, shoemaker, Oban, 1881–2
Type: AT531 'The Clever Horse'

This ship sailed to America with a great number of people who were going to reside in that country. It happened to them that they came near land at a part of the coast where there were many rocks and skerries; and all were lost except one man and his wife. These two got ashore on a broken piece of the ship, and they erected a tent above the shore. Sails and ropes belonging to the ship were going ashore; and they formed the tent of them. Some of the provisions that were in the ship were going ashore in hogsheads, such as biscuits and meat. Some books that were on board went also ashore. After they were there for some time what went ashore was spent; and they were in want.

It occurred to the man one day that he would go out through the country to try if he could see houses and men or anything that would please him; and he asked his wife not to be anxious. He set off, and went on, and passed through much wood. He took a bit of the bark off the trees as he went on. At last he got through the wood. He did not see any person or the appearance of any house. He saw a mountain at a considerable distance from him, and resolved to go to the top of it, because he would get a better view of the country. He reached the top of the mountain before he halted; and he was tired and hungry. A good part of the day was past by this time. He saw no appearance of anyone or of a house, as far as his eye could reach. He became so anxious that he said that he wished that he had not left his own little tent; and he was much afraid that he could not return on account of want of food.

As he was looking down the other side of the mountain he thought that he saw the appearance of a little hut at the foot of the mountain; and he said to himself, 'I will go down, and see what kind of house it is.' He went down, reached the hut, and entered a room in which there was a table covered with a large white tablecloth; and a bottle of wine and a loaf of wheaten bread were upon it. 'Well!' said he to himself, 'I am hungry, and know not what to do. If I touch this, perhaps I shall be to blame. I will, at any rate, venture to take a part of it.' He took hold of the bottle and took a mouthful or two out of it, and he took a bit out of the loaf and ate it. An old grey man then came in, and said to him, 'What is your news, stranger? What in the world has driven you in this direction?'

He told the old man every misfortune that he passed through, and said to him, 'I don't know but I have acted rudely by touching this; but I was hungry.'

'Not at all, not at all,' said the old man; 'take enough of it: it is there for such as you. Are you married?'

'I am,' said the other.

'Have you a family?' said the old man.

'We have not,' said the other; 'we never had any children.'

The old man said, 'The day is now past; and you have no time to return home tonight. Remain with me, and you shall get food and bed from me.'

He spent that night with the old man. They both rose in the morning; and the old man made breakfast for the other. He put a bottle of wine and a loaf of wheaten bread on the table, and said, 'Now make a good breakfast. You have a long distance to travel; and your wife is in great anxiety about you.'

When he was going away the old man spoke to him thus: 'What will you give me for the tablecloth? Every time that you spread it on your table you will get a bottle of wine, and a loaf of wheaten bread, and one or two other kinds of food besides.'

'Really,' said the other, 'I have nothing to give you for it.'

'Well!' said the old man, 'if you give me the first man or beast that will be born on your possession you shall get the tablecloth.'

The other, thinking that he would not have any children or beasts, said to the old man that he would give him what he asked. The old man said to him, 'Whatever it be, come here with it seven years from today.'

He then went away, and bade the old man goodbye, and returned home to his tent; and his wife was exceedingly pleased, for she did not expect ever to see him again. He took the tablecloth from under his arm, and spread it; and a bottle of wine and a loaf of wheaten bread were on the table, with many other kinds of food. 'Ah,' said his wife, 'where have you found this?'

He said, 'Fortune has bestowed it on me. We shall not be in want any more while we live.'

Thus day after day passed, till at last his wife had a young son, whom he named John. When he grew up to be a boy of about four or five years his father began to give him schooling. Time passed till it came to the seven years; and the man said to his wife, 'I am going away today, and going to take the boy with me, because it is he that I promised for the tablecloth.'

She began to weep and wail, and to reflect on him for doing such a thing. 'It cannot be helped,' said he. 'I must do it; I must go away today.'

His mother then rose, and kissed the boy, and let him away with his father. They arrived step by step at the little hut at the foot of the mountain where the old grey man was; and he went into the same room that he was in before; and a bottle of wine and a loaf of wheaten bread were on the table. It occurred to him that he would take a drop out of the bottle and a bit out of the loaf; and he and the boy took a little of them. Who came in but the old grey man! and he said to him, 'You have come as you promised.'

'Oo, yes,' said the other.

'Well!' said the old grey man, 'it behoved you to come today; for if you had not I would go for you tomorrow. I see that you have a boy with you this time, which was not the case before. What is his baptismal name?'

'John,' said the boy's father.

'May he enjoy his name; it is a good one,' said the old man. 'Has he any education?'

'He has a little: I have been teaching him myself,' said the boy's father.

The old man said, 'I will give him good schooling and instruction, and act towards him as if he were my own son. Perhaps I shall make a fortunate man of him yet.'

The boy's father remained with them that night at the foot of the mountain. After they had breakfast on the morrow his father bade the boy goodbye, and returned home. When he arrived his wife was sad and grieved after the boy. He was keeping up her spirits as he best could, in the hope that they would yet have another son. We will leave them there in comfort, and return to the old man at the foot of the mountain.

The boy grew up a big and handsome lad; and the old grey man gave him enough of schooling and instruction. He was more than twenty years with the old grey man; and the old grey man said to him, 'You and I are to go today to the top of the mountain up here. Look above the door, and you will find there a horse's bridle. Bring it with you.' Having reached the top of the mountain, the old grey man said to John, 'Shake the bridle towards me, and I shall turn into a horse, and you shall leap on my back.' John did as he was bid; and the old grey man turned into a horse. John leaped on his back; and the horse set off with him, and went at a terrible pace. Soft or hard ground was alike to him. They went on for the greater part of that day, and came to a big *aoineadh* at the sea-side; and the old grey man said to John, 'Come off my back, John.' John came off his back; and the old man said to him, 'Go to the cave up there, and you shall find three giants lying down in it, and dying of hunger; and look into my ear to see what you will find in it.' He looked, and found a bottle of wine and three loaves of wheaten bread. The old man said to him, 'Give them a loaf each, and divide the bottle among them; and when they partake of that, say to them that you hope that they will remember it to you yet.'

He went to the giants and gave them the wine and loaves. When they partook of them the chief giant said, 'We are now exceedingly well off.'

'If so,' said John, 'I hope that you will remember it to me yet.'

'Perhaps we will,' said the chief giant.

He went down where the old man was; and the old man said to him, 'Have you done as I bade you?'

'Yes, yes,' said John.

'Leap on my back, John,' said the old man.

They then set off, and reached the sea-side, where there was a great beach. 'Come off my back, John,' said the old man. 'Go down to the beach; there is a big fish there. Put it out on the sea, and say to it that you hope that it will remember it to you yet.'

He went down to the beach, and found the fish there, and he put it out on the sea, and said to it, 'I hope that you will remember it to me yet.'

'Perhaps I will,' said the fish.

He then returned to the old man, who said to him, 'Have you done as I bade you, John?' John said that he had; and the old man said to him, 'Leap on my back, John.' They set off then, and came to a large brazen castle; and the old man said, 'Come off my back, John. Go up to that castle, and enter it, and you shall see rooms full of gold and rooms full of silver; and by all that you have ever seen let not your hand touch any of it.'

John then entered the castle, and saw all the rooms of gold and silver that were in it; and when he was coming out he looked sideways, and saw a large bundle of goose feathers; and it occurred to him that one of them would suit well to make a pen; and he took one of them away with him. He did not tell the old man that he had done this. The old man said to him, 'Have you not had a good sight in there?'

'Yes,' said John.

'You have not touched anything or taken anything away with you,' said the old man.

'I have not,' said John.

'Leap on my back,' said the old man. John leaped on his back; and they set off, and reached the castle of a king that was there; and the old grey man said to him, 'Come off my back, John.' 'Yes, yes,' said John; and the old grey man said to him, 'Go in, and send word to the king, asking him if he wants a clerk.' John went in, and word came that a clerk was wanted under the command of the head clerk. John went out, and told this to the old man, who said, 'Accept of the office till you get a better.' John returned to the house and accepted the offer that he got. He then returned to the old grey man and told him that he had taken service with the king. The old grey man left him there, and said to him, 'Should any difficulty or hard lot overtake you, think of me, and I will come to you.'

He then went in, and began his work under the command of the head clerk. The pens that they had were not pleasing him, and remembering that he had taken the feather away with him from the brazen castle, he made a pen of it; and when he tried the pen he could write with it in such a manner as he himself never wrote, and as he never saw anyone writing. When the head clerk saw the writing he never saw the like of it, and he was terrified that John would get to be over him. One day that John happened to be out the head clerk came to try his pens, and having found this pen, he could write with it as well as John himself could. The head clerk went and told the king that it was John's pen that was doing the writing; and the king went and tried the pen himself, and he could write with it as well as John and the clerk could. The king sent for John, and said to him, 'Where did you get the pen that you have yonder?'

John said, 'I got the pen in the brazen castle on the day on which I came here.'

'I was thinking that,' said the king. 'You must go and bring the lady of the brazen castle to me here, that I may marry her.'

'I cannot do that,' said John.

'You must do it, or else you shall be hanged,' said the king.

John went to his own room, and began to weep; and he said to himself, 'How valuable would be the presence of the old grey man!' and who should in a moment come to him but the old grey man!

'What is the matter with you?' said the old grey man.

He told him what the king had said to him; and the old grey man said to him, 'I'll warrant that you touched something in the castle.'

'Indeed,' said John, 'I touched nothing except one feather; and I made a pen of it: and that is what has brought matters to this pass.'

'That is as bad for you as though you had touched a larger thing,' said the old grey man. 'I bade you not touch anything, and if you had not touched anything you would not have that to do today. However, come out, and leap on my back.'

John went out, and leaped on his back; and they set off, and came in sight of the brazen castle at the seaside. He then gave him a rod, and said, 'Strike me with the rod, and I shall become a ship; and you shall steer in a straight line to the front of the brazen castle, and cast anchor there, and you shall go ashore with the skiff, and keep looking about you to try what you will see, and walking backwards and forwards. The lady will put her head out at a window in the upper part of the castle, and say to you, "Whence have you come, sailor?" and you shall say to her that you have just come across from the Indies. She will say to you, "What cargo have you on board?" and you shall say to her that you have a cargo of silk, fashions newly come out, very fine for ladies. She will then say to you, "Bring in a good bundle of it, and I will buy a dress or two of it." You shall say to her, "I cannot guess what will please you; but as the day is calm and mild there is nothing better than that you come out yourself," and she will say to you that she thinks that that is best for her.'

He then went and struck the old man with the rod, and he turned into a ship; and they set off, and cast anchor in front of the brazen castle; and John went ashore with the skiff. He reached the castle, and was going round it backwards and forwards, hither and thither; and the lady put her head out at the window above, and said to him, 'Whence have you come, sailor?'

'I have just come across from the Indies,' said he.

'What cargo have you on board?' said she.

'A cargo of silk,' said he; 'every kind of new fashion, very suitable for dresses for ladies and great ladies.'

'I shall be obliged to you,' said she, 'if you will bring in a good bundle of it that I may buy a dress or two of it.'

'I cannot guess,' said he, 'what kinds will please you; you had better go out with me on board, as the day is calm and mild.'

'Indeed, I do not know,' said she, 'but it is best for me to do so.'

She went out with him; and he brought her down to the cabin, and set before her bundles of silk; and she took so much time looking over them, and thinking what kind she would take away with her, that when she came up on deck she was a great distance away from the castle.

'Ah!' said she, 'what have you done to me?'

'There is no fear of you yet,' said he.

'Well!' said she, 'I have now lost my brazen castle, my good home.' She put her hand in her pocket, and took out the keys of the castle, and threw them into the sea. 'Whatever befalls me,' said she, 'no other shall enter the castle after me.'

He steered the ship, and went ashore at the very spot from which he started. He took the lady of the brazen castle ashore in the skiff; and he shook the rod towards the ship; and it came to land, and became a horse. He set the lady of the brazen castle on the back of the horse; and they rode home to the palace; and he delivered her to the king. On the morrow he began his work as clerk.

The king told the lady of the brazen castle that he wished to marry her. She said to him, 'I will never marry you till you place the brazen castle at the end of this palace.'

'We shall make John do it,' said the king. He sent for John, and said to him, 'You must place the brazen castle at the end of this palace, or else you shall be hanged.'

Poor John betook himself to his own room, and began to think of the old grey man; and he came. The old grey man said, 'What is the matter with you today, John?'

'The king,' said he, 'bids me bring the brazen castle to the end of his palace here, or else I shall be hanged.'

'Did I not bid you,' said the old grey man, 'not touch anything in the castle? If you had not touched anything you would not have that to do today. Come out, and leap on my back.'

He went away with him till he brought him to the cave where the big giants were. 'There are many giants in it today,' said the old man. 'Ask them if they remember the day when they were dying of hunger, and you gave them wine and wheaten bread, and say to them that you hope that they will bring the brazen castle to the end of the king's palace for your sake.'

He went up; and the cave was full of giants, as the old man had told him; and he said to the chief giant, 'Do you remember the day when you were dying here of hunger, and I gave you a bottle of wine and loaves of wheaten bread?'

'Indeed, I think that such a thing happened,' said the chief giant.

'I hope that you will remember it to me today,' said John.

'What do you want?' said the chief giant.

'That you bring the brazen castle to the king's palace for my sake,' said John.

'Perhaps I will,' said the chief giant.

John then went down to the old grey man, who said to him, 'Have you done as I bade you, John?'

'I have,' said John.

'What did he say to you?' said the old grey man.

'He said, "Perhaps I will."'

'That is as good as though he made you more certain,' said the old grey man. 'Leap on my back, John.'

They returned all the way to the king's palace; and the old grey man said to him, 'Begin your work now; and should you at any time be in straits, think of me;' and he left him.

When the king rose next morning the brazen castle was at the end of his palace. The king then told the lady of the brazen castle that he wished to marry her; and she said, 'I will never marry you till I get the bundle of keys that I threw into the sea.'

The king said, 'We will make John get them.'

He sent for John to come to speak to him, and said to him, 'You must get for me the keys of the brazen castle that the lady threw into the sea on the day when you brought her away from the castle, or else you shall be hanged.'

John retired to his own room, and began to think of the old grey man; and he came and said, 'What does the king want now?'

'The keys of the brazen castle that the lady threw into the sea on the day when we took her away from the castle,' said John.

'Did I not bid you,' said the old man, 'not touch anything that was in the castle? If you had not touched anything you would not have that to do today. Come out and leap on my back.'

John then leaped on his back; and they set off, and reached the beach where was the fish that he put out in the sea; and the old man said to him, 'Go now, and call to the king of the fish, and when he comes, say to him, "Do you remember the day when you were left on the beach here by the receding tide, and I put you out?" The fish will say to you, "I think that I do. What do you want?" And you shall say to him that you want the keys of the brazen castle that the lady threw into the sea.'

John then went out on the sea, and called to the king of the fishes, and said to him, 'Do you remember the day when you were left here by the receding tide, and I put you out?'

'I do,' said the fish. 'What do you want?'

'I want the keys of the brazen castle that the lady threw into the sea,' said John.

The fish went in search of the keys, and took a considerable time to find them. John then returned with the keys, and went ashore; and the old man said to him, 'Have you found the keys?'

'I have,' said he.

'Leap on my back,' said the old man.

He leaped on his back, and went away with him to the king's palace, and gave the keys to the king; and the king gave them to the lady of the brazen castle. John went out, and returned to the old man, who said, 'Attend to your business as usual; and should you at any time be in straits, think of me.'

When the lady got the keys she said to the king, 'I will never marry till I get three bottles of the water of the well of virtues.'

'I cannot get that for you,' said the king; 'we will make John get it.'

John retired to his room, and began to think that it would be well if the old grey man would come. The old grey man came, and said, 'What is the matter with you today, John?'

'A great deal, and not a little,' said John. 'The king wants three bottles of the water of the well of virtues.'

'Come out and leap on my back; that is not easy to find,' said the old grey man.

John and the old grey man set off, and rode on a very great distance; and the old grey man said to John, 'John, come off my back, and get a good lump of a stone, and strike me in the root of the ear, and kill me (I cannot go farther); and when you kill me, rip up my belly, and go into it, and let part of my small intestines out at my side. Five ravens will come to eat them; and you shall put out your hand softly, and catch two of them; and the other three will say to you, "Let our brothers out to us." Say you to them that you will not let them out till they bring to you five bottles of the water of the well of virtues; and when they come with it, take care that they do not play you a trick. If it be the right water I shall rise alive on your pouring a quantity of it on me; but if it be not I shall not stir; and you shall threaten terribly that you will kill the two ravens that you have unless they bring the right water to you.'

John then went, and struck the old grey man with the stone in the root of the ear, and killed him. He ripped up his belly, and went into it. The five ravens came to eat the horse's intestines; and he put out his hand, and caught two of them; and the other ravens called to him to let their brothers out to them. 'I will not,' said he, 'till you bring to me here five bottles of the water of the well of virtues.'

They went away, and returned with the five bottles. 'Here,' said they, 'give up our brothers to us now.'

'I will not,' said he, 'till I know if it is the right water that you have.'

He threw a drop of it on the horse, but the horse did not stir. He then caught the two ravens that he had by their heads, and began to put them round, and said, 'I will take the heads off your necks unless you bring the right water to me.'

They set off for the water, and were a long time away before they returned, and they gave him the water; and he threw a quantity of it on the horse; and the horse rose, and came alive, and said to John, 'You have acquitted yourself well, John.' John then let the two ravens away with the others. The old grey man said, 'Leap on my back, John.' They then set off, and came home all the way to the king's palace; and the old grey man said to John, 'Give away three bottles and keep two; and should you be in any strait, think of me.'

He gave the three bottles to the king; and he gave them to the lady. She ordered a great cauldron full of water to be put on the fire to boil; and she went to a room alone, and washed herself from head to foot with the water of the three bottles. John was looking at her through the keyhole. She sprang into the cauldron, and said that she would never marry any man except one who would stand in the cauldron as long as she would. The king went, and sprang into the cauldron with her, and he was burned to death. John thought of the old grey man; and he came; and John told him what the lady did with the three bottles, how she and the king sprang into the cauldron, and the king was burned.

'Go you,' said the old grey man, 'and wash yourself with the water of the two bottles, which will be as effectual as though you had three, and go in where she is, and say to her that if she will marry you you will stand in the cauldron as long as herself.'

He washed himself, and went in where she was, and said to her, 'If you marry me I will leap into the cauldron with you.'

'I will marry you,' said she; and he leaped into the cauldron, and put his two hands round her, and began to kiss her. 'You are my man now,' said she. They came out of the cauldron, put on their clothes, and married; and he became king in place of the other. The old man bade him goodbye, and said to him, 'I have now done what I promised you: I have made a fortunate man of you.' Unless they have died since then, they are alive still.

KOISHA KAYN, OR, KIAN'S LEG

Source: D. MacInnes, *Folk and Hero Tales*
Narrator: Archibald MacTavish, shoemaker, Oban, 1881–2

There were five hundred blind men, and five hundred deaf men, and five hundred limping men, and five hundred dumb men, and five hundred cripple men. The five hundred deaf men had five hundred wives, and the five hundred limping men had five hundred wives, and the five hundred dumb men had five hundred wives, and the five hundred cripple men had five hundred wives. Each five hundred of these had five hundred children and five hundred dogs. They were in the habit of going about in one band, and were called the Cleeä-henachair. There was a knight in Eirin called O'Kroinikeard, with whom they spent a day and a year; and they ate up all that he had, and made a poor man of him. There was a king in Eirin called Brian Borr; and O'Kroinikeard went to him for help. When he arrived he went on his knees to the king; and the king said to him, 'What is your news, O'Kroinikeard?'

'I have but poor news for you, king.'

'What poor news have you?' said the king.

'That I have had the Cleeä-henachair for a day and a year, and they have eaten all that I had, and made a poor man of me,' said he.

'Well!' said the king, 'I am sorry for you; what do you want?'

'I want help,' said O'Kroinikeard; 'anything that you may be willing to give me.'

The king promised him a hundred cows. He went to the queen, and made his complaint to her, and she gave him another hundred. He went to the king's son, Murdoch Mac Brian, and he got another hundred from him. He got food and drink at the king's; and when he was going away he said, 'Now I am very much obliged to you. This will set me very well on my feet. After all that I have got there is another thing that I want.'

'What is it?' said the king.

'If I had a gun, yon greyhound kennel, and an ambler to ride home on, I would be satisfied,' said O'Kroinikeard.

'Ha!' said the king, 'it is your mightiness and pride that has caused the loss of your means; but if you become a good man you shall get these along with the rest.'

O'Kroinikeard bade the king goodbye, and set off with his gun, his dogs, and his ambler. As he was riding on the road home a hare met him; and he put a shot in the gun to kill it. When he put the gun to his eye he saw the hare in the form of a woman, and when he let down the gun she was a hare as before. He then went and set the dogs at her; and the dogs chased her at full speed. When she saw that the dogs were likely to overtake her she leaped up behind O'Kroinikeard, and became as beautiful a woman as he ever saw. She said to him, 'Call your dogs off me.'

'I will do so if you promise to marry me,' said O'Kroinikeard.

'If you keep three vows that I shall lay upon you I will marry you,' said she.

'What vows are they?' said he.

'The first is that you do not go to ask your worldly king to a feast or a dinner without first letting me know,' said she.

'Hoch!' said O'Kroinikeard, 'do you think that I cannot keep that vow? I would never go to invite my worldly king without informing you that I was going to do so. It is easy to keep that vow.'

'You are likely to keep it!' said she.

'The second vow is,' said she, 'that you do not cast up to me in any company or meeting in which we shall be together, that you found me in the form of a hare.'

'Hoo!' said O'Kroinikeard, 'you would not need to lay that vow upon me. I would keep it, at any rate.'

'You are likely to keep it!' said she.

'The third vow is,' said she, 'that you do not leave me in the company of only one man while you go out.' It was agreed between them that she should marry him.

They arrived at O'Kroinikeard's house. In those times the houses were very small. He and the woman married after going home. When he awoke on the following morning, and looked about him, he never saw so beautiful a room. He said to his wife, 'Where am I?'

'I am sure that you are surprised,' said she.

'I am indeed,' said he.

'You are in your own room,' said she.

'In my own room!' said he. 'I never had such a room.'

'I know well that you never had,' said she; 'but you have it now. So long as you keep me you shall keep the room.'

He then rose, and put on his clothes, and went out. He took a look at the house when he went out; and it was a palace, the like of which he had never seen, and the king himself did not possess. He then took a walk round the farm; and he never saw so many cattle, sheep, and horses as were on it. He returned to the house, and said to his wife that the farm was being ruined by other people's cattle and sheep. 'It is not,' said she; 'your own cattle and sheep are on it.'

'I never had so many cattle and sheep,' said he.

'I know that,' said she; 'but so long as you keep me you shall keep them. There is no goodwife whose tocher does not follow her.'

He was now in good circumstances, indeed wealthy. He had gold and silver, as well as cattle and sheep. He went about with his gun and dogs hunting every day, and was a great man. It occurred to him one day that he would go to invite the King of Eirin to dinner, but he did not tell his wife that he was going. His first vow was now broken. He sped away to the King of Eirin, and invited him and his great court to dinner. The King of Eirin said to him, 'Do you intend to take away the cattle that I promised you?'

'Oo! no, King of Eirin,' said O'Kroinikeard; 'I could give you as many today.'

'Ah!' said the king, 'how well you have got on since I saw you last!'

'I have indeed,' said O'Kroinikeard; 'I have fallen in with a rich wife who has plenty of gold and silver, and of cattle and sheep.'

'I am glad of that,' said the King of Eirin.

O'Kroinikeard said, 'I shall feel much obliged if you will go with me to dinner, yourself and your great court.'

'We will do so willingly,' said the king.

They went with him on that same day. It did not occur to O'Kroinikeard how a dinner could be prepared for the king without his wife knowing that he was coming. When they were going on, and had reached the place where O'Kroinikeard had met the hare, he remembered that his vow was broken, and he said to the king, 'Excuse me; I am going on before to the house to tell that you are coming.'

The king said, 'We will send off one of the lads.'

'You will not,' said O'Kroinikeard; 'no lad will serve the purpose so well as myself.'

He set off to the house; and when he arrived his wife was diligently preparing dinner. He told her what he had done, and asked her pardon. 'I pardon you this time,' said she; 'I know what you have done as well as you do yourself. The first of your vows is broken.'

The king and his great court came to O'Kroinikeard's house; and the wife had everything ready for them as befitted a king and great people: every kind of drink and food. They spent two or three days and nights at dinner, eating and drinking. They were praising the dinner highly, and O'Kroinikeard himself was praising it; but his wife was not. O'Kroinikeard was angry that she was not praising it, and he went where she was, and struck her in the mouth with his fist, and knocked out two of her teeth. 'Why are you not praising the dinner like others, you contemptible hare?' said he.

'I am not,' said she; 'I have seen my father's big dogs having a better dinner than you are giving tonight to the King of Eirin and his court.'

O'Kroinikeard got into such a rage that he went outside of the door. He was not long standing there when a man came riding on a black horse, who in passing caught O'Kroinikeard by the collar of his coat, and took him up behind him; and they set off. The rider did not say a word to O'Kroinikeard. The horse was going so swiftly that O'Kroinikeard thought the wind would drive his head off. They arrived at a big, big palace, and came off the black horse. A stableman came out, and caught the horse, and took it in. It was with wine that he was cleaning the horse's feet. The rider of the black horse said to O'Kroinikeard, 'Taste the wine to see if it is better than the wine that you are giving to Brian Borr and his court tonight.'

O'Kroinikeard tasted the wine, and said, 'This is better wine.'

The rider of the black horse said, 'How unjust was the fist a little ago! The wind that you emitted from your fist carried the two teeth to me.'

He then took him into that big, handsome, and noble house, and into a room that was full of gentlemen eating and drinking, and he seated him at the head of the table, and gave him wine to drink, and said to him, 'Taste that wine to see if it is better than the wine you are giving to the King of Eirin and his court tonight.'

'This is better wine,' said O'Kroinikeard.

'How unjust was the fist a little ago!' said the rider of the black horse.

O'Kroinikeard had dinner with them there. A musical instrument was sent round the table from man to man to see who would play on it best.

'Try you it, O'Kroinikeard, to see how you will play on it,' said the rider of the black horse.

O'Kroinikeard said, 'I have never played on such an instrument.' O'Kroinikeard played on it, and none of them could play on it better than he.

The rider of the black horse said, 'How unjust was the fist a little ago!'

When all was over the rider of the black horse said, 'Are you willing to return home now?'

'Yes,' said O'Kroinikeard, 'very willing.'

They then rose, and went to the stable; and the black horse was taken out; and they leaped on its back, and went away. The rider of the black horse said to O'Kroinikeard, after they had set off, 'Do you know who I am?'

'I do not,' said O'Kroinikeard.

'I am a brother-in-law of yours,' said the rider of the black horse; 'and though my sister is married to you there is not a king or knight in Eirin who is a match for her. Two of your vows are now broken; and if you break the other vow you shall lose your wife and all that you possess.'

They arrived at O'Kroinikeard's house; and O'Kroinikeard said, 'I am ashamed to go in, as they do not know where I have been since night came.'

'Hoo!' said the rider, 'they have not missed you at all. There is so much conviviality among them, that they have not suspected that you have been anywhere. Here are the two teeth that you have knocked out of the front of your wife's mouth. Put them in their place, and they shall be as strong as ever.'

'Come in with me,' said O'Kroinikeard to the rider of the black horse.

'I will not; I disdain to go in,' said the rider of the black horse.

The rider of the black horse bade O'Kroinikeard goodbye, and went away.

O'Kroinikeard went in; and his wife met him as she was busy waiting on the gentlemen. He asked her pardon, and put the two teeth in the front of her mouth, and they were as strong as ever. She said, 'Two of your vows are now broken.' No one took notice of him when he went in, or said 'Where have you been?' They spent the night in eating and drinking, and the whole of the next day.

In the evening the king said, 'I think that it is time for us to be going;' and all said that it was. O'Kroinikeard said, 'You will not go tonight. I am going to get up a dance. You will go tomorrow.'

'Let them go,' said his wife.

'I will not,' said he.

The dance was set a-going that night. They were playing away at dancing and music till they became warm and hot with perspiration. They were going out one after another to cool themselves at the side of the house. They all went out except O'Kroinikeard and his wife, and a man called Geur-mac-ul-Uai. O'Kroinikeard himself went out, and left his wife and Geur-mac-ul-Uai in the house. Then Geur-mac-ul-Uai rose, and shut the door, and said to her, 'I am surprised that so fine-looking a woman as you should have married a paltry, trifling fellow like O'Kroinikeard.'

'O'Kroinikeard is as good as you,' said she.

'He is not,' said he. 'What a great honour and credit it would be to you to be married to the king's brother-in-law!'

'It would be no great honour to me,' said she.

'You had better leave him, and you and I will get married,' said he.

'I would not take anyone in preference to himself,' said she.

He then rose, and took hold of her, and was going to be too free with her; and she gave a spring through the room, and became a big filly, and gave him a kick with her foot, and broke his thigh in two. She gave another spring, and smashed the door and went away, and was seen no more.

At daybreak next day poor O'Kroinikeard could only see the old house that he had before. Neither cattle nor sheep, nor any of the fine things that he had was to be seen. One awoke in the morning beside a bush, another beside a dyke, and another beside a ditch. The king only had the honour of having O'Kroinikeard's little hut over his head. The king knew that O'Kroinikeard's wife had been offended, and he began to inquire who had offended her. The men were searched for up and down to see if he could find out who the offender was. All of them had been found except Geur-mac-ul-Uai. The king vowed that whoever should be found out to be the offender would be put to death, one of his own family excepted. Geur-mac-ul-Uai was found lying across a big bog with his thigh broken, and unable to leave the spot. The king said to him, 'Is it you that has offended O'Kroinikeard's wife?'

'I cannot say that it is not,' said he.

The king told him how he had vowed to put anyone to death whom he should find out to be the offender, his own family excepted. 'What I will do to you,' said the king, 'is to send you to an island. A house shall be built for you there, and as much food shall be given you as will keep you for a month; and when that is spent you shall have to find food as you best can, or die.'

Geur-mac-ul-Uai was then borne away, and sent to an island,

and he was supplied with as much food as would keep him for a month, and with two crutches on which he would be going out and in as he might desire. At last the food was spent, and he was destitute. He was in the habit of going down to the shore, and gathering shellfish, and eating it.

As he was one day on the shore, he saw a big, big man landing on the island, and he could see the earth and the sky between his legs. He set off with the crutches to try if he could get into the hut before the big man would come upon him. Despite his efforts the big man was between him and the door, and said to him, 'Unless you deceive me in my good perception, you are Geur-mac-ul-Uai.'

Geur-mac-ul-Uai said, 'I have never deceived a man or good perception; I am the very man.'

The big man said to him, 'Stretch your leg, Kian, that I may apply to it leaves of herbs and healing. Pressure and business are upon me; and I am under the necessity of going to the big church of Rome tomorrow to listen to joy.'

Geur-mac-ul-Uai said, 'I will not stretch my leg that leaves of herbs and healing may be applied to it till you tell me why you have not a church of your own in Lochlann, so as not to be going to the church of Rome tomorrow to listen to joy. Unless you deceive me in my good perception, you are Machkan-an-ahar [son of the father], the son of the King of Lochlann.'

The big man said, 'I have never deceived any man or good perception; I am the very man. I am now going to tell you why we have not a church in Lochlann. Seven masons came to build a church, and they and my father were bargaining about the building of it. The agreement that the masons wanted was that my mother and sister would go to see the interior of the church when it would be finished. My father was glad to get the church built so cheaply. They agreed accordingly; and the masons went in the morning to the place where the church was to be built. My father pointed out the spot for the foundation. They began to build in the morning, and the church was finished before the evening. When it was finished they requested my mother and sister to go to see its interior. They had no sooner entered than the doors were shut; and the church went away into the skies in the form of a tuft of mist. Stretch your leg, Kian, that I may apply to it leaves of herbs and healing. Pressure and business are upon me; and I am under the necessity of going to the big church of Rome tomorrow to listen to joy.'

Geur-mac-ul-Uai said, 'I will not stretch my leg that leaves of herbs and healing may be applied to it till you tell me if you heard what befell your mother and sister.'

'Ah!' said the big man, 'the mischief is upon you; that tale is long to tell; but I will tell you a short tale about the matter. On the day on which they were working at the church I was away in the hill hunting game; and when I came home in the evening my brother told me what had happened, namely, that my mother and sister had gone away in the form of a tuft of mist. I became so cross and angry that I resolved to destroy the world till I should find out where my mother and sister were. My brother said to me that I was a fool to think of such a thing. "I'll tell you," said he, "what you'll do. You will first go to try to find out where they are. When you find out where they are you will demand them peaceably, and if you do not get them peaceably you will fight for them."

'I took my brother's advice, and prepared a ship to set off with. I set off alone and embraced the ocean. I was overtaken by a great mist, and I came upon an island, and there was a large number of ships at anchor near it; and I went in amongst them, and went ashore. I saw there a big, big woman reaping rushes; and when she would raise her head she would throw her right breast over her shoulder, and when she would bend it would fall down between her legs. I came once behind her, and caught the nipple of the breast with my mouth, and said to her, "You are yourself witness, woman, that I am the foster-son of your right breast." "I perceive that, great hero," said the old woman; "but my advice to you is to leave this island as fast as you can." "Why?" said I. "There is a big giant in the cave up there," said she, "and every one of the ships that you see he has taken in from the ocean with his breath, and he has killed and eaten the men. He is asleep at present, and when he wakens he will have you in a similar manner. A large iron door and an oak door are on the cave. When the giant draws in his breath the doors open, and when he emits his breath the doors shut; and they are shut as fast as though seven small bars, and seven large bars, and seven locks were on them. So fast are they that seven crowbars could not force them open." I said to the old woman, "Is there any way of destroying him?" "I'll tell you," said she, "how it can be done. He has a weapon above the door that is called the short spear, and if you succeed in taking off his head with the first blow it will be well; but if you do not, the case will be worse than it was at first."

'I set off, and reached the cave, the two doors of which opened. The giant's breath drew me into the cave; and stools, chairs, and pots were by its action dashing against each other, and like to break my legs. The door shut when I went in, and was shut as fast as though seven small bars, and seven large bars, and seven locks were on it; and seven crowbars could not force it open; and I was a prisoner in the cave. The giant drew in his breath again, and the doors opened. I gave a look upwards, and saw the short spear, and laid hold of it. I drew the short spear, and I warrant you that I dealt him such a blow with it as did not require to be repeated; I swept the head off him. I took the head down to the old woman, who was reaping the rushes, and said to her, "There is the giant's head for you." The old woman said, "Brave man! I knew that you were a hero. This island had need of your coming to it today. Unless you deceive me in my perception, you are Machkan-an-ahar, son of the King of Lochlann." "I have never deceived a man or good perception. I am the very man," said I. "I am a soothsayer," said she, "and know the object of your journey. You are going in quest of your mother and sister." "Well," said I, "I am so far on the way if I only knew where to go for them." "I'll tell you where they are," said she; "they are in the kingdom of the Red Shield, and the King of the Red Shield is resolved to marry your mother, and his son is resolved to marry your sister. I'll tell you how the town is situated. A canal of such a breadth surrounds it. On the canal there is a drawbridge, which is guarded during the day by one of the large serpents, so that no one can get in without being killed by it. When night comes the bridge is raised, and the serpent sleeps. A very high and big wall surrounds the king's palace." Stretch your leg, Kian, that I may apply to it leaves of herbs and healing. Pressure and business are upon me; and I am under the necessity of going to listen to the joy of Rome to-morrow.'

'Whether it be leg of Kian, or will be leg of anyone after him,'* said Geur-mac-ul-Uai, 'I will not stretch my leg that leaves of herbs and healing may be applied to it till you tell me if you went farther in search of your mother and sister, or if you returned home, or what befell you.'

'Ah!' said the big man, 'the mischief is upon you; that tale is long to tell; but I will tell you another tale. I set off, and reached the big town of the Red Shield; and it was surrounded by a canal, as the old woman told me; and there was a drawbridge on the canal. It was night when I arrived, and the bridge was raised, and the serpent was asleep. I measured two feet before me and a foot behind me of the ground on which I was standing, and I sprang on the end of my spear and on my tiptoes, and reached the place where the serpent was asleep; and I drew the short spear, and I warrant you that I dealt the serpent such a blow on the back of the head as did not require to be repeated. I took up the head and hung it on one of the posts of the bridge. I then went to the wall that surrounded the king's palace. This wall was so high that it was not easy for me to spring over it; and I set to work with the short spear, and dug a hole through it, and got in. I went to the door of the palace and knocked; and the door-keeper called out, "Who is there?" "It is I," said I. My mother and sister recognized my speech; and my mother called, "Oh! it is my son; let him in." I then got in, and they rose to meet me with great joy. I was supplied with food, drink, and a good bed. In the morning breakfast was set before us; and after it I said to my mother and sister that they had better make ready, and go with me. The King of the Red Shield said, "It shall not be so, but thus. I am resolved to marry your mother, and my son is resolved to marry your sister." "That is not to be the way of it," said I; "but if you wish to marry my mother, and if your son

* There is a play upon words here that cannot be represented in English.

wishes to marry my sister, let both of you accompany me to my home, and you shall get them there." The King of the Red Shield said, "So be it."

'We then set off, and came to where my ship was, went on board of it, and sailed for home. When we were passing a place where a great battle was going on, I asked the King of the Red Shield what battle it was, and the cause of it. "Don't you know at all?" said the King of the Red Shield. "I do not," said I. The King of the Red Shield said, "That is the battle for the daughter of the King of the Great Universe, the most beautiful woman in the world; and whoever wins her by his heroism shall get her in marriage. Do you see yonder castle?" "I do," said I. "She is on the top of that castle, and sees from it the hero that wins her," said the King of the Red Shield. I requested to be put on shore, that I might win her by my swiftness and strength. They put me on shore; and I got a sight of her on the top of the castle. Having measured two feet behind me and a foot before me, I sprang on the end of my spear and on my tiptoes, and reached the top of the castle; and I caught the daughter of the King of the Universe in my arms and flung her over the castle. I was with her and intercepted her before she reached the ground, and I took her away on my shoulder, and set off to the shore as fast as I could, and delivered her to the King of the Red Shield to be put on board the ship. All that were in the battle followed me in order to kill me. I turned back to meet them, and attacked them with the short spear, and did not leave a head on a neck of any of them. I then returned, and called to the King of the Red Shield to come in to the shore for me. Pretending not to hear me, he set the sails in order to return home with the daughter of the King of the Great Universe, and marry her. I measured two feet behind me and a foot before me, and sprang on the end of my spear and on my tiptoes, and got on board the ship. I then said to the King of the Red Shield, "What were you going to do? Why did you not come in for me?" "Oh!" said the king, "I was only making the ship ready and setting the sails to her before going on shore for you. Do you know what I am thinking of?" "I do not," said I. "It is," said the king, "that I will return home with the daughter of the King of the Great

Universe, and that you shall go home with your mother and sister." "That is not to be the way of it," said I. "Her whom I have won by my prowess neither you nor any other shall get."

'The king had a red shield, and if he should get it on, no weapon could make an impression on him. He began to put on the red shield, and I struck him with the short spear in the middle of his body, and cut him in two, and threw him overboard. I then struck the son, and swept his head off, and threw him overboard. Stretch your leg now, Kian, that I may apply to it leaves of herbs and healing. Pressure and business are upon me; and I am under the necessity of going to the big church of Rome tomorrow to listen to joy.'

'Whether it is leg of Kian, or will be leg of anyone after him, and if I am Geur-mac-ul-Uai, I will not stretch my leg that leaves of herbs and healing may be applied to it till you tell me why you have not a church of your own in Lochlann, so as not to be going to the big church of Rome tomorrow to listen to joy.'

'Ah! the mischief is upon you,' said the big man; 'I will tell you another short tale. I came home with my mother and sister, and the daughter of the King of the Universe, and I married the daughter of the King of the Universe. The first son I had I named Machkan-na-skaya-jayrika [son of the red shield]. Not long after this a hostile force came from the King of the Red Shield to enforce compensation for the King of the Red Shield, and a hostile force came from the King of the Universe to enforce compensation for the daughter of the King of the Universe. I took the daughter of the King of the Universe with me on the one shoulder and Machkan-na-skaya-jayrika on the other, and I went on board the ship and set the sails to her, and I placed the ensign of the King of the Great Universe on the one mast, and that of the King of the Red Shield on the other, and I blew a trumpet, and passed through the midst of them, and I said to them that this was the man, and that if they were going to enforce their claims, this was the time. All the ships that were there chased me; and we set out on the expanse of ocean. My ship possessed the quality of being equalled in speed by very few ships. One day a thick dark mist came on, and they lost sight of me. It happened that I came to an island called An Aluin Leuch [the Wet Mantle]. I built a hut there; and another son was born to me, and I called him Machkan-na-faluina-fleuicha [son of the Wet Mantle].

'I was a long time in that island; but there was enough of fruit, fish, and birds in it. My two sons had grown to be good lumps of boys. As I was one day going about killing birds, I saw a big, big man coming towards the island, and I ran to try if I could get into the house before he would arrive. He met me, and caught me, and put me into a bog up to the armpits, and he went into the house, and took out on his shoulder the daughter of the King of the Universe, and passed close to me in order to irritate me the more. The saddest look that I ever gave or ever shall give was that that I gave when I saw the daughter of the King of the Universe on the shoulder of another, and could not take her from him. The boys came out where I was; and I bade them bring me the short spear from the house. They dragged the short spear after them, and brought it to me; and I cut the ground around me with it till I got out.

'I was a long time in the Wet Mantle, even till my two sons grew to be big lads. They asked me one day if I had any word of going to seek their mother. I told them that I was waiting till they would become stronger, and that they should then go with me. They said that they were ready to go with me at any time. I said to them that we had better get the ship ready, and go. They said, "Let each of us have a ship to himself;" and we arranged accordingly. We three then gave the back to each other; and each went his own way.

'As I happened to be one day passing close to land I saw a great battle going on. Being under vows never to pass a battle without helping the weaker side, I went on shore, and set to work with the weaker side, and I knocked the head off every one with the short spear. Being tired, I lay myself down among the bodies, and fell asleep. Stretch your leg, Kian, that I may apply to it leaves of herbs and healing. Pressure and business are upon me; and I am under the necessity of going to the big church of Rome tomorrow to listen to joy.'

Geur-mac-ul-Uai said, 'I will not stretch my leg that leaves of herbs and healing may be applied to it till you tell me if you found the daughter of the King of the Universe, or if you went home, or what happened to you.'

'The mischief is upon you,' said the big man; 'that tale is long to tell; but I will tell another short tale. When I awoke out of sleep I saw a ship making for the place where I was lying, and a big giant with only one eye dragging it after him; and the ocean reached no higher than his knees. He had a big fishing-rod with a big strong line hanging from it on which was a very big hook. He was throwing the line ashore, and fixing the hook in a body, and lifting it on board, and he continued this work till the ship was loaded with bodies. He fixed the hook once in my clothes; but I was so heavy that the rod could not carry me on board. He had to go on shore himself, and carry me on board in his arms. I was then in a worse plight than I ever was in.

'The giant set off with the ship, which he dragged after him, and reached a big, precipitous rock, in the face of which he had a large cave; and a woman as beautiful as I ever saw came out, and stood in the door of the cave. He was handing the bodies to her, and she was taking hold of them, and putting them into the cave. As she took hold of each body she said, "Are you alive?" At last the giant took hold of me, and handed me in to her, and said, "Keep him apart; he is a large body, and I will have him to breakfast the first day that I go from home." My best time was not when I heard the giant's sentence upon me.

'When he had eaten enough of the bodies, his dinner and supper, he lay down to sleep. When he began to snore the woman came to speak to me; and she told me that she was a king's daughter, that the giant had stolen her, and that she had no way of getting away from him. "I am now," she said, "seven years except two days with him, and there is a drawn sword between us at night. He dared not come nearer me than that till the seven years would expire." I said to her, "Is there no way of killing him?" "It is not easy to kill him, but we will devise an expedient for killing him," said she. "Look at that pointed bar that he uses for roasting the bodies. At dead of night gather the embers of the fire together, and put the bar in the fire till it be red. Go, then, and thrust it into his eye with all your strength, and take care that he does not get hold of you, for if he does he will mince you as small as midges."

'I then went and gathered the embers together, and put the bar in the fire, and made it red, and thrust it into his eye; and from the cry that he gave I thought that the rock had split. The giant sprang to his feet, and chased me through the cave, in order to catch me; and I picked up a stone that lay on the floor of the cave, and pitched it into the sea; and it made a plumping noise. The bar was sticking in his eye all the time. Thinking it was I that had sprung into the sea, he rushed to the mouth of the cave; and the bar struck against the doorpost of the cave, and knocked off his brain-cap. The giant fell down cold and dead; and I threw him over the mouth of the cave into the sea.

'On the morrow I set out in quest of the daughter of the King of the Universe. I took the woman with me from the cave in one of the giant's boats, and left her in a place whence she might go wherever she should please. I said to her that if any trouble should come upon her, and if she should have a son she was to call him Machkan-an-uaigneas [son in secret]. I gave her a gold ring with my name on it, and I said to her that if it should be a boy that she would have, she was to give him the ring when he would be going to set off in quest of the daughter of the King of the Universe for Machkan-an-ahar, son of the King of Lochlann.

'I then set off to the place where I fought a battle, and found the short spear where I left it; and I was very pleased that I found it, and that the ship was safe. I sailed a day's distance from that place, and entered a pretty bay that was there, hauled my ship up above the shore, and erected a hut there, in which I slept at night. When I rose next day I saw a ship making straight for the place where I was. When it struck the ground, a big, strong champion came out of it, and hauled it up; and if it did not surpass my ship it was not a whit inferior to it; and I said to him, "What impertinent fellow are you that has dared to haul up your ship alongside of my ship?" "I am Machkan-na-skaya-jayrika," said the champion, "going to seek the daughter of the King of the Universe for Machkan-an-ahar, son of the King of Lochlann." I saluted and welcomed him, and said to him, "I am your father; it is well that you have come." We passed the night cheerily in the hut.

'When I rose on the following day I saw another ship making straight for the place where I was; and a big, strong hero came out of it, and hauled it up alongside of our ships; and if it did not surpass them it was not a whit inferior to them. "What impertinent fellow are you that has dared to haul up your ship alongside of our ships?" said I. "I am," said he, "Machkan-na-faluina-fleuicha, going to seek the daughter of the King of the Universe for Machkan-an-ahar, son of the King of Lochlann." "I am your father, and this is your brother; it is well that you have come," said I. We passed the night together in the hut, my two sons and I.

'When I rose next day I saw another ship coming, and making straight for the place where I was. A big, strong champion sprang out of it, and hauled it up alongside of our ships; and if it was not higher than they, it was not lower. I went down where he was, and said to him, "What impertinent fellow are you that has dared to haul up your ship alongside of our ships?" "I am Machkan-an-uaigneas," said he, "going to seek the daughter of the King of the Universe for Machkan-an-ahar, son of the King of Lochlann." "Have you any token in proof of that?" said I. "I have," said he; "here is a ring that my mother gave me at my father's request." I took hold of the ring, and saw my name on it: and the matter was beyond doubt. I said to him, "I am your father, and here are two half-brothers of yours. We are now stronger for going in quest of the daughter of the King of the Universe. Four plies are stronger than three plies." We spent that night cheerily and comfortably together in the hut.

'Who should come in where we were but Kruitean Ceòlar and another, the rider of the white horse. Every time that Kruitean Ceòlar would blow up the pipe he would set us asleep; and the rider of the white horse would rise now and then, and take the pipe out of his mouth. When the rider of the white horse saw that we were not finding fault with Kruitean Ceòlar, he allowed him to play on. We then fell asleep, and the rider stole the short spear. He came in the morning, and asked how we fared last night. We said that we fared but badly and sadly, that the short spear was stolen from us. The rider of the white horse said, "I'll tell you where it is: it is in a cave up there where two giants dwell."

'My three sons and I went to the cave, and called to the giants to send out the spear. When they saw the aspect of the heroes they got frightened, and threw the short spear out to us. We took it away, and returned to the hut where our ships were hauled up. The rider of the white horse came again where we were, and said to me, "Unless you deceive me in my perception, you are Machkan-an-ahar, son of the King of Lochlann. I am a soothsayer; and you are going in quest of the daughter of the King of the Universe. I will tell you where she is: she is with the son of the Blackbird, Carn Camaley."

'Machkan-na-skaya-jayrika then went and called for combat with a hundred fully trained heroes, or the sending out to him of the daughter of the King of the Universe. The hundred went out; and he and they began on each other, and he killed every one of them. Machkan-na-faluina-fleuicha called for combat with another hundred, or the sending out of the daughter of the King of the Universe. He killed that hundred with the short spear. Machkan-an-uaigneas called for combat with another hundred, or the daughter of the King of the Universe. He killed every one of these with the short spear. I then went out to the field, and sounded a challenge on the shield, and made the town tremble. Carn Camaley had not a man to send out: he had to come out himself; and he and I began on each other, and I drew the short spear, and swept his head off. I then went into the castle, and took out the daughter of the King of the Universe. It was thus that it fared with me. Stretch your leg, Kian, that I may apply to it leaves of herbs and healing. Pressure and business are upon me; and I am under the necessity of going to the church of Rome tomorrow to listen to joy.'

Geur-mac-ul-Uai stretched his leg; and the big man applied to it leaves of herbs and healing; and it was healed. The big man took him ashore from the island, and allowed him to go home to the king.

THE KING AND THE LABOURER

Source: Lord Archibald Campbell, *Records of Argyll*
Narrator: Archibald MacTavish, Oban; collected by 'D.'
Type: AT875 'The Clever Peasant Girl'

On a certain day, when the labourer was making drains, the king came where he was and said, 'You are at work?'

'I am,' said the labourer.

'Does the work pay you?'

'Sometimes it does and sometimes it does not,' was the reply; 'it depends on the ground.'

'Are you married?' said the king.

'I was married, but I am now a widower.'

'Have you a family?'

'I have one daughter.'

'How old is she?'

'Twelve years old.'

'I am going to put a question to you,' said the king.

'There is no use in putting questions to me, for I was never good at solving questions,' said the labourer. 'What question are you going to put to me?'

'The question that I am going to put to you is, how long will it take me to go round the world?'

'No man can solve that question,' said the labourer.

'Unless you solve it by twelve o'clock tomorrow you will be hanged.'

'It cannot be helped,' said the labourer.

The king then said, 'I am now going home, but will be back at twelve o'clock tomorrow; see to it that you be here to meet me.'

After saying this he went away and bid goodbye to the labourer, who went home in the evening sad and dejected. His daughter said to him, 'Is anything troubling you, father, for you are not so cheerful as usual?'

'The king came to me today and put a question to me,' said her father.

'What question did he put to you?'

'He put a question to me that I think no one can solve.'

'You might tell it to me,' said she.

'What is the use of telling it to you?'

'You do not know.'

'The question,' said the father, 'that he put to me is, what time will it take me to go round the world?'

'That question need not cause you uneasiness,' said the daughter. 'You had better take your supper, and I will solve the question for you when you are going to your work tomorrow.'

In the morning after breakfast he said to her, 'What am I to say to the king today?'

'You will say to him,' she answered, 'that he will go round the world in twenty-four hours, if he will be so clever as to sit astride on the sun or the moon.'

When he heard this he went off to his work in high spirits. The king came to him at twelve o'clock and said, 'You are at work?'

'I am, with your leave, king,' said the labourer.

'Have you solved the question?'

'I have made the attempt,' was the reply.

The king then said to him, 'How long will it take me to go round the world?'

'If you will do as I tell you,' said the labourer, 'you will go round the world in twenty-four hours.'

'Do you really think it possible for me to go round the world in twenty-four hours?' said the king.

'If you will sit astride on the sun or on the moon,' said the labourer, 'you will go round the world in that space of time.'

The king paused, looked up and down, and reflected. He then said to the labourer, 'I am afraid that neither you nor I will be able to sit astride on the sun or moon. But,' said the king further, 'you did not solve the question yourself.'

The labourer said, 'It does not matter who solved it, since you have got your answer.'

The king said, 'You have acquitted yourself well, for you have solved the question; but you must tell me who solved it for you, or you will be hanged tomorrow at twelve o'clock.'

The labourer got frightened when he heard this, and said, 'My daughter solved the question.'

The king said, 'Since you have so satisfactorily solved that question, I will put another to you today.'

'There is no use in putting more questions to me, for, although I have solved the last one, perhaps I cannot solve another. What question are you going to put to me today?'

'It is this,' said the king: 'what is the distance between the earth and the sky?'

'That is a more difficult question than the last; no one can solve it.'

The king said, 'Unless you solve it, you will be hanged tomorrow at twelve o'clock.' The king then bade the labourer goodbye, and said, 'I will be here tomorrow at twelve o'clock.'

When evening came the labourer went home, and, if he was sad before, he was much sadder this time. His daughter asked him how he got on with the king. He said that he got on very well, but that he put to him a much more difficult question than the last one.

'What question did he put to you?' said the daughter.

'I must tell him the distance between the earth and the sky,' said the father.

'Let not that question cause you any anxiety. When you are about to go to your work in the morning I will tell you the answer.'

This gave the old man great courage. When he was ready to go to his work next morning he said to his daughter, 'What shall I say to the king today?'

'Take the hatchet,' said she, 'and make two pins; you will then go to the king's palace, put off your coat, and put the pins in the ground with the hammer. The king will come out and say to you, "What are you going to do here?" and you will say to him, "I am, with your leave, O king, going to measure the distance between the earth and the sky; and since you are king and have plenty of gold and silver, buy for me a line that will reach from the earth to the sky, and I will measure the distance."'

He acted as his daughter directed. He went to the king's palace, put off his coat, and began to put the pins in the ground. The king saw him from a window, went out where he was, and said to him, 'What are you going to do here?'

The labourer said, 'I am, O king, with your leave, going to measure the distance between the earth and the sky, as you have desired, and I perceive that this is the most suitable place for the work; and as you are the king, and have plenty of gold and silver, buy for me a line that will measure it, and I will measure it.'

The king looked up and down, and reflected for a little. He then said, 'I am afraid that neither you nor I have enough of money to buy such a line, and so we shall let the matter pass. You have done well; but who solved the question for you?'

'I solved it myself,' said the labourer.

'You did not,' said the king; 'and you must tell me who solved it, or you will be hanged tomorrow at twelve o'clock.'

The labourer got frightened, and told the king it was his daughter that solved it. The king then said to him, 'How old is she?'

'Twelve years old.'

'She is clever, and has a good head,' said the king. 'You must allow her to come to my house to scour knives and do other light work.'

'What am I to do then?' said the labourer; 'for I have no other to keep my house in order, cook my food, and do my washing?'

'I must get her,' said the king, 'and I will be a good friend to you.'

He then went and brought his daughter to the king, and she began her work in the king's house. She grew to be a tall and elegant young woman. The other servants looked down upon her, and would only call her the poor man's daughter. This vexed her very much. Having met the king one day in front of the palace, she said to him that she was going to leave the house.

'Why?' said the king.

She answered, 'The other servants look down upon me, and call me constantly in the house the poor man's daughter.'

The king said to her, 'Wait you, and I will put a stop to that. I will make a knight of your father, and I'll wager that they will only call you then the knight's daughter.'

He sent for her father and made a knight of him. He sent the daughter to school and gave her education. After leaving school she was for a time waiting at the king's table. The king fell in love with her, and wished to marry her, and spoke to her about it; but she said to him, 'That is not likely, king, for you will get a wife out of a royal family, and perhaps I can get a husband to suit myself.'

'That is not the way it is to be,' said the king; 'you must marry me.'

'If I must, I will,' she replied.

'I have this to say to you,' said the king: 'if we marry, you must not give judgment in any matter in opposition to me.'

'That is well said; it would not be proper for me to give judgment in any matter in opposition to you.'

'Remember,' said the king, 'that the day you do so you will cease to be queen.'

She said, 'Remember, that if I be sent away, I must get, the day I leave, the three armfuls that I shall select, and you will give me writing for it.'

'You will get that,' said the king.

The matter was settled between them. They were married, and, I am sure, had a grand wedding. They had a young prince before the end of the year. Two men lived near the palace: one of them had a mare and foal, and the other had a white horse. The foal had the habit of following the white horse through the farm. The man who had the white horse alleged that the foal was his own. In consequence of this the men quarrelled, and went to the king for justice. The man who had the mare told the king that the other man was going to deprive him of the foal. The king said, 'Both of you claim the foal. This is how the matter is to be settled: put the horses into a park, and make a gap in the wall surrounding the park; and whichever of the horses the foal will follow, will have the foal.'

What the king commanded was done. After the horses were put into the park, the foal followed the white horse coming out at the gap – whereupon the man who had the mare dared not claim the foal any more. The man who had the mare recollected that the queen was related to him, and he resolved to go to her and lay his case before her. He went to the palace, and sent her word that he wished to see her. He saw her, and told her how he was treated.

'I see,' said the queen, 'that you have been wronged; but I dare not give judgment in any matter in opposition to the king – for if I do so, I shall cease to be queen. I will tell you what to do. Get a small basketful of peas; boil the peas, and put them back into the basket. Go then with the basketful of peas, and sow them when you see the king coming that way. The king will say to you, "What are you sowing there?" You will say to him, "I am sowing boiled peas;" and the king will say to you, "What a fool you are! Do you think that they will grow?" You will then say to him, "I think that they are as likely to grow as that an old white horse should give birth to a foal." The king will then look at you.'

He did as the queen directed. When he was sowing the peas, the king came the way and said to the man, 'What are you sowing here today?'

The man said, 'I am sowing boiled peas.'

The king said to him, 'What a fool you are! Do you think that they will grow?'

The man said to the king, 'I think they will.'

The king said to him, 'What proof will you give me that they will?'

'I think,' said the man, 'that they are as likely to grow as that an old white horse should give birth to a foal.'

'I do not say,' said the king, 'that you are not correct; but that idea did not originate in your own head. I understand who suggested it to you.' The king went away in a rage to the queen, caught her by the shoulder, and said to her, 'You are to be turned out today.'

'Why?' said she.

'Because you gave judgment contrary to mine in the case of the man who had the foal.'

'It is very likely, king, that I may have done so,' said the queen, 'because you did not give a righteous judgment.'

He then took hold of her, and said to her, 'You are now to be turned out.'

'Very well,' answered she; 'but remember that I am to get, before I go, the three armfuls you promised me.'

'You will get that,' said the king in a great rage.

'Now,' said she, 'put on your royal robe, and I will bid you goodbye.'

The king rose, got his robe, and put it on him. She then said to him, 'Sit now in your royal chair.' He did so. She then lifted both him and the chair, and put them outside the door. 'I have now,' said she, 'got my first armful outside the door.' She returned to the palace, and took the young prince, and put him in the king's lap. 'I have now two armfuls outside, and I want but another.' She entered the palace again, and took the charters of the kingdom, and put them in the young prince's lap. 'I have now, king, my three armfuls, and let what will befall what remains.'

The king then said to her, 'Ah, dearest of women, you and I will never part till death shall separate us!' He took her back to the palace. A servant was sent by the king to the man who had the foal, demanding of him to return it to its owner.

LASAIR GHEUG, THE KING OF IRELAND'S DAUGHTER

Source: Alan Bruford, 'A Scottish Gaelic Version of "Snow White"',
Scottish Studies, vol. 9, 1969
Narrator: Mrs Macmillan, Bridge Cottage, Strathtay, Atholl; taken down on 3 June
1891 by Lady Evelyn Stewart-Murray. Translated from the Gaelic by Alan Bruford
Type: AT709 'Snow White' mixed with AT706 'The Maiden Without Hands'

Note: the malicious old woman, the *eachrais ùrlair*, is a stock villain of
Gaelic folktale, the figure sometimes called the Henwife

There was a king once, and he married a queen, and she had a daughter. The mother died then, and he married another queen. The queen was good to her stepdaughter. But one day the *eachrais ùrlair* came in, and she said to the queen that she was a fool to be so good to her stepdaughter 'when you know that the day the king dies, your share of the inheritance will be a small one to your stepdaughter's share.'

'What can be done about it?' said the queen. 'If my stepdaughter does well, I will get a share.'

'If you give me what I ask,' said the *eachrais ùrlair*, 'I will do something about it.'

'What would you want, old woman?' said the queen.

'I have a little saucepan, I only put it on occasionally. I want meal enough to thicken it, and butter enough to thin it, and the full of my ear of wool.'

'How much meal will thicken it?'

'The increase of seven granaries of oats in seven years.'

'How much butter will thin it?' said the queen.

'The increase of seven byres of cattle in seven years.'

'And how much wool will your ear hold?'

'The increase of seven folds of sheep in seven years.'

'You have asked much, old woman,' said the queen, 'but though it is much, you shall have it.'

'We will kill the king's greyhound bitch and leave it on the landing of the stairs, so that the king thinks that it is Lasair Gheug [Flame of Branches] who has done it. We will make Lasair Gheug swear three baptismal oaths, that she will not be on foot, she will not be on horseback, and she will not be on the green earth the day she tells of it.'

The king came home, and saw the greyhound bitch on the landing. Roared, roared, roared the king: 'Who did the deed?'

'Who do you think, but your own eldest daughter?' said the queen.

'That cannot be,' said the king, and he went to bed, and he ate not a bite, and he drank not a drop: and if day came early, the king rose earlier than that, and went to the hill to hunt.

In came the *eachrais ùrlair*. 'What did the king do to his daughter last night?' she asked.

'He did nothing at all, old woman,' said the queen. 'Go home, and never let us see you again after the rage you put the king in last night.'

'I will be bound that he will kill his daughter tonight,' said the *eachrais ùrlair*. 'We will kill the king's graceful black palfrey, and leave it on the landing. We will make Lasair Gheug swear three baptismal oaths, that she will not be on foot, she will not be on horseback, and she will not be on the green earth the day she tells of it.'

The king came home, and saw the graceful black palfrey on the landing. Roared, roared, roared the king: 'Who did the deed?'

'Who do you think, but your own eldest daughter?' said the queen.

'That cannot be,' said the king. He went to bed, and he ate not a bite, and he drank not a drop: and if day came early, the king rose earlier than that, and went to the hill to hunt.

In came the *eachrais ùrlair*. 'What did the king do to his daughter last night?' she asked.

'He did nothing at all, old woman,' said the queen. 'Go home, and don't come here again, after the rage you put the king in last night.'

'I will be bound,' said the *eachrais ùrlair*, 'that he will kill his daughter tonight. We will kill your own eldest son,' said she, 'and leave him on the landing. We will make Lasair Gheug swear three baptismal oaths, that she will not be on foot, she will not be on horseback, and she will not be on the green earth the day she tells of it.'

The king came home, then, and saw his eldest son on the landing. Roared, roared, roared the king: 'Who did the deed?'

'Who do you think, but your own eldest daughter?' said the queen.

'That cannot be,' said the king. He went to bed, and he ate not a bite, and he drank not a drop: and if day came early, the king rose earlier than that, and went to the hill to hunt.

In came the *eachrais ùrlair*. 'What did the king do to his daughter last night?' she asked.

'He did nothing at all, old woman,' said the queen. 'Go home, and don't come here again, after the rage you put the king in last night.'

'I will be bound,' said the *eachrais ùrlair*, 'that he will kill his daughter tonight. You must pretend that you are sick, sore and sorry.'

Men leapt on horses and horses on men to look for the king. The king came. He asked the queen what in the seven continents of the world he could get to help her, that he would not get.

'There is something to help me,' said she, 'but what will help me you will not give me.'

'If there is something to help you,' said he, 'you shall have it.'

'Give me the heart and liver of Lasair Gheug, the King of Ireland's daughter,' said the queen.

'Well,' said the king, 'it hurts me to give you that, but you shall have that,' said the king. He went to the squinting sandy cook and asked him if he would hide his child for one night.

'I will,' said the cook. They killed a sucking pig, and they took out the heart and liver. They put its blood on Lasair Gheug's clothes. The king went home with the heart and the liver, and gave it to the queen. Then the queen was as well as she had ever been.

The king went again to the squinting sandy cook, and he asked him if he would hide his child for one night again. The cook said he would. Next day the king took with him the best horse in the stable, a peck of gold, a peck of silver, and Lasair Gheug. He came to a great forest, with no edge and no end, and he was going to leave Lasair Gheug there. He cut off the end of one of her fingers.

'Does that hurt you, daughter?' he said.

'It doesn't hurt me, father,' she said, 'because it is you who did it.'

'It hurts me more,' said the king, 'to have lost the greyhound bitch.' With that he cut off another of her fingers.

'Does that hurt you, daughter?'

'It doesn't hurt me, father, because it is you who did it.'

'It hurts me more than that to have lost the graceful black palfrey.' With that he cut off another of her fingers.

'Does that hurt you, daughter?' said the king.

'It doesn't hurt me, father,' said she, 'because it is you who did it.'

'It hurts me more,' said he, 'to have lost my eldest son.' He gave her the peck of gold and the peck of silver, and he left her there. He went home, and he lay down on his bed, blind and deaf to the world.

Lasair Gheug was frightened in the forest that wild beasts would come and eat her. The highest tree she could see in the forest, she climbed that tree. She was not there long when she saw twelve cats coming, and a one-eyed grey cat along with them. They had a cow and a cauldron, and they lit a fire at the foot of the tree she was in. They killed the cow and put it in the cauldron to cook. The steam was rising, and her fingers were getting warm. She began to bleed, and drop after drop fell into the cauldron. The one-eyed grey cat told one of the other cats to go up the tree and see what was there: for king's blood or knight's blood was falling into the cauldron. The cat went up. She gave it a handful of gold and a handful of silver not to tell that she was there. But the blood would not stop. The one-eyed grey cat sent every one of them up, one after another, until all twelve had been up, and they all got a handful of gold and a handful of silver. The one-eyed grey cat climbed up himself, and he found Lasair Gheug and brought her down.

When the supper was ready, the one-eyed grey cat asked her whether she would rather have her supper with him, or with the others. She said she would rather have her supper with him, he was the one she liked the look of best. They had their supper, and then they were going to bed. The one-eyed grey cat asked her which she would rather, to go to bed with him, or to sleep with the others. She said she would rather go with him, he was the one she liked the look of best. They went to bed, and when they got up in the morning, they were in Lochlann. The one-eyed grey cat was really the King of Lochlann's son, and his twelve squires along with him. They had been bewitched by his stepmother, and now the spell was loosed.

They were married then, and Lasair Gheug had three sons. She asked the king as a favour not to have them christened.

There was a well in the King of Ireland's garden, and there was a trout in the well, and the queen used to go every year to wash in the well. She went there this time, and when she had washed, she said to the trout, 'Little trout, little trout,' said she, 'am not I,' said she, 'the most beautiful woman that ever was in Ireland?'

'Indeed and indeed then, you are not,' said the trout, 'while Lasair Gheug, the King of Ireland's daughter, is alive.'

'Is she alive still?' said the queen.

'She is, and will be in spite of you,' said the trout. 'She is in Lochlann, and has three unchristened children.'

'I will set a snare to catch her,' said the queen, 'and a net to destroy you.'

'You have tried to do that once or twice before,' said the trout, 'but you haven't managed it yet,' said he, 'and though I am here now, many is the mighty water I can be on before night comes.'

The queen went home, and she gave the king a piece of her mind for making her believe that he had given her Lasair Gheug's heart and liver, when she was alive and well in Lochlann still. She wanted the king to go with her to see Lasair Gheug, but the king would not budge, and he would not believe that she was there. She sent her twelve maids-in-waiting to Lochlann, and she gave a box to her own maid to give Lasair Gheug, and she asked her to tell her not to open it until she was with her three unchristened children.

Lasair Gheug was sitting at the window, sewing. She saw her father's banner coming. In her delight she did not know whether to run out of the door or fly out of the window. They gave her the box, and she was so delighted with it that she did not wait to be with her three unchristened children. She opened the box when the others had gone home. When she opened the box, there were three grains in it ... one grain of ice stuck in her forehead and another in each of her palms, and she fell dead and cold.

The king came home and found her dead. That would have beaten a wiser man than he. He was so fond of her, he would not let her be buried. He put her in a leaden coffin and kept it locked up in a room. He used to visit her early and late. He used to look twice as well when he went in as when he came out. This had been going on for a while when his companions persuaded him to marry again. He gave every key in the house to the queen, except the key of that room. She wondered what was in the room, when he looked so poorly coming out, compared with the way he was when he went in. She told one of the boys one day, if he was playing near the king, to see if he could manage to steal that key out of his pocket. The lad stole the key and gave it to his stepmother. She went in, and what was there but the king's first wife. She looked her over; she saw the grain of ice in her forehead and she took a pin and picked it out. The woman in the coffin gave a sigh. She saw another one in one of her palms, and took it out. The woman sat up. She found another one in the other palm, and took it out. Then she was as well as she had ever been. She brought her out with her and put her in another room. She sent the boy with the key to meet his father coming home and put it back in his pocket without his knowledge.

The king came home. The first thing he did was to go into that room as usual. There was nothing there. He came out then to ask what had happened to the thing that had been in the room. The queen said she had never had the key of that room.

She asked what had been in the room. He said it was his first wife, and with the love he had for her he would not bury her: he liked to see her, dead though she was.

'What will you give me,' said the queen, 'if I bring you her alive?'

'I don't expect to see her alive,' said he, 'but I would be glad to see her even though she were dead.'

The queen went then and brought her in on her arm, alive and well. He did not know whether to laugh or cry with his delight. The other queen said then that she might as well go home, there was no more need for her there. Lasair Gheug said that she was not to go home: she should stay along with her, and should have food and drink as good as herself, every day as long as she lived.

At the end of this another year had gone by. The Queen of Ireland went to the well to wash there again.

'Little trout, little trout,' said she, 'am not I the most beautiful woman that ever was in Ireland?'

'Indeed and indeed you are not,' said the trout, 'while Lasair Gheug, the king of Ireland's daughter, is alive.'

'Is she alive still?' said she.

'Oh yes, and she will be in spite of you,' said the trout.

'I will set a snare to catch her,' said the queen, 'and a net to destroy you.'

'You have tried to do that once or twice before,' said the trout, 'but you haven't managed it yet,' said he. 'Though I am here now, many is the mighty water I can be on before night comes.'

The queen went home then, and she got the king moving, and they went to visit Lasair Gheug. Lasair Gheug was sitting at the window this time, but she showed no pleasure at all at the sight of her father's banner.

When Sunday came, they went to church. She had sent people to catch a wild boar that was in the wood, and others to get faggots and sticks and stuff to make a big fire. She got the wild boar; she got on to the boar's back, went in at one door of the church and out at the other door. She called her three unchristened children to her side.

'I am not going to tell my story to anyone at all,' said she, 'but to you three unchristened children.

'When I was in my own father's kingdom in Ireland, my stepmother and the *eachrais ùrlair* killed my father's greyhound bitch and left it on the landing. They made me swear three baptismal oaths, that I would not be on foot, I would not be on horseback, and I would not be on the green earth the day I told of it. But I am on the wild boar's back. They expected that my father would kill me, but my father has not killed me yet.'

She went in at one door, and she went out at the other door, and she called her three unchristened children along with her.

'I am not going to tell my story to anyone at all,' said she, 'but to you unchristened children.

'When I was in my own father's kingdom in Ireland, my stepmother and the *eachrais ùrlair* killed my father's graceful black palfrey and left it on the landing. They made me swear three baptismal oaths, that I would not be on foot, I would not be on horseback, and I would not be on the green earth the day I told of it. But I am on the wild boar's back. They expected that my father would kill me, but my father has not killed me yet.'

She went in at one door, and she went out at the other door, and she called her three unchristened children along with her.

'I am not going to tell my story to anyone at all,' said she, 'but to you three unchristened children.

'When I was in my own father's kingdom in Ireland, my stepmother and the *eachrais ùrlair* killed my eldest brother and left him on the landing. They made me swear three baptismal oaths, that I would not be on foot, I would not be on horseback, and I would not be on the green earth the day I told of it. But I am on the wild boar's back. They expected that my father would kill me, but my father has not killed me yet. Now,' said she, 'I have nothing more to tell you.'

The wild boar was set free. When they came out of the church, the Queen of Ireland was caught and burnt in the fire.

When the king was going home, he said to his daughter, Lasair Gheug, that she had done ill by him: he had come from home with a wife, and he was going home now without one. And Lasair Gheug said: 'It wasn't that way: you came here with a monster, but I have a woman friend, and you shall have her, and you will go home with a wife.' And they made a great, merry, mirthful, happy, hospitable, wonderful wedding; it was kept up for a year and a day. I got shoes of paper there on a glass pavement, a bit of butter on an ember, porridge in a creel, a greatcoat of chaff and a short coat of buttermilk. I hadn't gone far when I fell, and the glass pavement broke, the short coat of buttermilk spilt, the butter melted on the ember, a gust of wind came and blew away the greatcoat of chaff. All I had had was gone, and I was as poor as I was to start with. And I left them there.

GO BOLDLY, LADY,
AND DON'T GO BOLDLY, LADY

Source: Alan Bruford, 'Two More Stories from Atholl', *Scottish Studies*, vol. 10,
1966
Narrator: Mrs Campbell; taken down at Foss post office, Atholl, on 4 June 1891,
by Lady Evelyn Stewart-Murray. Translated by Alan Bruford, based on a rough
translation by Sorley Maclean
Type: AT955 'The Robber Bridegroom'

A suitor was coming to woo a lady, and he was very
handsome, he had twelve attendants, and her kin were
very willing that she should marry him, but she herself was not
willing to have him until she had looked around a little. She set
off one day, and she went on until she came to a wood. She
went into the wood, and kept on until she reached a fine house.
And what was there but a parrot in a cage hanging on the side
of the house. The parrot said to her: 'Go boldly, lady, and don't
go boldly, lady.'

She went in, and the first room she came to, there were
riddles full of oatcake and cheese. She took some of it with her
in her pocket. She went to another room, and it was full of
lovely gowns, and she opened a drawer and found rings and
earrings, and she went to another room and found ladies hanging
by their hair. Then she heard a noise coming. She ran away and
went into the back of the dog kennel, and she gave them a little
bread and cheese. Who should arrive now but her suitor and the
twelve men along with him, and who had they with them but
her father's brother's daughter. And the suitor said: 'Young
ladies are the better for having a drop of their blood drawn' –
and he put her cousin's feet in a tub of warm water, and kept on
saying to her: 'Young ladies are the better for having a drop of
their blood drawn.'

At last she said that she saw the house growing black, and one of the twelve men said: 'May God receive her soul,' and she died. They began to take the ring off her, and they could not, and they went and cut off the whole hand, and threw it to the dogs. The lady got hold of it, and she gave the dogs a piece with cheese to quiet them. They went off to hang her cousin by the hair with the other ladies in the room.

The lady managed to escape and ran away home. Nobody knew about this but herself. The suitor came again to woo her as before, himself and his twelve men. She said she would get engaged anyway, but she wanted her father's brother and his two sons to be at the betrothal, and that she should be allowed to sit between her uncle's two sons with her uncle himself opposite her. When she had this arranged, herself between her uncle's two sons and her uncle opposite, she said: 'I am going to tell you a dream. It is nothing but a dream,' said she. 'You mark me well, my uncle's sons.' She told them everything as it had happened, saying every now and then: 'Mark me well, but take it only as a dream.'

The man was very anxious to get away; he was very uneasy. She went on with the whole story, until she came to the hand; when she came to the hand, she took it out of her pocket, and said: 'If you don't believe me, look, here is the hand.'

And they were seized then and the suitor and eleven of them were hanged, but the man who had prayed for her cousin when she saw the house grow black was allowed to go free.

THE MARAICHE MAIRNEAL

Source: *Tocher* 29 (School of Scottish Studies tape SA 1974/26 B)
Narrator: Alasdair Stewart; recorded by D. A. MacDonald and Alan Bruford, 1974
Type: AT433b 'King Lindorm'

This was a young king, he was King of Ireland and, once again, he was a widower and he had a son. And then he married again. And now the lad, he was living with his father now, and his stepmother. And when he grew up then to be a big lad, his mother said to him – well, his stepmother – she told him that she was going to give him a present. And: 'Oh,' said the lad to her, 'I've never given *you* a present,' said he.

'Oh, that doesn't matter. I'm going to give you this.' And she came up and she had a shirt. Oh, the lad had never seen a shirt as beautiful as this one.

'There's a shirt for you,' she said.

And a day or two after that he was going to put on his best clothes and he put the shirt on. He was very proud of the new shirt he had got; it was so beautiful. But he hadn't had it on very long when he felt the shirt curling around his waist there and: 'What,' said he, 'what's wrong with the shirt?'

But it went on curling and curling and when it came up on him then and . . . till it was round his neck. And this, when it got round his neck, this turned out to be a great snake. 'Ah well,' said the lad, 'that's some present I've got!'

The king saw him then, his father, and he said to him, 'Oh,' said he, 'that's some present she's given you!'

And now, in these times, they had a woman whom they called the 'henwife'. And his father said to him, 'Run and see the henwife.'

'Oh,' said the woman to him, 'that's terrible, my poor lad,' said she, 'that thing that you've had put on you.'

'Is there anyone at all,' said he, 'who can cure me or take this off me?'

'Well,' said the henwife to him, 'there's only one person I know who can cure you, but how are you going to get there? There's a woman,' said she, 'on the summit of the island of Loch Leug, and if you were there, I think she might be able to cure you.' And: 'But,' said she to him, 'how are you going to get there? The only one who could get you there is the Maraiche Mairneal [the Weatherwise Mariner], and he – he's been bed-ridden for seven years and he's blind and deaf.'

But he took the thing along with him and they went to see the Maraiche.

'Oh,' said the Maraiche to them, 'I can't get up out of my bed and I can't do anything, but the boat is lying there and if you can get her out and afloat yourselves, you're welcome to have her.'

They went down to the boat then and they tried to get her out into the sea, but, oh, they couldn't do ... they couldn't move her. They came back then and told him that they could do nothing with the boat, they couldn't push her out.

'Oh well,' said the Maraiche to them, 'see if you can see my trousers.'

They brought him his trousers then and he got into his trousers and he put on his clothes and they took him down to the boat. And when they had got him down to the boat: 'Now,' said he, 'get my shoulder against her prow.' They set his shoulder against her prow and he gave her one shove and he sent her three times her own length out to sea. And they set out then, making for the summit of the island of Loch Leug. And when the woman saw them: 'Oh well,' said she, 'let him come from below or from above, but there's the mast-top of the Maraiche Mairneal's ship coming one more time.'

And she went out then and she gave the Maraiche a great welcome. 'What cargo,' said she to him, 'have you got this time?'

'Oh,' said he, 'I've got a cargo this time the like of which I've never had before. Here it is,' said he. He brought the lad up on deck and she had no sooner set eyes on him than: 'The sooner you take yourself off,' said she, 'you and your boat, out of this island . . . and may you . . . may you never . . .' said she. 'I'll send you and your boat to the bottom if you bring this fellow ashore here.'

'Ach well,' said the Maraiche, 'it's even worse than I thought,' said he. 'I hoped,' said he, 'that you could do something for him. Well, well,' said the Maraiche, 'we'll just go home then.'

But he said to this lad who had the snake round his neck: 'Run out then,' said he, 'and bring aboard two pails of water for us to have in the boat.' And when he had got the lad ashore, the Maraiche hoisted his sails and put the boat about and he headed back home.

And when the lad came back he looked around, and he had the two pails of water, and the boat was gone. But he threw the pails away then and turned back, and the woman of Loch Leug had a great garden. There was lots of fruit there – apples and the like. He was eating these – they were outside the wall, hanging over. He was eating some of them and the daughter of this woman came along. She looked and saw him and she said to him: 'Oh,' said she, 'come into the garden. Come in, come in,' said she, 'and eat the fruit.'

'Oh no,' said the lad, 'I won't go in,' said he. 'Well,' said he, 'I'm just like a wild beast,' said he, 'terrifying everyone,' said he, 'with this thing that's round me here. And I'm afraid,' said he, 'to go near anyone.'

'Oh, just you come in,' said she. And she ran into the house and she said to her mother: 'Oh,' said she to her mother, 'there's a boy out there,' said she, 'and I've never seen a boy better-looking than him. Won't you invite him into the garden?'

'Oh, tell him to come into the garden.' He came in then, and the other woman came out then – her mother. She looked at him: 'Come on,' said she. 'Come in,' said she.

'It seems that they've gone . . . They've left me in the island,' said he.

'Well, since they've left you,' said she, 'come in,' said she. She brought him in then. And, oh, this woman's daughter – she really fell for the lad and she couldn't live if she didn't get him. But her mother said to her: 'Would you lose a leg for him?'

'Yes.'

'Would you lose an arm for him?'

'Yes.'

'Would you lose a breast for him?'

'Yes.'

'Well, well then,' said she, 'we'll see what we can do when the morning comes.'

And she had three sons, this woman – she had the girl and . . . she had one daughter and three sons. And she said to one of the boys: 'Run out,' said she, 'and catch and kill the fattest wether you can find and bring it in for me.'

Day came then and the lads went out to the hill and they found this big wether and they killed it and skinned it and brought it in and gave it to their mother. She got a great big frying-pan and put it on the fire and she got the girl to sit facing the boy. They were sitting facing each other. And when she had her sitting down, she got her to expose her breast. And she kept turning this thing – the meat that was in the pan – and this brute, it was hungry and it wanted to eat this. And it loosed one coil and then it loosed another. But to make a short story of it, it gave [?] and came down and sprang into the pan – the frying-pan. Now the pan was hot enough to burn it. And it gave another spring but instead of going back round the boy's neck it fastened on to the girl's breast. And, oh, the woman was ready for it and she had a big knife and when it was on the girl's breast she slashed at it and cut off her breast and it fell to the floor and she put a basin over it and put her foot on top of the basin. And she took the girl away then and her wound was dressed and she was – she recovered all right. She was healed. The lad was now a lad just as he ought to be. The creature was off him and he was a fine-looking boy. He had got rid of the snake.

'Now,' said she to him . . . when she lifted the basin off the floor, the shirt was there again, as beautiful as ever you saw.

'There,' said she, 'is the present your stepmother gave you.'

And she put it in the fire. And the shirt went off with a bang when she put it in the fire and it blew off half the fireplace.

Well, the lad was there now along with the woman and they got married. And he was there along with these people in the

island – himself and his wife and his brothers-in-law and his
mother-in-law. And *they* had a henwife too, and her son. Now
the son of the henwife and this lad, they were quite often
together – very often together. And then the mother, she used
to look after this girl. And she knew everything about the girl.
And the henwife said to her own son: 'If you were smart,' said
she, 'you could be in his place.'

'Och,' said he, 'how could I be in his place ... the lad's
place?'

'Oh, quite easily. You could say to him that you have had
knowledge of his wife. And he asked [sic]: "What knowledge
have you of my wife?" "I'll tell you." Tell him: "Well, she has a
golden comb for combing her hair." "Och, you might just have
seen that." And the next thing you'll tell him: "If you don't
believe me, I'll tell you something else. She has a gold tip on her
breast." And I'll bet when he hears that he'll be consumed with
jealousy and you'll see that he'll do [?] and that he'll go away and
you'll get his place.'

And this was what happened then. He was outside [? one day]
and: 'Well,' said he to the lad, 'you've got a beautiful wife.'

'Oh yes,' said the lad, 'I know that – I have a beautiful wife
and a good wife.'

'Oh yes,' said he, 'though she's as good as all that, I've seen
her, and I've seen her combing her hair. I know what sort of
comb she has.'

'Och, you might have seen her combing her hair.'

'And I saw more than that. She's got a gold tip on her breast.'

'Oh you son of the Devil!' said he, and he struck him. And he
jumped up then and went home and he seized his wife and gave
her a terrible thrashing. And he kicked her. And then he set out
and went away. And he went away as a beggarman. He took up
his bundle and went away as a beggarman. He was wandering
from place to place. And one day he was going through a wood.
There was a path there and he was going through a wood and he
heard cries coming from the wood. He listened, and then he
heard the cry again. And he went towards it and here was a man
lying on the ground and he was very ill.

'Ho, what's the matter?' said he.

'Oh, I've got an illness,' said he, 'but there's a spring there and if I could get a drink from that spring I'd be as well as I ever was.'

'And can't you get a drink from the spring?' said the lad. 'Isn't it as . . . can't you get . . .?'

'Oh,' said he, 'the spring is guarded by wild animals,' and he said: 'Just now,' said he, 'there's a lion there and the lion has a cup under its paw. And if you can get that cup away from the lion's paw . . . Just now,' said he, 'they're asleep, and if you go and if you can get that for me, with a drink, I'll get well,' said he, 'and you'll have command of the whole world with that cup.'

'Well,' said the lad, 'I'll see what I can do.'

And, as he had said, the lion was sitting by the spring with this cup under its paw. The lad came up quietly and then, when he was almost upon it, he gave a leap and snatched the cup from the lion's paw. And they woke up with that, and he told the lion to clear out and leave the spring. Oh, as soon as he had this cup, every beast that was at the spring left – they fled. And he got a drink from it for the man then, and when he gave him the drink, a little while later the man rose to his feet and: 'Oh,' said the man, 'I'm very grateful to you. Now,' said he, 'I'm just as well as I ever was. And now,' said he, 'you've got a cup there, and any drink you wish for [you shall have], or any place in the world that you wish to be in, you'll be there,' said he, 'just in a flash. And,' said he, 'any kind of music there is, you've got it all with the cup.'

And then the lad thought about himself and: 'Well then,' said he to him, 'I'll go back now to the island of Loch Leug.'

And there he was, back at the estate of his mother-in-law and his wife. And now he was a beggarman. And he came in and, oh, not one of them recognized him. He had been so long away and he was changed beyond recognition with his beard and hair and everything else about him. He was making music for them. And his own wife had not been up, the girl, the wife he had married, she had not risen from her bed from the day he had left till the night he came back with the music. And at the sound of his music, she raised herself up on her elbow and she was listening to the music. They went then . . . Bedtime came and they went to bed, and when they had gone to bed the girl got up and came through to her brother, her youngest brother, and she said to him, 'What would you do now if my husband came back? What would you do to him?'

'Oh,' said he, 'if he came here,' said he, 'I'd break every bone in his body.' And she left him then and she went to the middle one and she said the very same thing to him: if her husband came what would he do to him?

'Oh,' said he, 'I'd put him' said he, 'on the [?].'

But then he [sic] went to the eldest brother. And he said to him [sic] when she went in to his room and knocked and:

'God save us,' said he to her, 'how have you managed to get up?' said he. 'It's years since you were last on your feet. How did you get up?'

'Oh, I don't know,' said she, 'but I found the strength tonight,' said she, 'and I've got up and I'm on my feet. But I'm going to ask you this,' said she. 'If my husband came back, what would you do to him? Would you treat him badly?' And:

'Oh,' said he, 'I wouldn't treat him badly. He was treacherously deceived himself, and lied to, and it was that,' said he, 'that led to that.'

And when she saw then that her eldest brother, that he agreed with her: 'Well then,' said she, 'that's him over there. He came tonight,' said she. 'Though none of you recognized him, I knew him.' And:

'Oh well,' said he, 'the one who made the wound has healed it.'

And then the morning came and when the morning came she told this to her mother. And then she told everyone that it was he, and, och well, everything ended all right then. She was up again and she was better.

And the henwife was seized then, and her son, and they were put in a barrel of tar and paraffin was poured over them and they were set alight with a match.

That's the end of that story. He stayed with her on the estate there and for all I know they may still be there.

THE THREE SHIRTS OF BOG COTTON

Source: *Tocher* 2 (School of Scottish Studies tape SA 1969/119 A2-B1)
Narrator: Donald Alasdair Johnson, Ardmore, South Uist; recorded by
Angus John MacDonald, 1969
Type: AT451 'The Maiden Who Seeks Her Brothers'

Well, I heard that there was a king once and he was married
and he had three sons and one daughter. And now his
wife died and he lived for some time like that and the children
were still young, or, at least, they were not very old. But,
anyway, he made up his mind now that he would get married –
that it would be better for him to marry again, and he did that:
he got married again. And the woman he married – she and the
children – they got on well enough together.

But, anyway, one day who should come that way but the
Eachlair Urlair: whatever sort of woman she may have been, she
was a bad woman anyway, who used to come to many places.
And she asked the queen, now, how she and the king were
getting on together. She said very well.

'Yes,' said she, 'are you and the children . . .?'

'Oh yes indeed,' said she, 'I treat the children, the dear things,
exactly as if they were my own.'

And: 'Indeed,' said she, 'you are very foolish.'

'Why?' said the queen.

'Indeed,' said she, 'supposing the king died tomorrow, your
share of this place wouldn't come to much.'

And: 'God knows,' said the queen, 'that I will do no harm to
the children whatever may become of me here.'

'Oh you needn't do anything wrong,' said she. 'You send
them up to me and you shall not be to blame for anything.'

And: 'Oh, I don't know,' said the queen.

But anyway she went on at her till . . . 'You will send them up
to me tomorrow,' said she, 'and send them to ask for the yellow

comb. Tell them they are going for the yellow comb,' said she.

Well, that is how it happened. Next day, anyway – the king used to go off hunting to the mountains and to go off here and there – she sent the oldest boy off and told him to go up to the house of the Eachlair Urlair – it could not have been far away, anyway – and to ask her to give him the yellow comb to bring down to her.

And this is what happened. The poor lad went off suspecting nothing. He went up and came to the house of the Eachlair Urlair and knocked at the door, and she asked him to come in. He went in.

'Yes,' said she. 'What do you want, my dear?'

'My stepmother sent me up,' said he, 'to get the yellow comb.'

'Go on, my dear,' said she, 'there it is over there on that dresser, and take it.'

He went across to the dresser and the comb was there – he could see it, the comb over on the dresser and he went across to the dresser and she just lifted her magic wand and as he picked the comb up she struck him with the wand and he was changed into a black raven. And he turned and went out of the house and as he was crossing the threshold he spat out a mouthful of blood and flew off from the door.

Well, there was no sign of him coming home and his stepmother said now to the next oldest boy: 'Goodness,' said she, 'your brother has not come back. You had better go up to see where he is and tell him to come . . . If you do not see him,' said she, 'ask for the yellow comb.'

And he set off and up he went and when the one who was a raven saw his brother coming he began to dart at him and kept on darting at him and he was almost taking his head off. Well, what he did was to start running to try and get into the house of the Eachlair Urlair before the raven could harm him. And he went in and asked her: 'Has my brother been here?' said he.

'Oh no, my dear,' said she.

'Well now,' said he, 'he came up to get the yellow comb. My stepmother sent him.'

'Well then,' said she, 'he has not been here at all, but there, my dear, is the comb over on the dresser, and you go and take it.'

The poor boy went across to the comb and when he was almost at the comb she swung round with the magic wand and he was changed into another black raven. And out he went from the house as his brother had done and as he went out he saw the blood at the door and he too spat out a mouthful of blood beside it.

Well, he went out and joined his brother and now they were getting uneasy about this one not getting back and the third one was sent up. And he came and the two ravens set upon him and they were almost taking ... They were not quite striking him but they very nearly were and they were darting at him and getting about his feet and getting in his way on all sides. And after all what he did was to start running to try and get inside before they could do him any harm. And he came into the house of the Eachlair Urlair and asked her: 'Were my brothers here?' said he.

'No indeed, my dear,' said she. 'None of your brothers was here. Were they coming here?'

'Yes,' said he. 'My stepmother sent them up to get the yellow comb.'

'Oh, none of them has been here,' said she. 'But there, my dear, the comb is over there on the dresser and you go across and take it.'

The poor boy went across and when he was – as happened to the others – when he was just going to pick up the yellow comb he was struck by the wand and changed into another black raven.

But, anyway, the girl, she was the oldest of them, and they were now getting anxious about the boys that they had not got back, and her stepmother said to the girl: 'Goodness,' said she, 'you had better see what has happened to the lads who have gone. Everyone is going and no one is coming back.'

Well, the girl went, and when they saw their sister coming, the three ravens set about her then and, here, before she got to the house it struck her that something was wrong and when she came to the door, then, she noticed the three mouthfuls of blood on the threshold. And she went in and she asked the Eachlair Urlair: 'Have you seen,' said she, 'any sign of my brothers here today?'

'Oh no, my dear,' said she.

'Have you not?' said the girl.

'Oh no,' said she.

'Well,' said she, 'my stepmother sent them up to get the yellow comb.'

And: 'Oh well,' said she, 'they have not been here at all, wherever they've gone, but the yellow comb is over on the dresser there and you go across, my dear, and take it.'

The girl went and as she went across she was keeping an eye on the woman who was behind her, and when she saw her lifting the wand – the magic wand – she sprang at her and seized the wand from her and she struck her with it on the crown of her head and turned her into a pillar of stone.

'Away,' said she. 'You can stay there.'

And she turned and went out and she did not take the comb or anything else. And as she crossed the threshold, she noticed the three mouthfuls of blood and she went with her handkerchief and took them up and wrapped them in the handkerchief. And she went out and when she went out the ones who were outside were almost taking her head off for joy that she had got back out. And it was almost nightfall.

Well, they headed south – the ravens – and she followed them on foot, and soon it got dark, and all she could do was to listen to where they were croaking in the sky above her and she followed them in that way. And so she went on, but then she lost them, and as she looked around her she saw a light and she headed straight for this light. And she came to a house and knocked at the door and there was no response. No one answered her knock. Then she opened the door and went in. There was a table there laid ready and she went in and sat down and she waited to see what . . . whether there was anyone at home or living in that house, and there was no sign of anyone appearing. But, anyway, she then heard the others croaking and coming towards the house and they came in and every one of them cast off his [raven] coverings and they came and sat at the table.

'Well,' said they, 'you got away with your life.'

'Oh yes,' said she.

And there was food on the table too and they had a meal and, now, after their meal they gathered round and then she said to them: 'Now is there anything in the world,' said she, 'that can break the spell that binds you?'

And the oldest one said: 'Oh yes, there is one thing,' said he, 'but I don't suppose you can do it.'

'Well,' said she, 'let me hear it.'

'Well, it's this,' said he. 'I have seen it in writing. You must make a shirt of bog cotton for each one of us, and from the day that you begin to pick the bog cotton to the day when you say, "Health to wear your shirt, sweet brother," you must not utter one single, solitary word in that time.'

'O yes,' said she, 'we shall see what can be done.'

Well, this is what happened. When daylight came they went off and when she had got the house in order – nobody came to disturb her, whatever sort of house it may have been – when she had got the house in order she took herself off to the hills and began to pick bog cotton. And she picked a sackful that day and she just left it where she had picked it and came back to the house, and then the others came; she was in before them and then they came home. Well, they threw off their coverings when they came in and turned into men and then came up to the room. And they began to try and catch her out then, and they kept trying to see if they could get her to speak. Not a syllable could they get all night long.

Well, next morning they went off and she herself went off that morning when she had got things in order – she went to the hills and she picked another sackful that day. And she put it with the one she had picked the day before and came back to the house. And they came and they were trying to catch her out to see if they could make her speak and not a syllable could they get.

But anyway, now, next morning they went off. They would go off in the morning: as soon as they had a meal – or whatever it may have been – they would go off, and she went earlier this day to see if she could make a sackful of it and carry it near to the road. And she was busy picking: all day she worked at this bog cotton, and she picked the sackful and now she considered to herself. It was fairly early in the evening. It had not got dark yet and [? she thought] that she would start to carry the sacks to the road. And she started to do that and she brought the three sacks there and by the time she had brought the three sacks there it had got dark – so dark that she could not make out which way she ought to go to get back to the house. And this is what she said to herself in her own mind: they would just be tormenting her anyway, even if she were to go home, to try to get her to speak, and she made up her mind that she would wait here in the shelter of the sacks until it was daylight and she could see.

Anyway, that was what she did and she stayed there in the shelter of the sacks and she was at the roadside. And suddenly she heard a horseman – hoofbeats coming. And this man came up and as he passed her, as if he had sensed something, he stopped. And he looked and thought he saw something that was not usually beside the road and he dismounted and went across and here he found her beside the sacks. He spoke to her. There was not a sound. He kept asking – he spoke to her two or three times and questioned her and she gave him no answer. Well, this is what he did: he went and lifted her up and set her behind him on the horse and off he went. And now he went on for some time till he came to a house – he came to his own house. And he lifted her down and put the horse into the stable and he brought her into the house, and there was no one living in this house but his mother and himself. And he was a gentleman, a great man. He had a fine house and all that.

Well, he told his mother how he had found the woman and everything and that she could not speak a word and he told his mother about the sacks she had left at the roadside and that he would have to bring them home. Well, anyway, they went to bed then. She got a room to herself and they went to bed and next morning, then, he got ready and went to fetch her sacks and he brought the three sacks home. And when he brought the sacks home, she set to work at the bog cotton, carding it and working it and spinning it, and I suppose it would be a distaff she had in these days; there would be no wheel to use.

But, anyway, she was working away there and what happened

to her next . . . what happened was that he went to bed with her and she became pregnant, and now she was working – despite everything, she was working away at the shirts. And the night before she was delivered of her first child she had the first shirt finished and she folded it and put it in a locker that she had up in her room. And that night she gave birth to a baby boy. And before morning came there was no trace of the child. He had been stolen. And she was dumb, and now it was suggested to the man that she herself had killed the child and that there was no saying what had been done to it.

Well, the man said that he would let her away with that, for the time being at least. And it seems to me, anyway, that she was a beautiful woman. And now she worked: she started then, when she had recovered after having the child, she started on the next shirt, carding it and combing it and doing all the work that had to be done to it, and spinning it.

And she became pregnant again, a second time, and the night before she was delivered she folded the second shirt and put it away along with the first one. And now there were midwives and women about the place but, despite that, before daybreak the child had been stolen – another boy. And now it was suggested to him again that it must be herself who was doing it and that she was killing the child, wherever she might be disposing of it.

Well, he said then: 'Well,' said he, 'we shall let her be this time again,' for others were saying that it was clear enough that a woman like her was not normal anyway, that she spoke not a word, yet she was such a good worker and everything, and that it must be that she was not normal.

And, oh, he never let on that he heard them. And when she had recovered then for the second time, she started on the third shirt. And what happened but that she became pregnant again and the night before she gave birth to the third child, and it was a boy again, she folded the third brother's shirt and put it away in the locker along with the others. And that night, anyway, she gave birth to another son and the next morning there was no sign of the boy, of the new-born child. It had disappeared.

And, oh well, word was sent to the man, and, oh well, there

was nothing else for it and his decision was that she should be burned since she was unnatural anyway. And a crowd gathered now; people began to gather and when it was just time for her to be brought out, they saw three horsemen approaching. And the gentleman, here, he asked the people to wait a moment, that here there were three horsemen approaching, and God knows but that someone might take it on himself to take her away out of his sight rather than have him do such a terrible thing to her.

And then the horsemen came up and, here, one of them had a child about three years old and another [a child] about two years old or a little under and the other with a baby in front of him on the horse. And now, the one who had the oldest child, he dismounted and he asked what was the meaning of all this. And the man told him about her.

'May I,' said he, 'have a word with this woman, myself and my brothers here?'

'Indeed you may,' said the gentleman. 'You may have a word with her and take her away with you if you so wish. Indeed, I hate to have to go and do the like of this. Yes,' said he, 'come in here.'

And he was taken into a room there and she was sent up there and she and her three brothers and the three children went up. And the gentleman – he went no further but closed the door behind him and they locked the door on the inside. And then she went across to her locker and took out the first shirt she had made and gave it to her oldest brother and told him to put the shirt on, and he started to put on the shirt and now when he had got it on she said to him: 'Health to wear your shirt, sweet brother,' said she.

'Good health to you, sweet sister,' said he, 'and here is your first child.'

The man who was there outside the door demanded that the door be opened when he heard her speaking, but her brother said it was not to be opened yet. And she went and brought out the second shirt and gave it to her brother – the second brother – and asked him to put it on. And he undressed and put the shirt on.

'Health to wear your shirt, sweet brother,' said she.

'Good health to you, sweet sister,' said he, 'and here is your second son.'

And the man outside demanded that the door be opened. They would not open it. He burst through the door where it stood and: 'Although I had everyone here who has ever lived,' said he, 'you are certainly not going away, since I have found out that you can speak. You will stay where you are,' said he.

Well, that is what happened, but she asked him to stand back for a moment till her third brother got it [i.e. the shirt] and she then brought out the third shirt and gave it to her brother and she asked him to undress and put this shirt on. And so he did. He took it off and put on her shirt.

'Health to wear your shirt, sweet brother,' said she.

'Good health to you, sweet sister,' said he, 'and here is your baby who was born last night.' And she took the child and held it. And all that remained to be done was to clear away the crowd outside who had been waiting to see the woman being burnt.

And now they stayed on in that place and he and she got married when they had got everything arranged, and her brothers were with them. Her brothers stayed on: she kept them there with her. And she and her three brothers were there and her three children – her three sons – and her husband and his mother. And, anyway, he was a wealthy man and they stayed on there and when she was recovered he married her.

And after the marriage they told the story – how the whole thing had happened from beginning to end – how the boys had been sent to the Eachlair Urlair, and when the gentleman found that out, they had to go then, the whole lot of them, and take themselves to the king's house – her father's house. And so they did.

And now when they reached the king's house the king was there, and since the day he had lost the children, never knowing what had happened to them, he had been unwell. But now when he found out who they were, then he began to improve all right. And he asked them then what had happened to them or what had taken them away. And then they told him of their adventures, how the Eachlair Urlair had made black ravens of the three boys when they went to fetch the yellow comb that their stepmother had sent them for. And she told of her own adventures and how it had occurred to her that there must be something odd about it when she saw the ravens and the fierce way they were attacking her to try and keep her away from the house.

And when the king heard this he sent her and men with her to the house of the Eachlair Urlair and he told her to strike her with the wand and wake her up – change her back from the pillar of stone to what she had been before, and bring her back to him.

And that was done. She went up and struck with the wand the pillar of stone in which the Eachlair Urlair still was as she had left her, and she came up as she had been before. And she was forced to come away with them – there were others with her – and the Eachlair Urlair was brought away and the king then gave judgment that she and the queen were to be burnt and their ashes scattered to the winds. And that was done.

When the Eachlair Urlair and the queen were burnt and their ashes scattered to the winds, I do not know what happened to him, but the gentleman and she and her children went back home and at that I parted with them.

FOUR HERO TALES

Source: J. MacDougall, *Folk and Hero Tales*
Narrator: Alexander Cameron, roadman between Duror and Ballachulish.
A native of Ardnamurchan, Cameron learned his stories 'from Donald McPhie
and other old men whom he had known in his boyhood, but who died
many years ago'
Types: These four tales of the Gaelic hero Finn are one narrator's contribution
to a great unwritten saga; each of them is also known in variant versions
from other storytellers

How Finn Kept His Children for the
Big Young Hero of the Ship,
AND HOW BRAN WAS FOUND

A day Finn and his men were in the hunting-hill they killed a great number of deer; and when they were wearied after the chase they sat down on a pleasant green knoll, at the back of the wind and at the face of the sun, where they could see everyone, and no one at all could see them.

While they were sitting in that place Finn lifted his eyes towards the sea, and saw a ship making straight for the haven beneath the spot on which they were sitting. When the ship came to land, a Big Young Hero leaped out of her on the shore, seized her by the bows, and drew her up, her own seven lengths, on the green grass, where the eldest son of neither land-owner nor [of holder] of large town-land dared mock or gibe at her. Then he ascended the hillside, leaping over the hollows and slanting the knolls, till he reached the spot on which Finn and his men were sitting.

He saluted Finn frankly, energetically, fluently; and Finn saluted him with the equivalent of the same words. Finn then asked him whence did he come, or what was he wanting? He answered Finn that he had come through night-watching and tempest of sea where he was; because he was losing his children, and it had been told him that there was not a man in the world who could keep his children for him but him, Finn, King of the Féinne. And he said to Finn, 'I lay on thee, as crosses and spells and seven fairy fetters of travelling and straying to be with me before thou shalt eat food, or drink a draught, or close an eye in sleep.'

Having said this, he turned away from them and descended the hillside the way he ascended it. When he reached the ship he placed his shoulder against her bow, and put her out. He then leaped into her, and departed in the direction he came until they lost sight of him.

Finn was now under great heaviness of mind, because the vows had been laid on him, and he must fulfil them or travel onwards until he would die. He knew not whither he should go, or what he should do. But he left farewell with his men, and descended the hillside to the seaside. When he reached that, he could not go farther on the way in which he saw the Big Young Hero depart. He therefore began to walk along the shore, but before he had gone very far forward, he saw a company of seven men coming to meet him.

When he reached the men he asked the first of them what was he good at? The man answered that he was a good Carpenter. Finn asked him how good was he at carpentry? The man said that, with three strokes of his axe, he could make a large, capacious, complete ship of the alder stock over yonder. 'Thou art good enough,' said Finn; 'thou mayest pass by.'

He then asked of the second man, what was he good at? The man said that he was a good Tracker. 'How good art thou?' said Finn. 'I can track the wild duck over the crests of the nine waves within nine days,' said the man. 'Thou art good enough,' said Finn; 'thou mayest pass by.'

Then he said to the third man, 'What art thou good at?' The man replied that he was a good Gripper. 'How good art thou?' 'The hold I once get I will not let go until my two arms come from my shoulders, or until my hold comes with me.' 'Thou art good enough; thou mayest pass by.'

Then he said to the fourth man, 'What art thou good at?' He answered that he was a good Climber. 'How good art thou?' 'I can climb on a filament of silk to the stars, although thou wert to tie it there.' 'Thou art good enough; thou mayest pass by.'

He then said to the fifth man, 'What art thou good at?' He replied that he was a good Thief. 'How good art thou?' 'I can steal the egg from the heron while her two eyes are looking at me.' 'Thou art good enough; thou mayest pass by.'

He asked of the sixth man, 'What art thou good at?' He answered that he was a good Listener. 'How good art thou?' He said that he could hear what people were saying at the extremity of the Uttermost World. 'Thou art good enough; thou mayest pass by.'

Then he said to the seventh man, 'What art thou good at?' He replied that he was a good Marksman. 'How good art thou?' 'I could hit an egg as far away in the sky as bowstring could send or bow could carry [an arrow].' 'Thou art good enough; thou mayest pass by.'

All this gave Finn great encouragement. He turned round and said to the Carpenter, 'Prove thy skill.' The Carpenter went where the stock was, and struck it with his axe thrice; and as he had said, the Ship was ready.

When Finn saw the Ship ready he ordered his men to put her out. They did that, and went on board of her.

Finn now ordered the Tracker to go to the bow and prove himself. At the same time he told him that yesterday a Big Young Hero left yonder haven in his ship, and that he wanted to follow the Hero to the place in which he now was. Finn himself went to steer the Ship, and they departed. The Tracker was telling him to keep her that way or to keep her this way. They sailed a long time forward without seeing land, but they kept on their course until the evening was approaching. In the gloaming they noticed that land was ahead of them, and they made straight for it. When they reached the shore they leaped to land, and drew up the Ship.

Then they noticed a large fine house in the glen above the beach. They took their way up to the house; and when they were nearing it they saw the Big Young Hero coming to meet them. He ran and placed his two arms about Finn's neck, and said, 'Darling of all men in the world, hast thou come?' 'If I had been thy darling of all the men in the world, it is not as thou didst leave me that thou wouldst have left me,' said Finn. 'Oh, it was not without a way of coming I left thee,' said the Big Young Hero. 'Did I not send a company of seven men to meet thee?'

When they reached the house, the Big Young Hero told Finn and his men to go in. They accepted the invitation, and found abundance of meat and drink.

After they had quenched their hunger and thirst, the Big Young Hero came in where they were, and said to Finn, 'Six years from this night, my wife was in child-bed, and a child was born to me. As soon as the child came into the world, a large Hand came in at the chimney, and took the child with it in the cap [hollow] of the hand. Three years from this night the same thing happened. And tonight she is going to be in child-bed again. It was told me that thou wert the only man in the world who could keep my children for me, and now I have courage since I have found thee.'

Finn and his men were tired and sleepy. Finn said to the men that they were to stretch themselves on the floor, and that he was going to keep watch. They did as they were told, and he remained sitting beside the fire. At last sleep began to come on him; but he had a bar of iron in the fire, and as often as his eyes would begin to close with sleep, he would thrust the bar through the bone of his palm, and that was keeping him awake. About midnight the woman was delivered; and as soon as the child came into the world the Hand came in at the chimney. Finn called on the Gripper to get up.

The Gripper sprang quickly on his feet, and laid hold of the Hand. He gave a pull on the Hand, and took it into the two eyebrows at the chimney.

The Hand gave a pull on the Gripper, and took him out to the top of his two shoulders. The Gripper gave another pull on the Hand, and brought it into the neck. The Hand gave a pull on the Gripper, and brought him out to the very middle. The Gripper gave a pull on the Hand, and took it in over the two armpits. The Hand gave a pull on the Gripper, and took him out to the smalls of his two feet. Then the Gripper gave a brave pull on the Hand, and it came out of the shoulder. And when it fell on the floor the pulling of seven geldings was in it. But the Big Giant outside put in the other hand, and took the child with him in the cap of the hand.

They were all very sorry that they lost the child. But Finn said, 'We will not yield to this yet. I and my men will go away after the Hand before a sun shall rise on a dwelling tomorrow.'

At break of dawn, Finn and his men turned out, and reached the beach, where they had left the Ship.

They launched the Ship, and leaped on board of her. The Tracker went to the bow, and Finn went to steer her. They departed, and now and again the Tracker would cry to Finn to keep her in that direction, or to keep her in this direction. They sailed onward a long distance without seeing anything before them, except the great sea. At the going down of the sun, Finn noticed a black spot in the ocean ahead of them. He thought it too little for an island, and too large for a bird, but he made straight for it. In the darkening of the night they reached it; and it was a rock, and a Castle thatched with eel-skins was on its top.

They landed on the rock. They looked about the Castle, but they saw neither window nor door at which they could get in. At last they noticed that it was on the roof the door was. They did not now know how they could get up, because the thatch was so slippery. But the Climber cried, 'Let me over, and I will not be long in climbing it.' He sprang quickly towards the Castle, and in an instant was on its roof. He looked in at the door, and after taking particular notice of everything that he saw, he descended where the rest were waiting.

Finn asked of him what did he see? He said that he saw a Big Giant lying on a bed, a silk covering over him and a satin covering under him, and his hand stretched out and an infant asleep in the cap of the hand; that he saw two boys on the floor playing with shinties of gold and a ball of silver; and that there was a very large deer-hound bitch lying beside the fire, and two pups sucking her.

Then said Finn, 'I do not know how we shall get them out.' The Thief answered and said, 'If I get in I will not be long putting them out.' The Climber said, 'Come on my back, and I will take thee up to the door.' The Thief did as he was told, and got into the Castle.

Instantly he began to prove his skill. The first thing he put out was the child that was in the cap of the hand. He then put out the two boys who were playing on the floor. He then stole the silk covering that was over the Giant, and the satin covering that was under him, and put them out. Then he put out the shinties of gold and the ball of silver. He then stole the two pups that were sucking the bitch beside the fire. These were the most valuable things which he saw inside. He left the Giant asleep, and turned out.

They placed the things which the Thief stole in the Ship, and departed. They were but a short time sailing when the Listener stood up and said, ''Tis I who am hearing him, 'tis I who am listening to him!' 'What art thou hearing?' said Finn. 'He has just awakened,' said the Listener, 'and missed everything that was stolen from him. He is in great wrath, sending away the Bitch, and saying to her if she will not go that he will go himself. But it is the Bitch that is going.'

In a short time they looked behind them, and saw the Bitch coming swimming. She was cleaving the sea on each side of her in red sparks of fire. They were seized with fear, and said that they did not know what they should do. But Finn considered, and then told them to throw out one of the pups; perhaps when she would see the pup drowning she would return with it. They threw out the pup, and, as Finn said, it happened: the Bitch returned with the pup. This left them at the time pleased.

But shortly after that the Listener arose trembling, and said: ''Tis I who am hearing him; 'tis I who am listening to him!' 'What art thou saying now?' said Finn. 'He is again sending away the Bitch, and since she will not go he is coming himself.'

When they heard this their eye was always behind them. At last they saw him coming, and the great sea reached not beyond his haunches. They were seized with fear and great horror, for they knew not what they should do. But Finn thought of his knowledge set of teeth, and having put his finger under it, found out that the Giant was immortal, except in a mole which was in the hollow of his palm. The Marksman then stood up and said: 'If I get one look of it I will have him.'

The Giant came walking forward through the sea to the side of the Ship. Then he lifted up his hand to seize the top of the mast, in order to sink the Ship. But when the hand was on high the Marksman noticed the mole, and he let an arrow off in its direction. The arrow struck the Giant in the death-spot, and he fell dead on the sea.

They were now very happy, for there was nothing more before them to make them afraid. They put about, and sailed back to the Castle. The Thief stole the pup again, and they took it with them along with the one they had. After that they returned to the place of the Big Young Hero. When they reached the haven they leaped on land, and drew up the Ship on dry ground.

Then Finn went away with the family of the Big Young Hero and with everything which he and his men took out of the Castle to the fine house of the Big Young Hero.

The Big Young Hero met him coming, and when he saw his children he went on his two knees to Finn, and said: 'What now is thy reward?' Finn answered and said, that he was asking nothing but his choice of the two pups which they took from the Castle. The Big Young Hero said that he would get that and a great deal more if he would ask it. But Finn wanted nothing except the pup. This pup was Bran, and his brother, that the Big Young Hero got, was the Grey Dog.

The Big Young Hero took Finn and his men into his house, and made for them a great, joyous, merry feast, which was kept up for a day and year, and if the last day was not the best, it was not the worst.

That is how Finn kept his children for the Big Young Hero of the Ship, and how Bran was found.

FINN'S JOURNEY TO LOCHLAN:
AND HOW THE GREY DOG WAS FOUND AGAIN

A day Finn and his men were in the hunting-hill, they killed a good number of deer; and when they were making ready to go home, they saw a Big Lad coming to the place where they were. He went to meet Finn, and saluted him frankly, energetically, fluently; and Finn saluted him with the equivalent of the same words.

Finn asked him whence did he come, or what was he wanting? He answered Finn and said, 'I am a Lad who came from east and from west, seeking a master.' Finn said to him, 'I want a Lad, and if we agree I will engage thee. What is thy reward at the end of a day and year?' 'That is not much,' said the Lad. 'I only ask that at the end of the day and year thou wilt go with me by invitation to a feast and a night's entertainment to the palace of the King of Lochlan; and thou must not take with thee a dog or a man, a calf or a child, a weapon or an adversary but thyself.' To shorten the tale, Finn engaged the Lad, and he was a faithful servant to the end of the day and year.

On the morning of the last day of his engagement the Big Lad asked of Finn whether he was satisfied with his service? Finn said to him that he was perfectly satisfied. 'Well,' said the Lad, 'I hope that I shall receive my reward, and that thou wilt go with me as thou didst promise.' 'Thou shalt get thy reward, and I will go with thee,' said Finn.

Then Finn went where his men were, and told them that that was the day on which he must go to fulfil his promise to the Lad, and that he did not know when he should return. 'But,' said Finn, 'if I shall not be back within a day and year, let the man of you who will not be whetting his sword be bending his bow for the purpose of holding one great day on the Great Strand of Lochlan, revenging my death.' When he had said this to his men, he left them farewell, and went in to his dwelling.

His Fool was sitting beside the fire, and he said to him, 'Poor man, art thou sorry that I am going away?' The Fool answered weeping, and said that he was sorry because he was going in the way in which he was going, but that he would give him an advice if he would take it. 'Yes, poor man,' said Finn, 'for often has the advice of the King been in the head of the Fool. What is thy advice?' 'It is,' said the Fool, 'that thou shalt take Bran's chain with thee in thy pocket; and it is not a dog, and it is not a man, it is not a calf, and it is not a child, and it is not a weapon, and it is not an adversary to thee. But thou shalt take it at any rate.' 'Yes, poor man,' said Finn, leaving him farewell and departing.

He found the Big Lad waiting him at the door. The Lad said to him if he was ready that they would depart. Finn said that he was ready, and told the Lad to take the lead, because he knew the way better.

The Big Lad went off, and Finn followed him. Though Finn was swift and speedy, he could not touch the Big Lad with a stick on the way. When the Big Lad would be going out of sight at one mountain-gap, Finn would be only coming in sight on the next mountain-ridge. And they kept in that position to each other until they reached the end of their journey.

They went into the palace of the King of Lochlan, and Finn sat down wearily, heavily, sadly. But, instead of a feast awaiting him, the chiefs and nobles of the King of Lochlan were sitting within putting their heads together to see what disgraceful death they would decree him. One would say we will hang him, another would say we will burn him, a third would say we will drown him. At last a man who was in the company stood up, and said that they would not put him to death in any of the ways that the rest mentioned. The men who first spoke turned towards him, and asked of him what way had he of putting Finn to death that was more disgraceful than any of the ways which they mentioned. He answered them and said: 'We will go with him, and send him up to the Great Glen (Glen More); and he will not go far forward there when he shall be put to death by the Grey Dog. And you know, and I know, that there is not another death in the world more disgraceful in the estimation of the Féinne than that their earthly king should fall by a cur of a dog.' When they heard the man's sentence, they all clapped their hands, and agreed with him in his sentence.

Without delay they went with Finn up to the Glen where the Dog was staying. They did not go very far with him into the Glen when they heard the howling of the Dog coming. They gave a look, and, when they saw him, they said that it was time for them to flee. They turned back quickly, and left Finn at the mercy of the Dog.

Now staying and running away were all one to Finn. If he ran away he would be put to death, and if he stayed he would only be put to death; and he would as soon fall by the Dog as fall by his enemies. And so he stayed.

The Grey Dog was coming with his mouth open, and his tongue out on one side of his mouth. Every snort which he sent from his nostrils was scorching [everything] three miles before him and on each side of him. Finn was being tormented by the heat of the Dog's breath, and he saw clearly that he could not stand it long. He now thought if there was any use in Bran's chain, that it was time to draw it [forth]. He put his hand in his pocket, and when the Dog was in a near distance of him he took it out and shook it towards him. The Dog instantly stood, and began to wag his tail. He then came on where Finn was, and licked every sore which he had, from the top of his head to the sole of his foot, until he healed with his tongue what he burned with his breath. At last Finn clapped Bran's chain about the Grey Dog's neck, and descended through the Glen, having the Dog with him in a leash.

An old man and an old woman, who used to feed the Grey Dog, were staying at the lower end of the Glen. The Old Woman happened to be at the door, and when she saw Finn coming with the Dog she sprang into the house, crying and beating her hands. The Old Man asked of her, what did she see or what did she feel? She said that she saw a great thing, as tall and as handsome a man as she ever beheld, descending through the Glen, having the Grey Dog with him on a leash. 'Though the people of Lochlan and of Ireland were assembled,' said the Old Man, 'among them all there would not be a man who could do that but Finn, King of the Féinne, and Bran's chain of gold with him.' 'Though it were that same,' replied the Old Woman, 'he is coming.' 'We shall soon know,' said the Old Man, as he sprang out.

He went forward to meet Finn, and in a few words they saluted each other. Finn told him, from beginning to end, the reason why he was yonder. Then the Old Man invited him to go into the house till he would throw off his weariness, and receive meat and drink.

Finn went in. The Old Man told the Old Woman the tale which Finn told him. And when the Old Woman heard the story, it pleased her so well that she said to Finn he was perfectly welcome to stay in her house to the end of a day and year. Finn gladly accepted the invitation, and stayed there.

At the end of a day and year the Old Woman went out, and stood on a knoll near the house. She was a while looking at everything she could see, and listening to every sound that she could hear. At last she gave a look down in the direction of the shore, and beheld an exceedingly great host standing on the Great Strand of Lochlan.

She ran quickly into the house, beating her hands and crying alas! [her despoiling!] while her two eyes were as large as a corn-fan with fear. The Old Man sprang to his feet, and asked of her, what did she see? She said that she saw a thing the like of which she never saw before. 'There is an innumerable host on the Great Strand down there; and in [the host] there is a squint-eyed, red-haired man [Oscar], and I do not think that his match in combat is this night beneath the stars.'

'Oh!' said Finn, as he sprang to his feet, 'there thou hast the companies of my love! Let me out to meet them!'

Finn, with the Grey Dog, went down to the Strand; and when his men saw him coming, alive and hale, they raised a great shout of rejoicing, which was heard in the four corners of Lochlan. Then they and their earthly king gave each other a friendly welcome. And if the welcome between them and Finn was friendly, not less friendly was the welcome between Bran and the Grey Dog; for this was his brother that was taken with him from the Castle.

Then they took vengeance on the men of Lochlan, because of the way they were going to treat Finn. They began at one end of Lochlan, and they stopped not till they went out at the other end.

After they had subdued Lochlan, they returned home, and, when they reached the Hall of Finn, they made a great, joyful, merry feast, which was kept up for a day and a year.

The Lad of the Skin Coverings

On a certain day of old, Finn thought that he would go to hunt to the White Glen. He took with him as many of his men as were at hand at the time, and they went to the Glen.

The hunt began, and when it was over no man who was present ever saw such a sight of dead deer.

It was a custom with the Fein [Féinne], after they had gathered together the deer they killed, to sit down and take a rest. They would then divide the deer among them, each man taking with him a small or large burden as he was able. But on this day they killed many more than all that were at the hunt could take with them.

While Finn was considering what he should do with the remainder, he gave a look, and saw a Big Lad coming over the side of the mountain, and making straight for the place in which they were assembled with so great speed that never before did they see a man so fast as he. 'Someone is coming towards us here,' said Finn, 'and 'tis before him his business is, or else I am deceived.' They all stood looking at the Big Lad who was coming, but he took not a long time till he was in their very midst.

He saluted Finn frankly, energetically, fluently; and Finn saluted him with the equivalent of the same words. Then Finn asked of him whence did he come, or whither was he going, or what was he wanting. He said that he was the Son of the Lady of Green Insh, and that he came from that as far as this seeking a Master. Finn answered, 'I have need of a servant, and I do not care although I engage thee if we agree about the reward.' 'That would not be my advice to thee,' said Conan. 'Conan, thou hadst better keep quiet, and mind thine own business; and I will do my business,' said the Big Lad. Everyone present was wondering at the Big Lad's dress, for it consisted of skin coverings. Not less did they wonder at the appearance of his great strength of body. And they were somewhat afraid that he would disgrace them before he would part with them. Finn then asked of him what reward would he be asking to the end of a day and year? The Big Lad said that he asked nothing but that there should be no apartness of meat or of drink between them at the table within, or on the plain without, or in any place in which they should take food to the end of the day and year. 'Thou shalt get that,' said Finn; and they agreed.

Then they began to lift the deer with them. One would take with him one, and another would take with him two, till all had their burdens except the Big Lad. But they left many more deer than they took with them. Finn then told the Big Lad to take with him a burden. The Big Lad began to pull the longest and the finest part of the heather that he could see, till he had a great heap beside him. Then he began to make a rope of the heather, and to place a deer on every deer's length that he would twine till he had every deer that was left in one burden.

When the burden was ready he told the rest to lift it on his back. They came, and as many went about the burden as could surround it; but though as many and as many more of the Fein would have been assembled as were present on that day they could not put wind between it and the earth. When the Big Lad saw this he told them to stand out of his way. He then took hold of the rope and put a turn of its end about his fist, he bent his back, put a balk on his foot, and threw the burden over his shoulder. Every one of the Fein looked at his neighbour, but spake not a word.

When the Big Lad got the burden steady on his back he said, 'I am but a stranger in this place; let one of you therefore go before to direct me in the way.' Every one looked at his neighbour to see who would go. At last Conan answered that he would go if the rest would carry his deer home. Finn said that his deer would be carried home if he would take the lead. Conan threw the deer off him, sprang before the Big Lad, and told him to follow him.

Conan went away as fast as he could, and the Big Lad went away after him. There were two big nails on the two big toes of the Big Lad, and they went but a short distance when he left not a hair's-breadth of skin on the back of Conan between the top of his two shoulders and the back of his two feet with the two big nails which were on his feet. At last Conan began to lose his distance, for he was growing weak with loss of blood; and in a short time he was under the necessity of stopping and of sitting down where he was. When the Big Lad saw that Conan yielded he went past him, and stop he made not till he let his burden go at the dwelling of Finn.

Then he sprang in, and put on a fire. He cooked food for every man who was at the hunt, and set the food of each man apart, except his own food and that of Finn. The Fein came home at last; and when they went in they wondered greatly to see the food ready before them, but they made no remark.

After the supper was over the Fein sent for Finn, and Conan spoke and said: 'Did I not tell thee that we should get disgraced by the Lad whom thou didst engage? His match in strength is not in the Fein. Thou must put him out of our way until his time shall be out.'

'Well,' said Finn, 'I do not know what I can do with him unless I send him away to Lochlan to seek the four-sided cup, and he has there a day and a year's journey however well he may walk.' They were all quite pleased with this, and told Finn to send him off as soon as he could. Finn answered and said: 'Before a sun shall rise on a dwelling he will get his leave to travel on the journey.'

Without delay he sent for the Lad of the Skin Coverings, and said to him that he was sorry to ask him to go on this long journey, but that he hoped he would not refuse. The Big Lad asked him on what business was he sending him, or whither had he to go. Finn said that he got word from Lochlan that he would get the four-sided cup if he would send a man for it. 'I sent them word to come and meet us with it, and that we would go and meet them. I am desirous that thou wilt go to seek it tomorrow, and I know that they will meet thee coming with it.' 'Well, Finn,' said the Big Lad, 'thou knowest and art assured that they shall not meet me with it, for numerous are the heroes who have shed their blood on the field beneath the spears of Lochlan for the sake of the four-sided cup which they have had since four-and-twenty years, and which thou hast not yet got. How now dost thou think, Finn, that I can take it out [of their hands] unassisted? But since I promised to do what thou wouldst ask me, I will go seek it for thee.'

On the next morning, before a sun shone, the Big Lad was ready for the journey. Then he lifted his own skin coverings on him, and strode away; and the swift March wind which was before him he would overtake, and the swift March wind which was behind him would not keep [pace] with him. At that rate of travelling onwards he did not slacken the speed of his chase till he struck his palm against a [door] bar at the palace of the King of Lochlan that night.

The palace of the King of Lochlan was kept by seven guards. The Big Lad knocked [at the gate of] the first guard, and the first guard asked him whence was he, or whither was he going? He replied that he was a servant who had come from Finn, King of the Fein, on a message to the King of Lochlan. Word went to the King that such a man was at the door. The King asked if any man was with him. The Lad-in-waiting said that there was not. The King then gave orders to let him in. The [gate of the] first guard was opened for him, and he got in, and in like manner every [gate with a] guard until he got through the seven guards. He was taken into the place where the King was, and the King told him to sit down. The Big Lad sat, for he was tired after the journey which he had made. He gave a look through the room, and noticed as beautiful a cup as he ever saw standing on a table. He said to the King of Lochlan, 'That is a beautiful vessel which thou hast there.' The King said that it was that, and also a cup of virtues. The Big Lad asked what virtues did it possess. The King answered that there was no fill that he would order to be in it which would not be in it immediately. The Big Lad, being thirsty after the journey which he had made, thought that its full of water on the table would be a good thing. Then he rose up, took hold of the cup, and drank all that was in it. He next turned his face to the door; and if he asked for an opening in, he asked not for an opening out, for he leaped over the seven guards, having the cup with him.

Then he lifted his own skin coverings on him, and strode away on the path on which he came; and the swift March wind which was before him he would overtake, but the swift March wind which was behind him would not keep [pace] with him. At that rate of travelling onwards he did not slacken the speed of his chase till he struck his palm against a [door] bar at Finn's dwelling on that night.

He went in, and handed the cup to Finn. 'Thou wert not long away,' said Finn. 'Did I not tell thee before thou didst leave that they would meet thee coming with it?' The Big Lad answered: 'Thou knowest and art assured that they did not meet me coming with it. But I reached Lochlan, and I got the cup in the King's palace, and I made the journey forward and back again.'

'Silence, babbler!' said Conan. 'There are some in the Fein who can run on ben-side or on glenstrath as well as thou canst, and they could not do the journey in double the time in which thou sayest thou didst it. But come to cut a leap with me as far as the Green Lakelet at the foot of Ben Aidan, and I will know if thou hast made the journey.' 'O, Conan! I am more needful of food and a little wink of sleep than of going to cut leaps with thee.' 'If thou wilt not go, we will not believe that thou hast made the journey,' said Conan.

The Big Lad rose and went with him; and they reached the Green Lakelet. Conan asked the Big Lad to cut a leap across the Lakelet. 'It is thou that brought me here, and I am tired,' said the Big Lad; 'therefore cut the first leap thyself.' Conan took a race and cut a leap, but sank to the balls of his two hips in the leafy marsh on the other side of the Lakelet. The Big Lad cut his leap without any race, and went over Conan's head on the hard ground on the other side of the Lakelet. He then leaped it back back-foremost, and forward front-foremost, before Conan got his haunches out of the bog.

When Conan got his feet on the hard ground he said that the roots gave way under his feet, and that he sank! 'But come and race with me to the top of Ben Aidan, and I will know if thou hast made the journey.' 'Conan, I am more needful of a little wink of sleep than of going to race with thee to the top of Ben Aidan.' However, he went. At a stride or two the Big Lad went past Conan, and gave not another look after him till he was on the top of the Ben. He then stretched himself on a green hillock and slept.

He knew not how long he slept, but it was the panting of Conan climbing the Ben which wakened him. He sprang quickly to his feet, and said, 'Did I make the journey now, Conan?' 'Come, wrestle with me, and I will know if thou hast made the journey,' said Conan. They embraced each other. Conan told the Big Lad to put his turn. 'Put thou thy turn first, Conan, for it is thou who wanted to begin.' Conan tried to put his turn, but he did not move the Big Lad.

The Big Lad then bent over Conan, and with his weight threw him, and bound his three smalls with his leather garter.

The Big Lad now took it as an insult that the most contemptible man in the Fein was despising and bullying him; and he gave a vow that he would not return to Finn any more. He went away, and left Conan bound on the top of the Ben.

The night was coming, and Finn was wondering that the two men who went away were not returning. At last fear struck him that the Big Lad had killed Conan, and therefore he told his men that they must go seek them. Before the sun rose on the next morning he divided his men in companies, and sent a company to each corner of the Ben, and told them to travel on till they should all meet on the top of the Ben. About the evening of the day they met, and found Conan bound by his three smalls in one thong.

Finn told one of his men to go over, and unbind Conan. Oscar went, and took a long time trying to do that, but for every knot which he would untie seven other knots would go on the thong. At last he said to Finn, 'I cannot loose this thong!' Then Goll sprang over, thinking that he could do better. He began to untie the thong; but, as happened to Oscar, it beat him. If it was not tighter when he ceased, it was not a bit looser. At last he lifted up his head in wrath, and said, 'There is not a man in the Fein who can unbind Conan!'

Finn now got afraid that Conan would be dead before they could get him released. But he remembered his knowledge set of teeth; and having put his finger under it he discovered that there was not a man in the world who could unbind him but the Smith of the White Glen, or else the man who bound him.

He then sent away Goll and Oscar to tell the Smith what befell Conan. They reached the Smith, and told him the business on which they were. The Smith told them to gather together every four-footed beast which was between the back of Ben Aidan and the top of the White Glen, and send them past the door of his smithy. 'And,' said he, 'if I then come out in peace good is my peace, but if I come out in wrath evil is my wrath.'

Oscar and Goll then returned to Finn, and told him what the Smith said to them. Finn said that the hunt must be started. The hunt was started, and that was the Great Hunt of the White Glen. Since the first hunt was started never was there so great a number of four-footed beasts assembled as were [together] on that day. Then they sent them past the door of the smithy. The Smith came out and asked what was yonder? They answered, all the four-footed beasts between the top of Ben Aidan and the head of the White Glen as he wanted. The Smith said, 'You have done well enough, but turn back every one of those creatures to the place from which you have taken them, and I will then go to unbind Conan.' They did that, and the Smith went to the top of Ben Aidan, and released Conan.

When Conan got released he was so ashamed on account of what befell him that he drew away down the Ben as fast as he could, and that he cast not a look behind him till he went out to the neck in the sea. Out of that, he would not come for Finn or for a man in the Fein. But the tide was rising at the time, and when the water began to enter his mouth he thought that it was better for him to go ashore, and return home after the rest.

On a certain evening after that, when Finn and his men were coming home from the hunting-ben they beheld a Lad coming to meet them. He took his way where Finn was, and said to him that he was sent from the Queen of Roy to Finn, King of the Fein, and that he was laying on him as crosses, and as spells, and as seven fairy fetters of travelling and straying, that he would neither stop nor take rest until he would reach the Queen of Roy's place. Having said this he turned towards them the back of his head, and departed; and they had not a second look of him.

The Fein looked at each other, for they thought that some evil was to happen to Finn, because no man was asked to go but himself. They said to him that they were sorry because he was going alone, and because they knew not when he would come, or where they would go to seek him. But Finn said to them that they were not to be anxious about his coming to the end of a day and year.

Out of that standing he departed with his arms on him. He travelled onward far long and full long over bens, and glens, and heights, and a stop went not on his foot till he came in sight of Green Insh. There he beheld a man going to lift a burden of rushes on his back. When he saw the man throwing the burden over his shoulder he thought that he was the Lad of the Skin Coverings. He began to approach him under cover [make earth-hiding on him] till he got near him. Then he showed himself, and when the man who was there looked at him in the face he knew that he was the Lad of the Skin Coverings. He sprang with a hasty step where he was, seized him in his two arms, and said, 'Darling of all men in the world! is it thou?' The Big Lad answered and said, 'If I were thy darling of all the men in the world, the most insignificant man whom thou hadst in the Fein would not have been bullying me, and making me the subject of mocking witticisms.' 'Well,' said Finn, 'I was sorry enough, but I could not help it. I was afraid that the men would rise up against me, and become unruly; I therefore left Conan in his opinion. But I knew thou didst make the journey, and we will be as good friends to each other as we ever were. Wilt thou go with me once more on this little journey?' 'Well,' said the Big Lad, 'I do not know. Look down in yonder hollow under us, and thou shalt see my mother on her knees cutting rushes, and a turn of her right breast over her left shoulder. If thou shalt get a hold of the end of the breast do not let it go till thou shalt get thy first request from her.'

Finn went away a while on his hands and feet, and another while dragging himself [along] on his belly, till he got within a distance to take a spring. Then he gave a spring, and got a hold of the end of the breast. The Lady of Green Insh cried who was there. He replied that Finn, King of the Fein, was there, asking his first boon of her. She said what boon would he ask that he would not get. He said, 'Let thy son go with me once more on this little journey.' The Lady said, 'If I had known that it was that which thou wouldst ask, thou wouldst not have got it though thou shouldst take the breast from my chest, but since I promised it thou shalt get it. But I will have one promise from thee before thou goest, and that is that thou shalt take home to me himself and all that shall fall with him.' 'I hope that the matter will not end in that way, and that he will return home whole.' 'If he will, good shall not befall thee, Finn. However, be off on your journey.'

Then Finn and the Big Lad went away on their journey, ascending hills and descending hollows, travelling over bens and glens and knolls till the gloaming of night was coming on them. They were growing weary, and were wishing to reach some place where they would get permission to take rest. They were but a short time travelling after that, when they beheld an exceedingly fine place before them, with fine large houses built on large green fields. Finn said to the Big Lad, 'Let us take courage, for we are not far from houses.' Shortly after that they reached the place.

Finn saw a man coming to meet them, and he knew that he was the very Lad who came with the message to him.

He asked of him what need had he of him now? The Lad answered and said that there were two big houses opposite him, one with doorposts of gold and doors of gold, and the other with doorposts of silver and doors of silver, that he was to take his choice of them to stay in, and that he would see when he would enter what he had to do there. The Lad having said this turned away from them, and left them where they were standing.

Finn looked in the face of the Big Lad, and said to him, 'Which one of these houses shall we take to stay in?' The Big Lad said, 'We will have the more honourable one; we will take the one with the doors of gold.'

They took their way over to the door. The Big Lad laid hold of the bar, and opened the door. Then they went in. When they looked there was a great sight before them, but the Big Lad thought nothing of it. There were eighteen score and eight Avasks standing on the floor. When they got Finn and the Big Lad inside the door they sprang towards it, and shut it; and put on it eighteen score and eight bars. The Big Lad went and put on it one great bar, and so firmly did he put the bar on that every bar they put on fell off. Then the Avasks made eighteen score and eight laughs; but the Big Lad made one great guffaw of a laugh and deafened all that they made. Then the Avasks said, 'What is the cause of thy laugh, little man?' The Big Lad said, 'What is the cause of your own laughter, big men all?' They said, 'The cause of our laughter is that it is a pretty, clustering, yellow head of hair which thou hast on thee to be used as a football out on yonder strand tomorrow.' 'Well,' said the Big Lad, 'the cause of my laugh is that I will seize the man of you with the biggest head and smallest legs, and that I will brain all the rest of you with him.' He then saw a man with a big head; and having laid hold of him by the smalls of his two feet he began braining them in one end of the band and stopped not till he went out at the other end. When he was done he had only as much of the feet as he held in his fists.

He and Finn put the dead bodies out, and made three heaps of them at the door. They shut the door then, and made food ready, for there was abundance of it in the house.

After they had taken the food the Big Lad asked of Finn, 'Whether wilt thou sleep or watch the door?' Finn answered, 'Sleep thou, and I will watch the door.' And so they did. But before the Big Lad slept Finn asked of him, 'With what shall I waken thee if distress shall come upon me at the door?' 'Strike the pillar [or block] of stone, which is behind the hearth, on me in the breast-bone, or else take with thy dirk the breadth of thy thumb from the top of my head.' 'Quite right,' said Finn, 'sleep on.'

Finn was watching the door, but for a long time he was feeling nothing coming. At break of dawn he noticed the conversation of ten hundred coming to the door. He lifted the block of stone, and struck the Big Lad with it in the chest. The Big Lad sprang quickly to his feet, and asked Finn what he felt. 'The conversation of ten hundred is at the door,' said Finn. 'That is right yet,' said the Big Lad, 'let me out.'

The Big Lad went out to meet them. He began in one end of them, attacked them violently below and above them, and left none of them alive to tell the evil tale, but one man with one eye, one ear, one hand, and one foot, and he let him go. Then he and Finn collected the dead bodies, and put them in the three heaps with the rest. They afterwards went in, and waited till the next night came.

After supper the Big Lad asked of Finn, 'Whether wilt thou sleep or watch tonight?' Finn said, 'Sleep thou, and I will watch.' The Big Lad went to sleep, and Finn was watching the door. A short time before sunrise, Finn heard the conversation of two thousand coming, or the Son of the King of Light alone. He sprang up, and with his dirk took the breadth of the face of his thumb from the top of the Big Lad's head. Instantly the Big Lad sprang to his feet, and asked of Finn what did he feel. Finn answered, 'The conversation of two thousand, or the Son of the King of Light alone is at the door.' 'Oh, then, I dare say that thou must be as good as thy promise to my mother,' said the Big Lad, 'but let thou me out.' Finn opened the door, the Big Lad went out, and it was the Son of the King of Light who was before him.

Then the two champions embraced each other, and wrestled from sunrise to sunset, but the one threw not the other, and the one spake not to the other during the whole time. They let each other go, and each one of them went his own way. Early next morning, before sunrise, the Big Lad went out, and his companion met him. They wrestled from sunrise to sunset, but the one threw not the other, and the one spake not to the other. They let each other go, and each one of them went his own way. The third day the heroes met, and embraced each other. They fought all day long till twilight, and the two fell side by side cold and dead on the ground.

Finn was dreadfully sorry for the Big Lad. But he remembered his promise to the Lad's mother, and said to himself that it must be fulfilled. He took out the silk covering which was over them where they slept, wrapped it about the two bodies, and took them with him on his back. He drew away with a hard step over bens and glens and hillocks, ascending hills and descending hollows, and stop or rest he made not till he reached the house of Green Insh.

The mother of the Big Lad met him at the door, and said to him, 'Hast thou come?' Finn answered that he had come, but not as he would wish. She said to him, 'Didst thou do as I told thee?' Finn said, 'Yes, but I am sorry indeed that I had to do it.' She said, 'Everything is right. Come in.' Finn went in, and laid the burden on the floor. He unloosed the covering, and the two lads were locked in each other's arms as they fell.

When the Lady of Green Insh saw the two lads she smiled and said, 'Finn, my darling, well is it for me that thou didst go on this journey.' She then went over into a closet, and having lifted a flag which was on the floor, took out a little vessel of balsam which she had there. She then placed the two lads mouth to mouth, face to face, knee to knee, thumb to thumb, and rubbed the balsam to the soles of their feet, to the crowns of their heads, and to all parts of their skins which touched each other. The two lads stood up on the floor kissing one another.

'Now, Finn,' said she, 'there thou hast my two sons. This one was stolen from me in his infancy, and I was without him till now. But since thou hast done as I told thee, thou art welcome to stay here as long as thou desirest.'

They were so merry in the house of Green Insh that the time went past unknown to them. On a certain night the Lady of Green Insh said to Finn, 'Tomorrow there will be a day and a year since thou didst leave the Fein, and they have given up hope of thee. The man of them who is not whetting his sword is pointing his spear tonight for the purpose of going away to seek thee. Make ready to depart tomorrow, and I will let my son go with thee. For if thou shalt arrive alone they will give thee such a tumultuous welcome that they will smother and kill thee. But when you will arrive my son will enter before thee, and say to them, if they will promise him that they will rise up one after another to give thee a quiet, sensible welcome, that he will bring their earthly king home whole and sound to them.'

Finn agreed to this with all his heart, and he and the Big Lad went away on their journey homewards on the morning of the next day. They had a long distance to go, but they took not long accomplishing it.

When they reached Finn's Hall the Big Lad went in first, and what his mother said proved true. Every man was getting ready his sword and spear. The Big Lad asked of them what were they doing. They told him that. Then the Big Lad said to them what his mother told him to say. They willingly consented to do that. He then called on Finn to come in. Finn came, and one rose after another as they promised. They got their earthly king back once more. The Big Lad returned home, and if he has not died since he is alive still.

How Finn was in the House of
Blar-buie [Yellow-field]
without the Power of Rising Up or of Lying Down

A day Finn and his men were in the hunting-hill they had done a great deal of travelling before they fell in with the deer, but before the close of the day had arrived they killed a good number of them. They then sat down to rest themselves, and consult each other to see what direction they should take next day.

While they were conversing, Finn gave a look down into the glen which was beneath them, and saw the appearance of a strong hero making straight towards them. He said, 'The appearance of a stranger is coming towards us here.' Conan replied, 'If he is coming without business, he will not leave without business.' But before they had much more conversation about him the young hero was standing before them.

He gave Finn the salutation of the day, and Finn saluted him courteously.

Finn then asked of him whence he came, or what business had he yonder. He said, 'I am a servant who has travelled far long and full long seeking a master, and I will not go further until you refuse me.' 'Well,' said Finn, 'I want a servant, and if we agree about the reward I do not care though I engage thee.' 'That would not be my advice to thee,' said Conan. 'I thought thou didst get enough of those wandering lads already.' 'Silence, rascal!' said the Lad; 'often has thy loquacity put thy head in trouble, and I am deceived if thou shalt not experience some trouble on account of the talk of this day.' 'Never mind,' said Finn, 'for thy appearance will answer for thee, at any rate. What is thy reward to the end of a day and year?' 'That you and your men will go on invitation with me to a feast and night's entertainment when my time will be out,' said the Lad. When Finn heard that his men were to go with him he took courage that no evil thing could befall them being together; and therefore he said to the Lad that he would get his reward.

When the time had passed, Finn and his men were in a house of conference considering which of them should go after the Lad, for he had a very swift appearance. Finn said, 'We will let Caoilte [Slender] after him, and I do not believe but that he will keep sight of him. Cuchulin will go after Caoilte, and we will follow them.' And so they did.

The Big Lad set off bare-headed, bare-footed, without strength for battle or for sane action, from gap to height, and from height to glen, and through glen to strath. Caoilte went after him, and when the Big Lad would be going out of sight on the first gap Caoilte would be coming in sight on the next ridge. Cuchulin was in the same distance to Caoilte, and all the men to Cuchulin. They kept in that order till they reached Blar-buie [or Yellow-field].

The Big Lad then stood till the last man of the Fein came on. Then he took his way over to a large, fine house, which stood opposite him. He opened the door of the house, and invited them to go in and be seated.

Finn went in first, and his men followed him. All of them got seats against the walls except Conan. He was behind, and because all the seats were full before he arrived he had no choice but to drop down and stretch himself on the hearth-stone. They were so tired after the journey which they had made that they were at first contented with the seats alone. But when they had a rest they began to grow impatient, because the feast was not coming. Finn at last told one of his men to go out and try if he could see any person coming with food to them. One or two attempted to rise from their seats, but could not. Their haunches stuck to the seats, the soles of their feet to the floor, and their backs to the walls. Each one of them then looked at his neighbour. Conan cried from the hearth-stone to which his back and hair were clinging, 'Did I not tell thee in good time what would happen to thee with thy wandering lads?' Finn spake not a word, because he was in great anxiety about the death-strait in which they were. But he remembered his knowledge set of teeth, and having put his finger under it, discovered that there was nothing that would release them from the place in which they were but the blood of the three sons of the King of Insh Tilly filtered through silver rings into cups of gold.

He did not know who would get the blood for him, but he remembered that Lohary, Son of the King of Hunts, and Oscar were that day absent from the company. He had the Wooden Crier [or whistle], which he never blew except when he happened to be in some death-strait or other. But when he would play on it, its sound would pass through the seven borders of the world, and to the extremity of the Uttermost World. And he knew that when Lohary and Oscar would hear the sound they would come from any quarter in which they would be.

He blew the Wooden Crier three times, and before the sun rose next day Oscar was crying outside the wall, 'Art thou here, Finn?' 'Who is there?' said Finn, inside the house. 'Thou art changed indeed when thou wouldst not know my voice while there is only the breadth of a house wall between us. I, Oscar, am here, and Lohary is with me. What have we now to do?'

Finn told them the situation and peril in which they were, and that nothing could release them from it but the blood of the three Sons of the King of Insh Tilly filtered through rings of silver into cups of gold. 'Where shall we watch for the purpose of finding them?' said Oscar. Finn said, 'Thou shalt watch well the ford-mouth of the river over yonder, at the going down of the sun. But it is yet early in the day. See if you can find food for us, for we are hungry. But, Oscar, remember to take thy Gaper [dart] with thee.'

Oscar and Lohary set their faces in the direction of the Big House which was over against them. When they arrived at the house the people residing there were making ready the dinner. Lohary said to Oscar, 'Take thou the lead.' Oscar took the lead, and was keeping his eye in every corner to see what he might behold. When he reached the cooking-place he looked in, and saw the appearance of a fierce hero lifting a quarter of a deer out of a cauldron. He said to Lohary, 'Follow me, and take the food with thee, and I will face the man.' He went in, but no man was now to be seen. By a look he gave he saw a large buzzard with outspread wings ready to pounce down on his head. He drew his Gaper, and darted it at the buzzard. He broke its wing off, and the buzzard itself fell on the floor, and he saw not another sight of it. He and Lohary now made the house their own, and took with them every bit of food of which they got hold.

They reached the house where Finn and his men were. They made a hole on the wall of the house, and threw in piece after piece for every man till all the men who were there got something, but Conan. He lay on his back on the hearth-stone, having his hands and feet together with his back bound to the flag-stone, so that they could not give him a bit except what they let down through the roof of the house, and which he then seized with his mouth. In this way he got a morsel or two.

Oscar then asked of Finn what had they to watch at the ford-mouth of the river besides the three Sons of the King of Insh Tilly. 'A great host will accompany them,' said Finn. 'And how shall we know the three Sons of the King of Insh Tilly from any other three men of the host?' 'They will walk apart from the host on the right hand, and have on them green apparel.' 'We will know them now,' said Oscar.

Then Oscar and Lohary went away to find the rings and cups for filtering and holding the blood. After they had found them they went to watch at the ford-mouth. At the going down of the sun they heard a loud sound coming. Oscar looked in the direction whence he heard the sound, and saw a great host coming in sight. He now called on Lohary to be ready. Lohary said, 'We will go ashore out of the water, and meet them on dry land.' And so they did.

When the great host came near they cried, 'Who are the two tall, uncomely Lubbers who are standing there at mouth of ford and beginning of night? Whoever they are it is time for them to be getting afraid.' Oscar cried, 'A third of your fear be on yourselves, and a small third of it be on us.' 'You will then wait to your hurt,' said the great host. Then they went to meet each other, but Oscar and Lohary assailed them violently under them and over them till they left not a man of them alive to tell the tale.

They turned back. Next morning they told Finn what befell them, but that they saw not the King's Sons. 'Where shall we watch next night?' said Oscar. 'Watch well the ford-mouth of the river tonight yet,' said Finn. 'But meantime get us food, for we are hungry. And remember to take with thee thy three-edged blade and thy shield today.'

The two heroes reached the Big House. Oscar was more guarded this day, because he knew not what might meet him. When he got a look of the Cooking-house he saw inside a dreadfully big man, having four hands, lifting the flesh out of the cauldron. He went in, but no man was now to be seen. He looked about the place, and saw a large eagle going to throw at him an egg which she held in her talon. He lifted his shield between him and the egg, but the blow sent him on one knee beside the cauldron. He saw that he could not be ready with his blade before the eagle would be at him; he therefore lifted the cauldron of soup which was on the floor, and poured it on her head. She gave a terrible shriek and went through the wall, and he had not a second look of her.

Then he and Lohary went away with the food, and succeeded in giving a share to every man as on the day before. But poor Conan's share was smaller.

When the time came they went away to the ford-mouth, and advanced further on the other side of the river than they went on the previous night. Shortly after they arrived they saw a very large host coming towards them. When they came near they cried, 'Who were the two tall, uncomely Lubbers who were standing yonder above the ford-mouth of the river in the evening? Whoever they are, it is time for them to be getting afraid.' 'Two thirds of your fear be on yourselves, and a little third of it be on us,' said Oscar. Then they assailed them on each side until they went out on the opposite side, and left not a man of them alive to tell the tale.

They turned back and told Finn that the King's children did not come that night yet. Finn told them that they were to get them food that day again. 'But, Oscar, remember thy spear and shield, and if thy spear will taste the blood of the Winged Dragon of Sheil, the King of Insh Tilly shall be without a son tonight.'

They went away, and turned their faces towards the Big House. Oscar took the lead, as he was accustomed to do. He was keeping his eye pretty sharply before him to see who would be in the Cooking-house this day. When he got a look of it he beheld a handsome, strong man with two heads and four hands lifting the flesh out of the cauldron. He said to himself that it was time for him to be ready. When he entered no man was to be seen; but a large Winged Dragon, having two serpent heads on her, was standing on the floor. Oscar whispered to Lohary, 'Make thou for the food, and I will make for the Dragon.' He then lifted his shield and drew his spear, and with one thrust he sent the spear through one head, and a bit of it through the other head of the Dragon. The Dragon fought terribly, but she was at last growing weak with the loss of blood. Then Oscar drew back the spear for the purpose of thrusting it again into the monster, but as soon as the spear came out of her flesh she went out of his sight, and he had not the next sight of her.

They got the food, and went away with it to their friends. When they arrived, Finn asked Oscar, 'Did thy spear taste blood?' 'A cubit length and hand-breadth of it drank greedily,' said Oscar. Then they managed to give a share of the food to every man as on the previous days. But Conan's share was still smaller.

As soon as the greying of the evening came, Finn said to Oscar, 'Let thy rings and cups be with thee tonight.'

Then the two heroes went away to the ford-mouth of the river. This evening they advanced farther on the other side of the river than they had yet gone. They were but a short time waiting when they beheld an exceedingly great host coming towards them, and on the right hand the three Sons of the King of Insh Tilly wearing green garments. Oscar asked Lohary, 'Whether wilt thou face the three Sons of the King of Insh Tilly or the great host?' Lohary said, 'I will face the three Sons of the King of Insh Tilly, and thou shalt face the great host.' When they approached each other the great host cried, 'Who were the two tall, uncomely Lubbers who were standing above the ford-mouth of the river in the evening? Whoever they are it is time for them to flee tonight.' 'Three thirds of your fear be on yourselves, and none at all of it on us,' said Oscar.

Then Oscar advanced to meet the great host, and Lohary faced the three Sons of the King. There was a hard fight between Oscar and the host; but he prevailed over them at last, and left not a man of them alive. Then he went in haste where Lohary was. Lohary had the three Sons of the King on their two knees, and they had Lohary on one knee. When Oscar saw that Lohary had the upper hand, it was not on helping him he directed his attention, but on the blood, for it was pouring out rapidly on the meadow. He began to filter it through the silver rings into the cups of gold, but before all the cups were full the bodies grew so stiff that out of them more would not flow.

The two heroes went away with what they had to the house in which Finn and his men were. When they reached it, Oscar cried that they had come, having the blood with them. 'Well,' said Finn, 'rub it to every bit of you which may touch the house, from the top of your heads to the soles of your feet.' They did that, and went in. They began to release the men by rubbing the blood to every bit of them which stuck to the seats, or the wall, or the floor. In that manner they released every man in the house but Conan. For him they left only the stain which remained on the cups, but that same sufficed to release every bit of him but the back of his head. The hair and skin stuck to the hearth-stone, and they had no alternative but to leave him bound as he was.

Finn and his men then went home, very happy that they escaped the great peril in which they were. They had not gone very far when they looked behind them, and saw Conan coming. They at once stood where they were until he came forward. There he was without a fibre of hair, or a strip of skin between the top of his head and the back of his neck. For when he perceived that the rest had gone away and left him behind, he gave his head a great pull and left his skin and hair bound to the hearth-stone. From that day forth people called him 'Bald Conan without hair'.

Finn and his men reached their home, and he gave word and oath that he would never again engage wandering lads.

OISEAN AFTER THE FEEN

Source: J. F. Campbell, *Popular Tales of the West Highlands*
Narrator: Unknown (Barra); collected by Hector MacLean in August 1859
Type: J. F. Campbell quotes a further five versions of this postscript to the Fenian
story; a more recent recording by David Clement from the narration of
Alasdair Stewart is printed in *Tocher* 29

Oisean was an old man after the [time of the] Feen, and he [was] dwelling in the house of his daughter. He was blind, deaf, and limping, and there were nine oaken skewers in his belly, and he ate the tribute that Padraig had over Eirinn. They were then writing the old histories that he was telling them.

They killed a right big stag; they stripped the shank, and brought him the bone. 'Didst thou ever see a shank that was thicker than that in the Feen!' 'I saw a bone of the blackbird's chick in which it would go round about.' 'In that there are but lies.' When he heard this, he caught hold of the books with rage, and he set them in the fire. His daughter took them out and quenched them, and she kept them. Oisean asked, with wailing, that the worst lad and dog in the Feen should lay weight on his chest. He felt a weight on his chest. 'What's this?' 'I, MacRuaghadh [son of the red, or auburn one].' 'What is that weight which I feel at my feet?' 'There is MacBuidheig [son of the little yellow].'

They stayed as they were till the day came. They arose. He asked the lad to take him to such a glen. The lad reached the glen with him. He took out a whistle from his pocket, and he played it. 'Seest thou anything going past on yonder mountain?' 'I see deer on it.' 'What sort dost thou see on it?' 'I see some slender and grey on it.' 'Those are the seed of the Lon Luath, swift elk; let them pass. What kind seest thou now?' 'I see some gaunt and grizzled.' 'Those are the seed of Dearg dasdanach, the red Fierce; let them pass. What kind seest thou now?' 'I see some heavy and sleek.' 'Let the dog at them, Vic Vuiaig!' MacBuidheig went. 'Is he dragging down plenty?' 'He is.' 'Now, when thou seest that he has a dozen thou shalt check him.'

When he thought he had them, he played the whistle, and he checked the dog. 'Now if the pup is sated with chase, he will come quietly, gently; if not, he will come with his gape open.' He was coming with his gape open, and his tongue out of his mouth. 'Bad is the thing which thou hast done to check the pup unsated with chase. When he comes, catch my hand, and try to put it in his gape, or he will have us.' He put the hand of Oisean in his gape, and he shook his throat out. 'Come, gather the stags to that knoll of rushes.' He went, and that is done; and it was nine stags that were there, and that was but enough for Oisean alone; the lad's share was lost. 'Put my two hands about the rushy knoll that is here.' He did that, and the great cauldron that the Feen used to have was in it. 'Now, make ready, and put the stags in the cauldron, and set fire under it.' The lad did that. When they were here ready to take it, Oisean said to him, 'Touch thou them not till I take my fill first.' Oisean began upon them, and as he ate each one, he took one of the skewers out of his belly. When Oisean had six eaten, the lad had three taken from him. 'Hast thou done this to me?' said Oisean. 'I did it,' said he; 'I would need a few when thou thyself hadst so many of them.' 'Try if thou wilt take me to such a rock.' He went down there, and he brought out the chick of a blackbird out of the rock. 'Let us come to be going home.' The lad caught him under the arm, and they went away.

When he thought that they were nearing the house, he said, 'Are we very near the house?' 'We are,' said the lad. 'Would the shout of a man reach the house where we are just now?' 'It would reach it.' 'Set my front straight on the house.' The lad did thus. When he was coming on the house, he caught the lad, and he put his hand in his throat, and he killed him. 'Now,' said he, 'neither thou nor another will tell tales of me.' He went home with his hands on the wall, and he left the blackbird's chick within. They were asking him where he had been since the day came; he said he had been where he had often passed pleasant happy days. 'How didst thou go there when thou art blind?' 'I

got a chance to go there this day at all events. There is a little
pet yonder that I brought home, and bring it in.' They went out
to look, and if they went, there did not go out so many as could
bring it home. He himself arose, and he brought it in. He asked
for a knife. He caught the shank, he stripped it, and then took
the flesh off it. He broke the two ends of the bone. 'Get now the
shank of the dun deer that you said I never saw the like of in
the Feen.' They got this for him, and he threw it out through the
marrow hole. Now he was made truthful. They began to ask
more tales from him, but it beat them ever to make him begin at
them any more.

3: HISTORICAL TRADITIONS

THE PECHS

Source: Robert Chambers, *Popular Rhymes of Scotland*
Narrator: 'Made up from snatches heard from different mouths'
Type: ML5010 'The Visit to the Old Troll', 'The Handshake'; (Irish types) 2412e
'Danish Heather Beer'

Long ago there were people in this country called the Pechs; short wee men they were, wi' red hair, and long arms, and feet sae braid, that when it rained they could turn them up owre their heads, and then they served for umbrellas. The Pechs were great builders; they built a' the auld castles in the kintry; and do ye ken the way they built them? – I'll tell ye. They stood all in a row from the quarry to the place where they were building, and ilk ane handed forward the stanes to his neebor, till the hale was biggit. The Pechs were also a great people for ale, which they brewed frae heather; sae, ye ken, it bood to be an extraornar cheap kind of drink; for heather, I'se warrant, was as plenty then as it is now. This art o' theirs was muckle sought after by the other folk that lived in the kintry; but they never would let out the secret, but handed it down frae father to son among themselves, wi' strict injunctions frae ane to another never to let onybody ken about it.

At last the Pechs had great wars, and mony o' them were killed, and indeed they soon came to be a mere handfu' o' people, and were like to perish aff the face o' the earth. Still they held fast by their secret of the heather yill, determined that their enemies should never wring it frae them. Weel, it came at last to a great battle between them and the Scots, in which they clean lost the day, and were killed a' to tway, a father and a son. And sae the King o' the Scots had these men brought before him, that he might try to frighten them into telling him the secret. He plainly told them that, if they would not disclose it peaceably, he must torture them till they should confess, and therefore it would be better for them to yield in time. 'Weel,' says the auld man to the king, 'I see it is of no use to resist. But there is ae condition ye maun agree to before ye learn the secret.' 'And what is that?' said the king. 'Will ye promise to fulfil it, if it be na onything against your ain interests?' said the man. 'Yes,' said the king, 'I will and do promise so.' Then said the Pech: 'You must know that I wish for my son's death, though I dinna like to take his life myself.

> My son ye maun kill,
> Before I will you tell
> How we brew the yill
> Frae the heather bell!'

The king was dootless greatly astonished at sic a request; but, as he had promised, he caused the lad to be immediately put to death. When the auld man saw his son was dead, he started up wi' a great stend, and cried: 'Now, do wi' me as you like. My son ye might have forced, for he was but a weak youth; but me you never can force.

> And though you may me kill,
> I will not you tell
> How we brew the yill
> Frae the heather bell!'

The king was now mair astonished than before, but it was at his being sae far outwitted by a mere wild man. Hooever, he saw it was needless to kill the Pech, and that his greatest punishment might now be his being allowed to live. So he was taken away as a prisoner, and he lived for mony a year after that, till he became a very, very auld man, baith bedrid and blind. Maist folk had forgotten there was sic a man in life; but ae night, some young men being in the house where he was, and making great boasts about their feats o' strength, he leaned owre the bed and said he would like to feel ane o' their wrists, that he might compare it wi' the arms of men wha had lived in former times. And they, for sport, held out a thick gaud o' ern to him to feel. He just snappit it in tway wi' his fingers as ye wad do a pipe stapple. 'It's a bit gey gristle,' he said; 'but naething to the shackle-banes o' my days.' That was the last o' the Pechs.

TWO SAINTS

Source: R. de B. Trotter, *Galloway Gossip*
Narrator: Unknown

JOHN THE BAPTIST

Ye maybe didna ken yt John the Baptist wus a residenter in the Glenkens, but they say it wus a fact. A canna say A believe't mysel, for the Bible gies a different accoont o' him.

It seems he wus a great man thereawa aboot the time o' the Persecution, an took the Bluidy Claverse by the neck an the heels, an half-roastit him on the het girdle yt he hail-roastit the Covenanter on.

He wus mairry't on yin o' the Kenmure leddies, an whun Archbishop Sharp got him beheidit for roastin Claverse, they bury't him in the Kenmure aisle amang the ither lords.

They didna bury him joost than, for the Kenmur lords wus a' stuff't, an they stuff't him too, an he wus set up on his en' in his coffin alang the wa' wi the lave o' them.

The coffins had a' a pen o' gless in the lids tae let ye see their faces, an the folk use't tae ken St John by the goold collar they put roon his neck tae hide whaur his heid had been haggit aff an sew't on again.

They wur a' bury't whun the aul' kirk wus dung doon, an the new yin biggit, an St John wus bury't alang wi them.

They hae some wunnerfu accoonts o' his adventurs aboot the Clachan, but they'r joost nonsense, sae A'll no mention them.

ST JOHNSTOUN

Queer stories is gaun in Gallawa aboot some o' the Saunts. A tell't ye afore aboot John the Baptist bein a residenter in the clachan o' Da'ry, but A forgot tae tell ye yt accordin tae the traditions, it wus him yt biggit the aul' kirk wi his ain hans; an there's a bit o't stannin yet, whut they ca' the Kenmure Aisle.

He brung the stanes on horses' backs frae the Airds Heugh near Balcary; an the lime frae Cocklehaen on the Water o' Orr.

There's a bit moss doon there yt they coost the peats oot o', an they made a bed o' gerse an whuns an dry sticks, wi sma peats on the tap o't, an than a thick layer o' cockle-shells, than peats again, than shells, an than peats again till they had as muckle as they wantit; than they happit the hailwor ower wi truffs an set lunt tae't on a kin o' wunny day, an whun it brunt oot they cool't it, an riddle't the brunt shells frae amang the asse, an sent it awa in pokes. They slocken't it whaur they wur gaun tae big; an it made awfu strong lime.

St John learnt the natives tae big hooses for theirsels, an he put up maist o' the auler hooses, an that's hoo they ca't it St John's Clachan.

LEGENDS OF ST COIVIN

Source: Lord Archibald Campbell, *Records of Argyll*
Narrator: Unknown (Kintyre)

St Coivin, to whom the church of Kilkerran is dedicated, is said to have allowed men who were not pleased with their wives to separate from them and make a second choice once a year in the following manner. At midnight a number of men and women were blindfolded, and started on a race promiscuously three times round the church, and at the moment they had finished, the Saint cried 'Seize!' whereupon every man laid hold of a woman, who became his wife for a year, after which he could again try his lot.

The following story is related of St Coivin.

A fair lady called Cathleen, descended of an illustrious race, and possessed of rich demesnes, having heard of the fame of St Coivin, who was at the time a youth, went to hear him preach, and fell in love with him. Tradition says, it was his intention to have built an abbey in a valley, but that the visits of Cathleen induced him to remove to a retreat where he might be freed from her interruptions, and he decided on Glendaloch; but just when he had established himself there, and supposed himself at rest for the remainder of his mortal career, the beautiful maid renewed her visits. Determined to avoid the temptations of her beauty and fidelity, and to spare her tender feelings, the Saint withdrew to the cave over the lake. Day after day Cathleen visited the wonted haunts of her beloved St Coivin, but he was nowhere to be found. One morning, however, as the disconsolate fair maid was walking along a path, St Coivin's favourite dog met her, fawned upon her, and turning, swiftly led the way to his master's abode. Here, then, follows the most uncharitable part of St Coivin's conduct; for awakening and seeing a lady leaning over him, although there was heaven in her eye, he hurled her from the rock. The next morning, says one traditionary historian, the unfortunate maid, whose unceasing affection seems to have merited a better fate, was seen for a moment on the margin of the lake wringing her flowing locks, but was never heard of more.

THE KING OF FINGALLS

Source: Lord Archibald Campbell, *Records of Argyll*
Narrator: Duncan Henderson, farmer, Kilmeny, Islay; collected by
Hector MacLean on 15 November 1883. Mr Henderson, a native of Southend,
Kintyre, was then aged seventy-two

Note: King of Fingalls = Righ Fionnghall, the King of the Norwegians,
or fair foreigners, whose descendants the Islesmen claimed to be

The King of Fingalls was a hard-hearted, bloody, vindictive man, and very oppressive on his tenantry. He was keen to destroy men. One day he left Sandell, the place where he resided, for the purpose of killing some persons whom he had fixed upon for destruction. Whenever he took a sword out of its sheath, he never liked to put it back without shedding blood. There was one man of whom he could not get the upper hand; and this was MacNeill, who was married to one of his sisters. For revenge he sent MacNeill to a moorland township called Gleann-reithe, where he could have no proper feeding either for himself or for his cattle; and he had to travel two miles before he could get to a road. MacNeill went to work in the harvest-time, and covered over the bushes of brushwood with corn, and thatched them, so as to appear like corn-stacks. When MacDonald had come to the place, he said to MacNeill, 'What a fine corn-yard you have! This is the best place I have yet visited. I must send you back to Killoran again.'

When MacNeill had left Killoran, MacDonald took from him all his horses in order to straiten him as much as possible. He thought now that MacNeill, being without horses, could not get on but ill at Killoran. MacNeill knew the day that the King of Fingalls had fixed upon to come to visit him at Killoran. So he gathered a great number of men, supplied with spades, and he sent a band of them to opposite sides of the field to dig it, as he had been deprived of his horses. They were to dig from the

233

opposite sides of the field until they should meet one another; and such a sight of spades was never seen in the place before. MacDonald asked for what purpose there was such a gathering of men with spades, and it was told him that it was MacNeill's ploughing team.

'Really! really!' exclaimed the King of Fingalls; 'there are as many men there as could dig the whole earth. The horses must be sent back to him again.'

MacNeill got back his horses; and whatever plan MacDonald tried, he could not be up with MacNeill. He now resolved to kill MacNeill. He went at night to MacNeill's house, intending to destroy him. He cried at the door, 'Rise, MacNeill of the porridge, that I might let your porridge out of you.'

'Wait a little! wait a little, MacDonald! You shall get in!' rejoined MacNeill.

MacNeill and his three sons got up. They put on their kilts only without their coats, and armed themselves with their swords. They put a large fire on. MacNeill opened the door and said to the King of Fingalls, 'Well, MacDonald, come in now!'

'Oh no!' replied MacDonald; 'you have an inhospitable appearance.'

'Come you in and you shall feel that!' continued MacNeill.

MacDonald would not go in; but, being mortified and enraged that he had not succeeded in killing MacNeill, he went to Capergan, which is within three miles of Dunaverty, where another sister of his lived, and was married. He went in through the night, and cut off the head of her husband in bed.

There was a wedding in the low part of the country. The daughter of Supar, of Ballymean, was the bride; and the King of Fingalls wished to assert his rights. There was a strong company of gentlemen at the wedding; and they considered it would be an insult to them were they to allow the King of Fingalls to have his way. When he had come near the place he raised his hand up to the side of his head. A gallant fellow who was at the wedding shot an arrow at his hand, and nailed it to his head. The whole of the men who were at the wedding rose up then and put him to flight. The custom which the MacDonalds of Kintyre had of lying the first night with every bride in the country, if he liked, was brought to an end that night.

STORIES OF HECTOR ROY
MACKENZIE,
FIRST LAIRD OF GAIRLOCH

※

Source: J. H. Dixon, *Gairloch in North-West Ross-shire*
Narrator: Unknown ('Gairloch seannachies')

During the later years of Alexander the Upright, his eldest son Kenneth Mackenzie, who was known as 'Kenneth of the Battle', led the clan in the many contests in which it was engaged. Hector Roy usually assisted his brother Kenneth in warfare. He took a leading part in the celebrated battle of Park, which gave Kenneth his appellation.

It seems that Kenneth of the Battle had married Margaret, daughter of John Macdonald of Islay, who laid claim not only to the lordship of the Isles, but also to the earldom of Ross. One Christmas eve Kenneth imagined himself, with some reason, to have been insulted by Alexander Macdonald, nephew and heir of John of Islay. In revenge for the insult Kenneth sent his wife (whom he did not love) back to Alexander, who was her cousin. The lady was blind of an eye, and she was sent away mounted on a one-eyed pony, accompanied by a one-eyed servant and followed by a one-eyed dog. The result was that John Macdonald of Islay determined on a great expedition to punish the Mackenzies. He mustered his followers in the Isles, and his relatives of Moidart and Ardnamurchan, to the number of three thousand warriors. Kenneth called out the clan Mackenzie, and strongly garrisoned Eileandonain Castle. Macdonald and his nephew Alexander marched to Inverness, reduced the castle there, left a garrison in it, and then plundered the lands of the sheriff of Cromarty. They next marched to Strathconan, ravaged the lands of the Mackenzies, put some of the inhabitants to the sword, and burned Contin church one Sunday morning, together with the aged people, women and children, and the old priest, who were worshipping in the church at the time.

Kenneth Mackenzie sent his aged father, Alexander the Upright, from Kinellan, where he was residing, to the Raven's Rock above Strathpeffer, and himself led his men, numbering only six hundred, to the moor still known as Blar na Pairc. The Macdonalds came to the moor to meet him. Between the two forces lay a peat moss, full of deep pits and deceitful bogs. Kenneth had his own brother Duncan, and his half-brother Hector Roy, with him. By the nature of the ground Kenneth perceived that Macdonald could not bring all his forces to the attack at once. He directed his brother Duncan with a body of archers to lie in ambush, whilst he himself advanced across the moss, being able from his knowledge of the place to avoid its dangers. The van of the enemy's army charged furiously, and Kenneth, according to his pre-arranged plan, at once retreated, so that the assailants following him became entangled in the moss. Duncan Mackenzie then opened fire from his ambush on the foe both in flank and rear, slaughtering most of those who had entered the bog. Kenneth now charged with his main body, and Macdonald's forces, thrown into confusion by the stratagem, were after a desperate battle completely routed. Kenneth was attacked by Gillespie, one of Macdonald's lieutenants, and slew him in single combat. Hector Roy, who commanded a division, fought like a lion, and most of the Macdonalds were slain. Those who fled before the victorious Mackenzies rallied on the following morning, to the number of three hundred, but Kenneth pursued them, and they were all killed or taken prisoners. Both Macdonald himself and his heir Alexander were taken prisoners, but Mackenzie released them within six months, on their promising that they would not molest him again, and that they would abandon all claim to the earldom of Ross.

During the battle a great raw ploughboy from Kintail was noticed by Hector Roy going about in an aimless stupid manner. The youth was Donnachadh Mor na Tuaighe, or Big Duncan of the Axe, commonly called Suarachan. He was one of the MacRaes of Kintail; you would have called him in English Duncan Mac-Rae. He received the name of Big Duncan of the Axe because, not having been thought worthy – much to his annoyance –

of being properly armed that morning for the battle, his only weapon was a rusty old battleaxe he had picked up. Hector Roy called upon Duncan to take part in the fight. In his chagrin at the contempt with which he had been treated, he replied, 'Unless I get a man's esteem, I shall not do a man's work.' Hector answered, 'Do a man's work, and you will get a man's share.' Big Duncan rushed into the battle, quickly killed a man, drew the body aside, and coolly sat upon it. Hector Roy noticed this extraordinary proceeding, and asked him why he was not engaged with his comrades. Big Duncan answered, 'If I only get one man's due, I shall only do one man's work; I have killed my man.' Hector told him to do two men's work and he would get two men's reward. Big Duncan went again into the fight, killed another man, pulled the body away, placed it on the top of the first, and sat upon the two. Hector Roy saw him again, and said, 'Duncan, how is this; you idle, and I in sore distress?' Big Duncan replied, 'You promised me two men's share, and I killed two men.' Hector quickly answered, 'I would not be reckoning with you.' On this Big Duncan instantly arose with his great battleaxe, and shouted, 'The man that would not be reckoning with me, I would not be reckoning with him.' He rushed into the thickest of the battle, where he mowed down the enemy like grass, so that that mighty chief Maclean of Lochbuy determined to check his murderous career. The heroes met in deadly strife; for some time Maclean, being a very powerful man clad in mail, escaped the terrible axe, but at last Duncan, with one fell swoop, severed his enemy's head from his body. Big Duncan accompanied his chief in the pursuit of the fugitives next day. That night when the triumphant chief, Kenneth of the Battle, sat at supper he missed Big Duncan, and said to the company, 'I am more vexed for want of my great *sgalag* this night than any satisfaction I had of the day.' One of the others said, 'I thought I saw him following some men [of the enemy] that ran up a burn.' He had scarcely finished speaking when Big Duncan entered, with four heads bound in a woodie and threw them before the chief. 'Tell me now,' says he, 'if I have not earned my supper.'

* * *

In 1499 a royal warrant was issued to the Mackintosh to put down and punish Hector Roy, who had become obnoxious to the government, as a disturber of the public peace. He was outlawed; a reward was offered for his capture, and MacCailean, Earl of Argyle, was appointed to receive his rents and account for them to the crown. A period of anarchy and disorder ensued. Hector, with his faithful bodyguard, took refuge in the hills, and MacCailean came down to gather the rents. The Caithness men, who at that time made frequent raids on Ross-shire, determined to destroy MacCailean and his force. When MacCailean looked out one morning the Caithness men were gathering above him, but he said to his followers, 'I am seeing a big man above the Caithness men, and twelve men with him, and he makes me more afraid than the Caithness men all together.' MacCailean and his men determined to cut through the Caithness men. When the combat began, Hector Roy and his twelve warriors came down and also attacked the Caithness men: few of them escaped. After the battle, Hector Roy and MacCailean went to speak to each other. MacCailean asked what he could do for Hector, who replied, 'It's yourself that knows best.' On this MacCailean bade him go to Edinburgh at such a time, and said he would meet him there.

Hector Roy went to Edinburgh and saw MacCailean, who told him to be in a certain place on such a day, and, when he should see MacCailean and the king walking together, to approach them and kneel before the king. MacCailean said the king would then lay hold of him by the hand to take him up, and Hector was to make the king remember that he had laid hold of him. Before this MacCailean and the king were talking together about Hector Roy: the king said Hector was a wild brave man, and it was impossible to lay hold of him. MacCailean replied, 'If you will grant my request, I will give you hold of his hand.' To this the king agreed. On the day fixed Hector Roy came to where the king and MacCailean were walking together, and kneeled before the king. The king took his hand to raise him up, when Hector Roy gave him such a grasp that the blood came out at the points of the king's fingers. 'Why did you not keep him?' said MacCailean, as Hector Roy turned away. 'There is no man in the kingdom would hold that man,' replied the king. Said MacCailean, 'That is Hector Roy, and I must now get my request.' 'What is it?' asked the king. 'That Hector Roy should be pardoned.' The king granted the pardon, and took a great liking to Hector Roy for his strength and bravery.

* * *

Many years ago there lived at Craig of Gairloch an old man named Alastair Mac Iain Mhic Earchair. He was a man of great piety and respectability, and was one of those who devote much of their time to religious exercises, and are called 'the men'. He is remembered by old people now living. It was in the first quarter of the nineteenth century that early one morning Alastair went out for a load of bog fir for firewood. When he came to the peat moss where the wood was to be found, there suddenly appeared before him a tall fair-haired man attired in the Breacan an fheilidh, or belted plaid; with him were twelve other men similarly dressed; their plaids were all of Mackenzie tartan, and their kilts were formed of part of the plaid pleated and belted round the waist as was the manner in the old days. The fair-haired one, who from his noble bearing was manifestly a chief, inquired, 'How fare the Gairloch family?' Alastair replied, 'They are well.' Then they departed. When they were leaving him, Alastair heard not the sound of their tread nor saw them make a step, but they passed away as if a gust of wind were bending down the tall grass on the hillside. Alastair, to his dying day, declared and believed that he had had a vision of the great chief Hector Roy with his bodyguard of twelve chosen heroes.

CANOBIE DICK

Source: Sir Walter Scott, 'Appendix to the General Preface', *Waverley*, 1829
Narrator: Sir Walter Scott from unknown sources
Type: AT766 'The Seven Sleepers'

Now, it chanced many years since, that there lived on the Borders a jolly, rattling horse-cowper, who was remarkable for a reckless and fearless temper, which made him much admired, and a little dreaded, amongst his neighbours. One moonlight night, as he rode over Bowden Moor, on the west side of the Eildon Hills, the scene of Thomas the Rhymer's prophecies, and often mentioned in his story, having a brace of horses along with him which he had not been able to dispose of, he met a man of venerable appearance, and singularly antique dress, who, to his great surprise, asked the price of his horses, and began to chaffer with him on the subject. To Canobie Dick, for so shall we call our Border dealer, a chap was a chap, and he would have sold a horse to the devil himself, without minding his cloven hoof, and would have probably cheated Old Nick into the bargain. The stranger paid the price they agreed on, and all that puzzled Dick in the transaction was, that the gold which he received was in unicorns, bonnet pieces, and other ancient coins, which would have been invaluable to collectors, but were rather troublesome in modern currency. It was gold, however, and therefore Dick contrived to get better value for the coin than he perhaps gave to his customer. By the command of so good a merchant, he brought horses to the same spot more than once, the purchaser only stipulating that he should always come by night, and alone. I do not know whether it was from mere curiosity, or whether some hope of gain mixed with it, but after Dick had sold several horses in this way, he began to complain that dry bargains were unlucky, and to hint, that since his chap must live in the neighbourhood, he ought, in the courtesy of dealing, to treat him to half a mutchkin.

'You may see my dwelling if you will,' said the stranger; 'but if you lose courage at what you see there, you will rue it all your life.'

Dicken, however, laughed the warning to scorn, and having alighted to secure his horse, he followed the stranger up a narrow footpath, which led them up the hills to the singular eminence stuck betwixt the most southern and the centre peaks, and called from its resemblance to such an animal in its form, the Lucken Hare. At the foot of this eminence, which is almost as famous for witch meetings as the neighbouring windmill of Kippilaw, Dick was somewhat startled to observe that his conductor entered the hillside by a passage or cavern, of which he himself, though well acquainted with the spot, had never seen or heard.

'You may still return,' said his guide, looking ominously back upon him; but Dick scorned to show the white feather, and on they went. They entered a very long range of stables; in every stall stood a coal-black horse; by every horse lay a knight in coal-black armour, with a drawn sword in his hand, but all were as silent, hoof and limb, as if they had been cut out of marble. A great number of torches lent a gloomy lustre to the hall, which, like those of the Caliph Vathek, was of large dimensions. At the upper end, however, they at length arrived, where a sword and horn lay on an antique table.

'He that shall sound that horn and draw that sword,' said the stranger, who now intimated that he was the famous Thomas of Hersildoune, 'shall, if his heart fail him not, be king over all broad Britain. So speaks the tongue that cannot lie. But all depends on courage, and much on your taking the sword or the horn first.'

Dick was much disposed to take the sword, but his bold spirit was quailed by the supernatural terrors of the hall, and he thought to unsheath the sword first might be construed into defiance, and give offence to the powers of the Mountain. He took the bugle with a trembling hand, and a feeble note, but loud enough to produce a terrible answer. Thunder rolled in stunning peals through the immense hall; horses and men started to life; the steeds snorted, stamped, grinded their bits, and tossed on high their heads – the warriors sprung to their feet, clashed their armour, and brandished their swords. Dick's terror was extreme at seeing the whole army, which had been so lately silent as the grave, in uproar, and about to rush on him. He dropped the horn, and made a feeble attempt to seize the enchanted sword; but at the same moment a voice pronounced aloud the mysterious words:

'Woe to the coward, that ever he was born
Who did not draw the sword before he blew the horn!'

At the same time a whirlwind of irresistible fury howled through the long hall, bore the unfortunate horse-jockey clear out of the mouth of the cavern, and precipitated him over a steep bank of loose stones, where the shepherds found him the next morning, with just breath sufficient to tell his fearful tale, after concluding which he expired.

TRADITIONS OF
ALASDAIR MACDONALD

Source: Lord Archibald Campbell, *Records of Argyll*
Narrators: As described

JOHN CAMPBELL, LAIRD OF BRAGLIN

From the Gaelic of Angus Campbell, Oban; supplied by 'D.'

In the turbulent times of old, when the rule was, that they should take who had the power, and they should keep who could, there lived a laird of Braglin, who was commonly called Iain Beag MacIain 'ic Dhòmhnuill, i.e., little John, son of John, son of Donald. He was celebrated in his day for his dauntless bravery and fertility in resource, of which the following incidents are notable illustrations.

His house having been on one occasion surrounded by a party of soldiers under Alexander MacDonald, Montrose's lieutenant, he made a hole in the roof in order to escape. When he made his appearance on the top of the house MacDonald called out to him, 'How would you act towards me if I were similarly situated?' 'I would place you,' said John, 'in the middle of my men, and give you a chance of breaking through them if you could.' Whereupon, leaping off the house sword in hand, he bounded backward and forward till he found out the weakest point in the ranks, when he dashed through them, and made his escape. Twelve of the swiftest and most resolute of MacDonald's men started in pursuit. After running till they were nearly exhausted, John slackened his pace till the foremost of his pursuers was close up to him, when he turned upon him and cut him down. He acted in this manner throughout the pursuit till all were slain except one, whom he allowed to return to his party.

A feud having broken out between John and MacDougall of Lorne, the latter attacked him with overwhelming numbers, and compelled him to flee for his life. He took refuge in Ireland, where he was safe from pursuit. After the lapse of some time he returned to Argyleshire, and made his way by night to Braglin. He found his mother at home, and was welcomed by her. Having partaken of food and got the news of the country, he set out for Benderloch, where MacDougall had sent his cattle for greater security. Having found out the password of the shepherds, and thus won their confidence, he took the first opportunity that presented itself of attacking and killing them. He then drove the cattle across Loch Etive; he himself got across by clinging to the bull's tail. When intelligence of this daring exploit had reached MacDougall, he sent a party of men to Braglin to recover the cattle and seize John. Apprised of their coming, he drew up his people, both men and women, on an eminence, disposing them in such a manner that they appeared much more numerous and formidable than they in reality were. In consequence of this, the MacDougalls deemed it prudent to come to terms with him. John and the MacDougalls appear to have lived amicably after this.

The following incident, equally with the above, is characteristic of the man and his times. The English who were in the country at the time, and whose conduct it is said was connived at by some of his neighbours, were in quest of John with the design of killing him. Not knowing him by sight, they inquired about him of such persons as they met. While they were thus employed, who should meet them but John himself? They asked him if he knew John Beag. He answered that he did, and that if they would go with him and help him to split a tree, he would undertake to give them him by the hand. They accompanied him. John had partially split the tree by driving wedges into it. He now asked the strangers to pull it asunder. While they were endeavouring to do so, John managed adroitly to remove the wedges, so that they were caught by the fingers. He then told them who he was; and having taken the sword of one of them, he cut off the heads of all of them except one, whom he spared that he might, after going home, relate what had occurred.

The laird of Braglin was buried in the churchyard of Kilbride, where his curiously carved gravestone is still to be seen.

ALEXANDER MacDONALD, ALIAS ALASDAIR MacCHOLLA, AND JOHN CAMPBELL OF BRAGLIN, ALIAS IAIN BEAG MACIAIN 'IC DHÒMHNUILL

From the Gaelic of William Campbell White, Oban; supplied by 'D.'

Colla Chiotaich [i.e., left-handed Coll] was a prisoner in Dunstaffnage Castle, and was hanged at a place called Tom-a-Chrochaidh, between Connel and Dunstaffnage. The country road now passes through the place. Coll had a son called Alasdair MacCholla. In his youth, this Alasdair lived for some time with the laird of Auchinbreak. On a certain day he went to the hill to cut brackens. He was alone, and under the impression that he was unobserved. While cutting the tops of the brackens with a hook, he would say the one time, 'If you were a Campbell, I would treat you in that manner!' and the other time, 'If you were a Campbell, I would treat you in this manner!' He was thus employed, when he perceived that he was observed by some persons from behind a hillock near him. Fearing that his words were heard, and would be reported to Auchinbreak, he took to flight, and went over to Ireland. He eventually raised a strong body of men, and crossed with them to the Highlands of Scotland, which he ravished with fire and sword.

On a certain occasion, he was with his men crossing a moor above Kilmichael Glassary, in Argyleshire. In the moor there was a lake called Loch-leathan, and a castle, fragments of which are still to be seen. When they were passing the castle (early in the morning of May-day), there was shot from it an arrow that killed one of the men. Alasdair turned round and looked at him, without showing the least concern for his fate. He called to his men to move on, and that he would follow them. As they went marching along they met John Campbell of Braglin, who was alone, but armed. Alasdair and John recognized each other, and John was made prisoner. Alasdair then said to John, 'How would you treat me, little John, were you with your men to meet me alone, as you have been met today?' 'I would,' said John, 'make a circle of my men, and place you in the centre of it; and, on my word of honour, I would allow you to escape if you could break through either on my right hand or on my left.' 'On my word of honour,' said Alasdair to John, 'I will treat you today in a similar manner.' Looking round the circle, John drew his sword, cleared a passage for himself, and got off scathless. Whereupon Alasdair said to John, 'Little John, you have got free today; but we shall meet again.' The two heroes had more than once before tried each other's mettle.

Through fear of Alasdair and his men, John was for some time after this in the habit of passing the night in the moor. It so happened that he was one evening detained in Braglin House longer than usual, waiting for his supper, which consisted of mashed potatoes and milk. Losing patience, he said to the servant who was preparing the supper, 'The potatoes are mashed enough; bring them to me, lest Alasdair MacCholla and his men come upon me if I wait longer for them.' The servant answered, 'If Alasdair MacCholla's head were as mashed as the potatoes, you might remain in your house tonight.' 'You have spoken wickedly, you senseless woman!' said John. 'It would be a great pity that so brave a man's head should be as mashed as that.' Alasdair, who had in the meantime surrounded the house with his men, and heard at the window the conversation that had taken place between John and the servant, cried out, 'On account of your generous words, little John, I and my men will depart from your house tonight and do you no harm.'

ALASDAIR MACDONALD AND THE MACDOUGALLS

From the Gaelic of John Clerke, Kilbride; supplied by 'D.'

When Alasdair MacDonald had left Ederline, after having fought a successful battle with big Sachary MacCallum of Poltalloch, he marched northwards, went round the head of Loch Melfort and called at Ardanstuir, the residence of the Campbells of Melfort. Melfort was then absent with most of his men. When it was known that MacDonald was coming, Mrs Campbell prepared a sumptuous feast for him, which she placed in proper form on a table. Having done this, she and her household fled to the woods, leaving the door of the house open. When MacDonald arrived, he was agreeably surprised to find his wants so bountifully provided for, and partook heartily of the viands on the table. He was so pleased with the courtesy shown him that he gave strict orders that no injury should be done to anything belonging to the Melfort family. When he was on the top of the hill above the house he happened to look back, and saw that the house was on fire. When his men came up he called out, 'Which of you has dared to commit this act contrary to my orders?' Inquiry having been made, the criminal was found out, and sentenced to be hanged on the first tree that they should meet.

This episode over, they resumed their march, crossed the hill at a place called Doire-nan-cliabh, and descended on Ardmaddy, passing the night with John Maol Macdougall. Next morning they left Ardmaddy, marched through Glenrisdale, and came down upon Raray. When they came in sight of Gleniuächair, MacDonald ordered the pipers to play '*A'mhnathan a' Ghlinne so's mithich dhuibh éiridh*' ['Women of this glen, it is time for you to rise']. When he had reached Laganmòr, he was met by John Campbell of Braglin, and his nephew, the Baron of Dunach, with their men. MacDonald and Campbell attacked each other with their swords. Campbell was getting the better of MacDonald, when a Macdougall follower of the latter came behind the former and struck him about the legs, which compelled him to give in. Thrusting his sword into its scabbard, MacDonald said to John, 'It is a pity that you are a Campbell.'

These two men appear to have entertained a genuine respect and regard for each other; and they showed on more than one occasion a generosity of feeling towards each other that is seldom to be met with among opponents in time of civil war. And yet the same men could commit the most barbarous atrocities. Macdougall, fearing the consequences of his act, took to his heels. In his flight he met a herd keeping cattle, and said to him, 'Give me your coat and bonnet, and I will give you my hat and cloak.' The herd agreed to the exchange. It was no sooner made than the Baron of Dunach came where they were, and mistaking the herd for Macdougall, cut his head off. After the battle, Mac-Donald marched through Laganmòr. Having heard that some women and children were hidden in a barn, he ordered it to be set on fire. The consequence was, that all in the barn were burned, except one woman, who succeeded in breaking through the roof. She was allowed to escape. On the night of the battle she gave birth to twins in the wood of Fearrnagan, near Sabhal nan Cnàmh. When, about ten years ago, the farmer of Laganmòr was digging the foundation of the barn for stones, he came upon a large quantity of bones.

MacInnes and His Treasure

From the Gaelic of Dugald MacDougall of Soraba; supplied by 'D.'

On the farm of Airdeorain, on the west side of Loch-faochan, and opposite Cnìopach mòr, there is a jutting promontory, called the promontory of MacInnes's house. On this promontory are to be seen the ruins of a house, called the ruins of MacInnes's house. This MacInnes lived during the period of the civil war carried on under the generalship of the Marquess of Montrose. He was possessed of considerable wealth, amounting to a foal's skinful of gold and silver coins. When Alasdair MacDonald, commonly called in the Highlands Alasdair MacCholla, came to Argyleshire, ravaging, burning, and slaying, MacInnes bethought him of hiding his money, that it might not fall into MacDonald's hands. He said one day to his big son that they would take the skin with the money in their boat across to Cnìopach, and hide it in one of the caves or holes that abound in that rugged place. Before leaving the house he directed his wife to put a light in the window; for the distinguishing mark he wished to have of the spot where his money was to be hid was, that it should be in a direct line with the light in the window. On their way back from Cnìopach, the evil thought arose in his mind that his son might steal the money, and that he would be reduced to poverty. With this thought agitating and maddening him, he attacked his son and killed him, and cast him into the loch. When he reached home, his wife was surprised to find that her son did not return with him. She questioned him sharply about the lad, but failed to get satisfaction. The purport of the dialogue that took place between them is given in the following song:

> *She.* My Duncan has gone to the hill,
> My Duncan has gone to the hill,
> My Duncan has gone to the hill,
> And has not come home.
>
> *He.* Thou bad woman, without sense,
> Thou bad woman, without sense,
> Thou bad woman, without sense,
> Keep thy marriage badge and cap on thee.
>
> *She.* He was my Duncan,
> He was my Duncan,
> He was my Duncan,
> What has happened is my loss.
>
> *He.* His feet are to a burn,
> His feet are to a burn,
> His feet are to a burn,
> And his head leans on a support.
>
> *She.* My Duncan has gone to the hill, &c.

Alasdair MacDonald having come the way, he forced Mac-Innes to join his ranks. MacInnes went afterwards to Ireland and was taken prisoner there. He never returned to Airdeorain, or sent for his treasure. He revealed to certain persons in Ireland, before his death, where it was to be found; but these never came over to search for it. Many spent some time searching for it. It was prophesied that the treasure would yet be found, and that one of those engaged in finding it would lose his life, since a life was lost when it was hid. It is said that a herd-boy in Ballino once saw a number of coins somewhere under Cniopach rock; but instead of taking them away with him, he ran home to tell about them. Some of the people of the farm went with the boy for the coins, but he could not find the spot where he saw them. In the long winter nights, when people used to gather in each other's houses, the old men in Glenfaochan often told the youth that the treasure was guarded by a large serpent.

LOCHBUIE'S TWO HERDSMEN

Source: J. G. Campbell, *Clan Traditions and Popular Tales of the Western Highlands and Islands*
Narrator: Donald Cameron, Rudhaig, Tiree
Type: AS1791 'The Sexton Carries the Parson'

Note: *Dubh-brochan* is a thin mixture of oatmeal and water

In 1602 Lochbuie had two herdsmen, and the wife of one herdsman went to the house of the other herdsman. The housewife was in before her, and had a pot on the fire. 'What have you in the pot?' said the one who came in. 'Well there it is,' she said, 'a drop of *brochan* which the goodman will have with his dinner.'

'What kind of *brochan* is it?' said the one who came in.

'It is *dubh-brochan*,' said the one who was in.

'Isn't he,' said she, 'a poor man! Are you not giving him anything but that? I have been for so long a time under the Laird of Loch Buie, and I have not drank *brochan* without a grain of beef or something in it. Don't you think it is but a small thing for the Laird of Loch Buie though we should get an ox every year. Little he would miss it. I will send over my husband tonight, and you will bring home one of the oxen.'

When night came she sent him over. The wife then sent the other away. The one said, 'You will steal the ox from the fold, and you will bring it to me, and we will be free; I will swear that I did not take it from the fold, and you will swear that you did not take it home.'

The two herdsmen went away. In those days they hanged a man, when he did harm, without waiting for law or sentence, and at this time Lochbuie had hanged a man in the wood. The herdsmen went and kindled a fire near a tree in the wood as a signal to the one who went to steal. One sat at the fire, and the other went to steal the ox.

The same night a number of gentlemen were in the mansion at Loch Buie. They began laying wagers with Lochbuie that there was not one in the house who would take the shoe off the man who had been hanged that day. Lochbuie laid a wager that there was. He called up his big lad MacFadyen, and said to him was he going to let the wager go against him. The big lad asked what the wager was about. He said to him that they were maintaining that there was no one in his court who could take the shoe off the one who had been hanged that day. MacFadyen said he would take off him the shoe and bring it to them where they were.

MacFadyen went on his way. When he reached, he looked and saw the man who had been hanged warming himself at a fire. He did not go farther on, but returned in haste. When he came they asked him if he had the shoe. He told them he had not, for that yon one was with a withy basket of peats before him, warming himself. 'We knew ourselves,' said the gentlemen, 'that you had only cowards.'

The lameter, who was over, said, 'It is a wrong thing you are doing in allowing him to lose the wager. If I had the use of my feet, I would go and take his leg off as well as his shoe before I would let Lochbuie lose the wager.'

'Come you here,' said the big lad, 'and I will put a pair of feet that you never had the like of under you.' He put the lameter round his neck, and off he went. When they came in sight of the man who was warming himself the lameter sought to return. MacFadyen said they would not return. They went nearer to the man who was warming himself. The one that was at the fire lifted his head and observed them coming. He thought it was his own companion, the one who had gone to steal the ox, who was come. He spoke and said, 'Have you come?' 'I have,' said MacFadyen. 'And have you got it?' 'Yes,' said MacFadyen. 'And is it fat?'

'Whether he is fat or lean, there he is to you,' and he threw the lameter on to the fire.

MacFadyen took to his heels and fled as fast as ever he did. Off went the lameter after him. He put the four oars on for making his escape. The one at the fire rose, thinking there were some who had come to pry upon himself, and that he was now caught. He went after the lameter to make his excuses to the Laird of Loch Buie. The lameter was observing him coming after him, feeling quite sure that it was the one who had been hanged.

MacFadyen reached, and they asked him if he had taken the shoe off the man. He said they did not; that he asked him if the lameter was fat, and that he was sure he had him eaten up before now. The lameter came, and that cry in his head for to let him in, for that yon one was coming. He was let in. The moment this was done, the one who had been on the gallows knocked at the door, to let him in. Lochbuie said he would not.

'I am your own herdsman.' They now let him in. He then began to tell how he and the other herdsman went to steal the ox, and that he thought it was the other herdsman who had returned, and it was that made him ask if he was fat. Lochbuie and his guests had much sport and merriment over this all night. They kept the herdsman till it was late on in the night telling them how it happened to him.

The one who went to steal the ox now came back and reached the tree where he left the other herdsman, but found no one. He began to search up and down, and became aware of the one dangling from the tree.

'Oh,' said he, 'you have been hanged since I went away, and I will be tomorrow in the same plight that you are in. It has been an ill-guided object, and the tempting of women that sent us on the journey.'

He then went over and took the man off the tree to take him home. He went away with him and never got the like, going through hill, and through mud and dirt, till he came to the house of the other woman. He knocked at the door. The wife rose and let him in.

'How have things happened with you?' 'Never you mind, whatever; but, alas! he has been hanged since we went away.'

The wife took to roaring and crying.

'Do not say a word,' he said, 'or else you and I will be hanged tomorrow. We will bury him in the garden, and no one will ever know about it. And now,' he said, 'I will be returning to my own house.'

The one that was in Loch Buie thought it was time for him now to go home. He knocked at his own door. His wife did not say a word. He then called out to be let in.

'I will not,' said the wife, 'for you have been hanged, and you will never get in here.'

'I have not yet been hanged,' he said.

'Be that as it may to you,' she said, 'you will never come here.'

The advice he gave himself was to go to the house of the other herdsman. He called out at that one's door to let him in.

'You will not come in here. I got enough carrying you home on my back, and you after being hanged.'

There was a large window at the end of the house. He went in at the window. 'Get up,' he said, 'and get a light, and you will see that I have not been hanged any more than yourself.' When he saw who he had, he kept him till morning, till day came. They then talked together, telling each other what had happened to them on both sides, and thought they would go to Lochbuie, and tell him all that occurred to them. When Lochbuie heard their story, there was not a year after that but he gave each of them an ox and a boll of meal.

THE APPIN MURDER

Source: J. Dewar, *The Dewar Manuscripts*, vol. 1
Narrator: Unknown (Appin), 1860s

Note: These four tales preserve a traditional account of a Highland *cause célèbre*,
the Appin murder which is the central event of R. L. Stevenson's *Kidnapped*.
Stevenson made enquiries of local people in 1881 when he thought of
writing a paper on the Appin murder to support his bid for the Chair of
Constitutional Law at Edinburgh University. He writes in the dedication to
Kidnapped, 'To this day you will find the tradition of Appin clear in Alan's favour.
If you inquire, you may even hear that the descendants of "the other man"
who fired the shot are in the country to this day. But that other man's name,
inquire as you please, you shall not hear.' The stories he heard were probably
much like those Dewar collected, though the man named in them as Glenure's
murderer, Donald Stewart, seems an unlikely suspect. Stevenson suggests
in his novel that 'it must have been a Cameron from Mamore that did the act',
and Sir William MacArthur seems to share this view in his account of this
complex affair, *The Appin Murder*. The records of *The Trial of James Stewart*
have been edited by D. N. Mackay in the series Notable British Trials

COLIN OF GLENURE

When the lands of the rebels were confiscated, factors were put over them to manage them, to let them to tenants, to give leases, and to gather in the rents. Colin Campbell of Glenure was made factor of the lands of Lochiel and of the lands of the Stewarts of Appin. Colin was a son of the laird of Barcaldine by his second wife, the daughter of Cameron of Lochiel. He was in the King's army putting down the rebels in the years 1745 and 1746.

He was marked as being very vicious against those who rose with the Prince. When the laird of Kinlochmoidart and the brother of MacDonald of Keppoch were taken, they were among the common soldiers. They had put off every mark of distinction by which they should be known as officers, thinking that they would not be recognized, and that they would get home with the common soldiers. Some of the officers of the Red Army were sent for in order to see if they knew any of them. The officers went through the prisoners; and although some of the officers knew Kinlochmoidart and Keppoch they were friendly to them for old acquaintance' sake, and they did not let on that they knew them. Colin of Glenure came forward after that. He looked at the prisoners and said, 'O! here is the laird of Kinlochmoidart who was a major in the army of the Prince: and here is, also, the brother of MacDonald of Keppoch who was an officer in the army of Prince Charles.'

The two young gentlemen were immediately seized and put in prison.

They were afterwards tried, found guilty, and condemned. They were first put up on a gallows and taken down before they were dead; then their breasts were torn open, and their hearts were pulled out of them and thrown in their faces. Their heads were then cut off, after which their bodies were burnt and the ashes were thrown away with the wind. It is said that two hearts were found in MacDonald.

When Colin got to be factor of the lands of Lochiel and Ardsheil he was very covetous of managing matters in such a way as to conduce to his own profit. At that time there were Campbells who had extensive farms in Glen Etive, and when their leases had expired the laird of Fasnacloich took the lands over their heads for persons of the name of MacLaurin who were related to the Stewarts. The Campbells were related to Colin of Glenure, and when he heard that the laird of Fasnacloich had taken the land of his friends over their heads, he said, 'I will be upsides with these men! I will yet see that a clod of land in Appin shall not be possessed by a Stewart, and that a clod of the land of Lochaber shall not be possessed by a Cameron.' This language excited great anger and hatred in the people of Appin and Lochaber against Colin of Glenure.

The cousin of Charles Stuart, laird of Ardsheil, Iain Glas Stewart by name, had large farms in Strathfillan and in Glendochart. Ben More was in his land. He was killed at Culloden. Some MacColls, relatives of his, took away a drove of his cattle to prevent them from being taken for the King. Colin of Glenure understood that the cattle were taken away and he made inquiry until he ascertained that they were taken away by the

MacColls. Iain Glas left a young family, but it was not known whether it was for these or for themselves that the MacColls took away the cattle. Colin gave the MacColls up to the Law. The MacColls were then outlawed as thieves. Messengers-at-arms and soldiers were sent to seize them and they were obliged to flee and leave the country, and they never returned. One of these fugitives was married to the daughter of a farmer at a hamlet named Candalach, in Benderloch, in the land of Barcaldine. This fugitive was staying in the house of his father-in-law. Colin of Glenure got information of his being there and he went with a party to seize him. When they reached Candalach, the fugitive understood that they had come to seize him and he fled. Colin drew a gun to shoot the fugitive in preference to letting him escape. The goodwife of Candalach ran between Colin and her son-in-law, thinking that he would not fire at her, and exclaimed, 'O! Colin! Colin! Let him go with his life.' Colin fired the gun in the breast of the woman herself and killed her; and he was not taken up for killing the woman, because she had no right to go between him and the person of whom he was in pursuit.

Another time Colin was going to seize an outlaw. When the outlaw understood that he was for seizing him he fled. Colin would rather kill him than let him go, so he fired after him and killed him. Such deeds as these excited great hatred against Colin in those who were friendly to the people who rose with the Prince, and they wished Colin dead. They gathered together as one body of people to try to conceal from the King's men where the outlaws were wont to hide and find means of sending food to them. Times were very hard in the Highlands in those days. Both rich and poor who rose in the cause of Prince Charles were plundered. Neither cow nor horse, sheep nor goat was left to them. The blankets were taken off their beds; any part of their body-clothes that was worth was taken from them; and even the skeins of yarn were taken out of the dye-pots, and their houses were put on fire. The result was that the people who were rebels were poorly off. When once the soldiers took their property from them, if they got an opportunity of taking it back and did so, and the soldiers found it in their possession, this was considered theft, a violation of law, and they were obliged to flee. The rebels were badly off many times with cold and hunger.

When a company of the rebels would come into a house, were there any that did not sympathize with them there, the one who knew this would say, 'Take care, men, the roof in this house leaks.' This gave warning that there was someone in who was not friendly, and that they were not to talk of anything that should be kept secret, lest there should be information given about it. It was usual when anyone went to a neighbour's house to speak of any matter, that the first thing he did was to look round through the house and ask, 'Is the roof of this house leaking?' Were there none in but friends it was said to him 'No,' but were it otherwise the reply was 'Yes. Watch where you sit.'

They were generally very faithful to one another. They shared their means with one another and they endeavoured to conceal one another's affairs from those who were on King George's side. Nevertheless, as happens always to the weaker union, there were false persons among them who gave information concerning them.

James Stewart, the half-brother of Charles Stuart of Ardsheil, who had taken a lease of the estate from Charles, wished to retain the lease and to pay the rent to Colin of Glenure for the King, and the case was allowed to remain so at first; but Ardsheil was cheaply rented, and James Stewart sought not to keep any of the profit for himself. He first paid the rent to Colin of Glenure, and then gave the remainder of the income of the estate to his brother's lady and children for their maintenance. There was, however, some glib-tongued person who informed Colin of Glenure that James of the Glen had Ardsheil too cheap and that he was giving all the income, except as much as paid the rent, to the lady of Ardsheil. Colin of Glenure searched out how the case was until he discovered that James of the Glen had given money to the lady of Ardsheil.

Colin gave up the case to the Law, and the manner in which the case was settled was that James of the Glen was a servant of Charles Stuart, laird of Ardsheil before the laird of Ardsheil joined the rebels; that he always continued a servant; and as a proof of that, that he was giving the income of the place to the lady of Charles Stuart.

The cattle of Ardsheil were confiscated and the provision store was taken from James of the Glen. Colin of Glenure let Ardsheil to a man of the people of Breadalbane whose name was Peter Campbell. He dwelt in a place called the Achadh and he was called Paruig an Achaidh. Colin of Glenure gave him a lease of three nineteen years of Ardsheil. It caused great loss to James of the Glen that the store was taken from him. He had had the store in his own hand: he got some of the provisions on credit, and he was after paying money for the rest of it. He became much addicted to drink thenceforth, and when he would be drunk, as often he was, he reviled Colin of Glenure, spoke of his ill will to him, threatened that he should do as much harm to Colin of Glenure as Colin had done to him, and he did not conceal his resentment.

There was a brother of Cameron of Lochiel dwelling in a place of the name of Fassifern. He did not rise at all with the Prince, although his brother did. When the Prince and those who were with him lost, Lochiel was obliged to flee from the kingdom along with the Prince, and his lands were forfeited. Fassifern got one Charles Stewart, a notary, to write a false charter of some of the lands of Lochiel for him. When Colin of Glenure, who was factor of the lands of Lochiel, went to collect the rents, Fassifern showed him the charter which he had of part of the lands of Lochiel. Colin examined a farmer who was acquainted with the case, and searched out until he got proof that the laird of Fassifern had only a false charter. Although the laird of Fassifern was Colin of Glenure's cousin, Colin gave him up to the Law. Fassifern was brought to court, and it was found out there that it was Charles Stewart, the notary, who wrote the false charter. Instead of seizing the man who got the charter written, however, and who showed it to claim that which did not belong to him, it was the man who wrote the false charter that was seized. Charles Stewart, the notary, was seized and put in prison in Edinburgh, there to be kept until he should be tried by the Red Lords, the Lords Justices.

When the day of trial was near, Alexander, the notary, was willing to go to Edinburgh, although he was an old man at the time, to plead the cause of his son. It was not allowed at that time to wear the Highland dress, but Alexander, the notary, put on a dress as Highland as he durst. He put on a coat and a pair of breeches of homespun. He reached Edinburgh, and on the day of trial went to the court-house. He said, 'I am the father of the prisoner who is to be tried, shall I get leave to speak in his behalf?'

The Chief Judge of the court said that he should. Alexander, the notary, said, 'I am deaf. I must speak to you in writing.' The lawyers about the court thought that he was but an old farmer without much intelligence, and they actually began to make a laughing-stock of him. He took a paper out of his pocket, gave it to them, and said, 'Here is a paper for you and read it.' They put the paper round among them, and one after the other of them read it, and they began to laugh about it and make a mock of it. They gave him back his paper and said to him, 'There is your paper for you – your paper will not do you much good.' They went on then with the business of the court. A short time after that he took out another paper from his pocket and said, 'Here is another paper for you, were you to be so good as to read it,' and he handed the paper to the lawyers. The paper went round among the lawyers, and they read it one after the other, and they handed it up to the Lord who was sitting in the court chair. The Lord read the paper and said to the lawyers, 'You may stop your laughing; there is something you did not think of in the old fellow's head, and you will see that yet.' The paper was handed back to Alexander, the notary, and it was said to him, 'There is your paper for you. That paper will not do you much good either.' The notary took another paper out of his pocket and said, 'Here is another paper yet, if you do not think it troublesome, were you to be so good as to read it,' and he gave the lawyers the paper; but instead of laughing at it, they were shaking their heads at one another, and the paper was handed to the Lord Justice Clerk. He read it two or three times, and handed it up to the Judge who was sitting in the judgment chair. The Judge looked at the paper and said to Alexander, the notary, 'I do think myself that your son is but a fool.' Alexander replied, 'That is known, indeed. My son was but a fool since he was born. He would do what was desired of him, and he was not wise. See you to what you are doing; the Law does not allow that an irresponsible person shall suffer for his foolish deeds. It was a foolish deed that my son did, and he did but what he was asked to do.'

The lawyers then got the forged charter which was written by Charles Stewart, the notary, and it was written as correctly as any lawyer could write it. What the lawyers of the court made of it was that the false charter was written sensibly, and that that was the deed of a wise man; and they went on with the trial. When all the lawyers had said all which they meant to say, Alexander, the notary, then began to speak on behalf of his son, and he ended his speaking by saying, 'It is known that my son is not wise; he did the deed of an unwise man; he wrote as he was asked to do; and although it is so, it was not wise of him to do that; and although it is the law that the hand shall be cut off him who commits forgery, the law does not bear out that a drop of his blood shall be shed. According to the law of Moses, blood shall not be shed but for blood. If a person stole he was obliged to pay four times as much again; and to make a false title deed is but as theft. Although it is allowed you to cut the hand off my son, it is not allowed you to shed a drop of his blood; and if you do there will be speaking about it hereafter.'

The Judge listened until Alexander ceased speaking, and then he gave judgment that the manner in which the hand should be taken off Charles Stewart was that he durst not thenceforth be a notary; that he durst not thenceforth write any bond, charter, covenant or contract, or anything else which related to mutual agreement between people; or if he did, that the law was that he should be hanged. When the judge had pronounced the sentence, he said, 'Deliver his son to the man again.'

Charles was released without having his hand cut off; but, notwithstanding, the means of earning his bread were taken from him, for he durst not afterwards be either a notary or a notary's clerk.

*

Colin of Glenure would show no indulgence whatever to the old natives of Lochaber or of Appin. The people of the country sent two gentlemen to him to try if they could get him to make peace with them; and as they were left destitute by the King's people already that he would show them kindness in such a way as to let them have a living, but Colin's reply to them was, 'I will not stop from what I am doing until I leave not a clod of land in the possession of a Stewart in Appin, or of a Cameron in Lochaber.' This language spread through the whole of Appin and Lochaber. There was hatred and anger against Colin before, and the people would sincerely wish him dead; but when they heard his language anew they would earnestly wish to kill him themselves. The people of Appin and Lochaber often talked of how ill-disposed Colin of Glenure was; how he ransacked out and got information of the poor rebels and gave them up to Law; and that if he continued to do as he was doing, that it would not be long until the old inhabitants might leave the country. Colin had a certain place where he walked by himself in the afternoon. Some of the people of Lochaber learned of this place, and of the time of day when he took his walk in it. The laird of Callart got a gun and went purposely to try if he could get an opportunity of putting a bullet through him. He reached the place and hid himself near it. He waited until Colin should come, for the purpose of shooting him. That day, however, when Colin was on his way to the place where he was wont to take his walk, a gentleman met him, with whom he returned to the house, and he did not go out of his house that night. The laird of Callart went to the house of the laird of Fasnacloich that night, took his supper there, and stayed all night. It is not known what conversation took place that night about the affair between the two lairds; but the laird of Callart went home to his own house next day.

Shortly after this the people of Appin and Lochaber made up that some of the principal men in the two countries should meet, and that they should take counsel what they ought to do, and how they settled the case was: they fixed a day to meet together in Glenstockdale in Appin. There were some men in the country who had not given up their arms to the King, and these were the most esteemed in the country. Every man who had a gun was to bring his gun with him, in order that its goodness might be tested. The place they chose for trying the guns was a place called Lag bhlair an lochain, because the sound of the guns fired there would not be heard far off.

There were three guns in Appin and Glencoe at that time. John Stewart who dwelt at Caolas nan Con had a gun, and the name he had for it was 'a' Chuilbhearnach'. It was a Spanish gun, a very good one of its kind. The laird of Fasnacloich had a two-barrelled gun. There was another man in Appin of the name of Dugald MacColl, by some called 'Dugald of the Whisker', who had a big, long, Spanish gun, and his name for it was 'an t-Slinneanach'. It was an excellent gun for casting bullets.

They met on the day which they had appointed at the place where they were to meet, but before they began firing they swore to each other that they would keep the affair about which they were going secret: and that those who had the guns were to give them up to those who were the best shots. The best shot was to get the best gun and to do the special hunting. They tried the guns and the Slinneanach, Dugald MacColl's gun, was the best. It would put a bullet and swan shot within two inches of each other near the middle of the target at the distance of a hundred yards. A man called Donald Stewart, a nephew of the laird of Ballachulish, was the best hand at the gun. He could put the ball and swan shot in the middle of the mark with the Slinneanach. Dugald MacColl delivered the Slinneanach to him, and Donald was chosen as the man for the shooting of Glenure. The laird of Fasnacloich was the second best shot; he was also chosen to be Donald Stewart's comrade.

Colin of Glenure had to go to Lochaber on a certain day to settle affairs, and Mungo, his nephew, was to go with him: he was for making this Mungo a factor under him in Lochaber. The associates who were to do the killing got information of the day on which he was going thither; and they made up that they would watch him on his return from Lochaber and kill him.

When the day that Colin was to go to Lochaber had come, those who were to do the killing put themselves in order as they were to be. Donald Stewart and the laird of Fasnacloich were to be in Appin to wait for him, and the Camerons were to wait for him in Lochaber. Colin went to Lochaber to look after the lands of Lochiel and put matters as he liked them to be. Mungo, his nephew, was along with him and he had a gillie of the name of MacKenzie with him of the people of Onich in Lochaber. He put his nephew, Mungo, as factor on the lands of Lochaber, for he was beginning to be afraid of staying in Lochaber himself because he knew that many of the people there were ill-disposed towards him. When he had finished his business in Lochaber, he went off for going home. Mungo, his nephew, and MacKenzie, the gillie, were riding on horseback along with him. The avengers knew that he was coming and they were on the watch, ready, waiting for him. The lairds of Callart and Onich were to watch at Onich. Big Donald Og MacMartin of Dochanassy was to be in another place to wait for an opportunity to shoot Colin as he was passing. The laird of Fasnacloich and Donald Stewart were together at a big black rock which is between Ballachulish and Lettermore. There was a large birch tree where they were, and a large bough stretched outwards from it. They cut a portion of the branches and twigs off the bough to enable them to rest their guns upon it, and they stayed there until they got an opportunity of doing the deed about which they had come.

Big Donald Og of Dochanassy had not come forward in time, and before he had reached where he was to be on watch, Colin of Glenure and his companions passed the place. He asked the companion who was to be with him, 'How have you let Colin of Glenure pass?' His companion responded, 'I was asleep when he came and he passed unknown to me.'

Mackenzie, the gillie that Colin had, learned that some were near the road with guns, seeking an opportunity to shoot his master, and he kept as close as he could to Colin. When they were passing Onich he was between his master and those who were lying in wait for him with guns, and because the gillie himself was of the people of Onich, and the son of a neighbour, they were afraid to fire at Colin, lest they should kill Mackenzie along with him. For this reason Colin got past Onich as he did the other place previously.

Big Donald Og went after Colin until he reached Onich, and when he saw that Colin had got past Onich, as he did the other place, he was angry, and said, 'How have you let the rogue pass without giving him his desert?' They answered, 'Mackenzie, the gillie, was between us and him, and we did not get firing at him as we were afraid that we might kill Mackenzie with him.' Donald said, 'Were I here when he passed I should fire the shot, although Mackenzie would be killed along with him. Mackenzie should not prevent me from killing him. I am sure that the able men on the other side will not be so slack as those on this side. They will not let him pass so easily as the men on this side have done, and I will not leave this place until I hear the sound of the firing.' Then Donald sat down to wait whether he should hear the firing of a gun on the other side of the loch.

Colin of Glenure and those who were with him reached Caolas Mhic Pharuig where the ferryman was Archibald Mac-Innes. He had but one eye, so that he was called the One-eyed Ferryman by some. Some maintained that he was gifted with the second sight, and that he knew of things that were to happen before they came to pass; but let that be as it may, he learned that some were ill-disposed to Colin and that they sought an opportunity for killing him, so he said to him, 'Colin, if you will take my advice, you will not at all go down the side of Loch Leven tonight, but go home through Gleann an Fhiudhaich, so that no harm may happen to you.' Colin rejoined, 'I will not do that, but I will go down the way of Ardsheil – I have business there, and I will go that way. The One-eyed Ferryman remarked, 'Well, my advice to you is to take a boat, and go down the middle of the loch, and to keep as far from the land as you can, so that a ball may not reach you.' Colin replied, 'I am not in the least afraid of that; but, assuredly, I was afraid in Lochaber. I had enough fear of my mother's clan; but now, since I have got whole from the country of my mother, I am not the least afraid.'

The One-eyed Ferryman sent Colin, Mungo and Mackenzie, the gillie, across the ferry, they and their horses. They mounted the horses and went off. They had not gone far when they met the laird of Ballachulish, and he said to Colin, 'It is better for you to stay in my house tonight, Colin, to take a night's hospitality from me, and to go away in the morning.' Colin replied, 'I will not stay, I am in a hurry to go to Ardsheil, and I am desirous of being forward as soon as I can.' 'You are welcome,' said the laird of Ballachulish, 'to stay a night with me if you like, and I do think it were better for you to stay.' 'It is going forward that I will do,' said Colin, 'I have business to settle in Ardsheil.'

Colin of Glenure and Mungo went onwards, and the laird of Ballachulish and Colin's gillie went off together after them, but Colin and Mungo were going faster, so that Ballachulish and the gillie lost sight of them.

When Colin and Mungo reached opposite the black rock where the laird of Fasnacloich and Donald Stewart were hiding, and were passing with their back to them, Donald Stewart fired the Slinneanach at Colin of Glenure, and the two balls struck him in the left side between his crooked ribs and the armpit. Colin's horse was not accustomed to shot and he jumped, and was inclined to run away. Colin fell with a lurch to the one side of the horse and exclaimed, 'O Mungo! Mungo! Flee! Flee as fast as the legs of the horse will permit. I am shot.'

There was a gate across the highway a little further on from the place where Colin was shot. The horse when it reached the gate was close to one side of the road, and Colin, bent down over the side of the horse, struck against the pillar of the gate. This hastened his death. He fell off the horse and never spoke again.

The laird of Ballachulish and Colin's gillie heard the shot, and Ballachulish said, 'That shot has done harm! I hope that Colin of Glenure is safe, that he went down by the shore.' With that the laird of Ballachulish returned while Mackenzie hastened onwards to see how it fared with his master.

The shot was heard at Onich and Big Donald Og remarked, 'My business is done now. I may go home. I knew that the gallant men on the other side would not let the rogue pass them in such a silly manner as the men on this side did.'

When Mackenzie reached the place where Colin of Glenure and Mungo Campbell were, Colin was lying at the side of the road, dead and shedding blood, while Mungo, his nephew, was standing at his side. Mungo said to Mackenzie, 'Go on till you reach the house of James of the Glen, as fast as the legs of the horse will bring you, and try if you will get him and others with him to lift Colin of Glenure.'

Mackenzie took fright, but he applied the spur to the horse he had and went onwards until he reached the house of James of the Glen, and struck at the door. James of the Glen and his serving-man had been sowing barley that day. The ground was soft and James was dirty with clay over the knees. He was standing with his back to the fire warming himself when Colin of Glenure's gillie came to the house, and when the latter struck at the door he went into the chamber. The gillie saw him, but he did not let on that he did; he asked, however, if the goodman was in, and it was told him he was not. Then the gillie told that his master was killed between Ballachulish and Lettermore. When James of the Glen got clean clothes on he went into the presence of Colin's gillie. The gillie told James how his master was killed between Ballachulish and Lettermore, and he asked James to go at once to lift him. James himself was willing to go, but his wife was opposed to it; and then he refused and did not go.

After Colin's gillie had gone for men to lift his master, Mungo Campbell was standing at his side trying to quench the blood. A woman came past him and a handkerchief over her shoulders. Mungo said to her, 'Were you to be so good, woman, as to give me your handkerchief, I would pay you for it.' 'I will not, indeed,' said the woman. 'It is in the shop that I bought my handkerchief: and go you to the shop and buy a handkerchief as I did.' 'There is a man here,' said Mungo, 'who has been killed by a shot which someone has fired at him, and it is for quenching the blood that I ask for the handkerchief.' The woman rejoined, 'Let the hunter now drink the soup,' and she went away.

Colin's gillie got men, and he came back to the place where Mungo and his master's body were. They took the body with them to the house of the miller at Kintallen, where they put it in a barn, and they let it lie there until they got a bier made for it. The body was embalmed, taken away and buried.

The relations of Glenure and many gentlemen of the Clan Campbell were very angry about his murder, and they were ransacking through the country trying if they could find out those who had ill will to him.

James of the Glen was wont to be often in the public house; and as has been said, after Colin of Glenure had taken the provision store and Ardsheil from him, when he was drunk, as often he was, he traduced Colin of Glenure for being so maliciously disposed against those who had risen with Prince Charles, and he especially reviled him for the harm he had done to himself. He often threatened that, if he got the opportunity, he would do as much harm to Colin as Colin had done to him.

It happened that, some time, James was in the company of some people at a public house of whom one proposed the health of Colin of Glenure. James of the Glen said, 'I will not myself drink the health of Colin of Glenure.' The other man asked, 'Well, what would you do then?' 'Were he on the gallows I would draw down his feet,' James rejoined. There was notice taken of this remark and it was kept in remembrance. When, therefore, a large reward was offered to any person who should give information of those who had ill will to Colin, there was information given of the language which James of the Glen had spoken, and he was seized and sent to jail.

There was also information given to the Sheriff of Inveraray that the laird of Fasnacloich was seen going to the moor armed the same day that Colin of Glenure was killed. It was suspected that Fasnacloich had a hand in the killing of Colin of Glenure, and he was brought to court about the affair. Fasnacloich had sent his serving-man on a message to William Stewart, usually called Uilleam Mor MacDhonnachaidh Fhuideir, to Fort William. The serving-man got a little parcel from Uilleam Mor to bring to the laird of Fasnacloich. When the latter opened the parcel the serving-man cast his eye on it: and the contents were a few balls and a mould for making them on which was marked the number of the gun. When Fasnacloich was brought to Inveraray the serving-man fled out of the country and did not return for three or four years. It is not known what evidence that serving-man might bring against the laird of Fasnacloich were he found – but he was not found.

There was a man dwelling in Inverpoll of the name of Donald

MacIntyre, called Domhnall Ban Mac Iain. He was away with the Prince and had been at the battle of Culloden. He was summoned against Fasnacloich, put on oath, and examined. The Sheriff asked him, 'Did you see the laird of Fasnacloich going to the moor in arms the same day that Colin of Glenure was killed?' Donald replied, 'No.' They had no more witnesses upon that point, so they were obliged to stop the trying of Fasnacloich and to set him at liberty.

A while after the laird of Fasnacloich had been set at liberty, he was passing Inverpoll. He saw Domhnall Ban Mac Iain at work and called upon him. 'Come hither, Domhnall Ban, I want to have a little talk with you.'

Donald went where he was. There was another of the name of Donald MacMichael working near them and the laird of Fasnacloich called to him, 'Come you hither, also, Donald MacMichael, that you may hear what shall be said.' Donald MacMichael went where Fasnacloich and Domhnall Ban were. The laird of Fasnacloich said to Domhnall Ban Mac Iain, 'I am much obliged to you, Donald MacIntyre, for having perjured yourself to save me at Inveraray.' Donald rejoined, 'O Devil's spawn. Would you say that I perjured myself for you?'

'Well, then, tell me, Donald,' remarked Fasnacloich, 'how you clear yourself.' 'The Sheriff asked me,' said Donald, ' "Did you see the laird of Fasnacloich in arms on the day on which Colin of Glenure was killed?" I said, "No." Neither did I see you have but a gun; and you know that one gun is not arms. It is but an arm.' 'Right enough,' said Fasnacloich, 'you clear yourself that way.'

JAMES STEWART OF THE GLEN

James Stewart of the Glen was a prisoner in Fort William and his friends were very anxious about him. One of his daughters was married and dwelt at Keil opposite Eilean nan Gobhann. Her face resembled very much that of her father and she was of the same size. She went to the prison to see him. She got in where he was and they were left alone. When they spoke to one another for a short time, she said to him, 'Since we resemble each other so much in features, we might exchange clothes. They would not distinguish us from one another and I should remain in prison in your place, and you might escape.'

The reply of James of the Glen was, 'Since I am innocent I will not put on myself any appearance of guilt. I will stay in the prison and stand my trial. Although they can destroy my life they cannot destroy my soul.' So James remained in the prison to stand his trial.

There were not many of the gentlemen, or of others who were somewhat respected that rose with Prince Charles, either in Lochaber or in Appin of MacIain Stiubhart, who were not someway connected with the plot against the life of Colin of Glenure. They were now under fear that there should be a ransacking out about it, and that there should be information of their connection with it obtained, so they devised a plan to put those who were in search of evidence off the scent.

There was a man of a respectable family whose name was Allan Stewart, usually called Allan Breck. He received a reward for fleeing and allowing the killing of Colin of Glenure to be imputed to him, for the purpose of lessening inquiries concerning the rest of the gentlemen by directing suspicion to himself (Allan Breck) and sending those who sought for the guilty to search the country for him. He went to Kinlochbeg and stayed there for a while, and he was a while in Glen Lyon keeping himself in concealment; and the people of the country were all faithful to him for, while he was not taken, he was concealing the guilt of those who did the ill deed. At last Allan found means of leaving the country and going to France.

He enlisted in the French army and got to be an officer in it, and when he understood that he was safe from British Law he sent a letter to his own country telling that he was the man who killed Colin of Glenure. The letter did not reach soon enough to be of use to James of the Glen.

James Stewart, James of the Glen, was brought to Inveraray where he was tried before the court. The trial lasted three days without anything being found against him that would make him guilty. On the third day John Breck MacColl, one of the people of Glenduror, was brought as witness against him. John MacColl had been left an orphan in the beginning of his youth; he was left without mother, father or means, and it was James of the Glen who pitied him, brought him into his own house, and reared him till he was able to do for himself. He was for a long time a serving-man to James of the Glen. He was wont to be along with the latter at the public house. He heard much of the abusive language that James uttered against Colin of Glenure when drunk. John Breck MacColl did not object to telling every harsh word that he remembered James of the Glen say against Colin of Glenure. The latter, however, was not condemned on account of any of the evidence that was at that time given against him by John Breck, who was then allowed to leave the witness-box.

When John Breck MacColl had gone out of the court-house, he and his wife met each other, and they began to talk of the evidence which John had given before the court. His wife asked him, 'Did you tell them that you heard James of the Glen saying once when he was drunk, that he would go a mile on his knees on the ice to make a black cock of Colin of Glenure?' 'Indeed, I did not remember that,' said John. 'Well,' said his wife, 'you had better return in yet and tell it to them.' 'I do not like to return to the court-house again, since I did not remember it when I was in,' replied John. John Breck was not willing to go in again to the court-house, but his wife persuaded him. He returned to the court and said, 'I forgot something when I was in before, gentlemen. There is a little thing that I did not remember to tell you.'

'Come on, then,' they said to him, 'and enter the witness-box, and tell what you have to say.' John Breck entered the witness-box and said, 'I heard the prisoner before you, James Stewart, say, once when he was drunk, that he would go three miles on his knees on the ice to make a black cock of Colin of Glenure.' When the Judge heard this he gave sentence, that James Stewart was to be hanged on a gallows at Cnap a' Chaolais; that his body was to be left hanging until it fell down and that his bones were to be put up again and left hanging to the gallows until they should decay with time. So many days were allowed James Stewart of the Glen to live in prison.

After James Stewart of the Glen had been condemned to be hanged and was confined in prison under sentence of death, Donald Stewart, the nephew of the laird of Ballachulish, was exceedingly sorry about it, thinking that although he was the man by whom Colin of Glenure was killed, yet that it was James of the Glen, a man innocent of it, who was to suffer death by hanging for the deed. Donald was disposed to give himself up to be hanged instead of James of the Glen, and he told his friends what he was inclined to do.

When the friends of Donald Stewart heard that he was intending to inform about himself, they were much afraid that he would give himself up, and that information might be obtained of everyone who had joined in the plot for killing Colin of Glenure. They gathered round him to advise him to keep secret all that could be kept secret of the affair. They pointed out to him that Allan Breck Stewart had already feigned that he was the person who killed Colin of Glenure, but that that had done no good to James of the Glen, and granting that he (Donald) should deliver himself up, it would only make matters worse; that it would be better that one innocent man should be put to death, than that a common destruction should be brought on all the people of the country; that even were he to give himself up, it would not save James from the gallows but that both of them should be hanged; that there was danger that all connected with the plot should in this case be discovered and that those of them who were not slaughtered should be exiled from the kingdom.

The gentlemen managed with great difficulty to prevent Donald Stewart giving himself up, but he grew sick with grief-fever; he took to his bed and lay in it for a long time thereafter.

A gallows was erected at Cnap a' Chaolais, James of the Glen was hanged on it and he was left hanging on it. The place where he was hanged was very trying to his friends. It was in sight of the place where the house of his widow was and there was not a time that she looked the way of Ballachulish or Glencoe, that she did not see her husband hanging on the gallows at Cnap a' Chaolais. There was a sister of James of the Glen married at Callart and another at Invercoe, and the houses of those sisters were in sight of Cnap a' Chaolais. There was not a time that they looked towards Ardsheil that they did not see their brother hanging on the gallows at Cnap a' Chaolais; and the gallows was within a short distance of the house of Ballachulish, and all the friends were grieved about it.

About those times Duke Archibald died, and General John Campbell of Mamore was the heir. It was he who got to be Duke after Duke Archibald. He was the second Duke John that was on Argyll.

Duke John was highly esteemed by the King who made him Chief Governor of all the castles in Scotland; and he was wont to go on a circuit once a year to see in what order the castles were kept.

One time that he was on his journey to survey the castles, the bones of James of the Glen fell, and there was a rumour that the ruling men of the garrison at Fort William were going to prepare irons to hang up the bones to the gallows again. This was an annoyance to every person who dwelt in sight of Cnap a' Chaolais. There was a man of the people of Lochaber who was not quite sane, called Mad Macfie, who was wont to go occasionally to Appin. It happened that he went to Ballachulish about those times. Someone went and felled the gallows and Mad Macfie was blamed for the deed. Macfie owned that he did it; yet the people of the country were not free from fear that when the Duke would come round he should be angry about the felling of the gallows, and that he should raise a quarrel about the matter.

Iain Buidhe was the name which some gave to John Stewart who was laird of Ballachulish at that time. He thought that he would try to win the good graces of the Duke by humbling himself and offering friendship. He gave orders to the people of Aird nan Saor, when the Duke reached to send a messenger to Ballachulish to inform him of his arrival, in order that he might meet him and declare his business.

When the Duke was going his round he reached Aird nan Saor and the night before he was to leave this place, a messenger was sent to Ballachulish to inform Iain Buidhe that the Duke was going the way next day. The next day the laird of Ballachulish was at Caolas Mhic Pharuig waiting until the Duke should come. When the Duke came forward a page and four white dogs were going before his coach. When the Duke crossed the ferry of Caolas Mhic Pharuig, Ian Buidhe, the laird of Ballachulish, met him in a cheerful and welcoming manner, and he offered his hand to the Duke to salute him. The Duke said to him, 'Who are you? I do not myself know you.' Iain Buidhe replied, 'John Stewart is my name. I have a little estate here at Ballachulish, and I should consider it a favour if you would come and pass a night with me.' The Duke asked him, 'Have you a comfortable place for me if I go with you?' Iain Buidhe replied, 'I have but a small house, as becomes a man who has but a small estate, and without much luxury within it; nevertheless, I think that I can give a night's hospitality to a Duke and his following.' The Duke said, 'It seems to me that it comes to my recollection that I saw you before. I will go with you tonight.'

The Duke and his following went with the laird of Ballachulish to pass a night with him in his house. The laird and lady of Ballachulish had made ready for having the Duke a night in their house in passing; and they had everything in a suitable manner with a place for the servants, the horses, and the dogs; and the Duke got good hospitality in the house of Ballachulish. Plenty of oats and food was given to the horses, and porridge was made for the dogs. The lady of Ballachulish got a quarter of a stone of butter, and made two halves of it, and she put one half in the dogs' porridge; and next day there was porridge made for the dogs, and the lady put the rest of the butter in it.

After the Duke and Iain Buidhe had finished their meal of meat, the Duke said to John, 'Is there anything in my power to do for you that you wish me to do?' 'Well,' rejoined John, 'I have a female neighbour, and I should like to get leave to put her away.' The Duke remarked, 'Is not Ballachulish your own and can you not do your own pleasure on your own lands?' John answered, 'I cannot. I have one female neighbour that I cannot put away without your consent, and that is the gallows on which James of the Glen was hanged. It is opposite my eyes every day that I rise and it causes me very much annoyance.'

'Do not let on anything,' replied the Duke, 'but put it away. It was not in accordance with my wish that it was ever there. I did all I could against its being placed there at all, but he who was

Duke of Argyll then did as he liked; but put away your neighbour in a quiet manner, and I promise you that I shall not say a word about it. I feel affronted by that case, and it were better in my estimation had it never happened.'

The Duke left Ballachulish that day and went to Ardchattan. He had his four white dogs along with him. They were put in an outside house and there was not but poor food given them. As they had got good food at Ballachulish the previous night and that morning itself before they left, they were not pleased at Ardchattan. They broke out of the house in which they were and went back to Ballachulish.

In the morning, when the Duke's gillie got up and went to see about the dogs, they were away. He went and told the Duke that the dogs had left him. The Duke asked him, 'What food did they get last night?' 'They got brawn and water,' remarked the gillie. 'And what food,' asked the Duke, 'did they get when they were at Ballachulish?' The servant told, 'They got their fill of oatmeal porridge and plenty of butter in it.' Then the servant told the quantity of butter that the goodwife of Ballachulish had put in the porridge.

'O! Then,' said the Duke, 'you may go to Ballachulish to seek the dogs and you will get them there. It is likely, however, that the laird of Ballachulish will send a gillie with the dogs to bring them to me. Go you onwards until the gillie meets you, and wherever he will meet you, tell him to come on to Inveraray with the dogs along with you.'

The Duke went home to Inveraray and the gillie returned for the dogs. And when he was going forward by the side of the Linn of Seil the gillie of Ballachulish met him with the dogs. The Duke's gillie told the other gillie that the Duke wished him to go on to Inveraray, that he had some particular business with him. The two went onwards together till they reached Inveraray, and the Duke gave a gift to the gillie of Ballachulish. It is not known how much he gave him, but the gillie of Ballachulish went home and did not consider his journey to have been in vain.

A short time after these things happened the Duke and Duchess were together by themselves, and the Duchess asked the Duke where he had met with the best hospitality when he was on his journey. The Duke replied, 'Well, it was at Ballachulish from Iain Buidhe, laird of Ballachulish.' 'Just so; you are wealthy enough to put a heel-piece on his shoe for that.'

The Duke had a right to a share of the woods of Appin, and when the woods were cut his own share of the price of the timber was set apart for him. There was a wood of native fir which grew from the top of Duraig to a place called Lag a' Ghiubhais, and when that wood was cut MacCailein's share of it was left standing on a plain called after that Leirg Mhic Cailein. The Duke gave up the fir that was on that plain to the laird of Ballachulish. There was a piece of land between Drochaid na Larach, or as it was called at that time Uisge-fheadhain, and Port Eachainn in Glencoe which the Duke gave to the lady of Ballachulish as a dowry.

After the Duke had been a night in the house of Iain Buidhe, laird of Ballachulish, the Stewarts and Campbells grew more friendly to one another than they had been for a while prior to that and for a long time subsequent to the death of Colin of Glenure.

ALLAN BRECK STEWART

After Allan Breck Stewart had got to France, he sent back a letter saying that he was the man who killed Colin of Glenure, and that James Stewart, called James of the Glen, was innocent. There was then a complaint made to the High Rulers of the kingdom about the trial of James of the Glen. There was ransacking about the case, and there was a change made as to the manner in which prisoners were tried in the shire of Argyll after that. Instead of gentlemen of the shire sitting in the Chair of Judgment, there were judges called the Red Lords going once a year to Inveraray to be judges in the court of the sheriffdom. Allan Breck Stewart was in the army of France, and he was in America during the period of the war between Britain and France in America. One time some of the Red Army were nearly taken prisoners by him. He was an officer in the French army. There were some of the men of Argyll in the Red Army, and the heart of Allan Stewart warmed towards the men of his country. He went at night to their tents and told them who he was, and in his conversation with them he told them that he had no hand whatever in the killing of Colin of Glenure; that it was to relieve the gentlemen of Appin that he took upon himself that he had killed him; and when he got to flee to France, that it was a false letter that he sent home to his country people saying that he was the murderer, but that he had no hand in it. He told the Scots officers that he would leave a breach for them to escape next night. He left a breach, as he said, by which the Scotsmen escaped from the snare in which they were.

DONALD STEWART

Donald Stewart, the laird of Ballachulish's nephew, and Alexander Campbell, brother to Colin of Glenure, and their dogs and gillies with them, went to the moor of Rannoch to hunt deer. Donald had the long Spanish gun called the Slinneanach with him. They travelled through the moor of Rannoch during the whole day without seeing a deer. When it was near evening, they sat in a hollow to eat some food which they had with them. While they were eating the food they were looking around them, and they observed something resembling the antlers of a deer on a precipice between them and the horizon, at the top of the place where they were. For a while at first they were in doubt whether they saw the antlers of a deer or a bush of willow. At last Donald Stewart rested his long gun called the Slinneanach and said to his gillie, 'Whistle.' The gillie whistled and nothing whatever moved. 'Whistle more vigorously,' said Donald. The gillie whistled louder and a deer rose. They were his antlers which they saw. Donald aimed at the deer while it was stretching itself before taking a leap. Alexander Campbell, son of the laird of Barcaldine, said to him, 'Fool! Do you think that you can do it at that distance?' Donald fired the shot and the deer fell. 'You have made it out,' said Alexander Campbell, 'and I did not think that there was any gun that could do the turn at the distance.'

They went to the place where the deer lay and they looked where he had been struck. The holes of the two balls which had been in the gun were about twice the breadth of the two balls from one another, halfway between the back of the shoulder and the short rib.

Alexander looked at the manner in which the deer was struck for a short time and then said, 'That is exactly the very manner in which Colin my brother was struck; and I am deceived, or else it is the same gun that did the deed.' 'Do you think,' said Donald Stewart, 'that it was I who killed your brother?' 'I do not say in whose hand the gun was,' rejoined Alexander Campbell, 'but I say that I am deceived, if that is not the very gun by which the killing was done.' 'Were I to think that you imagined that it was I who killed your brother, you should not go home living on your own feet.' 'I do not say that it was you who killed my brother; but I remark that the gun, which you have, has put the two balls at the same distance from one another as those which were put in my brother were, and much in the same manner.' 'If I thought that you were suspecting me,' replied Donald, 'of having killed your brother, you should not go home to say that to another.' 'O! I do not suspect you,' said the other, 'I do but say that the shots were like each other.'

The talk produced a coldness between the two. They separated, and each of them chose a road for himself to go home, and they did not thenceforth go to hunt together.

The people of Ballachulish after this gave a bad report of the gun called the Slinneanach; that any house in which it was should take fire. They would not keep it in a Ballachulish house any longer nor give it again to those to whom it belonged. They kept it for a while in an outhouse, taking as an excuse that it was not to be kept in Ballachulish House for fear of its going on fire. At last they sent the Slinneanach to the north, to friends that they had there, and they did not give it back again to the MacColls, although the MacColls were very desirous of getting it. The North Country men were not the least afraid that their house should take fire when the Slinneanach was brought into it.

Donald Stewart went to sea and did not return again until he was an old man. It is said that he died in a shealing-hut in Gleann na h-Iola; that many of the gentlemen of the country were in with him the night that he died; that the gentlemen took fear; that they fled out; that they did not go in again until day; but that when they went in they found Donald Stewart dead.

The son of Donald Stewart went to sea. It was on a ship of war that he was. The laird of Ballachulish was very desirous that he should come home and marry his daughter, in order that the estate should continue in the true line of Stewarts; but the son of Donald Stewart did not come home in time, and the daughter of the laird of Ballachulish made up with one of the name of Dugald Stewart who had a commission in the army. Dugald Stewart got the daughter of Ballachulish with child, and the son of Donald Stewart would not take her then, and she married Dugald Stewart. The laird of Ballachulish was not willing to give the estate to Dugald Stewart, and he made a will leaving the land of Ballachulish to Donald Stewart, his brother's son, and leaving only the money saved to his daughter. He repented of this again, however, and he made a new will leaving the land of Ballachulish to his own daughter. The two wills raised a dispute.

The son of Donald Stewart was an officer on board a ship of war, and he laid by much money. When he came home, he supposed that as he was the male who was nearest related to the laird of Ballachulish he was the rightful heir. After the death of the laird of Ballachulish, he went to try law with Dugald Stewart and the daughter of the laird of Ballachulish. He tried to break the will which the laird of Ballachulish had made, but he failed in that. The lawsuit lasted for many years and the son of Donald Stewart left himself without much. He went to sea again and never returned. The lawsuit cost so much money to Dugald Stewart that he put the estate in debt. As he kept up a great rank he left the estate deeply in debt at the time of his death.

Charles was the name of Dugald's son. He was obliged to sell Ballachulish and a Low Country gentleman bought it. The land was let in large farms to farmers, and many of the old natives were obliged to leave the place. It was then that they grew indifferent about the gentlemen who were in the country in the days of old, and that they would tell any tale at all that they knew about them.

THE HERRING-FISHER AND
THE PRESS-GANG

Source: Cuthbert Bede, *The White Wife*
Narrator: Unknown (Kintyre), 1861–5

Note: Stories of the press-gang are still vividly recalled, and many are given
in a feature on 'The Press-Gang' in *Tocher* 29

My father had gone out with a herring fleet from Campbelton, and on a certain day they were all safe in harbour at
the Island of Barra. They had not been there long when a man-
of-war popped in upon them. Knowing the fate that was in store
for them, the fishers took to their heels and made for the hills,
with the press-gang after them.

Now it happened that my father had been up all night at the
boat, and, when he had come ashore in the morning to the
public house, he had been glad to go to rest for a while to sleep
away his fatigue, so that when the press-gang came he had
turned in in his shirt. But his comrades gave him the note of
warning and roused him from the bed, telling him that the press-
gang were on him. At this intelligence my father was so alarmed
that he at once jumped up and ran out of the door; and seeing
that the press-gang were just then being put on shore from the
man-of-war's boat, and that not a moment was to be lost, he did
not tarry by returning for his clothes, but at once set off to run
to the hills in his shirt.

Being thus so slightly clad and unencumbered with superfluous
apparel, and being also very strong and swift, my father soon
outstripped his own companions and distanced the press-gang.
After he had scudded along for some distance, and was getting
tired with his running, and could not meet with any cave or
secret place wherein he dared to hide himself, he lighted upon a
house, and, as it was a miserable-looking place, he made bold to

lift the latch and enter without losing time by knocking or ceremony. He found two people inside the house, an old woman who was spinning, and a young woman who was stirring the pot over the fire. They looked scared at seeing a man with nothing but his shirt on thus entering in upon them so suddenly. The lassie squealed, and lifting up her spoon in surprise, let the pot boil over into the fire, while the old wife nearly fell off her stool in affright.

My father was too much out of breath to waste many words in explanation, but he gasped out, 'The press-gang! save me!' and they understood him at once. 'Get you in here, decent man, and you shall be safe,' said the old wife, as soon as she could get herself together; and she led my father to a bed in a little room which had no glass window, but only a hole in the mud wall, into which straw had been thrust. My father crept into the bed, and hid himself there in the darkness, listening anxiously to every sound of approaching footsteps. But he had only one fright, and that was when the goodman came in from his work; all the rest of the day he was not interfered with, and heard nothing of his pursuers. It was soon explained to the old man that he had got a new tenant in his house, and, as everyone hated the press-gang, the goodman's sympathies were at once enlisted for my father, and he brought him a good supper and a glass of whisky to keep up his courage.

They had all gone to bed, when, about midnight, my father heard the sound of hard English outside the house, and, presently, there was a great thumping at the door. My father knew at once that it was the press-gang, and cast about what he should do for his escape. The thumping and the English were going on, and the old man, crying to my father to lie close, unbarred the door. My father heard the press-gang enter, and, somewhat to his relief, instead of asking for him, they said to the old wife, 'Where is your daughter?' Now my father understood their language, but the old wife had got no English; so when she caught the word 'daughter', she fancied they were seeking a doctor, and she therefore replied, '*Cha' neil dotair an so*' ['There is no doctor here']. The press-gang did not understand her, and they pushed about, looking for the daughter. Her bed was just on the other side of the thin partition, against which my father had crept, and he could hear her trembling all over while the men were searching the rest of the room. They soon found her, and the poor lassie set up a great scream as they dragged her forth.

My father thought that the noise that was being made would be favourable for his escape; so, as he could not render any help to the lassie, he pushed the straw out of the hole in the mud wall, squeezed himself with some difficulty through the narrow aperture, and took to running with the greatest speed. But before he had got many yards from the house, and before he had lost the hearing of the poor lassie's cries, he heard a great shout, and found that he had been discovered by one of the press-gang who had, perhaps, been left outside the house to keep watch. It was a bright moonlight night; and my father wished that his shirt had been anywhere else than on his back, for it mainly assisted to guide his enemies in their pursuit. Half a dozen of them were now in pursuit of him, shouting and yelling, and even firing pistols at him, though, perhaps, this was only to intimidate him. As his shirt made him to be so conspicuous in the moonlight, my father thought it would be the best plan to throw it away and run in his buff; and this he did. This proceeding probably saved him, for his pursuers made for his shirt, imagining, most likely, that he was inside it, and had fallen from exhaustion, and my father, at the same time, had doubled like a hare in another direction. Thus his pursuers were thrown off the scent; and, as good luck would have it, they took the very opposite road to that which my father took; and one of the men fell over a rock, crying, 'My bones are broken.'

My father travelled on until he met a haystack, where he made a place for himself; but he did not remain in it long, for he began to feel very cold. So, as all seemed safe, he crept out, and once more took to running, until he came to a barn; and there he covered himself with straw, and remained till daylight. When the farmer came to the barn in the morning he was greatly surprised to find a naked man lying asleep amidst the straw; and crying out that it was a murder, he with his noise not only brought his men to his assistance, but also aroused my father from his heavy slumber. My father was more frightened than the farmer and his men; for, at first, he imagined that they were the press-gang; and he would have once more taken to running if he had seen any hole or door through which he could have escaped. But there was none; so he jumped out of the straw, intending to ask the farmer for protection. But when the farmer and his men saw a wild-looking, stark-naked man thus advancing upon them, with straws sticking in his hair, they viewed him in the light of an imbecile, or lunatic; and snatched up forks wherewith to defend themselves from his attacks.

Of course each side soon found out the mistake they were making, and when my father explained to them how it was that he came to be dressed in his buff, the farmer at once understood all about it, and gave him his coat to wrap around his loins, like a kilt, and led him to his house, which was close at hand. There he furnished my father with a full suit of the Highland garb, until he should get his own clothes; and he also set before him a good breakfast, and sent one of his men to spy out if the man-of-war was still off the island. When it was reported to have sailed, my father knew that he was safe, and he therefore bade farewell to the friendly farmer, and went back to the boats, where he found that nearly all his companions had been captured by the press-gang and taken on board the man-of-war. The shortness of hands obliged him to do double work; and, as they left the island the next day, he was unable to search out the house in which he had first taken refuge, and to learn what had befallen the poor lassie. My father did not afterwards take a part in the herring-fishery voyages, so that he escaped any further adventures with the press-gang.

JAMES MACKENZIE'S GAIRLOCH STORIES

Source: J. H. Dixon, *Gairloch in North-West Ross-shire*
Narrator: James Mackenzie of Kirkton, born 1808

WILLIAM ROY MACKENZIE

William Roy Mackenzie was stopping at Innis a bhaird. This was in the eighteenth century, before they commenced making whisky in Gairloch. William used to go to Ferintosh with his two horses with crook saddles, carrying a cask of whisky on each side. He always went there about Christmas. At that time Christmas was observed in Gairloch; now its observance is given up. William had two horses, a white and a black; one of them was fastened behind the tail of the other, the white horse foremost. On the other side of Achnasheen there was an exciseman waiting to catch William on his way home with four casks of whisky. The exciseman hid himself until William came past. Then he jumped out from his hiding-place, and caught the white horse by the halter, saying, 'This is mine.' Says William, 'I do not think you will say that tomorrow; let go my horse.' 'No,' says the exciseman. 'Will you let him go,' says William, 'if you get a permit with him?' 'Let me see your permit,' says the exciseman, still dragging at the white horse. 'Stop,' says William; 'let go the horse, the permit is in his tail.' He would not let go; so when William saw that, he loosed the black horse from behind the grey, that he might get at the permit. Then he lifted his stick and struck the old grey so that he plunged and jumped, and in the scrimmage one of the casks of whisky struck the exciseman and knocked him down on the ground. Says William, 'There's the permit for you.' The exciseman lay helpless on the ground; so William Roy got clean away with all the whisky, and came home with it to Innis a bhaird.

KENNETH AND JOHN MACKENZIE OF RONA

One of the Mackenzies of Letterewe had a daughter who was married to a man in Badfearn in Skye. A daughter of theirs became the wife of William Mackenzie of Rona, who was one of the Mackenzies of Shieldaig of Gairloch. He had a son named Kenneth; and Kenneth had two sons, called Kenneth and John. They were out fishing in a smack of their own, when they were attacked and taken by the press-gang. They were carried off, and placed in a hulk lying in the Thames below London. One night they were together on the same watch, and they then made a plan to escape. A yacht belonging to a gentleman in London was in the river; she was out and in every day, and always anchored alongside the hulk. The gentry from the yacht were going ashore every night, and leaving only a boy in her. The night the two brothers Kenneth and John were on the watch, the boy was alone in the yacht. What did they do but decide to carry out their plan of escape there and then! So they went through the gun-ports, one on each side of the hulk, and swam to the yacht. Then they got the yacht under weigh, the boy sleeping all the time. They got safe away with the yacht, and worked her as far as to Loch Craignish, on this side of Crinan. There they went ashore in the night, and left the yacht with the boy. They left the yacht's gig ashore in Loch Craignish, and set off on their way home. When the laird of Craignish saw the gig, and the yacht lying in the loch, he went out in the gig to see what kind of yacht she was. The brothers had left the papers of the yacht on the cabin table, that it might be found out who she belonged to. So the laird of Craignish wrote to the owners in London, and advised them to send orders to him to sell the yacht and send the boy home with the money. The owners did so, and the yacht was sold. She became the mail-packet between Coll and Tobermory. I saw her long ago on that service.

The two brothers, Kenneth and John Mackenzie, got safe back to Rona, and soon got another smack. They were going south with a cargo of fish, through the Crinan Canal; the smack was lying in the basin after you pass the first lock. There was a plank put to the shore from the gangway of the vessel; by this they went ashore to the inn at Crinan. A girl in the house went to the vessel and took the plank out; the two Mackenzies, on going back to the smack in the dark, for want of the plank fell into the basin, and were both drowned. They were relations of my mother. I saw them when I was a boy at Mellon Charles. They were fine men.

JOHN MACGREGOR OF LONDUBH

John Mackenzie, son of William Mackenzie, the fourth laird of Gruinard, by Lilias, daughter of Captain John Mackenzie of Kinloch (or Lochend), was a captain in the 73rd Regiment in the end of the eighteenth century. The Gruinard family had holes and presses in their houses at Udrigil and Aird, where they kept men whom they had caught until they agreed to enlist in the army. Gruinard got money for catching men for the army. There was a man in Londubh named Ruaridh Donn or Rorie Macgregor, of the Macgregors of Kenlochewe; he was an old man, and was still strong. He had a son, John, who was a very strong bold man. Gruinard gathered a gang of twelve men to catch John Macgregor. So Mackenzie Lochend sent him down with a letter to Mackenzie Gruinard. John went with the letter, and gave it to Mrs Mackenzie, Gruinard's wife. 'Come in, John,' she said, 'till you get some meat before you go away to Poolewe.' So John went in, and she made a piece for him: she gave him a slice of bread and butter, and put a sovereign between the bread and butter so that he might get it. When John was eating he found the gold in his mouth; he put it in his pocket. So when he had finished eating, he came out of the house to go away home, and there he saw the gang of twelve men ready to catch him. Mrs Mackenzie told him he had got the king's money. 'It's not much,' said he. 'I wish I would get more of it.' Says she, 'You'll get that by and by.' 'I'm not so sure of that,' says John. Then the gang took him. 'If you're going to keep me,' says John, 'send word to my old father, that I may see him as I pass by: he is old and weak, and I will never see him again.' So Mrs Mackenzie sent on word to his father to meet him. John was sent away with the gang, and as they passed the garden at Londubh, Ruaridh Donn came down to the road to meet his son, leaning on his staff as if he were weak. 'Goodbye! are you going away, John?' says he. 'Oh yes! goodbye to you, I'll never see you again,' says John. Then the old man got a hold of John, and put him between himself and the wall. The old man was shaking on his stick. John lifted his two hands and put them over his father's shoulders, and began laughing and mocking the gang. So the twelve men dare not go near them, and they left John to go home with his money.

Captain John Mackenzie, son of Captain John Mackenzie, Kinloch, and brother of Mrs Mackenzie, Gruinard, went to Skye to marry a daughter of the minister of Cambusmore. He went in a boat with a crew of six men, and Duncan Urquhart, his own valet. John Macgregor was one of the crew. They went ashore at Port Golaig, near Ru Hunish, the point of Skye furthest north. The captain and Duncan walked up to Cambusmore, but the crew stopped with the boat. The captain and Duncan were in the minister's house all the week. On the Saturday John Macgregor was sent up to the manse by the rest of the crew to see what was keeping them. It was late when John got to the manse. The captain came out and scolded John, asking what business he had there, and saying he might go away any time he pleased for all he cared. Then the minister came out, and said John must stop in the house until the Sabbath, for it would not be safe for him to return to the boat through the night. But John would go away back, and he fell over the high rock near Duntulm Castle and was killed. When the minister rose in the morning, he sent Duncan Urquhart to see if John had arrived at the boat. When Duncan was going he saw part of John's kilt caught on a point of rock, and found his dead body below. So Duncan turned to the house and told the bad news. The minister said to the captain, 'You may go home; you will not get my daughter this trip.' John Macgregor's body was taken home in a box, and buried in the churchyard at Inverewe. He left two daughters; one of them was married to Murdo Crubach Fraser in Inverkerry, and was the mother of Kenneth Fraser and John Fraser now living at Leac-nan-Saighead. A daughter of Murdo Crubach's is the wife of Christopher Mackenzie, Brahan, and a son of theirs is piper with the Mackintosh.

MURDO MACKENZIE, OR MURDO'S SON

There was a Mackenzie of an old Gairloch stock living in Ullapool, Loch Broom. He was called in Gaelic 'Murchadh mac Mhurchaidh', or, 'Murdo the son of Murdo': I will call him 'Murdo's son'. He was a very fine, good-looking man, and very brave. He had a small smack, and he was always going with her round the Mull of Kintyre to Greenock with herrings from Loch Broom. Returning with the vessel empty, he put into a place called Duncan's Well, in the Island of Luing, on the other side of Oban. This island belongs to Lord Breadalbane to this day. Murdo's son went ashore at night. There was a ball going on in a house, and Lord Breadalbane's daughter was there. She fell in love at once with the good-looking Murdo's son, and he fell in love with her. He took her away with him that very night, and before daybreak they set sail for Ullapool. When they got to Ullapool they were married, and he took her to his house at the place now called Moorfield, where the banker lives in the present day.

There was no name on Murdo's son's smack at that time; there were no roads nor newspapers then; and no one knew where the smack had gone with Lord Breadalbane's daughter, only that she had left with Murdo's son. Lord Breadalbane could find out nothing more. He went to the king and got a law made that from that time every vessel should have a name on it; there were no names on vessels before then in Scotland. Lord Breadalbane offered a reward of three hundred pounds to anyone who would find where his daughter had gone. When Murdo's son got the report of this reward he started off at once, dressed in his best kilt and plaid, with his dirk in his belt, and walked all the way to Lord Breadalbane's castle at Taymouth. He knocked at the door, and a man came and asked what he was wanting; he told him he wanted to see the lord. So the man went in, and soon the lord came in his slippers to the door. He asked Murdo's son what he was wanting there. He told him he came to tell him where his daughter was, that he might get the reward. Says the lord, 'You will get the money if you tell me where she is. Where is she?' 'Well,' says Murdo's son, 'I'll tell that when I get the money.' 'There's your money for you then.' When he got the money, he said, 'She's at Ullapool, at Loch Broom, and if you will give me other three hundred pounds I will put the hand of the man that stole her into your hand.' The lord gave him other three hundred pounds. Says he, 'Keep out your hand. There,' says he, putting his hand in the lord's hand, 'is the hand that took your daughter from the Island of Luing;' and Lord Breadalbane was so pleased with his pluck and appearance, that he accepted him as his son-in-law, and gave him the full *tocher* of his daughter. I remember seeing their son and daughter; the daughter married John Morrison, who was the farmer at Drumchork, about 1850.

Murdo's son was going in the same smack with herrings from Loch Broom to sell them. After coming round the Mull of Kintyre he anchored at Crinan for the night. There was lying there a lugger full of gin and brandy; she had been captured near Cape Wrath by a government cutter; the crew had been put ashore at Cape Wrath. Six men of the cutter's crew were bringing the lugger to deliver her at Greenock. She came alongside Murdo's son at Crinan, as she was going south and he coming north. Murdo's son asked them, 'What craft is that?' They told him it was a smuggler they had caught at Cape Wrath. 'Surely you have plenty drink on board,' says he. 'Oh, yes,' they said, 'she is choke full.' Says he, 'You had better all of you come over and see if the stuff I have is better than what you have got.' So they came over, all hands, to his smack. He tried the jar he had, and made them all drunk. They could not leave his cabin. When they were in this state he and his crew went to the lugger, took possession of her, and set sail, leaving her drunken crew in his own smack. Murdo's son came to Ullapool with the lugger, and when he had taken the cargo out of her he set fire to her and destroyed her. A son of Murdo's son was married to Mrs Mackenzie of Kernsary before Mr Mackenzie married her, and had two sons, both now dead, and buried in Cil-lean, in Strath Garve.

Donald Morrison, of Drumchork, was a grandson of Murdo's son and Lord Breadalbane's daughter. He went to see the Lord Breadalbane of his day, a descendant of the lord whose daughter was married to Murdo's son. Lord Breadalbane gave Donald Morrison three hundred pounds when he went to the castle. Rorie Morrison also went to see Lord Breadalbane, but he did not get anything. Donald was a very fine, tall, handsome man, and looked grand in his kilt and plaid; there was no one like him in the country, so good-looking and so well shaped for the kilt!

ANECDOTE OF SIR HECTOR MACKENZIE

The law that a name should be put on every vessel brings to my mind an anecdote of Sir Hector Mackenzie of Gairloch. Macleod of Raasay had a boat that had no name on her when the law was made requiring names. So the boat was taken from him, and he was cited to a court at Inverness, that he might be fined for not putting a name on the boat. When Sir Hector heard of this he went to the court. Macleod was there; the judge told him he was fined so much for not having the boat named. Sir Hector said, 'Macleod's boat is the coach to his house, and he can never get home without it, and if you are going to fine him for not having his boat named, you must put a name on your own coach when you go out.' Said the judge, 'If that be the case he can go home.' Thus Macleod got clear.

MACKENZIE KERNSARY AND MY GRANDFATHER

I can remember Mr and Mrs Mackenzie of Kernsary. They lived in the house where I now live. Rorie, as Mackenzie Kernsary was called, was a strange eccentric man; he died a good while before his wife, and was buried in the chapel in the Inverewe burial ground close by. They had only one son, Sandy, and it was he who built the house at Inveran; he was married to a daughter of the Rev. Roderick Morison, minister of Kintail, the best-looking woman in the north of Scotland at that time; her nephew is the present minister of Kintail. Sandy had three sons and three daughters. One son became Established Church minister at Moy; one daughter married Mr Mactavish, a lawyer in Inverness; another daughter married one Cameron, a farmer; and another son was at sea. My grandfather, John Mackenzie, was a cattle drover; he was always going through the country buying cattle; an old Hielan'man, with his blue bonnet and old Hielan' coat. He bought cattle between Poolewe and Little Loch Broom. At times he bought a large number. One time he went to the Isle of Gruinard and bought a fat grey cow from one Duncan Macgregor there. He sent a man on with the drove to Gairloch to go to the market, and stopped behind himself that day. When the cows were passing Londubh, Mackenzie Kernsary was out on the brae; he saw the cattle passing, and he asked the man with them to whom did they belong. The man replied, 'To John Mackenzie, the drover.' 'Oh!' says he, 'they could not belong to a better man. You'll turn that grey cow up here till I kill her for Mrs Mackenzie.' 'No,' says the herd, 'that'll no be the case; we'll know which is the best man first.' 'That tells you that the cow will be mine,' says Kernsary. And so it was; Mackenzie took the cow from him, drove her to the byre, got the axe, and killed her in a minute. He went in and told Mary his wife to send a man to bleed the cow before it would get cold. So Mary said, 'What cow is it?' 'Never mind,' says he, 'you'll know that before Saturday.' And so she did. The old drover himself came by next day. Mrs Mackenzie saw him passing, and called him up. She took him into the house and gave him a glass of mountain dew. Then she told him what her husband did yesterday on a grey cow of his, and that she was going to pay him. She asked him what was the value of the cow. He replied, 'Nothing but what I paid for it;' and she paid him.

THE WHALE IN LOCH EWE

In the year 1809 Loch Ewe was the most famous loch known for haddock. Boats came even from the east coast, from Nairn and Avoch; indeed until the following occurrence Loch Ewe was unrivalled in the north of Scotland for its haddock fishing.

It was a beautiful day, and all the boats were fishing on the south-west side of Isle Ewe opposite Inverasdale. A new boat was put off the stocks at Mellon Charles, and was taken out that day for the first time. Seven men went out in her, viz., Duncan Mackenzie, Ronald Mackenzie, Rorie Maclean, Murdo Mackenzie, Donald Maclennan, John Chisholm, and Hector Macrae, all Mellon men. They went to the back of Sgeir an Fharaig, much further out towards the open than the other boats. It was so calm the oars were laid across the boat. Suddenly they saw a whale coming in from the ocean making straight at them. One of the men suggested they had better put the oars straight and pull out of her way. And this they did; but as they worked to one side, the whale cut across straight after them, and soon came up with them. She struck the boat in the bow, and made a crack about a yard long in the second plank above the keel. Six oars were then manned, and, with one man keeping his coat to the crack, they rowed for their lives; but as the crack was in the bow, the water forced itself in notwithstanding the efforts of the man with his coat. They were making for the nearest land, when the boat filled. When Ronald, who had been a soldier, saw this, he stripped and jumped overboard to swim for it. He swam some distance when the whale struck him below; so then he turned back to the water-logged boat. When he reached the boat, three of the men had been drowned, viz., Murdo Mackenzie, Donald Maclennan, and John Chisholm. After that the whale disappeared, or at least ceased to molest them. It was a small whale.

A man at Mellon Charles had noticed the incident; he ran through the township to procure help; but no boat was to be found, and there were only women and children at home. He went as far as Drumchork; there an old boat was found, that had been turned keel up for two years. Seven men were found to attempt an expedition for the rescue of the wrecked fishermen. They had only one oar, and on the other side of the boat worked bits of board, whilst two of the men were employed baling. In this way they reached the water-logged boat, and rescued the four survivors of its crew. Ever since this fatal occurrence it has been the popular belief in the country that whales attack new boats or newly tarred boats. When the boat was got ashore a large piece of the whale's skin was found in the crack in the bow.

A Story of Rob Donn

Rob Donn, the great Reay bard, was bard and ground-officer to Mackay Lord Reay, in the middle of the eighteenth century. He would always be going out with his gun, and secretly killing deer. Lord Reay found this out, and sent for Rob. He said, 'I'm hearing, Robert, you are killing my deer.' 'Oh, no,' says he, 'I am not killing them all, but I am killing some of them; I cannot deny that.' Lord Reay then said, 'Unless you give it up, I must put you away out of the place; you must get a security that you will not kill any more.' 'Oh,' says Rob to him, 'I must go and see if I can get a surety.' So he left the room. Outside the door he met Lord Reay's son. 'Will you,' said Rob to the boy, 'become security for me that I will not kill more deer on your father's property?' 'Yes,' replied the boy. Rob caught him by the hand and took him to Lord Reay. 'Is that your security, Robert?' said his lordship. 'Yes,' said Robert, 'will you not take him?' 'No, I will not,' answered his lordship. 'It is very strange,' replied Rob, 'that you will not take your own son as security for one man, when God took his own Son for all the world's security.' It need scarcely be added that Rob Donn remained bard and ground-officer to Lord Reay. This story I believe to be perfectly true.

The Lochbroom Herring Fishing

About ninety years ago the British Fishery Society built the pier at Ullapool, and the streets of unfinished and unoccupied houses there which to this day give it the appearance of a deserted town. There were great herring fisheries then in Lochbroom, and Woodhouse from Liverpool started a large curing establishment in Isle Martin; so did Rorie Morrison at Tanera, and Melville at Ullapool. The Big Pool of Loch Broom was the best place for herrings in Scotland at that time, and there would be a hundred and fifty ships from all parts to buy herrings there –

from Saltcoats, Bute, and Helensburgh, Greenock and Port Bonachie, East Tarbert and West Tarbert. Melville built two ships in Guisach, which he named the *Tweed* and the *Riand*. That place was full of natural wood at the time; it was in a rocky spot at Aultnaharril, opposite to Ullapool, where the ferry is. Melville was bound to take the herrings from all the fishermen's boats. They were so plentiful that he could not cure them all, so he made middens of them, and he also boiled quantities for the oil from them. After that season Lochbroom was nineteen years without a hundred herrings in it, and the fishery has never recovered to this day.

THE OTHER ROB ROY MACGREGOR

Kenneth Mackenzie, the last laird of Dundonnell of the old family, was descended from the first Lord Mackenzie of Kintail, and was a connection of the Gairloch Mackenzies. He was a peculiar man; he had a large flock of hens, and used to make every tenant pay him so many hens at the Martinmas term along with their rent. My grandfather's brother, Sandy M'Rae, who was tenant of the Isle of Gruinard, had to pay four hens every year to the laird. Kenneth Mackenzie, in 1817, married Bella, daughter of one Donald Roy Macgregor, belonging to Easter Ross; they had no family. She had a brother called Rob Roy Macgregor, who was a lawyer in Edinburgh. When Kenneth was on his deathbed his wife and Rob Roy wanted him to leave the Dundonnell estate to the latter. The dying laird was willing to do so, because he did not care for his only brother Thomas Mackenzie; but he was so weak that he could not sign his name to the will, and it is said that Rob Roy Macgregor held the laird's hand with the pen, and that the wife was keeping up the hand while Rob Roy made the signature.

The laird died soon after, and left nothing at all to his brother Thomas. When the will became known there was a great feeling of indignation among all the Mackenzies and the gentry of the low country, as well as among the tenantry on the Dundonnell estates, against Rob Roy Macgregor, who now took up his residence at the old house of Dundonnell. The whole of the tenantry were opposed to him, except one man at Badluachrach named Donald Maclean, commonly called Donald the son of Farquhar. He was the only man that was on Rob Roy's side. His neighbours made a fire in the bow of his boat in the night time and burnt a good part of it. He sent the boat to Malcolm Beaton, a cousin of his own at Poolewe, to repair it; the night after it was repaired (whilst still at Poolewe) there was a fire put in the stern, and the other end of her was burnt. The Dundonnell tenants rose against Rob Roy Macgregor, and procured firearms; they surrounded the house, and fired through the shutters by which the windows were defended, hoping to take his life; one ball or slug struck the post of his bed. The next night he escaped, and never returned again. His barn and his stacks of hay and corn were burnt, and the manes and tails of his horses were cut short. Thomas Mackenzie commenced law against Rob Roy Macgregor for the recovery of the estate. In the end it was decided that it belonged to him, but it had become so burdened by the law expenses that it had to be sold.

CASES OF DROWNING IN LOCH MAREE

It would be before 1810 that Hector Mackenzie of Sand was living in a house at Cliff, on the west side of the burn at Cliff House. Sir Hector Mackenzie of Gairloch had given him lands at Inverasdale. He went up Loch Maree in a boat to fetch wood to build a house close to the shore at Inverasdale. He took for a crew his son Sandy, a young lad, and also William M'Rae from Cove, and William Urquhart, called William Og, and his son, who lived at Bac Dubh. They reached Kenlochewe and loaded the boat. Just before they started back, Kenneth Mackenzie, a married man, and Rorie Mackenzie, a young man, who were returning to Gairloch with hemp for nets, asked for a passage down the loch. Hector said there was too much in the boat already. He was not for them to go in the boat, so they went off; but William Og said to Hector, 'You had better call the men back; you don't know where they will meet you again.' William Og called for them to come back. Kenneth Mackenzie came back, but Rorie would not return; he had taken the refusal amiss, and it was good for him that he had done so. The boat with the six of them started from the head of Loch Maree. Opposite Letterewe she was swamped, from being so heavy. All hands were lost except William M'Rae and Sandy the son of Hector, they were picked up by a boat from Letterewe.

Two sons of Lewis M'Iver, of Stornoway, came to Kenlochewe on their way back from college. It was before the road was made from Gairloch to Poolewe. They took a boat down Loch Maree. Four Kenlochewe men came with them; they were all ignorant of sailing. Between Ardlair and the islands there was a breeze, and they put the sail up. One of the Kenlochewe men stretched himself upon the middle thwart of the boat; a squall came, and he went overboard head foremost and was drowned.

Kenneth Mackenzie from Eilean Horrisdale and Grigor M'Gregor from Achtercairn were employed sawing at Letterewe. They were put across to Aird na h'eighaimh, the promontory that runs out from the west shore of Loch Maree to near Isle Maree, by a boat from Letterewe. One of them had a whip saw on his shoulder. On landing they started to walk to Gairloch. There was then no bridge over the river at Talladale. The stream was swollen by rain; they tried to wade it, but were carried off their legs and taken down to the loch, where they were drowned. Their bodies were never recovered. This was more than eighty years ago.

Donald Maclean from Poolewe and John M'Iver, called John M'Ryrie, and often known as Bonaparte, from his bravery, were in a sailing boat in Tagan Bay at the head of Loch Maree, when a squall upset the boat. John M'Ryrie went down, and was drowned. Donald Maclean got on the keel of the boat. Rorie Mackenzie had a boat on the stocks at Athnanceann. She had only seven strokes in her, but there was no other boat, so they took her down to the loch, and Donald Maclean was saved by means of her. John M'Ryrie's body was recovered, and buried in the Inverewe churchyard.

It would be about 1840 that Duncan and Kenneth Urquhart, two brothers from Croft, sons of Kenneth Urquhart the miller, were coming down Loch Maree one Saturday evening after dark. There was smuggling going on in the islands at that time.

It was a very dark night, and there was a stiff breeze blowing down the loch and helping to propel the boat. Duncan was rowing the bow oar, and Kenneth the other. Duncan called to his brother to go to the stern and steer the boat with his oar. Kenneth jumped on the seat in the stern, and from the way that was on the boat, and his own spring, he went over the stern. He called to Duncan, but he had only the one oar left, and with the wind so strong he could do nothing for his brother, so Kenneth was drowned. His body was found nine days afterwards in the middle of Loch Maree; the oar came ashore at a spot called An Fhridhdhorch, or 'the dark forest', where the scrubby wood now is near a mile to the north of Ardlair. Duncan came ashore with the boat on the beach in Tollie Bay.

When Seaforth bought the Kernsary estate some forty years ago Mrs M'Intyre was living at Inveran. It was after Duncan Fadach had lived there. Two years after Seaforth made the purchase he sent two lads to repair the house at Inveran. One of them was Sandy Mackenzie from Stornoway. The two lads went to bathe at the rock called Craig an t' Shabhail, or 'the rock of the barn', where the River Ewe begins; there was a barn long ago on the top of this rock. Immediately Sandy entered the water he went down, and was drowned. The other lad hastened to the house, and a sort of drag was made with a long stick and a crook at the end of it, and with this the body was lifted. Sandy was of the stock of George Mackenzie, second laird of Gruinard, who had thirty-three children. Sandy's brother is the present Free Church minister of Kilmorack.

THE STORNOWAY PACKET AND THE WHALE

The smack *North Britain*, Captain Leslie, was carrying the mails between Poolewe and Stornoway for eighteen years. Leslie had four of a crew besides himself. Murdo Macdonald was at the helm when the smack struck a whale. She was running with a two-reefed mainsail and slack sheet. She ran on the back of the whale and cut it through to the backbone; seven feet was put out of the cutwater of the packet: it was a severe stroke! When the smack ran up on to the back of the whale her stern went under to the companion. The whale sank down, and so the smack went over her, but made so much water in the hold that they were obliged to run her ashore. They got her to Bayhead, inside the pier at Stornoway. The whale went ashore in Assynt, and they found the cut on her. I had this account from Leslie and others of the crew.

THE WRECK OF M'CALLUM'S SCHOONER AT MELVAIG

About 1805 John M'Callum, a decent man from Bute, had a schooner and carried on a trade in herrings; he had been to Isle Martin. He had one pound in cash to purchase every barrel of herrings with. The herrings were so plenty he got them for five shillings a barrel. He had a smack called the *Pomona* as well as the schooner, and he would be sending the smack to Greenock with cargoes of herrings whilst he stayed at Isle Martin curing herrings. At the end of the season, as there was a great demand for small vessels, he sold the *Pomona* for three hundred pounds to Applecross men. Then he himself started home in the schooner, with a crew of seven sailors. He came to Portree from Isle Martin, and left Portree for home, intending to go through Kyleakin. When he got through the sound of Scalpay it came on a hurricane from the south. The vessel would not take the helm, and became unmanageable. She was running down the coast in that state, and at last the wind shifting to the west put her on the rocks at Melvaig.

The mate went to M'Callum, who was in the cabin, and told him to come up, that they were going to be lost, and he should try and get ashore. M'Callum was old and weak, and replied that he was so frail that he would have no chance, and that his days were gone at any rate; so he remained below. One of the crew went out on the jib boom, and as she struck he let himself down by a rope from the jib boom to a shelf on a rock, and was quite safe. Another of the crew jumped out, but could not get ashore on account of the surf. The Melvaig people saw him swimming a mile off; then he turned back; he seemed to be a good swimmer; when he was in the surf and saw a big sea coming, he would dive through it; at last he disappeared. The ship went to pieces, and all hands were lost except the man who had got on the shelf of rock. All the bodies were washed ashore, and were buried in Melvaig, near the house of Murdo Mackenzie, called Murdo Melvaig. A Melvaig man, named John Smith, stripped the sea boots from one of the bodies and took them home with him. When the man who was saved heard this, he said it would have been enough for him to take them off when he was alive! The man who came ashore told the Melvaig people that the three hundred pounds realized for the sale of the *Pomona*, as well as the balance of the money the captain had had to buy herrings, was in a box. The captain had had one pound to buy each barrel of herring, and as he had only to pay five shillings a barrel he must have had nearly four hundred pounds balance. The whole of the money was found in a box, as the man had said. The man went away home, but he did not get the money with him.

A SEA CAPTAIN BURIED IN ISLE EWE

About twelve years ago some gentlemen in a steam yacht came to Isle Martin, and inquired there whether anyone knew of a place where the captain of a ship had been buried in one of the Summer Isles. They thought he had been buried in one of the small islands off Loch Broom. They offered fifteen pounds to anyone who could inform them, but no one could tell them anything of the place. Here is the true account of this captain and his death and burial. It was about 1822 that I was living with my father in Mellon Charles house. A schooner going to Newcastle with bars of brass put in for shelter to the sound of Isle Ewe. She lay opposite the dyke on the island; that is still the safest anchorage, the best holding ground in a storm. Two of the crew came ashore at Aultbea, and said the captain had got ill, and they were seeking a doctor; there was no doctor then in the country. My father used to go and see some who would be sick, and would bleed them if they would require it. So the two sailors were told to go to him, and they took him out to the schooner. He found the captain lying dead in his cabin, and there were cuts in different parts of his head as if he had been killed by his men. He was buried in the old churchyard in the

Isle of Ewe, still enclosed by a dyke; there is a headstone yet standing at his grave. No other sea captain has been buried in this district for many years, except John M'Callum, John M'Taggart, and this captain buried in Isle Ewe.

THE LOSS OF THE *GLENELG*

It was about 1825 that the mail-packet called the *Glenelg of Glenelg* was lost. A year before that the Right Honourable Stewart Mackenzie, who had in 1817 married Lady Hood, the representative of the Seaforth family and proprietrix of the Lews, bought the *Glenelg* to ply with the mails between Poolewe and Stornoway. Poolewe is the nearest port on the mainland to Stornoway. There had been packets on the same service generations before. The *Glenelg* was a smack of about sixty tons. Her crew consisted of two brothers, Donald and John Forbes, and a son of Kenneth M'Eachainn, of Black Moss (Bac Dubh), now called Moss Bank, at Poolewe. Donald was the master, and John the mate. She was going to Stornoway about once every week, but she had not a fixed time. It was on a Saturday, either the end of November or beginning of December, that the Rev. Mr Fraser, who was minister of Stornoway, returned to Poolewe from the Low Country. He had come down Loch Maree in a boat. The master of the *Glenelg* was ashore at the inn, which was then at Cliff House. Mr Fraser came to Donald Forbes, and told him he would require to be at Stornoway that evening to preach on the morrow. Donald said it was not weather to go. Mr Fraser said he would prosecute or punish him for not going; then Donald said he should take care before he would not punish himself, and that he knew his business as well as Mr Fraser knew his own. At last Mr Fraser persuaded him to go; and there were two other passengers, Murdo M'Iver from Tigh na faoilinn, who was going to be a Gaelic teacher in a parish near Stornoway, and Kirstie Mackenzie from Croft. They started about nine o'clock in the morning, with two reefs in the mainsail. Donald M'Rae from Cove was out on the hill for a creel of peats and saw the *Glenelg* loosing some of her canvas after going out of Loch Ewe. Nothing more was seen of her. M'Iver's box was washed ashore at Scoraig in Little Loch Broom, and two hand-spikes and the fo'scuttle. Another packet was afterwards put on the same service.

WRECK OF THE *HELEN MARIANNE* OF CAMPBELTON

John M'Taggart from Campbelton had a smack called the *Helen Marianne*. He used to come to Glen Dubh buying herrings, and he had two fishing boats of his own worked with the smack. I saw him in Glen Dubh when I was fishing there; it would be about 1850. One Sabbath night he left Loch Calava at the entrance to Glen Dubh, and set sail for home, thus breaking the Sabbath. A storm from the north-east came on, and in the night he struck on the Greenstone Point, at the other side of Oban, or Opinan, there, and all hands were lost. Donald Mackenzie and Kenneth Cameron, the elder of the church, both living in Sand, had the grazing of Priest Island. On the Tuesday they went out to that island to see the cattle, and there they found the dead body of John Taggart, along with an empty barrel. They thought he must have been washed off the deck, as the vessel had been carried past Priest Island before she was wrecked. They brought the body to Sand, and buried it in the churchyard with the rest of the crew, whose bodies were all recovered. There would be six or seven of them in all, for the crews of the fishing boats were with the smack, the two boats being on deck, one on each side.

WRECK OF THE *LORD MOLYNEUX* OF LIVERPOOL

Farquhar Buidhe, who was one of the Mathesons of Plockton, and brother of Sandy Matheson the blind fiddler there, was the owner and master of the trawler *Lord Molyneux*, a smack he had bought at Liverpool. He used to come to Glen Dubh for the herring fishery. It was two or three years before the wreck of the *Helen Marianne* of Campbelton that Farquhar set sail for home one Sabbath night. Before daylight he was lost upon a rock at the end of the island of Oldany. These two ships were both lost from Sabbath-breaking.

John Macdonald, the Drover of Loch Maree

It was about 1825 that John Macdonald lived at Talladale. He was a cattle drover, and was always known as 'the drover of Loch Maree'. He was a fine tall man; I remember seeing him. He wore a plaid and trousers of tartan, and a high hat. He used to go to the Muir of Ord market with the cattle he bought in Gairloch. At that time large quantities of smuggled whisky were made in Gairloch and Loch Torridon. John Macdonald got the loan of an open boat at Gairloch. She was a new boat, with a seventeen-foot keel: I remember seeing her. He worked her round to Loch Torridon, and then he took a cargo of whisky for Skye. Two Torridon men accompanied him. A storm came on from the south or south-west, and they could not make Skye. The boat was driven before the wind till she reached the shore of Assynt, on the south side of Stoir Head. There they came ashore; the boat was found high and dry, and quite sound, above high-water mark. John Macdonald and his companions were never seen again, and some Assynt men said that they had been murdered for their whisky. Assynt was a wild country then, and long before.

The Murder of Grant, the Peddler

It was about 1829 there lived in a house some three hundred yards above the present parks at Tournaig a man named Grant. He had three sons, William and Sandy, and another, who was the youngest, whose Christian name I forget. He was a peddler, a good-looking lad, about twenty-three years of age at the time. He used to carry his pack on his back through the country. He often went to Assynt, and was acquainted with one M'Leod, who lived near Loch Nidd, to the north of Stoir Head. M'Leod was a kind of teacher; he was a great favourite with the women. Grant, the peddler, was stopping in a house near M'Leod's, and M'Leod was seeing him. One morning, after breakfast, Grant left his lodgings to walk across to Lochinver with his pack on his back. M'Leod joined him, to convoy him out of the township. When they were out of sight of the houses M'Leod struck the peddler with a small mason's hammer, which he had concealed in his breast. He struck him at the back of the ear, and killed him clean. When M'Leod saw the peddler was dead, he would have given three worlds to have made him alive again, as he afterwards said; but it was too late. M'Leod put the body in a small loch, still called from this circumstance Loch Torr na h' Eiginn, or 'the loch of the mound of violence', and he put stones on the body to keep it from floating. A man in the township had a dream that the peddler had been murdered and put in this loch, and he went with his neighbours and found the body there. The neighbours thought this man had killed Grant, because he knew where the body was. The poor man was apprehended, and taken to the gaol at Dornoch, where he was kept for a year, and his sufferings caused his hair to come from his head. He was not set free till M'Leod confessed the murder. The men of the place were all anxious to find out the murderer of the peddler, that they might clear their own families.

M'Leod, soon after the murder, hid the peddler's pack in a stack of peats. He took part of the goods out of it to give to some of his sweethearts, of whom he had too many! The girl that was in the house where Grant had lodged had taken notice of the contents of the pack. She saw some of the things after the murder with a girl who was a neighbour, and whom M'Leod was courting. She said to this girl, 'It must have been you, or someone belonging to you, that killed Grant.' This girl was taken to Dornoch gaol, and another girl who was seen with a piece of cloth that had been in Grant's pack was also taken to gaol. The neighbours were all against each other, trying to discover the murderer. At last these two girls gave evidence that they had received the things from M'Leod, and upon their testimony he was found guilty of the murder before the judge at Inverness. He would not confess to the murder, until the Rev. Mr Clark, minister of a church in King Street, in Inverness, who was attending on the condemned man, worked upon him so that he told the whole truth. It was not until this confession that the man who had had the dream was released from Dornoch gaol. Poor man, he never got over it. M'Leod was hung at Inverness, and on the gallows he sang the fifty-first Psalm in Gaelic. The two brothers of the murdered peddler, and their sister, who had married a MacPhail, got up a ball at Inverness on the night M'Leod was hung. It was a foolish thing.

Death of the Shieldaig Shoemaker and his Companions at Lochinver

It was long after the murder of Grant, the peddler, in Assynt, that three men from Shieldaig of Applecross went in their smack to fish with long lines for cod at Lochinver. One of them was a shoemaker. It is said that they came ashore to the inn there. After their return to the smack, three days passed without any smoke from the vessel, and the people on shore did not know what was the cause of it. So they went to see what was wrong, and they found the three men dead, two of them among the barrels in the hold, and one at the hearth in the fo'castle. They came ashore, and a letter was sent to M'Phee, the fishing-officer at Shieldaig of Applecross, reporting the case. Three Shieldaig men went first to Lochinver and brought the vessel home. I saw them as they passed Poolewe. Some thought that the three fishermen had had poison given them in the inn. After the disappearance of John Macdonald, the Loch Maree drover, and his two companions, and the murder of Grant the peddler, in Assynt, it was considered dangerous for men from Gairloch and the neighbourhood to visit that wild country.

FOUR LOCAL ANECDOTES
FROM HARRIS

Source: Kenneth Jackson, 'Four Local Anecdotes from Harris'; *Scottish Studies*,
vol. 3, 1959
Narrator: Angus Macleod ('Angus the Tailor') of Malaclett, Sollas, North Uist;
recorded in Gaelic in 1951 by Professor Jackson using phonetic script.
Mr Macleod was then sixty-six
Types: (II) ML6045 'Drinking Cup Stolen from Fairies'

I

About eighty years ago and before that, there used to be many
sailing vessels coming into Loch Tarbert, Harris, at the end of
autumn; they used to stay there till the beginning of spring. It
was from the mainland of Europe they used to come, and they
sailed then to America and to other countries. They used to sell
every kind of drink. The crofters used to give them birds'
feathers, eggs, hens, and meat in exchange for drink; but it was
in secret that this traffic was carried on. The customs boats used
to be looking out for smuggling, and they had to be careful.
They sometimes buried casks of wine and rum and whisky on
the small islands that are in the loch. They got many other
things from these people.

There was a stout fellow in Caolas Scalpaidh whom they
called Big Kenneth MacAskill. He himself and his mates got
three casks and hid them on an island called Sgeotasbhaidh.
After a while, when the whisky that they had was used up, they
thought of going to fetch the three casks that were on the
island. They left at nightfall. It seemed that the captain of
the customs boat got information in some way about the trip the
men were going on. When Big Kenneth was half-way across
the sound, they saw the customs boat coming. They rowed
hard – they wanted to get ashore before the customs boat

appeared – and you may say that they made haste. They got ashore and succeeded in getting the casks out of the boat when the customs boat appeared. They had no time to do anything, because the crew of the customs boat would see them if they tried to hide the casks. Big Kenneth went and took off one of his shoes and removed his sock; he gave a blow to each cask in turn, and you would not have known them from the rocks of the beach. The customs boat came in where they were, and the captain asked them where the casks were. 'Casks?' said Big Kenneth, 'we have nothing of the sort at all. You have only to look at our boat, and if you see anything at all there that ought not to be there, take it with you.' The crew of the customs boat searched the boat, and looked round all over the beach, but they did not see a sign of anything but the rocks of the beach. The captain excused himself and went back to Tarbert. No sooner had he gone out of sight than Big Kenneth took off his shoe again, took his sock off, and struck the rocks. They turned into three casks of whisky as they had been before; and you may say that both young men and old had a great night in Caolas that night.

II

Many generations ago there was a man in the west of Harris; he had livestock – cattle and sheep. He used to drive them to the hill, and it was his custom, when he was driving the cattle, that he used to cry, 'Ho, ho!' and 'Stop here!' He was a man with whom matters prospered very well, and he had a wife who was exceedingly good at carrying forward their affairs.

One fine summer day he was going off with the cattle, and he was calling, 'Ho, ho!' and 'Stop here!' in the usual way. Every time he called he heard a voice answering him; the voice was saying, 'Ho, ho! Stop here! A safe return to you and a safe journey to you!' He stood still and called, 'Ho, ho!' again. The voice answered, 'Ho, ho! May you come back safe and may you go safe!' He kept going and did not pay any further attention to the voice that was answering him.

At last he reached a green knoll; he heard music and melody, and he stopped and saw an open door in the side of the knoll. He went in. A beautiful woman came and welcomed him in. A little old man came over where he was with a golden cup full of whisky. He asked the man to drink every drop of it, for the fairies had a great feast that day, and all who were inside had drunk from the cup but himself; and the old man left him and went among the company. While the man was drinking no one troubled him. The girl who welcomed him in gave him the hint to work his way to the door little by little, because when he had drunk all that was in the cup they would take it from him, and the door would be shut and he would never get out again. This is what he did; he was taking one sip after another from the cup and continually working his way to the door. Finally the last mouthful was left in the cup. He leaped suddenly out of the door and took to his heels homewards, with the golden cup in his hand and the last mouthful in the cup not drunk. The troop of fairies followed after him.

When they were coming close to him he cried, 'Ho, ho! May you come back safe, and may you go safe!' The fairies stood still, but when they stood he ran away; no sooner did he run away than they were in pursuit again. Every time they were about to catch him he called out the same thing, 'Ho, ho! May you come back safe! A safe arrival to you!' At last he was in sight of his own house. His wife heard the uproar outside, and stood in the doorway. As soon as the man saw her he cried, 'Flora, Flora, out with the chamber-pot!' She rushed in, and in a trice she was out; the man was coming in, and the fairies were almost upon her. She dashed what was in the pot on the troop of fairies; the one in front got a torrent of urine from the pot – he was blinded and choked at the same time. He went to the right about, himself and those with him; and they never troubled the man or his wife further.

Macleod of Dunvegan heard about the golden cup, and he came to look at it. The cup pleased him so much that the man gave it to him, and Macleod gave him a farm rent-free in return for the cup. The cup is at Dunvegan still, to the present day; it may be seen by anyone who goes that way. There you have the story of the golden cup of Dunvegan.

III

There was a man in Rodil in Harris who married a woman from Strond. She came of well-to-do people, but she suspected that he was nothing but a blackguard. A brother of hers came to visit her, and was going to stay the night. The man of the house began to make fun of the Strond folk. Now the wife's brother had sold him a heifer the year before, and the man of the house had never paid him for it. His taunting enraged him. He turned on him and said, 'You ought to pay for the spotted heifer.' 'I'll do that, but you'll be well paid for it before morning comes.'

His wife realized that he was planning mischief, and she stayed awake. She pretended to be asleep. When he thought she was asleep he got up and killed his brother-in-law. His wife jumped up and took to her heels, and made for her relatives. Out through the bedroom window she went; she got out unknown to her husband. When he returned to bed after doing the dreadful deed he was going to kill the woman too; but when he saw she was not in bed when he got there he realized she had gone to get help, and he ran away, for he knew he would be pursued.

He got a boat and made for Dunvegan in the hope that Macleod would protect him. He reached Dunvegan. Macleod saw that he must be escaping after doing some wickedness, and he questioned him, and the answers he gave did not satisfy him. He told him he should have food and drink and a bed, until he got information from Harris about what wrong he had done. The man stayed in the castle; he got food and drink, and was badly in need of them.

But he got up before day dawned and took himself off. He set out for Sleat to see whether MacDonald would protect him. MacDonald promised to do this, but he would not keep him in the castle on any account, but put him with a shepherd who had a house among the mountains. He did not do a handsturn along with the shepherd. He went to hide every morning in the heather within sight of the shepherd's house, for he was afraid he would be pursued. The shepherd was afraid of him, as he had weapons – a dagger and arrows. He had to have meat every night when he came home.

When the woman reached her father's house she told him what had happened. The Strond men gathered every young able-bodied man and made for the house of the murderer, but when they got there they found nothing but the withy on which the fish had been – the murderer had fled. They searched every nook and cranny, but they found that the boat he had taken with him was missing, and they understood that the murderer had gone to Skye. They got a galley and set off for Dunvegan. They arrived and went to the castle and told the Chief what had happened. He answered them and told them how the man had come to the castle asking for protection, because his enemies were after him. He told them what he himself had done and how the man had fled, but that he supposed that he had gone to Sleat; and he said to them, 'This is what I will do, I will send a messenger to MacDonald of Sleat telling him to hand the murderer over to him, or if he won't hand him over –!'

The messenger set off and told MacDonald what sort of man he had given protection to; he told him the message Macleod sent him. MacDonald replied and said the man was on his lands, and let Macleod come and seek him; 'But if he comes –!' The messenger returned home and told Macleod how he had fared, and the reply MacDonald had given him. Macleod was seized with rage. He gathered his men to him, and all the Harris men who were along with them; there was a great host there.

Macleod set off with them and they reached MacDonald's land. When the people of the country saw them coming under arms they quickly sent word to MacDonald that a great host was coming and that they were not ready for them; and that they were unwilling to go and fight for an alien murderer. MacDonald at once sent a messenger to Macleod, telling him where the murderer was in hiding, and saying he should take him away and no one in his lands would hinder him; but that he would have to be cautious, as the man was exceedingly cunning.

This is what Macleod did; he sent two men to the shepherd's house to ask about the man he had staying with him. The shepherd was utterly sick of the stranger whom MacDonald had sent him. The men told the shepherd what sort of man he had in the house, and the shepherd told them about him; that he had a dagger and a bow and arrows; how he used to hide all day in the heather; how he used to come at nightfall, and he had to have meat for him. 'But this is what I will do; when he comes home tonight I'll have no meat but a sheep's head, and I'll ask him for his dagger to break up the sheep's head. If he gives it to me I will call to you to come in.' He told them how they could get close to the house without anyone seeing them. That is what the young men did; they went to the shepherd's house at nightfall, and got safely close to the shepherd's house without anyone seeing them.

The murderer came home, and asked the shepherd who were the couple of men that had been at the house that day. The shepherd answered that they were nothing but people who were travelling the road. Then he said, the man of the house, that he had no meat but a sheep's head, and that he had no knife which would cut it, but if he would give him his dagger he would break up the sheep's head with it. The murderer was not willing to give it to him, but he was hungry, and he thought there was no one pursuing him for miles round. He handed his dagger reluctantly to the shepherd. The shepherd succeeded in cutting the bow-string unobserved, and he then tried the dagger on the sheep's head; and the people outside heard the crack that the dagger made as it went through the bones, and in they came. They were on the murderer's back before he was able to look.

They bound him and took him away with them. They got him safely to Rodil. Macleod was the judge. He gave his sentence that he was to be hanged. They did that; he was hanged outside. There was a pair of new shoes on the murderer; they left them on him, and his clothes, and that very night the shoes were stolen off him; but he was left hanged until the flesh fell away from his bones. There was a young lad going by one dark night, and he heard the creaking of the bones as the wind swung the body back and forth, and the lad was seized with fright. He ran home; he did not stop to open the door but dashed the door and the doorposts in on the floor, and went to bed behind his father with his shoes and clothes on, and remained for a month

without getting up. After that they took the body down from
the gallows and buried it.

IV

For centuries it was the custom in Harris to keep Hallowe'en
with drinking and music and dancing. They used to gather in
one place and pass the night pleasantly together. One night they
had gathered in the house of an old man; there were many
women there but there was no man there but the man of the
house. The young men had left the house, and were in a nearby
hamlet, and they expected to come to the old man's house after
midnight. They had had their supper. The old man put a sheep's
jawbone in the fire and began to 'read' it. He suddenly jumped
up and shouted; he told the women to escape, that enemies were
very close at hand to them and that he himself would go and
keep them back as long as he could.

The women set off quickly and were off in a moment, to try
to get to where the men were gathered, to see if they would be
in time to help the old man before the enemy arrived. The
women reached where the men were and told them what had
happened, and said they should arm themselves at once. There
was no delay about the matter, but alas, they were too late – they
came upon the old man dead. He had used up all his arrows.
They did not meet the enemy at all.

They began to try to find them; they found the oars of the
galleys in a hollow, and they call it Lag nan Ràmh [The Hollow
of the Oars] to the present day. They went off with the oars and
hid them. They went after the enemy; they encountered them
and fought a bloody battle. The strangers were MacNeills. The
MacNeills fled to where they had left their oars, and found
nothing but the withy on which the fish had been, and they fled
to the shore. The fight became so hot for them that they had to
jump out into the sea. They call it Cath a' Bhàdhaidh [The Battle
of the Drowning] to the present day.

They buried the valiant old man where he fell, as it was their
custom to do in those days; and to prove that this story is true
Lag nan Ràmh is still there, and Cath a' Bhàdhaidh where the

strangers jumped out into the sea. About forty years ago they were making a new high road through Rodil, and they came upon the bones of a man. They recognized that it was the bones of the old man that they had found. They buried him in the graveyard at Rodil.

4: JESTS AND ANECDOTES

ANECDOTE OF JAMES V

Source: Robert Chambers, *Scottish Jests and Anecdotes*
Narrator: Unknown

King James the Fifth, in one of his pedestrian tours, is said to have called at the village of Markinch in Fife, and going into the only change-house, desired to be furnished with some refreshment. The gudewife informed him that her only room was then engaged by the minister and schoolmaster, but that she believed they would have no objection to admit him into their company. He entered, was made very welcome, and began to drink with them. After a tough debauch of several hours, during which he succeeded in completely ingratiating himself with the two parochial dignitaries, the reckoning came to be paid, and James pulled out money to contribute his share. The schoolmaster, on this, proposed to the clergyman that they should pay the whole, as the other had only recently acceded to the company, and was, moreover, entitled to their hospitality as a stranger. 'Na, na,' quoth the minister, 'I see nae reason in that. This birkie maun just pay higglety-pigglety wi' oursels. That's aye the law in Markinch. Higglety-pigglety's the word.' The schoolmaster attempted to repel this selfish and unjust reasoning; but the minister remained perfectly obdurate. King James at last exclaimed, in a pet, 'Weel, weel, higglety-pigglety be't!' and he immediately made such arrangements as ensured an equality of stipend to his two drinking companions, thus testifying his disgust at the meanness of the superior, and his admiration of the generosity of the inferior functionary. Till recent times the salaries of the minister and schoolmaster of Markinch were nearly equal – a thing as singular as it may be surprising.

Our authors for this story, as Pitscottie would say, are fifteen different clergymen, resident at different corners of the kingdom, all of whom told it in the same way, adding, as an attestation of their verity, that they heard it discussed in all its bearings, times innumerable, at the breakfasts given by the Professor of Divinity; on which occasions, it seems, probationers are duly informed of the various stipends, glebes, etc., of the parishes of Scotland, as they are instructed, at another period of the day, in the more solemn mysteries of their profession.

DAVID HUME

Source: Robert Chambers, *Scottish Jests and Anecdotes*
Narrator: Unknown

This distinguished philosopher was one day passing along a narrow footpath which formerly winded through a boggy piece of ground at the back of Edinburgh Castle, when he had the misfortune to tumble in, and stick fast in the mud. Observing a woman approaching, he civilly requested her to lend him a helping hand out of his disagreeable situation; but she, casting one hurried glance at his abbreviated figure, passed on without regarding his request. He then shouted lustily after her; and she was at last prevailed upon by his cries to approach. 'Are na ye Hume the Deist?' inquired she, in a tone which implied that an answer in the affirmative would decide her against lending him her assistance. 'Well, well,' said Mr Hume, 'no matter; you know, good woman, Christian charity commands you to do good, even to your enemies.' 'Christian charity here, Christian charity there,' replied the woman, 'I'll do naething for ye till ye turn a Christian yoursel; ye maun first repeat baith the Lord's Prayer and the Creed, or faith I'll let ye groffle there as I faund ye.' The sceptic was actually obliged to accede to the woman's terms, ere she would give him her help. He himself used to tell the story with great relish.

Hume one night came too late to one of the little supper parties given by his friend Mrs Cockburn (authoress of a fine song to the tune of the 'Flowers of the Forest'), and it so happened that the good lady's slender pantry had been almost completely desolated before he arrived. Mrs Cockburn informed him of this fact; but, at the same time, told him she would do her best. 'Oh, trouble yourself very little,' said the metaphysician, 'about what you have, or how it appears; you know I am no *epicure*, but only a *glutton*.'

'Pray sir,' said Lady Wallace to David Hume, 'I am often asked of what age I am – what answer should I make?' Mr Hume, immediately guessing her ladyship's meaning, said, 'Madam, when you are asked that question again, answer, that you are not yet come to years of discretion.'

David Hume and Lady Wallace once crossed the Firth from Kinghorn to Leith together, when a violent storm rendered the passengers apprehensive of a salt-water death; and her ladyship's terrors induced her to seek consolation from her friend, who, with infinite *sang froid*, assured her he thought there was great probability of their becoming food for fishes. 'And pray, my dear friend,' said Lady Wallace, 'which do you think they will eat first?' 'Those that are gluttons,' replied Hume, 'will undoubtedly fall foul of me, but the epicures will attack your ladyship.'

During Hume's last illness, he was waited on by a female member of the Berean Congregation, who supposed she had a message from heaven to deliver to him, regarding the state of his soul. On learning her object, the good-natured philosopher ordered a bottle of wine and some other refreshments to be brought in, observing, that they could not well proceed to discuss a matter of such importance 'dry-lippit'. The woman was prevailed upon to take two glasses of wine; and, as she was sipping it, Mr Hume questioned her about her situation and business in life. Understanding that her husband was a candle-maker at Leith, he desired her to send him two stone weight of his best moulded candles, for which the money would be paid on delivery. The lady thought no more of the high commission she had been intrusted with, but hastened home to inform her husband of the order she had received, and quite forgot the conversion of Mr Hume.

When the New Town had reached that street which since bears the name of the tutelar saint of Wales, the house at the south-west corner of St Andrew Square, but entering from the street, was first occupied by David Hume. One day when passing, the Rev. Dr W— waggishly chalked on the corner, *Saint David* Street. The housekeeper having noticed this mark, with eyes like saucers, ran into her master's study, and told him how he had been quizzed. 'Never mind, Jenny,' quoth David, 'a better man than I am hath been made a saint of before me.'

A KEY TO THE RESURRECTION

Source: Robert Chambers, *Scottish Jests and Anecdotes*
Narrator: Unknown

Dr John Brown, author of the Brownonian System of Physic, a man of somewhat coarse manners, on passing the monument of David Hume, in the Calton burying-ground, observed to a mason who was laying a pavement stone for it, 'Friend,' said he, 'this is a strong and massy building; but how do you think the honest gentleman can get out at the resurrection?' The mason archly replied, 'Sir, I have secured that point, for I have put the *key under the door*!'

RUSTIC NOTION OF THE
RESURRECTION

Source: Robert Chambers, *Scottish Jests and Anecdotes*
Narrator: Unknown

It is the custom in Scotland for the elders to assist the minister in visiting the sick; and on such occasions they give the patient and the surrounding gossips the benefit of prayers. Being generally well acquainted in the different families, they often sit an hour or two after the sacred rites, to chat with those who are in health, and to receive the benefit of a dram. On one of these occasions, at the house of Donald M'Intyre, whose wife had been confined to her fireside and armchair for many years, the elder and Donald grew *unco gracious*. Glass after glass was filled from the bottle, and the elder entered into a number of metaphysical discussions, which he had heard from the minister. Among other topics was the resurrection. The elder was strenuous in support of the rising of the same body; but Donald could not comprehend how a body once dissolved in the dust could be re-animated. At last, catching what he thought a glimpse of the subject, he exclaimed, 'Weel, weel, Sandy, ye're richt sae far; you and me, that are strong, healthy folk, *may* rise again; but that *peer* thing there *far* she sits' [that poor thing there where she sits] '*she'll* ne'er rise again.'

CHURCH CANDIDATES

Source: Robert Chambers, *Scottish Jests and Anecdotes*
Narrator: Unknown

At a church in Scotland, where there was a popular call, two candidates offered to preach, of the names of Adam and Low. The last preached in the morning, and took for his text, 'Adam, where art thou?' He made a most excellent discourse, and the congregation were much edified. In the evening Mr Adam preached, and took for his text, 'Lo, here am I!' The *impromptu* and his sermon gained him the church.

THE WEE BOY AND THE
MINISTER GREY

Source: Katharine Briggs, *A Dictionary of British Folk-Tales*
Narrator: J. Robertson; recorded by Hamish Henderson, School of
Scottish Studies
Type: AT1735a 'The Bribed Boy Sings the Wrong Song'

One day when the Minister Grey was out walking he over-heard a wee boy singing a song. This wee boy made up songs out of his own head. And the minister listened, and the wee boy's song went:

> 'My father stole the minister's sheep,
> Plenty of pies and puddings to eat,
> Since he stole the minister's sheep,
> It was on a merry Christmas.'

Now the minister had lost some of his sheep lately, so he knew the wee boy was telling the truth. So he said: 'That's a bonny song, my wee laddie. Just sing it again.' The wee laddie didn't know what to do, so he just sang it again. The minister said: 'That's such a bonny song, I'd like the whole congregation to hear it. So I'll give you two pound, and a change of clothing, if you'll sing it out in the kirk on the Sabbath.' 'I will,' said the boy, 'if you'll give me the two pound now.'

The minister gave the wee boy the two pound, and some clothing, and he thought he had the sheep-stealers now. But the wee boy knew well enough his father would get into trouble for that song. So he climbed up a tree that looked over the manse and the glebe, and he keeked about till he saw what he wanted to see. On the Sabbath, at the end of the service, the minister stood up, and he said: 'I've a wee boy here, who's a very good singer, and I want you to listen to his song, for it's every word true, and not a word of a lie in it. So sing up, my wee boy, and sing the truth.' So the wee boy stood up and he sang:

'As I strolled out one fine summer's day,
Who did I spy but Minister Grey;
He was rolling Molly amongst the hay;
He was tossing her upside downwards.'

And so the wee boy sang his song without a word of a lie in
it, and he won his two pound and a new suit for making a fool
of the minister.

FOUR STORIES OF WATTY DUNLOP

Source: Dean Ramsay, *Reminiscences of Scottish Life and Character*
Narrator: Unknown (third story supplied by Rev. William Blair, Dunblane)

Many anecdotes of pithy and facetious replies are recorded of a minister of the south, usually distinguished as 'Our Watty Dunlop'. On one occasion two irreverent young fellows determined, as they said, to 'taigle' the minister. Coming up to him in the High Street of Dumfries, they accosted him with much solemnity. 'Maister Dunlop, dae ye hear the news?' 'What news?' 'Oh, the deil's dead.' 'Is he,' said Mr Dunlop, 'then I maun pray for twa faitherless bairns.'

On another occasion Maister Dunlop met, with characteristic humour, an attempt to play off a trick against him. It was known that he was to dine with a minister, whose manse was close to the church, so that his return home must be through the churchyard. Accordingly, some idle and mischievous youths waited for him in the dark night, and one of them came up to him, dressed as a ghost, in hopes of putting him in a fright. Watty's cool accost speedily upset the plan. 'Weel, Maister Ghaist, is this a general rising, or are ye juist taking a daunder frae your grave by yersell?'

I have received from a correspondent another specimen of Watty's acute rejoinders. Some years ago the celebrated Edward Irving had been lecturing at Dumfries, and a man who passed as a wag in that locality had been to hear him. He met Watty Dunlop the following day, who said, 'Weel, Willie man, an' what do ye think of Mr Irving?' 'Oh,' said Willie contemptuously, 'the man's crack't.' Dunlop patted him on the shoulder, with the quiet remark, 'Willie, ye'll aften see a light peeping through a crack!'

* * *

Rev. Walter Dunlop of Dumfries was accompanying a funeral one day, when he met a man driving a flock of geese. The wayward disposition of the bipeds at the moment was too much for the driver's temper, and he indignantly cried out 'Deevil choke them.' Mr Dunlop walked a little farther on, and passed a farmstead, where a servant was driving out a number of swine, and banning them with 'Deevil tak them.' Upon which, Mr D. stept up to him, and said, 'Ay, ay, my man, your gentleman'll be wi' ye i' the noo; he's just back the road there a bit, choking some geese till a'man.'

DRAWING THE LONG BOW

Source: J. D. Carrick, *The Laird of Logan*
Narrator: Unknown
Type: AT1920 'Contests in Lying'

Note: The 'Laird of Logan' is a convenient fiction to whom Carrick attributed
all manner of traditional and witty retorts

One day, Logan happened to dine at the Earl of E—'s along with some English gentlemen, when the conversation chanced to turn on the comparative fruitfulness of the northern and southern divisions of Britain. The laird, who was always a steady stickler for the honour and general superiority of Scotland, displayed on this occasion the full bent of his national predilections. One of the gentlemen, however, wishing to come to particulars, requested to know how much wheat an acre of the best land in Scotland would produce. Logan, wishing to astonish his opponent, named a quantity which he thought would have that effect. 'Pooh, pooh!' said the Englishman, 'that's not more than half what is reaped from the very commonest of our lands in the south.' 'But now tell me,' continued he, still addressing the laird, 'what quantity of beans will the same extent of ground produce?' 'Na, na, frien',' said Logan, seemingly piqued at being put down, 'lee about is fair play – it's your turn to speak first now.'

THE TWO STORYTELLERS

Source: Robert Chambers, *Scottish Jests and Anecdotes*
Narrator: Unknown
Type: AT1920 'Contests in Lying'

The clergymen of two adjoining parishes in Forfarshire were both alike remarkable for an infinite fund of anecdote, as well as for a prodigious willingness, or rather eagerness, to disclose it. When one of them happened to be present in any company he generally monopolized, or rather prevented, all conversation; when both were present, there was a constant and keenly contested struggle for the first place. It fell out on a certain morning that they breakfasted together, without any other company; when the host, having a kind of right of precedence, in virtue of his place, commenced an excellent, but very long-winded story, which his guest was compelled to listen to, though disposed, at the end of every sentence, to strike in with his parallel, and far more interesting tale. As the host proceeded with his story, he poured hot water into the teapot; and, so completely was he absorbed in the interest of what he was relating, or rather perhaps so intent was he to engage the attention of his listener, that he took no note of what he was doing, but permitted the water first to overflow the vessel into which he was pouring it, then the table, and finally the floor. The guest observed what was going on; but, being resolved for once to give his rival ample scope and verge enough, never indicated by word, or look, or gesture, that he perceived it, till at last, as the speaker brought his voice to a cadence, for the purpose of finishing the tale, he quietly remarked, 'Ay, ye may stop noo – it's rinnin' oot at the door!'

A SCOTCH MÜNCHHAUSEN

Source: Robert Chambers, *Scottish Jests and Anecdotes*
Narrator: Unknown
Type: AT1889 'Münchhausen Tales', AT1889c 'Fruit Grows from Head of Deer',
AT1920a 'Contests in Lying'

Mr Finlayson, town clerk of Stirling in the latter part of the seventeenth century, was noted for the marvellous in conversation. He was on a visit to the last Earl of Monteith, in his castle of Talla, and was about taking leave, when he was asked by the Earl whether he had seen the Sailing Cherry Tree. 'No,' said Finlayson, 'what sort of thing is it?' 'It is,' replied the Earl, 'a tree that has grown out at a goose's mouth, from a stone the bird had swallowed, and which she bears about with her in her voyages round the loch; it is now in full fruit of the most exquisite flavour. Now, Finlayson,' he added, 'can you, with all your powers of memory and fancy, match my story of the Cherry Tree?' 'Perhaps I can,' said Finlayson, clearing his throat, and adding, 'When Oliver Cromwell was at Airth, one of his cannon sent a ball to Stirling, and lodged it in the mouth of a trumpet which one of the men in the castle was sounding in defiance.' 'Was the trumpeter killed?' inquired the Earl. 'No, my lord,' said Finlayson; 'he blew the ball back, and killed the artilleryman who had fired it.'

BILZY YOUNG

Source: John Monteath, *Dunblane Traditions*
Narrator: Bilzy Young
Type: AT1889 'Münchhausen Tales', AT1889c 'The Split Dog', AT 1920a
'Contests in Lying'

Bilzy Young was one of those chattering, unsettled, work-little, dingy, and gill-drinking mortals, who may be found in almost every town and village about the size of Dunblane. Cities of greater extent have their varieties of the same characters, modified by circumstances and the peculiarities of their gibberish. Bilzy was a spare black-visaged creature, about the middle-size. He was a shot-about weaver to trade, resided in the vicinity of a public house, and where, on account of his peculiar humour, he was invited too frequently, treated to as many gills as he could desire, and where his stories were told with the greatest glee. Bilzy used to pique himself most upon telling wonderful stories. He would engage to tell 'the greatest lee' of any man in company, and found always plenty to back him when he took a bet on that score with a stranger.

One time an English traveller was treating his customers to a bowl in the Auld Smith's, when some of the party mentioning Bilzy's eccentricities, the Englishman desired to see him, confident, he said, he should tell a more improbable and wonderful story than any which Bilzy could invent. Bilzy was in consequence sent for, and soon arrived. The glass went freely round, and Bilzy soon fell in close confab with the Englishman. 'Ye'll be a merchant, noo?' said Bilzy. 'A nailer – a manufacturer of *large* nails, my friend,' said the Englishman; 'I have this day only arrived here from *the moon*, where I was employed driving one of my nails through that orb, to prevent her from falling asunder.' 'Indeed!' exclaimed Bilzy, readily, 'then ye wad surely see *me* – it was *me*, man, that stood at the back o' the auld shaird and *rooved* yer nail.' 'There's a *nailer* for ye, lad,' added Bilzy in triumph; and a loud gaffaw from the assembled guests announced the defeat of the Englishman, which he courteously acknowledged, with a compliment to Bilzy for his ready wit; and the conversation was again resumed by the Englishman. 'You would hear,' he observed, while the company listened, 'of the extraordinary cabbage lately reared by a gentleman in Yorkshire, second only to the great tree in the ancient King of Babylon's dream – it was a mile in height, and a league in circumference – and under the shade of which the whole British army might have found shelter from a hurricane?' Bilzy said he had not heard of that prodigy, but he could now divine the use for the immense *capper* which, during all last summer, had been making at Carron. 'It was sae wide,' he said, 'that the men workin' at the tae side couldna hear the men chappin' at the tither, an' sae deep, that when ane o' the men let fa' his hammer aff the lip o't, it took an hour to fa' to the boddom.' 'Beat again!' exclaimed the Englishman, 'your capper shall boil my cabbage,' and he called in liquor until every one present was as drunk as a piper, and Bilzy carried hame in a hurl-barrow.

On one occasion Bilzy was likely to be out-Heroded in the marvellous by an old Nimrod, whose exploits, as related by himself, left those of Baron Münchhausen in the shade. Bilzy, however, determined to equal him even as a hunter, and related the following in the character of himself.

He said he knew there were two large hares in a park near by, and he determined to have them both. Arriving at the gate, with his dog, early in the morning, he fixed his large gully-knife in the passage, in such a way as he thought would secure the death of one of the hares, while he knew his dog would be certain to catch the other. Having done this, he sent his dog through the park to start the game, which was speedily done, and the dog in full cry after the two hares direct for the gate. But he said he miscalculated the proper position for erecting his gully betwixt the gateposts, for one hare passed by one side of it, and the other the other side, while his dog, after running straight against the knife, severing himself exactly in two *perpendicularly*, caught both hares in an adjacent park, the several halves of the dog turning to the right and left of the gully, pursuing each its own hare, and killing it.

Bilzy Young died about 1800 – 'waur to water than corn' till the last. He was an amusing pot-companion, a garrulous story-teller, and never in his element but in the presence of his drouthy cronies and their little-stoup.

JOHN FRASER THE COOK

Source: Dean Ramsay, *Reminiscences of Scottish Life and Character*
Narrator: Unknown
Type: AT785a 'The Goose with One Leg'

There was a waggish old man cook at Duntrune for sixty years, and during three generations of its owners. In 1745–6, when his master was skulking, John found it necessary to take another service, and hired himself to Mr Wedderburn of Pearsie; but he wearied to get back to Duntrune. One day the Laird of Pearsie observed him putting a spit through a peat – it may have been for the purpose of cleaning it – be that as it may, the laird inquired the reason for so doing, and John replied, 'Indeed, sir, I am just gaein to roast a peat, for fear I forget my trade.' At the end of two years he returned to Duntrune, where he continued to exercise his calling till near the close of life.

One day he sent up a roast goose for dinner which he or someone had despoiled of a leg before it came to table; on which his master summoned him from the kitchen to inquire who had taken the leg off the goose. John replied that all the geese here had but ae leg. In corroboration of his assertion, he pointed to a whole flock before the window, who were, happily, sitting asleep on one leg, with a sentinel on the watch. The laird clapped his hands and cried *whew*, on which they got upon both legs, and flew off. But John, no way discomfited, told his master, if he had cried *whew* to the one on the table, it would most likely have done the same!

FIVE FABLES

Source: J. F. Campbell, *Popular Tales of the West Highlands*
Narrators: 1, J. MacLeod, fisherman, Sutherland. 2, D. M. and J. MacLeod,
Sutherland. 3, collected by C. D. Sutherland. 4, John Dewar, Inveraray,
27 August 1860. 5, collected by C. D. Sutherland
Types: 1, AT6 'Animal Captor Persuaded to Talk'. 2, AT62 'Peace among
the Animals'. 3, AT56 'The Fox through Sleight Steals the Young Magpies'.
4, AT61 'The Fox Persuades the Cock to Crow with Closed Eyes'.
5, AT2 'The Tail-Fisher'

I

One day the fox succeeded in catching a fine fat goose asleep by
the side of a loch, he held her by the wing, and making a joke of
her cackling, hissing and fears, he said:

'Now, if you had me in your mouth as I have you, tell me
what you would do?'

'Why,' said the goose, 'that is an easy question. I would fold
my hands, shut my eyes, say a grace, and then eat you.'

'Just what I mean to do,' said Rory, and folding his hands,
and looking very demure, he said a pious grace with his eyes
shut.

But while he did this the goose had spread her wings, and she
was now half-way over the loch; so the fox was left to lick his
lips for supper.

'I will make a rule of this,' he said in disgust, 'never in all my
life to say a grace again till after I feel the meat warm in my
belly.'

2

One day the fox chanced to see a fine cock and fat hen, off
which he much wished to dine, but at his approach they both
jumped up into a tree. He did not lose heart, but soon began to
make talk with them, inviting them at last to go a little way with

334

him. There was no danger, he said, nor fears of his hurting them, for there was peace between men and beasts, and among all animals. At last after much parleying the cock said to the hen, 'My dear, do you not see a couple of hounds coming across the field?'

'Yes,' said the hen, 'and they will soon be here.'

'If that is the case, it is time I should be off,' said the sly fox, 'for I am afraid these stupid hounds may not have heard of the peace.'

And with that he took to his heels and never drew breath till he reached his den.

3

A fox had noticed for some days a family of wrens, off which he wished to dine. He might have been satisfied with one, but he was determined to have the whole lot – father and eighteen sons – and all so like that he could not tell one from the other, or the father from the children.

'It is no use to kill one son,' he said to himself, 'because the old cock will take warning and fly away with the seventeen. I wish I knew which is the old gentleman.'

He set his wits to work to find out, and one day seeing them all threshing in a barn, he sat down to watch them; still he could not be sure.

'Now I have it,' he said. 'Well done the old man's stroke! He hits true,' he cried.

'Oh!' replied the one he suspected of being the head of the family, 'if you had seen my grandfather's strokes, you might have said that.'

The sly fox pounced on the cock, ate him up in a trice, and then soon caught and disposed of the eighteen sons, all flying in terror about the barn.

4

A fox one day met a cock and they began talking.

'How many tricks canst thou do?' said the fox.

'Well,' said the cock, 'I could do three; how many canst thou do thyself?'

'I could do three score and thirteen,' said the fox.

'What tricks canst thou do?' said the cock.

'Well,' said the fox, 'my grandfather used to shut one eye and give a great shout.'

'I could do that myself,' said the cock.

'Do it,' said the fox. And the cock shut one eye and crowed as loud as ever he could, but he shut the eye that was next the fox, and the fox gripped him by the neck and ran away with him. But the wife to whom the cock belonged saw him and cried out, 'Let go the cock; he's mine.'

'Say thou, "'Se mo choileach fhein a th' ann' [it is my own cock],"' said the cock to the fox.

Then the fox opened his mouth to say as the cock did, and he dropped the cock, and he sprung up on the top of a house, and shut one eye and gave a loud crow; and that's all there is of that sgeulachd.

I find that this is well known in the west.

5

One day the wolf and the fox were out together, and they stole a dish of crowdie. Now the wolf was the biggest beast of the two, and he had a long tail like a greyhound, and great teeth.

The fox was afraid of him, and did not dare to say a word when the wolf ate the most of the crowdie, and left only a little at the bottom of the dish for him, but he determined to punish him for it; so the next night when they were out together the fox said:

'I smell a very nice cheese, and (pointing to the moonshine on the ice) there it is too.'

'And how will you get it?' said the wolf.

'Well, stop you here till I see if the farmer is asleep, and if you keep your tail on it, nobody will see you or know that it is there. Keep it steady. I may be some time coming back.'

So the wolf lay down and laid his tail on the moonshine in the ice, and kept it for an hour till it was fast. Then the fox, who had been watching him, ran in to the farmer and said: 'The wolf is there; he will eat up the children – the wolf! the wolf!'

Then the farmer and his wife came out with sticks to kill the wolf, but the wolf ran off leaving his tail behind him, and that's why the wolf is stumpy-tailed to this day, though the fox has a long brush.

BENEFIT OF OBEYING A WIFE

Source: Robert Chambers, *Scottish Jests and Anecdotes*
Narrator: Unknown
Type: AT1409 'The Obedient Husband'

A clergyman, travelling through the village of Kettle, in Fife, was called into an inn to officiate at a marriage, instead of the parish minister, who, from some accident, was unable to attend, and had caused the company to wait for a considerable time. While the reverend gentleman was pronouncing the admonition, and just as he had told the bridegroom to love and honour his wife, the said bridegroom interjected the words, 'and obey', which he thought had been omitted from oversight, though that is part of the rule laid down solely to the wife. The minister, surprised to find a husband willing to be henpecked by anticipation, did not take advantage of the proposed amendment; on which the bridegroom again reminded him of the omission, 'Ay, *and obey*, sir – love, honour and obey, ye ken!' and he seemed seriously discomposed at finding that his hint was not taken. Some years after, the same clergyman was riding once more through this village of the culinary name, when the same man came out and stopped him, addressing him in the following remarkable words: 'D'ye mind, sir, yon day when ye married me, and when I wad insist upon vowing to *obey* my wife? Weel, ye may now see that I was in the richt. Whether ye wad or no, I *hae* obeyed my wife; and, behold, I am now the only man that has a *twa-storey house* in the hale toun!'

A REPAIRABLE LOSS

Source: Dean Ramsay, *Reminiscences of Scottish Life and Character*
Narrator: Unknown

A countryman had lost his wife and a favourite cow on the same day. His friends consoled him for the loss of the wife; and being highly respectable, several hints and offers were made towards getting another for him. 'Ou ay,' he at length replied, 'you're a' keen aneuch to get me anither wife, but no yin o' ye offers to gie me anither coo.'

THE HIGHLANDER TAKES
THREE ADVICES FROM THE
ENGLISH FARMER

Source: Cuthbert Bede, *The White Wife*
Narrator: Unknown (Kintyre), 1861–5
Type: AT910b 'The Servant's Good Counsels'

In one of the glens of Cantire there lived a young and loving pair who were blessed with one child, a fine healthy lad. They strove hard to provide themselves with the necessaries of life; but their croft was sterile and their crops scanty: and, after many bitter and serious consultations, it was agreed that they should separate for a season, with the hope to make their circumstances better, and that the wife should shift for herself and the lad, and that the husband should travel in search of a situation where he would have food and wages. Their separation was painful; but they comforted themselves with the promise to be true to each other, and to meet again in better circumstances.

The husband had an aversion to become a soldier; so he sailed to Greenock, and from thence made his way into England, and travelled on until he met with a worthy farmer, with whom he agreed to work. The bargain was made by signs, for the Highlander had no English; but after a time they came to understand each other quite well, and the Highlander learned a little English. His master respected his servant very much; and the servant was steady, honest, and industrious in his service.

Time passed on, year after year; and every year the Highlander left his wages in his master's hands, until he had a pretty round sum to take. At length he prepared to return home to Cantire; and his master laid down all his wages on the table, and said, 'Whether will you lift all your money, or take three advices in its place?'

The Highlander replied, 'Sir, your advices were always good to me, and I think it better to take them than to lift the money.'

So the master took away the money, and gave him these three advices:

I. When you are going home keep on the highway, and take no byway.

II. Lodge not in any house in which you see an old man and his young wife.

III. Do nothing rashly until you have well considered what you will do.

Besides these three advices, the English farmer gave the Highlander sufficient money to carry him home; and he also gave him a loaf, which he was not to break until he could eat it with his wife and son. Then they bade farewell.

After travelling several miles the Highlander overtook a pedlar, who was on his way to Scotland; so they agreed to keep company with one another, and to lodge at a certain town that same night. But as they were travelling quite agreeably, they came upon a byway which was a great length shorter than the high road, and the pedlar proposed that they should take it; but the Highlander would not, for he thought of his master's first advice. Then the pedlar said that he was tired with his burthen, and that he would take the short byway, and wait until his companion had come forward. So they went each their way, and the Highlander kept to the highway until he had come to the place appointed. There he found the pedlar weeping, and without his pack, for he had been robbed in the byway. So this was the benefit that the Highlander got by following the first advice of the English farmer.

Then they walked on together to the town, the pedlar weeping for the loss of his pack, and saying that he knew where they would get good lodgings. But, when they got to the house, the Highlander saw an old man and a young wife; so he would not lodge there, for he remembered his master's second advice. But the pedlar remained in the house, and the Highlander crept into a coal-house in the entry. At midnight he felt someone coming in at the door, and, after remaining a short time, going out again; but, as he passed him in the dark, the Highlander, with his knife, cut a bit from the wing of his coat, and kept it. In the morning the cry of murder was heard, and it was found that the old man who kept the house had been killed. The authorities of the town came and saw the dead body, and found the pedlar sleeping in a room; and when they searched his pockets, there was a bloody knife found in them; and as he had no pack or money, they concluded he was a false pedlar, and had murdered the old man to get his wealth. So the pedlar was apprehended and condemned to be hanged; and the Highlander accompanied him to the scaffold, and observed among the crowd a young man walking with the young wife of the murdered man; and the young man's coat was of the same colour as the swatch he had cut from it in the coal-house in the entry. 'Hang me!' said the Highlander, 'if you pair are not the murderers.' So they were apprehended, and acknowledged their crime, and were hanged; and the pedlar was set at liberty. And this was the benefit that was got from the Highlander following the second advice of the English farmer.

It was midnight when the Highlander got back home. He rapped at the door, and his wife got up, and recognized her husband, and lighted a candle. Upon that, the Highlander saw a fine young man lying in the bed; and he was purposing to step up and kill him, apprehensive that another had taken his place. But he thought on his master's advice, and said, 'Who is yon man?'

'It is our son!' said his wife; 'he came home from his service last evening, and slept in that bed.'

'I should have slain him but for the master!' said the Highlander. So this was the benefit he got from following the third advice of the English farmer.

The Highlander's joy was now at its height. His son arose from the bed; more peats were put on, and a large fire kindled; and the Highlander then sought a knife to cut the loaf that he had carried all the way from England. With the first slice he found silver money; and when he had cut all the loaf, he found therein all the wages that would have been paid him by his master. So the Highlander got the money and the three advices also; and with the money he stocked a farm and lived comfortably till the end of his days.

WE THREE HIGHLANDMEN

Source: Robert Chambers, *Scottish Jests and Anecdotes*
Narrator: Unknown
Type: AT1697 'We Three: For Money'

Three young Highlanders, about fifty years ago, set out from their native hills, to seek a livelihood amongst their countrymen in the Lowlands. They had hardly learnt any English. One of them could say, 'We three Highlandmen': the second, 'For the purse and penny siller': and the third had very properly learnt, 'And our just right too'; intending thus to explain the motives of their journey. They trudged along, when, in a lonely glen, they saw the body of a man who had been recently murdered. The Highlanders stopped to deplore the fate of the unhappy man, when a gentleman, with his servant, came up to the spot. 'Who murdered this poor man?' said the gentleman. 'We three Highlandmen,' answered the eldest of the brothers (thinking the gentleman inquired what they were). 'What could induce you to commit so horrid a crime?' continued the gentleman. 'For the purse and the penny siller,' replied the second of the travellers. 'You will be hanged, you miscreants!' 'And our just right too,' returned the third Highlander. And the poor men were, on their own evidence and presumption of guilt, condemned and executed.

AN ANECDOTE OF RAB HAMILTON,
THE AYR SIMPLETON

Source: Dean Ramsay, *Reminiscences of Scottish Life and Character*
Narrator: Unknown
Type: AT1738 'The Dream: All Parsons in Hell'

Dr Auld often shewed him kindness, but being once addressed by him when in a hurry and out of humour, he said, 'Get away, Rab; I have nothing for you today.' 'Whaw, whew,' cried Rab in a half howl, half whining tone, 'I dinna want onything the day, Mister Auld; I wanted to tell you an awsome dream I hae had. I dreamt I was deed.' 'Weel, what then?' said Dr Auld. 'Ou, I was carried far, far, and up, up, up, till I cam to heeven's yett, where I chappit and chappit and chappit, till at last an angel keekit out, and said, "Wha are ye?" "Am puir Rab Hamilton." "Whaur are ye frae?" "Frae the wicked town o' Ayr." "I dinna ken ony sic place," said the angel. "Oh but I'm joost frae there." Weel, the angel sends for the Apostle Peter, and Peter comes wi' his key and opens the yett, and says to me, "Honest man, do you come frae the auld toun o' Ayr?" "Deed do I," says I. "Weel," says Peter, "I ken the place, but naebody's cam frae the town o' Ayr, no since the year"' so and so – mentioning the year when Dr Auld was inducted into the parish. Dr Auld laughed, and told him to go about his business.

DAFT SANDY AND THE MARE'S EGG

Source: Previously unpublished, School of Scottish Studies tape SA 1978/90/B4
Narrator: Duncan Williamson; recorded by Linda Williamson in 1978
Type: AT1319 'Pumpkin Sold as Ass's Egg'

Now there are so many good humorous tales. And Jack was always the hero or he was always lazy or silly. But the most important ones along the West Coast were the 'Daft Sandy tales'. Sandy was the village fool and Sandy was supposed to be daft, but he wasn't really as daft as people were led to believe. And this is the story I'm going to tell you, I hope you'll enjoy it.

So Sandy got a wee job, he was to shaw neeps* at the back of the dyke. Oh, and it's a sore job shawing neeps! He was doing this all day for to keep him and his mother in a wee bite of meat. But he's close to the road and who comes along but an Irishman, an Irish tramp.

But on the road coming over a bridge what did the Irish tramp find but a gold watch and chain! Now the Irish tramp had never seen a gold watch and chain before in his life. And the Irish tramp's name was Mick. He saw the watch lying and he got a stick, stuck it through the chain and he held it up. It was going 'tick-tick-tick, I'll kill Mick-I'll kill Mick'!

He said, 'You'll no kill me, beast!' and he held it on the stick. He came walking along and Sandy was standing at the side of the dyke looking over. The tramp said, 'Mister, could you tell me, son, what's *that*?'

Oh, Sandy looked at it – great gold watch and chain – Sandy knew right away. He said, 'That is a very funny thing . . . I'm warning you to keep away from it!'

'I know, trusting my soul I'm keeping away from it,' the

---

* shaw neeps: cut the shaws off turneeps (turnips)

Irishman said. 'Listen what it's saying! It's saying "tick-tick tick-tick, I'll kill Mick-I'll kill Mick!" It's not going to kill me!'

'Well,' Sandy said, 'the best thing you can do is get rid of it, because it'll definitely – it will kill you through time!'

'Well,' he said, 'it's no going to kill me,' and Mick's standing with the watch and chain. 'But,' he said, 'what is it you're doing in there? What is that things, that big red things you're cutting in there?'

'Well,' said Sandy, 'they're mares' eggs.'

'Well trustin my soul,' he said, 'I never saw mares' eggs before in my life.' (Big swedes, you see, big neeps!) He said, 'If I give you this "tick-tick", will you give me a mare's egg?'

'Oh,' said Sandy, 'I'll give you a mare's egg for that thing – but I'm no very sure of it myself.'

He said, 'I'll place it on the dyke to you, and you give me a mare's egg!'

Sandy said, 'Right, put it there on the dyke and I'll watch it!' And Sandy picked a big neep. 'Now,' he said, 'you take that – there's a mare's egg for you!'

'Ah, but,' he said, 'you'll have to tell me how to get a foal!'

'Oh,' Sandy said, 'I'll tell you how to get a foal, no bother at all. You'll never need to tramp the roads no more. You'll get a beautiful foal!'

'Well you can keep that "tick-tick" if you tell me how to get a foal!'

Now along by where Sandy was shawing neeps there was a steep hill and it was full of whins and brackens. It was about October month, an early winter. Sandy says, 'You're Irish, aren't you?'

'Aye, I'm an Irishman,' he says.

'And you never saw mares' eggs? Well,' Sandy says, 'look, tonight about twelve o'clock you go up to the top of that steep hill, right to the top! And place your mare's egg on the top of the hill, right! And take down your trousers and sit on it, sit for three hours and hatch it! You'll get yourself a wee foal!'

'Well trustin my soul, I'll just do that! I could do with a foal. I would never need to walk the roads no more.'

'You do that,' says Sandy, 'and you'll get yourself a beautiful wee foal!' Sandy waits till he goes away with a big wet neep below his oxter. Sandy catches the gold watch and chain, looks at the time and puts it in his waiskit pocket. He said, 'The very thing I was needing!' It was late in the day so Sandy went home.

About midnight away goes the Irishman to the top of the hill. He places the neep down. He says, 'I've longed for a foal. All my people in Ireland have horses, but I've never owned a horse in my life. Well I'm going to own one now!' Down comes his trousers. He says, 'I'll sit here suppose I sit till daylight,' and he gets *down* on top of the neep. And he sat and he sat and he sat. The moon came up and he was still sitting. It was a cold cold frosty night and he's looking down, he's shivering with the cold. His legs were frozen, his trousers still round his knees, but he wouldn't move! He said, 'I'll not be long now – I can feel it moving. Wouldn't I love a beautiful wee hairy foal!' Then the moon came right out, you could see to gather needles and pins on the ground it was that clear! But it got that cold as he was shifting, trying to shift back and forward from hip to hip, but him moving with the cold – didn't he move the neep!

And the neep moved down the hill with the decline – what goes up must come down – and away goes the neep. He's after it – he pulls up his trousers and he's off! He's running and running and running trying to catch the neep. The neep's rolling rolling rolling down the brae. And the neep rolled into a big whin bush. What was lying sound asleep in the whin bush but a big brown hare! And when the neep came in the hole where the hare was, the neep stopped. The hare got a fright and cut out the other side of the bush, and it's off! He looks, 'Oh my God, trusting my soul in my God! If I had have sat for another ten minutes I would have had a lovely wee foal. I'll never catch her now, she's gone for ever. Gone for ever – my beautiful foal!' He was nearly in tears. He lost his foal, he never knew the neep was still in the bush.

Back at his house Sandy showed his mother the beautiful watch and he tellt her the trick. She said, 'It's a shame what you done on that poor Irishman. Probably that poor cratur's frozen to death.'

But the Irishman went on his way the next day. He never got his foal, but Sandy still had his gold watch! That's the last of my story.

JOCK AND HIS MOTHER

Source: Robert Chambers, *Popular Rhymes of Scotland*
Narrator: Written down by Andrew Henderson from an unknown narrator
Type: AT1696 'What Should I Have Said (Done)?'

There was a wife that had a son, and they ca'd him Jock; and she said to him: 'You are a lazy fallow; ye maun gang awa' and do something for to help me.' 'Weel,' says Jock, 'I'll do that.' So awa' he gangs, and fa's in wi' a packman. Says the packman: 'If ye carry my pack a' day, I'll gie ye a needle at night.' So he carried the pack, and got the needle; and as he was gaun awa' hame to his mither, he cuts a burden o' brakens, and put the needle into the heart o' them. Awa' he gaes hame. Says his mither: 'What hae ye made o' yersel' the day?' Says Jock: 'I fell in wi' a packman, and carried his pack a' day, and he ga'e me a needle for't; and ye may look for it amang the brakens.' 'Hout,' quo' she, 'ye daft gowk, ye should hae stuck it into your bonnet, man.' 'I'll mind that again,' quo' Jock.

Next day he fell in wi' a man carrying plough socks. 'If ye help me to carry my socks a' day, I'll gie ye ane to yersel' at night.' 'I'll do that,' quo' Jock. Jock carries them a' day, and gets a sock, which he sticks in his bonnet. On the way hame, Jock was dry, and gaed awa' to tak a drink out o' the burn; and wi' the weight o' the sock, it fell into the river, and gaed out o' sight. He gaed hame, and his mother says: 'Weel, Jock, what hae ye been doing a' day?' And then he tells her. 'Hout,' quo' she, 'ye should hae tied a string to it, and trailed it behind you.' 'Weel,' quo' Jock, 'I'll mind that again.'

Awa' he sets, and he fa's in wi' a flesher. 'Weel,' says the flesher, 'if ye'll be my servant a' day, I'll gie ye a leg o' mutton at night.' 'I'll be that,' quo' Jock. He gets a leg o' mutton at night; he ties a string to it, and trails it behind him the hale road hame. 'What hae ye been doing?' said his mither. He tells her. 'Hout, ye fool, ye should hae carried it on your shouther.' 'I'll mind that again,' quo' Jock.

Awa' he goes next day, and meets a horse-dealer. He says: 'If ye will help me wi' my horses a' day, I'll gie ye ane to yersel' at night.' 'I'll do that,' quo' Jock. So he served him, and got his horse, and he ties its feet; but as he was not able to carry it on his back, he left it lying on the roadside. Hame he comes, and tells his mother. 'Hout, ye daft gowk, ye'll ne'er turn wise! Could ye no hae loupen on it, and ridden it?' 'I'll mind that again,' quo' Jock.

Aweel, there was a grand gentleman, wha had a daughter wha was very subject to melancholy; and her father gave out that whaever should make her laugh would get her in marriage. So it happened that she was sitting at the window ae day, musing in her melancholy state, when Jock, according to the advice o' his mither, came flying up on the cow's back, wi' the tail owre his shouther. And she burst out into a fit o' laughter. When they made inquiry wha made her laugh, it was found to be Jock riding on the cow. Accordingly, Jock is sent for to get his bride. Well, Jock is married to her, and there was a great supper prepared. Amongst the rest o' the things there was some honey, which Jock was very fond o'. After supper, they were bedded, and the auld priest that married them sat up a' night by the fireside. So Jock waukens in the night-time, and says: 'O wad ye gie me some o' yon nice sweet honey that we got to our supper last night?' 'O ay,' says his wife; 'rise and gang into the press, and ye'll get a pig fou o't.' Jock rises, and thrusts his hand into the honey-pig for a nievefu' o't; and he could not get it out. So he came awa' wi' the pig on his hand, like a mason's mell, and says: 'Oh, I canna get my hand out.' 'Hout,' quo' she, 'gang awa' and break it on the cheek-stane.' By this time the fire was dark, and the auld priest was lying snoring wi' his head against the chimney-piece, wi' a huge white wig on. Jock gaes awa', and ga'e him a whack wi' the honey-pig on the head, thinking it was the cheek-stane, and knocks it a' in bits. The auld priest roars out 'Murder!', Jock taks down the stair as hard as he can bicker, and hides himsel' amang the bees' skeps.

That night, as luck wad have it, some thieves came to steal the bees' skeps, and in the hurry o' tumbling them into a large gray plaid, they tumbled Jock in alang wi' them. So aff they set, wi' Jock and the skeps on their backs. On the way, they had to cross the burn where Jock lost his bannet. Ane o' the thieves cries: 'O I hae fand a bannet!' and Jock, on hearing that, cries out: 'O that's mine!' They thocht they had got the deil on their backs. So they let a' fa' in the burn; and Jock, being tied in the plaid, couldna get out; so he and the bees were a' drowned thegither.

If a' tales be true, that's nae lee.

JOHN GLAICK, THE BRAVE TAILOR

Source: *Folk-Lore Journal*, vol. 7, 1889
Narrator: Contributed by Walter Gregor, who had it from Mr W. Copland,
an Aberdeenshire schoolmaster who heard it from his father forty-five
years previously
Type: AT1640 'The Brave Tailor'

John Glaick was a tailor by trade, but like a man of spirit he grew tired of his tailoring, and wished to follow some other path that would lead to honour and fame. This wish showed itself at first rather in dislike to work of all kinds than in any fixed line of action, and for a time he was fonder of basking idly in the sun than in plying the needle and scissors. One warm day as he was enjoying his ease, he was annoyed by the flies alighting on his bare ankles. He brought his hand down on them with force and killed a goodly number of the plague. On counting the victims of his valour, he was overjoyed at his success; his heart rose to the doing of great deeds, and he gave vent to his feelings in the saying:

> 'Weel done! John Glaick.
> Killt fifty flees [flies] at ae straik.'

His resolution was now taken to cut out his path to fortune and honour. So he took down from its resting-place a rusty old sword that had belonged to some of his forebears, and set out in search of adventures. After travelling a long way, he came to a country that was much troubled by two giants, whom no one was bold enough to meet, and strong enough to overcome. He was soon told of the giants, and learned that the king of the country had offered a great reward and the hand of his daughter in marriage to the man who should rid his land of this scourge. John's heart rose to the deed and he offered himself for the service. The great haunt of the giants was a wood, and John set out with his old sword to perform his task. When he reached the wood, he laid himself down to think what course he would follow, for he knew how weak he was compared to those he had undertaken to kill. He had not waited long, when he saw them coming with a waggon to fetch wood for fuel. He hurriedly hid himself in the hollow of a tree, thinking only of his own safety. Feeling himself safe, he peeped out of his hiding-place, and watched the two at work. Thus watching he formed his plan of action. He picked up a pebble, threw it with force at one of them, and struck him a sharp blow on the head. The giant in his pain turned at once on his companion, and blamed him in strong words for hitting him. The other denied in anger that he had thrown the pebble. John now saw himself on the highway to gain his reward and the hand of the king's daughter. He kept still, and carefully watched for an opportunity of striking another blow. He soon found it, and right against the giant's head went another pebble. The injured giant fell on his companion in fury, and the two belaboured each other till they were utterly tired out. They sat down on a log to breathe, rest, and recover themselves. While sitting, one of them said, 'Well, all the king's army was not able to take us, but I fear an old woman with a rope's end would be too much for us now.' 'If that be so,' said John Glaick, as he sprang, bold as a lion, from his hiding place, 'What do you say to John Glaick wi' his aul roosty soord?' So saying, he fell upon them, cut off their heads, and returned in triumph. He received the king's daughter in marriage and for a time lived in peace and happiness. He never told the mode he followed in his dealing with the giants.

Some time after a rebellion broke out among the subjects of his father-in-law. John, on the strength of his former valiant deed, was chosen to quell the rebellion. His heart sank within him, but he could not refuse, and so lose his great name. He was mounted on the fiercest horse that 'ever saw sun or wind', and set out on his desperate task. He was not accustomed to ride on horseback, and he soon lost all control of his fiery steed. It galloped off at full speed, but, fortunately, in the direction of the rebel army. In its wild career it passed under the gallows that stood by the wayside. The gallows was somewhat old and frail, and down it fell on the horse's neck. Still no stop, but always forward at furious speed towards the rebels. On seeing this strange sight approaching towards them at such a speed they were seized with terror, and cried out to one another, 'There comes John Glaick that killed the two giants with the gallows on his horse's neck to hang us all.' They broke their ranks, fled in dismay, and never stopped till they reached their homes. Thus was John Glaick a second time victorious. Happily he was not put to a third test. In due time he came to the throne and lived a long, happy, and good life as king.

DAVID FRASER

Source: Hugh Miller, *My Schools and Schoolmasters*
Narrator: Unknown masons. Miller knew Fraser's brother John as 'a shrewd, sarcastic old man, much liked, however, by his fellow workmen'.

David Fraser I never saw; but as a hewer he was said considerably to excel even his brother John. On hearing that it had been remarked among a party of Edinburgh masons, that, though regarded as the first of Glasgow stone-cutters, he would find in the eastern capital at least his equals, he attired himself most uncouthly in a long-tailed coat of tartan, and, looking to the life the untamed, untaught, conceited little Celt, he presented himself one Monday morning, armed with a letter of introduction from a Glasgow builder, before the foreman of an Edinburgh squad of masons engaged upon one of the finer buildings at that time in the course of erection. The letter specified neither his qualifications nor his name: it had been written merely to secure for him the necessary employment, and the necessary employment it did secure.

The better workmen of the party were engaged, on his arrival, in hewing columns, each of which was deemed sufficient work for a week; and David was asked, somewhat incredulously, by the foreman, if he could hew? O yes, *he thought* he could hew. Could he hew columns such as these? O yes, *he thought* he could hew columns such as these. A mass of stone, in which a possible column lay hid, was accordingly placed before David, not under cover of the shed, which was already occupied by workmen, but, agreeably to David's own request, directly in front of it, where he might be seen by all, and where he straightway commenced a most extraordinary course of antics. Buttoning his long tartan coat fast around him, he would first look along the stone from the one end, anon from the other, and then examine it in front and rear; or, quitting it altogether for the time, he would take up his stand beside the other workmen, and, after looking at them with great attention, return and give it a few taps with the mallet, in a style evidently imitative of theirs, but monstrously a caricature. The shed all that day resounded with roars of laughter; and the only thoroughly grave man on the ground was he who occasioned the mirth of all the others.

Next morning David again buttoned his coat; but he got on much better this day than the former: he was less awkward and less idle, though not less observant than before; and he succeeded ere evening in tracing, in workmanlike fashion, a few draughts along the future column. He was evidently greatly improving. On the morning of Wednesday he threw off his coat; and it was seen that, though by no means in a hurry, he was seriously at work. There were no more jokes or laughter; and it was whispered in the evening that the strange Highlander had made astonishing progress during the day. By the middle of Thursday he had made up for his two days' trifling, and was abreast of the other workmen; before night he was far ahead of them; and ere the evening of Friday, when they had still a full day's work on each of their columns, David's was completed in a style that defied criticism; and, his tartan coat again buttoned around him, he sat resting himself beside it. The foreman went out, and greeted him. 'Well,' he said, 'you have beaten us all: you certainly *can* hew!' 'Yes,' said David; 'I *thought* I could hew columns. Did the other men take much more than a week to learn?' 'Come, come, *David Fraser*,' replied the foreman; 'we all guess who you are: you have had your joke out; and now, I suppose, we must give you your week's wages, and let you away.' 'Yes,' said David; 'work waits for me in Glasgow; but I just thought it might be well to know how you hewed on this east side of the country.'

THREE WITTY EXPLOITS
OF GEORGE BUCHANAN,
THE KING'S FOOL

❈

Source: Sir George Douglas, *Scottish Fairy and Folk Tales*
Narrator: Written down by Dougal Graham for *John Cheap the Chapman's Library*
Types: 1, AT1612 'The Contest in Swimming'. 2, AT821b 'Chickens from Boiled
Eggs'. 3, AT926c 'Cases Solved in a Manner Worthy of Solomon'

I

One night a Highland drover chanced to have a drinking bout
with an English captain of a ship, and at last they came to be
very hearty over their cups, so that they called in their servants
to have a share of their liquor. The drover's servant looked like
a wild man, going without breeches, stockings, or shoes, not so
much as a bonnet on his head, with a long peeled rung in his
hands. The captain asked the drover how long it was since he
catched him? He answered, 'It is about two years since I hauled
him out of the sea with a net, and afterwards ran into the
mountains, where I catched him with a pack of hounds.' The
captain believed it was so. 'But,' says he, 'I have a servant,
the best swimmer in the world.' 'Oh, but,' says the drover, 'my
servant will swim him to death.' 'No, he will not,' says the
captain; 'I'll lay two hundred crowns on it.' 'Then,' says the
drover, 'I'll hold it one to one,' and staked directly, the day
being appointed when trial was to be made.

Now the drover, when he came to himself, thinking on what a
bargain he had made, did not know what to do, knowing very
well that his servant could swim none. He, hearing of George
being in town, who was always a good friend to Scotsmen, went
unto him and told him the whole story, and that he would be
entirely broke, and durst never return home to his own country,

for he was sure to lose it. Then George called the drover and his man aside, and instructed them how to behave, so that they should be safe and gain too. So accordingly they met at the place appointed. The captain's man stripped directly and threw himself into the sea, taking a turn until the Highlandman was ready, for the drover took some time to put his servant in order. After he was stripped, his master took his plaid, and rolled a kebbuck of cheese, a big loaf and a bottle of gin in it, and this he bound on his shoulder, giving him directions to tell his wife and children that he was well, and to be sure he returned with an answer against that day se'nnight. As he went into the sea, he looked back to his master, and called out to him for his claymore. 'And what waits he for now?' says the captain's servant. 'He wants his sword,' says his master. 'His sword,' says the fellow; 'what is he to do with a sword?' 'Why,' says his master, 'if he meets a whale or a monstrous beast, it is to defend his life; I know he will have to fight his way through the north seas, ere he get to Lochaber.' 'Then,' cried the captain's servant, 'I'll swim none with him, if he take his sword.' 'Ay, but,' says his master, 'you shall, or lose the wager, take you another sword with you.' 'No,' says the fellow; 'I never did swim with a sword, nor any man else, that ever I saw or heard of. I know not but that wild man will kill me in the deep water; I would not for the whole world venture myself with him and a sword.' The captain seeing his servant afraid to venture, or if he did he would never see him again alive, therefore desired an agreement with the drover, who at first seemed unwilling; but the captain putting it in his will, the drover quit him for half the sum. This he came to through George's advice.

2

A poor Scotchman dined one day at a public house in London upon eggs, and not having money to pay, got credit till he should return. The man, being lucky in trade, acquired vast riches; and after some years, happening to pass that way, called at the house where he was owing the dinner of eggs. Having called for the innkeeper, he asked him what he had to pay for the dinner of eggs he got from him such a time. The landlord, seeing him now rich, gave him a bill of several pounds, telling him, as his reason for so extravagant a charge, that these eggs, had they been hatched, would have been chickens, and these laying more eggs, would have been more chickens, and so on, multiplying the eggs and their product, till such time as their value amounted to the sum charged. The man, refusing to comply with this demand, was charged before a judge. He then made his case known to George, his countryman, who promised to appear in the hour of cause, which he accordingly did, all in a sweat, with a great basket of boiled pease, which appearance surprised the judge, who asked him what he meant by these boiled pease? Says George, 'I am going to sow them.' 'When will they grow?' said the judge. 'They will grow,' said George, 'when sodden eggs grow chickens.' Which answer convinced the judge of the extravagance of the innkeeper's demand, and the Scotsman was acquitted for two-pence halfpenny.

3

Two drunken fellows one day fell a-beating one another on the streets of London, which caused a great crowd of people to throng together to see what it was. A tailor being at work up in a garret, about three or four storeys high, and he hearing the noise in the street, looked over the window, but could not well see them. He began to stretch himself, making a long neck, until he fell down out of the window, and alighted on an old man who was walking on the street. The poor tailor was more afraid than hurt, but the man he fell on died directly. His son caused the tailor to be apprehended and tried for the murder of his father. The jury could not bring it in wilful murder, neither could they altogether free the tailor. The jury gave it over to the judges, and the judges to the king. The king asked George's advice on this hard matter. 'Why,' says George, 'I will give you my opinion in a minute: you must cause the tailor to stand in the street where the old gentleman was when he was killed by the tailor, and then let the old gentleman's son, the tailor's adversary, get up to the window from whence the tailor fell, and jump down, and so kill the tailor as he did his father.' The tailor's adversary hearing this sentence passed, would not venture to jump over the window, and so the tailor got clear off.

THE PROFESSOR OF SIGNS

Source: 'Notes', *The Folk-Lore Record* 3, 1880
Narrator: Unknown; remembered by James Napier as told in his youth, *c.* 1820
Type: AT9248 'The Language of Signs Misunderstood'

A learned Professor from Spain having visited Aberdeen University for some purpose put the question to the Senators if they had a professor of signs? Although they did not know what this meant, still to keep up the character of the University they answered in the affirmative, thinking the Professor would not wait, and expressed their regret that he was out of town. But the Professor expressed his determination to see him before leaving, which put the Senators in great difficulty. Now, there lived in the town a sharp-witted shoemaker, who, when he had a glass, was ready for any project. The affair was stated to him, and he was willing to do anything for the honour of the city. The examination day came, and the shoemaker, in a Professor's dress, was introduced and seated opposite the Spanish Professor, with instruction he was not to speak but to sign his replies. So the Professor held up an orange, when the shoemaker at once held up a piece of oatcake; the Professor then held up his forefinger, the shoemaker instantly held up two fingers; the Professor now held up three fingers and thumb, which was followed by the shoemaker holding up his clenched fist in a menacing manner. The Professor then bowed his satisfaction, and the shoemaker withdrew.

When the Professor said that he had never met such an educated man, such a man in his country would soon realize a fortune, seeing how easy they could communicate without language, the other professors of Aberdeen were anxious to hear an explanation of the signs, which were afterwards explained thus: 'I held up an orange to say that my country produces such fruit; he held up a cake in reply that your country produced the staff of life. I held up one finger to say I believe in one God; he held up two, to say Father and Son. I then held up three and the thumb, to say Father, Son, and Holy Ghost are yet only one; he held up his entire hand, carrying out the full meaning of our creed, saying the same in substance, wisdom, and power.' The Professor then retired. The Senators were now anxious to hear the shoemaker's version of the signs, who being brought in to explain, said with triumphant glee, 'You'll be nae mair fash wi' that character. He held up an orange, saying can you match that? I held a piece of cake, as much as to say that's worth all your oranges. He looked me in the face and pointing with his finger, as much as to say ye have but a'e e'e. I held up two to tell him my ane was worth his twa. He then held up three fingers and thumb, meaning that our three would only mak ane good one. This was too much, so I shook my neeve in his face, and he was glad to stop the quarrel that would have taken place.'

THE BLACK THIEF AND HIS
APPRENTICE

Source: Cuthbert Bede, *The White Wife*
Narrator: Unknown (Kintyre), 1861–5
Type: AT1525 'The Master Thief'

It was a long time ago, when An Gadaidhe Dubh, 'the Black Thief', perambulated Cantire with his Apprentice.

Now, these thieves were not punished by law; but, rather, were respected on account of their ingenuity and dexterity; and the only preventative was, for every person to take care of his own goods and cattle. Indeed the thieves were often praised for their courage and activity; and they seldom failed in obtaining their prize.

One day, when the Black Thief and his Apprentice were on their avocation, and were looking after game, they observed a man on the way, driving a fine fat sheep before him. The Apprentice laid a bet with his Master that he would steal the sheep from the man on the way. So, the Apprentice ran some distance on the road, and dropped one of his shoes on the way. The man came up to the place and saw the shoe, and said, 'Here is a good shoe; but it is of no use to me without its morrow.' So he passed along. But, after travelling a small distance on a winding road, he came up to the other shoe that the Apprentice had dropped; and he saw the shoe and said, 'Here is the morrow.' So he tied the fine fat sheep to a post, and he returned himself for the other shoe. And the Apprentice lost no time, but loosed the sheep and took it away to his Master.

The next day, the same man was coming the same way with another fine fat sheep; and the Apprentice took it in hand to steal it also. So, when the man had come to the place where he had tied the sheep the last day, the Apprentice went into the wood, bleating like a sheep. 'Oh!' says the man, 'this is my sheep, which broke away yesterday.' So he tied the sheep, even as he did unto the other; and the Apprentice jumped out, and stole away the sheep. And in this way the man lost his two sheep.

At another time the Apprentice laid a bet with his Master that he would steal a fine horse belonging to a gentleman who took great care of him and locked him safely in the stable every night and kept the key of the stable-door in a secret place lest anyone should go by craft and take away his horse while he slept. The Master thought that, as the gentleman took so much pains, the Apprentice would not be able to succeed; but the Apprentice laid a bet that he would do it, and gain the gentleman's horse for his Master.

They waited till Hallowe'en, and then went to the gentleman's house; and, taking care that they were not seen, climbed up into the *farradh*, or loft, over the kitchen, where the hen-roost was, and where was a store of good peats to make light at night when the people wanted oil to give them light, and where all kinds of articles were put to be out of the way. Into this loft the Master and his Apprentice quietly crept, and they watched diligently to see if they would find out where the key of the stable-door was placed. Down below in the kitchen, the people were busy with their Hallowe'en sports, burning and cracking nuts, dropping eggs, and performing other rites and ceremonies that were in fashion on that night, expecting that in their dreams they would have a knowledge of futurity, and, more particularly, that the young would gain a view of their future companions and helpmates.

On the loft the Apprentice was not idle. Here he sewed to his Master's coat-tail an old dry hide that was in the loft, without letting his Master know what he had done; and then whispered him that he was going to crack a nut, on account of its being Hallowe'en. The Master told him to do nothing of the kind, or they would be discovered. But the Apprentice cracked the nut, and the noise of it was heard by the people in the kitchen below, who looked up, afraid that the house was going to fall; but, seeing all safe, went on again with their amusements.

The Apprentice again whispered his Master, that he would not let Hallowe'en pass without keeping it a little; and that he was going to crack another nut. The Master said he was a stupid fellow; and that the people down below would be sure to hear the noise, and would examine the loft and discover them. But this did not prevent the Apprentice: he cracked a nut, and the people started. 'Oh!' says one of them; 'I'll bet it's the Gadaidhe Dubh.' So they got a ladder and a light in order to search the loft. The Master found that it was time for him to take to his heels; so, he leaped down from the loft, dragging with him the dry hide, which made a rustling noise after him. At first, the people were alarmed, supposing him to be an evil spirit; but, presently, they all ran out after him, and gave him chase.

The Apprentice remained in the loft, until everyone had gone in chase of his Master except the old lady of the house. Then he came down, and he asked her for the key of the stable-door, until he would catch the thief. The old lady gave him the key, not knowing, in the hurry, who it was to whom she gave it. Whereupon the Apprentice went to the stable, unlocked the door, and took out the gentleman's fine horse, upon which he galloped off, and so won his wager; feeling sure that his Master would make way for himself and get safe home; which, indeed, proved to be the case.

HIGHLAND THIEVES

Source: J. D. Carrick, *The Laird of Logan*
Narrator: Unknown
Type: AT1791 'The Sexton Carries the Parson'

Dugald M'Caul was a professed thief in the Highlands, and sometimes took young lads into his service as apprentices to the same business. With one of these hopeful youths, who had recently engaged with him, he agreed one night to proceed upon an excursion, the apprentice to steal a wedder, and Dugald himself to steal kale. It was also agreed that they should, after being in possession of their booty, meet in the kirkyard, where they were pretty sure of not being molested, as it got the name of being haunted by a ghost. Dugald, as it may well be supposed, arrived first at the place of rendezvous, and, sitting on a gravestone, amused himself with eating kale-custocks until the apprentice should arrive with the wedder. In a neighbouring farmhouse, a cripple tailor happened to be at work, and the conversation having turned upon the story of the kirkyard being haunted, the tailor boldly censured some young men present, for not having the courage to go and speak to the supposed apparition, adding, that if he had the use of his limbs, he would have no hesitation in doing it himself. One of the young men, nettled at the tailor's remarks, proposed taking the tailor on his back to the kirkyard; and, as the tailor could not well recede from what he had said, off they went. The moment they entered the kirkyard, Dugald M'Caul saw them, and thinking it was the apprentice with a wedder on his back, he said, in a low tone of voice, as they approached him, 'Is he fat?' 'Whether he be fat or lean,' cried the young man, 'there he is to you:' and throwing down the tailor, ran off as hard as he could. To his utter astonishment, he found the tailor close at his heels, on entering the farmhouse, intense fear having supplied him with the long-lost use of his limbs, which it is said he retained ever after.

5: TALES OF THE SUPERNATURAL

THE GREY PAW

Source: J. G. Campbell, *Witchcraft and Second Sight in the Highlands and Islands of Scotland*
Narrator: Unknown; Campbell notes, 'This is perhaps the most widely known and most popular story in the Highlands . . . There is hardly an old church in the Highlands where the event has not been said to have occurred'

In the big church of Beauly (*Eaglais mhor na manachain*, i.e. of the Monastery) mysterious and unearthly sights and sounds were seen and heard at night, and none who went to watch the churchyard or burial-places within the church ever came back alive. A courageous tailor made light of the matter and laid a wager that he would go any night, and sew a pair of hose in the haunted church. He went and began his task. The light of the full moon streamed in through the windows, and at first all was silent and natural. At the dead hour of midnight, however, a big ghastly head emerged from a tomb and said, 'Look at the old grey cow that is without food, tailor.' The tailor answered, 'I see that and I sew this,' and soon found that while he spoke the ghost was stationary, but when he drew breath it rose higher. The neck emerged and said, 'A long grizzled weasand that is without food, tailor.' The tailor went on with his work in fear, but answered, 'I see it, my son, I see it, my son; I see that and I sew this just now.' This he said drawling out his words to their utmost length. At last his voice failed and he inhaled a long breath. The ghost rose higher and said, 'A long grey arm that is without flesh or food, tailor.' The trembling tailor went on with his work and answered, 'I see it, my son, I see it, my son; I see that and I sew this just now.' Next breath the thigh came up and the ghastly apparition said, 'A long, crooked shank that is without meat, tailor.' 'I see it, my son, I see it, my son; I see that and I sew this just now.' The long foodless and fleshless arm was now stretched in the direction of the tailor. 'A long grey paw without blood, or flesh, or muscles, or meat, tailor.' The tailor was near done with his work and answered, 'I see it, my son, I see it, my son; I see that and I sew this just now,' while with a trembling heart he proceeded with his work. At last he had to draw breath, and the ghost, spreading out its long and bony fingers and clutching the air in front of him, said, 'A big grey claw that is without meat, tailor.' At that moment the last stitch was put in the hose, and the tailor gave one spring of horror to the door. The claw struck at him and the point of the fingers caught him by the bottom against the doorpost and took away the piece. The mark of the hand remains on the door to this day. The tailor's flesh shook and quivered with terror, and he could cut grass with his haunches as he flew home.

REV. THOMSON AND THE DEVIL

Source: Andrew Jervise, *The History and Traditions of the Land of the Lindsays*
Narrator: Unknown; Jervise notes that, 'Although uniformly ascribed to
Mr Thomson, these stories are scarcely in accordance with his real character'

But it would seem, if tradition can be relied upon, that, about the beginning of last century (during the incumbency of the Rev. Mr Thomson), man's great adversary had enjoyed a kind of respite from his thousand years' captivity, and taken up his abode in the quiet glen of the West Water. 'Twere idle to relate a tithe of the stories yet told of his perambulations, and the various shapes in which he appeared to the minister, as well as to many of his less educated neighbours; but an instance or two will sufficiently shew the credulity both of the pastor and his flock.

One of these stories is based on a quarrel which took place between the farmer of Witton and a fellow parishioner. Witton had long a craving to be revenged on his neighbour, and on learning one evening that the object of his hatred was from home, and would not return until a late hour, he went away to meet him. Before departing on his unhallowed expedition, however, his excited appearance, and the unusually late hour, so alarmed his wife, that she tried every means to dissuade him from his journey, and all protestation having failed, she enquired, as a last resort, and in a piteous tone, who was to bear her company during his absence? To this he answered gruffly, and in a frantic manner – '*The devil if he likes!*' – and immediately went forth on his errand of revenge. So, sure enough, in the course of an hour or two, his Satanic majesty rose from the middle of the earthen floor of the chamber where the poor disconsolate woman sat, and presented himself to her astonished gaze! Whether he attempted to do her any injury is not related; but having had presence of mind to put her son, a mere boy, out at a back window for the minister, his reverence and the boy, with some of the neighbours, made way for the house. When within a short distance of it, Mr Thomson, supposing that he felt the odour of 'brimstane smeik', was so impressed with the belief of the bona fide presence of Beelzebub, that he retraced his steps to the manse, and arrayed himself in his black gown and linen bands, and taking the Bible in his hand, went boldly forth to vanquish the master fiend! On entering the ill-fated chamber, he charged the intruder with the Spirit of the Word, when, in the midst of a volume of smoke, and uttering a hideous yell, he shrunk aghast, and passed from view in much the same mysterious way as he had appeared; and an indentation in the ground floor of the farmhouse was long pointed out as having been caused by the descent of Satan!

Nor had the sanctity of the manse any effect in deterring this prowling and tormenting emissary. Even there, poor Mr Thomson was annoyed out of all patience: if he sat down of an evening to write or read, his book or paper soon became a darkened and unseemly mass, and the candle burnt so faintly before him, that he could barely see from one end of his little chamber to the other; and so bent was his enemy to do him injury, that his last interview with him was attended with disastrous and serious consequences. It was on a dark winter evening – the storm howled apace – and the snow had previously fallen so plentifully, that great wreaths were blown against the manse and church, and the minister was sitting by the fire writing, when a tremendous gust of wind suddenly shook the house from top to bottom – a peculiar sound was heard in the chimney – and amidst much din and confusion, his tormentor entered the minister's *sanctum sanctorum* in the shape of a large black cat! How he found his way, none could divine, for the minister didn't see him enter, and saw nothing of him save his long hairy fangs, which suddenly extinguished the candle! Running in pursuit, however, he saw him clear the steep and narrow stair which led to the lower flat of the house, and, falling from head to foot of it himself, Mr Thomson was so greatly injured from bruises and fright, that he never fully recovered!

THE WHITE ADDER

Source: Andrew Jervise, *The History and Traditions of the Land of the Lindsays*
Narrator: Unknown
Type: ML3030 'The White Serpent'

The wonderful gift of seeing into the firmly sealed volume of futurity was supposed to be innate in some person; but the 'broo' or broth of the white adder had the same magical effect on the partaker, as if he had been born heir to the gift. This was the manner in which Brochdarg, the celebrated Prophet of the North, was endowed with the marvellous power of diving into futurity, and of knowing the persons who 'cast ill' on their neighbours. Going to the Continent in youth as the servant of a second Sidrophel, he got a white adder from his master to boil one day, and was admonished on the pain of his existence not to let a drop of the 'broo' touch his tongue. On scalding his fingers, however, he inadvertently thrust them into his mouth as a soothing balm, when he instantly beheld the awful future stretched out before him. Fearing the ire of his master, he fled from his service, and, domiciling himself among his native mountains in Aberdeenshire, was consulted by all the bewitched and lovesick swains and maidens far and near, and died an old wealthy carle about eighty years ago!

THE TALE OF SIR JAMES RAMSAY
OF BAMFF

Source: Robert Chambers, *Popular Rhymes of Scotland*
Narrator: Unknown
Type: ML3030 'The White Serpent'

Weel, ye see, I dinna mind the beginning o' the story. But the Sir James Ramsay o' Bamff of that time was said to be ane o' the conspirators, and his lands were forfaulted, and himsel' banished the country, and a price set upon his head if he came back.

He gaed to France or Spain, I'm no sure which, and was very ill off. Ae day that he was walking in a wood, he met an oldish man wi' a lang beard, weel dressed and respectable-looking. This man lookit hard at Sir James, and then said to him that he lookit ill and distressed like; that he himsel' was a doctor, and if Sir James would tell his complaints, maybe he might be able to do him good.

Syne Sir James said he was not ill but for want o' food, and that all the medicine he needed was some way to earn his living as a gentleman. The auld doctor said till him he would take him as an apprentice if he liked; that he should live in his house and at his table, and learn his profession. So Sir James went hame wi' him, and was very kindly tret. After he had been wi' him a while, his master said till him ae day that he kend how to make the best and most wonderful medicine in the world – a medicine that would make baith their fortunes, and a' that belanged to them; but that it was a difficult business to get the materials that the medicine was made of – that they could only be gotten frae the River —, that ran through the county of —, in Scotland, and at a particular part of the river, which he described; and that it would need to be some canny person, that kend that pairt o' the

country weel, to gang wi' ony chance o' success. Sir James said
naebody kend that pairt o' the country better than himsel', for it
was on his ain estate o' Bamff, and that he was very willing to
run the risk o' going hame for his master's sake, that had been
sae kind to him, and for the sake o' seeing his ain place again.

Then the doctor gied him strict directions what he was to do,
and how he was to make sure o' getting the beast that he was to
make the medicine o'. He was to gang to a pairt o' the river
where there was a deep pool o' water, and he was to hide himsel'
behind some big trees that came down to the waterside for the
three nights that the moon was at the full. He would see a white
serpent come out o' the water, and go up to a big stane, and
creep under it. He maun watch till it came out again, and catch it
on its way back to the water, and kill it, and bring it awa' wi'
him.

Weel, Sir James did a' that he was bidden. He put on a
disguise, and gaed back to Scotland and to Bamff, and got there
without onybody kenning him. He hid himsel' behind the trees
at the waterside, and watched night after night. He saw the
white serpent come out the first twa nights, and creep under the
stane; but it aye got back to the water afore he could catch it;
but the third night he did catch it, and killed it, and brought it
awa' wi' him to Spain to his master. His master was very glad to
get it, but he wasna sae kind after to Sir James as he used to be.
He told him, now that they had got the serpent, the next thing
to do was to cook it, and he maun do that too. He was to go
down to a vault, and there stew the serpent till it was turned into
oil. If onybody saw him at the wark, or if he tasted food till it
was done, the charm would be spoiled; and if by ony chance he
was to taste the medicine, it would kill him at ance, unless he
had the proper remedy. Sae Sir James gaed down to the vault,
and prepared the medicine just as he had been ordered; but when
he was pouring it out o' the pan into the box where it was to be
keepit, he let some drops fa' on his fingers that brunt them; and
in the pain and hurry he forgot his master's orders, and put his
fingers into his mouth to suck out the pain. He did not die, but
he fand that his een were opened, and that he could see through
everything. And when his master came down at the appointed

time to speer if the medicine was ready, he fand he could see into his master's inside, and could tell a' that was going on there. But he keepit his ain secret, and never let on to his master what had happened; and it was very lucky, for he soon found out that his master was a bad man, and would have killed him if he had kend that he had got the secret o' the medicine. He had only been kind to him because he kend that Sir James was the best man to catch the serpent.

However, Sir James learnt to be a skilfu' doctor under him; and at last he managed to get awa' frae him, and syne he travelled over the warld as a doctor, doing mony wonders, because he could clearly see what was wrang in folk's insides. But he wearied sair to get back to Scotland, and he thought that naebody would ken him as a doctor. Sae he ventured to gae back; and when he arrived, he fand that the king was very ill, and no man could find out what was the matter wi' him. He had tried a' the doctors in Scotland, and a' that came to him frae far and near, but he was nane the better; and at last he published a proclamation, that he would gie the princess, his daughter, in marriage to ony man that would cure him. Sae Sir James gaed to the court, and askit leave to try his skill. As soon as he came into the king's presence, and looked at him, he saw there was a ball o' hair in his inside, and that no medicine could touch it. But he said if the king would trust to him, he would cure him; and the king having consented, he put him sae fast asleep, that he cuttit the ball o' hair out of his inside without his ever wakening. When he did waken, he was free from illness, only weak a little frae the loss o' blood; and he was sae pleased wi' his doctor, that Sir James kneeled down and tell't him wha he was. And the king pardoned him, and gied him back a' his lands, and gied him the princess, his daughter, in marriage.

DONALD DUIBHEAL MACKAY

Source: Rev. George Sutherland, *Folk-Lore Gleanings*
Narrator: Unknown; collected for a competition run by the Wick branch of
the Comunn Gaidhealach
Type: ML3000 'Escape from the Black School of Witteburg', ML3020
'Inexperienced Use of the Black Book, Ropes of Sand'

Donald Duibheal Mackay was a notable wizard in his day, and ought to be, for he studied the black art in Italy under a no less distinguished professor than Satan himself. The fee that this notorious personage demanded for his professorial work was that at the end of the session, when the students would be dispersing, the last one to go out at the door should be his perquisite. On dismissal day Donald happened to be the last to leave the room. Satan made a grab at him, but Donald protested that he was not the last, and, turning round, he pointed to his shadow and said, 'De'il tak' the hindmost.' Satan looked round and seized Donald's shadow, but before he realized its unsubstantiality Donald was away. Donald's shadow was the only fee Satan got for that session's work.

His education being now finished, Donald came home to the Reay country. The observant and sharp-witted people of his native district quickly noticed that he was uncanny, for they saw that he did not cast a shadow. Shortly after coming home he went into the famous cave of Smoo in Durness, and was resolved to explore its subterranean recesses where no foot of man had ever trod. He climbed the face of the cliff that forms the back wall of the magnificent outer cave and entered the opening that gave access to the dark underground part of the cave. He found that a lake, fed by a stream that poured through a hole in the roof, barred further progress. But a man that was so clever as to outwit the devil was not to be baulked in his purpose by an underground pool of water. A small boat launched on this pool would overcome the difficulty. The tiny boat soon materialized. It was hoisted up into the entrance hole and pushed into the water. Donald and his dog went aboard. For some distance the passage was narrow, and at one point the roof was so low that he could not sit upright in the boat. He squeezed past the low narrow part, and passed the point where the stream was pouring through a hole in the roof into the cave. After passing these obstacles the cave widened out and also increased in height, and after a few more yards the boat touched dry land. He and the dog landed. As he was feeling his way through a passage dark as a wolf's throat he heard a voice ordering him to halt. The dog had run on into the dark passage a considerable distance in front of him, but soon returned howling from pain and fear. Donald and the dog got into the boat again, and in a few minutes more they were back into the light, when to his horror Donald saw that the dog was stripped naked of all his hair.

As Donald was leaving the cave the queen of the fairies met him. She commanded him to give up all thought of exploring the cave of Smoo, and instructed him to go to a certain place which she named where he would find a box which he was on no account to open until he would get further instructions. Donald went to the place and found the box, but disobeyed the injunction not to open it. Hundreds of fairies swarmed out of the open box, and were calling out, 'Work, work, work.' To stop their clamour Donald bade them go to the hillside and strip off the heather, twist it into ropes, and wind the ropes into large clews. With amazing rapidity they went about this work, and the clews of heather ropes were tumbling down the hillside like a shower of gigantic hailstones. The hillside was stripped bare in no time, and, if rumour speaks true, nothing ever grew on that hillside again.

This job having been finished, Donald's imps were clamouring as insistently as before for work. While the fairies were busy at the heather affair, he was busy planning what to set them to next. It was believed that a pot full of gold was hid in the loch on the east side of Clash Breac in Brubster. To set his energetic workers the task of drying the loch would keep them for some time from being troublesome, and besides, there was a sporting chance of finding the pot of gold and of making him the happy possessor of it. He accordingly gave the order to drain the loch. The fairies or imps, or whatever they were, laboured at their task with great vigour, and were making good progress, as may be seen to this day by the two hills – Craigmore and Craigbeg – formed by the rock and soil which they excavated from the canal that they were digging. One day while the work was progressing satisfactorily, the Cailleach of Clash Breac [the Carline of Clash Breac] came along and shouted to the workers: 'In the name of God, what are you doing here?' In an instant the labourers vanished – they could not endure the mention of the Sacred Name. Donald's rage was boundless. He picked up a spade, and there and then he split the Cailleach's head with it. When the workers threw down their tools a loud noise like thunder reverberated among the hills. The unfinished work is still to be seen in the form of a deep ravine extending for about two hundred feet in the direction of the loch, but not reaching it. On the north side of this ravine there is a standing stone with the top part of it cleft in twain. This is said to be the Cailleach with the cloven skull now turned into stone.

Donald and his workers often visited Caithness, and were always ready for a job. On one of such visits he came to the farm of Lythmore. It was the middle of the harvest season, but the weather was cold and stormy, and the harvest work was still undone. Donald undertook to cut the farmer's corn, to bind it in sheaves, and to stook it – and all this to be finished by next evening. The morning came but Donald was still in bed, and seemed to be in no hurry to begin the work. The farmer was becoming anxious, and went to his bedside and told him that it was a good harvest day and that he would like to see him getting on with the work. Donald gave little heed to the farmer's remonstrances, and lay in bed till the evening. He then went quite leisurely to the field, hook in hand, and cut as much corn as would make a stook. He bound it in sheaves, and set up the sheaves in a stook. He then clapped his hands and said: 'Everyone like that.' No sooner were the words uttered than stook after stook was springing up, and in an incredibly short time all the corn on the farm was in stooks. On that night there was a great cutting-off feast and high revelry at the farmer's house; and, of course, Donald was handsomely paid for his services.

On another occasion he was on his way to Caithness, and it happened to be on a Sunday. When he came to the split stone at Drumholiston he sat down on a boulder to rest, when to his surprise he saw Satan standing beside him with a beautiful set of bagpipes under his arm. While he was resting Satan regaled him with some bagpipe music, after which they continued their journey to Reay. As they were approaching Reay they saw the people gathering to church. Satan and Donald also made for the church, and having arrived at the sacred building, they took their stand at the door and tried to dissuade the people from going into a killjoy place like that, and urged them to recruit into Satan's jolly service. To the great credit of the Reay people, not one of them listened to Satan's appeal or to that of his henchman. The tradition does not say how this rebuff affected Donald's feelings, but evidently it did not break his heart, for shortly after he turned up in the best of spirits at the house of a Reay farmer and agreed to thresh his corn.

In those days there were no threshing mills in Caithness, the threshing was done by flails, and the farmer was glad to avail himself of the services of Donald Duival's imps and so avoid the drudgery of the flail. Donald went to bed for the night in the farmer's house. Next morning the farmer, carrying out the instructions given him, had a considerable number of people assembled at the barn. One set of people was needed to loosen the sheaf bands and to throw the loosened sheaves on to the threshing floor. The other set was needed for removing the threshed straw and grain out of the way of the flails. Seeing that the fairies themselves were so efficient, it is not clear why they should bother with such a crowd of clumsy humans. The morning hours were passing, midday came, but Donald was still in bed. In the late afternoon he turned up at the barn and gave orders to have everything ready for the threshers. Then he gave the mystic signal, and instantly many flails were at work. The men could not throw the sheaves on to the floor quickly enough, and it was as much as the other set could do to clear away the threshed straw and grain. Early that evening every screw in the cornyard was threshed and Donald and his gang were ready for another bout of work, and before dusk on the same evening they cleared another cornyard in that neighbourhood, and then disappeared. That afternoon lived long in the Reay tradition as 'The day of the big threshing', and it became an era from which local events were dated.

By far the biggest job that Donald and his workers ever took in hand was the attempt to bridge the Pentland Firth. The bridge was to be made of ropes woven from the sands of Dunnet Bay. Surely a sufficiently difficult enterprise, yet for a time it promised to be a success. In obedience to Donald's orders his workers succeeded in making what was to be the main rope for supporting the bridge. When trying to manoeuvre it into position, and getting it stretched from shore to shore, it snapped in the middle. The fairies were now raging at Donald for giving them work that transcended their powers. They turned on him in fierce rebellion, and would have torn him limb from limb, but Donald was too clever for them. He quickly changed himself into a black horse and fled from them with lightning speed into the town of Thurso.

As fairies are not permitted to quit their job until it is finished, they are presumably fumbling among the Dunnet sands to this day, and trying to twist them into ropes.

THE TALE OF MICHAEL SCOT

Source: John MacInnes, 'The Tale of Michael Scot', *Scottish Studies*, vol. 7, 1963
Narrator: Duncan MacInnes (Donnachadh Nan Sgeulachdan, Duncan of
the Stories), seventy-three, a fisherman of Eriskay, South Uist; taken down on
12 July 1933 by Donald MacDonald for the Irish Folklore Commission
Type: AT756b 'The Devil's Contract'

Michael Scot was an evil man. He had the devil for a horse
to ride and he acted in this way for a long time. When
they went across the sea, the Adversary used to ask Michael how
it was that he was able to ride him, so that he could shoot him
off his back. Michael would cry, 'Mount higher, Devil!' Anyhow,
as I have already said, he acted in this way for a long time.

There was a priest who was studying at a college, but before
he had gone to college he had had a sweetheart. He remained at
college until he took his vows. Then he left college and made to
return home. He came to a lodging-house and said to himself
that he would spend the night there, and asked for a room. He
was reading in his room all alone when the door opened and a
woman came in with a veil over her face. The priest raised his
head and looked at her but he said nothing to her.

'You don't recognize me at all,' said she.

'I think I recognize you,' said he.

Who was it but his old sweetheart? 'You'd better renounce
these things you've taken,' said she, 'and you and I will get
married.'

'That's not easy for me,' said he.

'It's easy enough,' said she, 'if you want to.'

She nagged at him until she made him write it down on paper
that he would marry her. When the woman got this she bolted
out of the door. After she had gone it came into his mind that
she was a spirit come from the Devil to tempt him. The
following day he went home and told his father about the thing

he had done and said that he was going off to see if he could seize the pledge he had given her.

'Go to Michael Scot,' said his father. 'If anyone knows of the evil place and where it is, he does.'

Anyway, the priest came to Michael Scot and told him what he was looking for. 'I have no more idea where it is, my boy, than you have yourself – though I have been there twenty times. But if you do go looking for it keep your face to the north.'

Off went the priest. Day and night he journeyed on and there was no sign that he was going to find anything. Then he came to a glen, and he kept being aware of the most unpleasant smell in the glen. At the head of the glen he observed a mound of a house. He went in and there was an old grey-headed man inside.

'I know the object of your journey very well,' said the old man.

'I'm glad to hear that,' said the priest. 'Can you tell me how far I've still got to go?'

'You don't have to go much farther,' said the old man, 'it's only a little way beyond this. You will see a dark-blue stone in the ground: that is the door. Take a candle with you and light it. When the door opens, call her by name – Catriona MacLeod – and if she is not there or is unwilling to give you the paper, step one pace forward with the candle.'

The priest went off, came to the flagstone and struck it and the flagstone was opened. The priest lit the candle. The person working the door-chain called out to hurry up and announce to him whatever it was he wanted.

The priest called for Catriona MacLeod and nine times nine women of her name came to the door. She was not there at all. He called again and another nine times nine came and she was not there at all. He called again and another nine times nine came and there she was.

'Give me the pledge I gave you,' said he.

'No,' she said, 'not I.'

He moved in a step with the candle. The person working the chain shouted, 'Hurry up and give him whatever he wants or else you will go to Michael Scot's bed tonight!' When Catriona heard this she tossed the pledge to the priest.

'Well now,' said he, 'since I have come here – and may God bring me safely out of it – you must show me Michael Scot's bed.'

They showed it to him; it had walls of ice on the one side and green flame on the other.

The priest left and went back the way he had come. He went home to his father's house with the pledge in his possession. Michael Scot heard of his arrival and came to see him. Michael asked him how things had gone with him. 'Very well for me,' replied the priest, 'but God help you the day you leave here!'

'Did you see my bed?' asked Michael Scot.

'Yes,' he said.

'I knew it was there,' said Michael, 'but they never let me see it myself. Oh God,' said he, 'forgive Thou me for all I have done. I will never do one thing ever again but go about on my two knees asking forgiveness from God till I drop dead!'

He turned to the priest. 'When I die,' said he, 'you will make a fire and you will cast my body on it and burn me. You'll see a dove and a raven approaching. If the raven bears away the ashes, scatter them to the winds, but if the dove bears them away, take care of them and bury them.'

When Michael died, the priest burnt his body and it soon turned to ashes. A raven came and a dove came and they sailed above Michael's ashes.

'What sent you here?' said the raven to the dove. 'It was for me he did everything he ever did.'

'Yes,' said the dove, 'but it was for me he did the last.'

The dove descended on the ashes and bore away a mouthful. The priest took care of the ashes and buried them.

There was a holy man worshipping God in a rocky cave for twenty years, and a bird used to come to him with food from Heaven. One day the bird was late in coming and the holy man asked it what had kept it late.

'No small thing,' said the bird, 'is that which has kept me late today. We had a feast today in Heaven and great joy with the arrival there of the soul of Michael Scot.'

'Michael Scot!' said the holy man. 'The most accursed man

who ever lived – whereas I have been here worshipping God for twenty years!'

The holy man went off in a blaze of fire to the skies.

He got Michael Scot's place in Hell and Michael Scot got his place in Heaven.

THE BLACK HORSEMAN

Source: R. de B. Trotter, *Galloway Gossip*
Narrator: Unknown

Ey! an there wus a kin' o' ghaist or spectre use't tae be seen at Dalarran, yt they ca't the Black Horseman, an folk said it wus the king o' the Danes yt wus kill't an bury't aneath the muckle leck, an couldna rest acause he wusna bury't at the Fintilach, at the ither side o' the water.

There wus yin George M'Millan, a son o' Brocklach's in Carsephairn, yt saw't, an he tell't the doctor a' aboot it. It's no sae mony year sin he wus leevin in Manchester. It wus in 1809, an he wus takin his sister tae Dumfries tae the Boardin-skule, an she wus sittin ahint him on the beast; for it wus the fashion than for the women tae ride on the horse ahint the man, on a pillion. It wus the grey o' the mornin, for the Black Horseman wus never seen at nicht like ither ghaists, but ey whun it wus nearly daylicht. There wus nae brig ower the Garpel than, but just a ford, an whun they wur crossin't they heard the fit o' a beast comin doon the burn, an jaupin the water aboot it wi its feet. They never thocht o' the Black Horseman, but wunner't wha could be comin doon the burn at that time i'e mornin, an sae they stoppit till it cam up.

They had har'ly stoppit whun it cam bye them, no half a dizzen yairds aff, an keepit strecht on doon the burn, sae yt they had a gude sicht o' him. The horse wus a big black yin, the biggest they had ever seen, an had an awfu queer saddle on, an something like airmour on its neck, but there wus naething fleysome aboot it; an the man wus a perfet giant, wi gude features an black hair, an he wus dress't in black airmour, an had on a helmet wi feathers on't, an he cairry't a big sword. He took nae notice o' them, an never loot on they wur there, an whun he had gane doon the burn a bit, he turn't on tae the haugh, an strecht for Dalarran stane. He stoppit there a minute, an then gaed richt across the holm, an through the Ken, an up the hillside.

Geordie wus curious tae ken whaur he gaed tae, an follow't him, but his horse walkit that fast they could har'ly keep up wi't. He gaed richt up the hill till he wun tae the muckle leck yt use't tae stan ablow the Fintilach hoose, an he stoppit there an gradually fadit awa oot o' their sicht.

Mony a yin had seen him at the ford, but naebuddy ever follow't him afore, an they a' gied the same description o' him, an thocht he had a verra melancholy coontenance. A haena heard o' him bein seen sin his grave wus hokit up. Folk said he wus the king o' the Danes yt wus kill't by Grier o' Lag at the time o' the Persecution.

THE LADY OF BALCONIE

Source: Hugh Miller, *Scenes and Legends of the North of Scotland*
Narrator: Unknown

The house and lands of Balconie, a beautiful Highland property, lie within a few miles of the chasm. There is a tradition
that, about two centuries ago, the proprietor was married to a
lady of very retired habits who, though little known beyond her
narrow circle of acquaintance, was regarded within that circle
with a feeling of mingled fear and respect. She was singularly
reserved, and it was said spent more of her waking hours in
solitary rambles on the banks of the Auldgrande, in places where
no one else would choose to be alone, than in the house of
Balconie. Of a sudden, however, she became more social, and
seemed desirous to attach to herself, by acts of kindness and
confidence, one of her own maids, a simple Highland girl; but
there hung a mysterious wildness about her – a sort of atmosphere of dread and suspicion – which the change had not
removed; and her new companion always felt oppressed, when
left alone with her, by a strange sinking of the vital powers – a
shrinking apparently of the very heart – as if she were in the
presence of a creature of another world. And after spending with
her, on one occasion, a whole day, in which she had been more
than usually agitated by this feeling, and her ill-mated companion
more than ordinarily silent and melancholy, she accompanied
her, at her bidding, as the evening was coming on, to the banks
of the Auldgrande.

They reached the chasm just as the sun was sinking beneath
the hill, and flinging his last gleam on the topmost boughs of the
birches and hazels which then, as now, formed a screen over the
opening. All beneath was dark as midnight. 'Let us approach
nearer the edge,' said the lady, speaking for the first time since

she had quitted the house. 'Not nearer, ma'am,' said the terrified girl; 'the sun is almost set, and strange sights have been seen in the gully after nightfall.' 'Psha,' said the lady, 'how can you believe such stories? Come, I will show you a path which leads to the water: it is one of the finest places in the world. I have seen it a thousand times, and must see it again tonight. Come,' she continued, grasping her by the arm, 'I desire it much, and so down we must go.' 'No, lady!' exclaimed the terrified girl, struggling to extricate herself, and not more startled by the proposal than by the almost fiendish expression of mingled anger and fear which now shaded the features of her mistress, 'I shall swoon with terror and fall over.' 'Nay, wretch, there is no escape!' replied the lady, in a voice heightened almost to a scream, as, with a strength that contrasted portentously with her delicate form, she dragged her, despite of her exertions, towards the chasm. 'Suffer me, ma'am, to accompany you,' said a strong masculine voice from behind; 'your surety, you may remember, must be a willing one.' A dark-looking man, in green, stood beside them; and the lady, quitting her grasp with an expression of passive despair, suffered the stranger to lead her towards the chasm. She turned round on reaching the precipice, and, untying from her belt a bunch of household keys, flung them up the bank towards the girl; and then, taking what seemed to be a farewell look of the setting sun, for the whole had happened in so brief a space that the sun's upper disk still peeped over the hill, she disappeared with her companion behind the nearer edge of the gulf. The keys struck, in falling, against a huge granitic boulder, and sinking into it as if it were a mass of melted wax, left an impression which is still pointed out to the curious visitor. The girl stood rooted to the spot in utter amazement.

On returning home, and communicating her strange story, the husband of the lady, accompanied by all the males of his household, rushed out towards the chasm; and its perilous edge became a scene of shouts, and cries, and the gleaming of torches. But, though the search was prolonged for whole days by an eager and still increasing party, it proved fruitless. There lay the ponderous boulder impressed by the keys; immediately beside it yawned the sheer descent of the chasm; a shrub, half uprooted, hung dangling from the brink; there was a faint line drawn along the green mould of the precipice a few yards lower down; and that was just all. The river at this point is hidden by a projecting crag, but the Highlanders could hear it fretting and growling over the pointed rocks, like a wild beast in its den; and as they listened and thought of the lady, the blood curdled at their hearts. At length the search was relinquished, and they returned to their homes to wonder, and surmise, and tax their memories, though in vain, for a parallel instance. Months and years passed away, and the mystery was at length assigned its own little niche among the multitudinous events of the past.

About ten years after, a middle-aged Highlander, the servant of a maiden lady who resided near the Auldgrande, was engaged one day in fishing in the river, a little below where it issues from the chasm. He was a shrewd fellow, brave as a lion and kindly natured withal, but not more than sufficiently honest; and his mistress, a stingy old woman, trusted him only when she could not help it. He was more than usually successful this day in his fishing; and picking out some of the best of the fish for his aged mother, who lived in the neighbourhood, he hid them under a bush, and then set out for his mistress with the rest. 'Are you quite sure, Donald,' inquired the old lady as she turned over the contents of his basket, 'that this is the whole of your fishing? – Where have you hid the rest?' 'Not one more, lady, could I find in the burn.' 'O Donald!' said the lady. 'No, lady,' reiterated Donald, 'devil a one!' And then, when the lady's back was turned, off he went to the bush to bring away the fish appropriated to his mother. But the whole had disappeared; and a faintly marked track, spangled with scales, remained to show that they had been dragged apparently by some animal along the grass in the direction of the chasm.

The track went winding over grass and stone along the edge of the stream, and struck off, as the banks contracted and became more steep and precipitous, by a beaten path which ran along the edge of the crags at nearly the level of the water, and which, strangely enough, Donald had never seen before. He pursued it, however, with the resolution of tracing the animal to its den. The channel narrowed as he proceeded; the stream which, as he entered the chasm, was eddying beneath him in rings of a mossy brown, became one milky strip of white, and, in the language of the poet, 'boiled, and wheeled, and foamed, and thundered through'; the precipices on either hand beetled in some places so high over his head as to shut out the sky, while in others, where they receded, he could barely catch a glimpse of it through a thick screen of leaves and bushes, whose boughs, meeting midway, seemed twisted together like pieces of basket work. From the more than twilight gloom of the place, the track he pursued seemed almost lost, and he was quite on the eve of giving up the pursuit, when, turning an abrupt angle of the rock, he found the path terminate in an immense cavern. As he entered, two gigantic dogs, which had been sleeping one on each side of the opening, rose lazily from their beds, and yawning as they turned up their slow heavy eyes to his face, they laid themselves down again. A little further on there was a chair and table of iron apparently much corroded by the damps of the cavern. Donald's fish, and a large mass of leaven prepared for baking, lay on the table; in the chair sat the lady of Balconie.

Their astonishment was mutual. 'O Donald!' exclaimed the lady, 'what brings you here?' 'I come in quest of my fish,' said Donald, 'but, O lady! what *keeps* you here? Come away with me, and I will bring you home; and you will be lady of Balconie yet.' 'No no!' she replied, 'that day is past; I am fixed to this seat, and all the Highlands could not raise me from it.' Donald looked hard at the iron chair; its ponderous legs rose direct out of the solid rock as if growing out of it, and a thick iron chain red with rust, that lay under it, communicated at the one end to a strong ring, and was fastened round the other to one of the lady's ankles. 'Besides,' continued the lady, 'look at these dogs – O! why have you come here? The fish you have denied to your mistress in the name of my jailer, and his they have become; but how are you yourself to escape?' Donald looked at the dogs. They had again risen from their beds, and were now eyeing him with a keen vigilant expression, very unlike that with which they had regarded him on his entrance. He scratched his head. ''Deed, mem,' he said, 'I dinna weel ken; I maun first durk the twa tykes, I'm thinking.' 'No,' said the lady, 'there is but one way;

be on the alert.' She laid hold of the mass of leaven which lay on the table, flung a piece to each of the dogs, and waved her hand for Donald to quit the cave. Away he sprang; stood for a moment as he reached the path to bid farewell to the lady; and after a long and dangerous scramble among the precipices, for the way seemed narrower, and steeper, and slipprier than when he had passed by it to the cave, he emerged from the chasm just as the evening was beginning to darken into night. And no one, since the adventure of Donald, has seen aught of the lady of Balconie.

THE GREEN LADY

Source: Hugh Miller, *Scenes and Legends of the North of Scotland*
Narrator: Hugh Miller's uncle James

The wife of a Banffshire proprietor, of the minor class, had been about six months dead, when one of her husband's ploughmen, returning on horseback from the smithy in the twilight of an autumn evening, was accosted, on the banks of a small stream, by a stranger lady, tall and slim, and wholly attired in green, with her face wrapped up in the hood of her mantle, who requested to be taken up behind him on the horse, and carried across. There was something in the tones of her voice that seemed to thrill through his very bones, and to insinuate itself in the form of a chill fluid between his skull and the scalp. The request, too, seemed a strange one; for the rivulet was small and low, and could present no serious bar to the progress of the most timid traveller. But the man, unwilling ungallantly to disoblige a lady, turned his horse to the bank, and she sprang up lightly behind him. She was, however, a personage that could be better seen than felt; and came in contact with the ploughman's back, he said, as if she had been an ill-filled sack of wool. And when, on reaching the opposite side of the streamlet, she leaped down as lightly as she had mounted, and he turned fearfully round to catch a second glimpse of her, it was in the conviction that she was a creature considerably less earthly in her texture than himself. She opened, with two pale, thin arms, the enveloping hood, exhibiting a face equally pale and thin, which seemed marked, however, by the roguish, half-humorous expression of one who had just succeeded in playing off a good joke. 'My dead mistress!' exclaimed the ploughman. 'Yes, John, *your mistress*,' replied the ghost. 'But ride home, my bonny man, for it's growing late; you and I will be better acquainted ere long.' John accordingly rode home, and told his story.

Next evening, about the same hour, as two of the laird's servant-maids were engaged in washing in an outhouse, there came a slight tap to the door. 'Come in,' said one of the maids; and the lady entered, dressed, as on the previous night, in green. She swept past them to the inner part of the washing-room; and seating herself on a low bench, from which, ere her death, she used occasionally to superintend their employment, she began to question them, as if still in the body, about the progress of their work. The girls, however, were greatly too frightened to reply. She then visited an old woman who had nursed the laird, and to whom she used to show, ere her departure, considerably more kindness than her husband. And she now seemed as much interested in her welfare as ever. She inquired whether the laird was kind to her; and, looking round her little smoky cottage, regretted she should be so indifferently lodged, and that her cupboard, which was rather of the emptiest at the time, should not be more amply furnished.

For nearly a twelvemonth after, scarce a day passed in which she was not seen by some of the domestics – never, however, except on one occasion, after the sun had risen, or before it had set. The maids could see her in the grey of the morning flitting like a shadow round their beds, or peering in upon them at night through the dark window-panes, or at half-open doors. In the evening she would glide into the kitchen or some of the out-houses – one of the most familiar and least dignified of her class that ever held intercourse with mankind – and inquire of the girls how they had been employed during the day; often, how-ever, without obtaining an answer, though from a different cause from that which had at first tied their tongues. For they had become so regardless of her presence, viewing her simply as a troublesome mistress who had no longer any claim to be heeded, that when she entered, and they had dropped their conversation, under the impression that their visitor was a creature of flesh and blood like themselves, they would again resume it, remarking that the entrant was 'only the green lady'. Though always cadaverously pale and miserable-looking, she affected a joyous disposition, and was frequently heard to laugh, even when invisible. At one time, when provoked by the studied silence of a servant girl, she flung a pillow at her head, which the girl caught up and returned; at another, she presented her first acquaintance, the ploughman, with what seemed to be a handful of silver coin, which he transferred to his pocket, but which, on hearing her laugh immediately after she had disappeared, he drew out again, and found to be merely a handful of slate-shivers. On yet another occasion, the man, when passing on horseback through a clump of wood, was repeatedly struck from behind the trees by little pellets of turf; and, on riding into the thicket, he found that his assailant was the green lady. To her husband she never appeared; but he frequently heard the tones of her voice echoing from the lower apartments, and the faint peal of her cold unnatural laugh.

One day at noon, a year after her first appearance, the old nurse was surprised to see her enter the cottage, as all her previous visits had been made early in the morning or late in the evening; whereas now, though the day was dark and lowering, and a storm of wind and rain had just broken out, still it *was* day. 'Mammie!' she said, 'I cannot open the heart of the laird, and I have nothing of my own to give you; but I think I can do something for you now. Go straight to the White House [that of a neighbouring proprietor], and tell the folk there to set out, with all the speed of man and horse, for the black rock at the foot of the crags, or they'll rue it dearly to their dying day. Their bairns, foolish things, have gone out to the rock, and the sea has flowed round them; and if no help reach them soon, they'll be all scattered like seaware on the shore ere the fall of the tide . . . But if you go and tell your story at the White House, mammie, the bairns will be safe for an hour to come; and there will be something done by their mother to better you, for the news.' The woman went as directed, and told her story; and the father of the children set out on horseback in hot haste for the rock – a low, insulated skerry, which, lying on a solitary part of the beach, far below the line of flood, was shut out from the view of the inhabited country by a wall of precipices, and covered every tide by several feet of water. On reaching the edge of the cliffs, he saw the black rock, as the woman had described, surrounded by the sea, and the children clinging to its higher crags. But, though the waves were fast rising, his attempts to ride out through the surf to the poor little things were frustrated by their cries, which so frightened his horse as to render it unmanageable; and so he had to gallop on to the nearest fishing village for a boat. So much time was unavoidably lost, in consequence, that nearly the whole beach was covered by the sea, and the surf had begun to lash the feet of the precipices behind; but, until the boat arrived, not a single wave dashed over the black rock; though immediately after the last of the children had been rescued, an immense wreath of foam rose twice a man's height over its topmost pinnacle.

The old nurse, on her return to the cottage, found the green lady sitting beside the fire. 'Mammie,' she said, 'you have made friends to yourself today, who will be kinder to you than your foster-son. I must now leave you: my time is out, and you'll be all left to yourselves; but I'll have no rest, mammie, for many a twelvemonth to come. Ten years ago, a travelling pedlar broke into our garden in the fruit season, and I sent out our old ploughman, who is now in Ireland, to drive him away. It was on a Sunday, and everybody else was in church. The men struggled and fought, and the pedlar was killed. But though I at first thought of bringing the case before the laird, when I saw the dead man's pack with its silks and its velvets, and this unhappy piece of green satin (shaking her dress), my foolish heart beguiled me, and I bade the ploughman bury the pedlar's body under our ash tree, in the corner of our garden, and we divided his goods and money between us. You must bid the laird raise his bones, and carry them to the churchyard; and the gold, which you will find in the little bole under the tapestry in my room, must be sent to a poor old widow, the pedlar's mother, who lives on the shore of Leith. I must now away to Ireland to the ploughman; and I'll be e'en less welcome to him, mammie, than at the laird's; but the hungry blood cries loud against us both – him and me – and we must suffer together. Take care you look not after me till I have passed the knowe.' She glided away as she spoke in a gleam of light; and when the old woman had withdrawn her hand from her eyes, dazzled by the sudden brightness, she saw only a large black greyhound crossing the moor. And the green lady was never afterwards seen in Scotland. But the little hoard of gold pieces, stored in a concealed recess of her former apartment, and the mouldering remains of the pedlar under the ash tree, gave evidence to the truth of her narrative.

THE GHOST OF GAIRNSIDE

Source: Katharine Briggs, *A Dictionary of British Folk-Tales*
Narrator: John Higgins, 1955; recorded by Hamish Henderson, School of
Scottish Studies

Tell us, John, what is this story about the Ghost of
Gairnside?

Ah, well, jist about a crofter and his son at the top of
Gairnside.

The crofter, he had a son, and his son was carryin' on with his
sweetheart for over a year, and he'd always over a mile and a
half to go down to meet her every Sunday night. He always met
her about half-past ten every Sunday night, and this meetin'
lastit for over a year, and he was workin' aboot the farm in [?]
Auld Ringie. His father used to say to him, say to his mother,
like, 'I dout there's something happent to John.' For he was
always a cheery chap when he was workin', whistlin' aboot and
aathing when he was plewin' up the ground and that, 'Ach,' he
says, 'he's jist like oorsels when we were young – perhaps he's
makin' it up to get married, or something.'

Oniegait, when he was away down come Sunday, he had to
go down to meet his sweetheart. So he went away down and
aathing, and he's always meetin' her at a certain place at the back
of a bush, aboot four and a half mile frae his own place. So
when he went down to where he was always meetin' his sweetheart, there was a white lady stannan up against a gate. So when
he lookit up tae her, he says, 'What are ye doin' staundin' there?'

She says tae him, 'Where are ye goin'?'

'Oh,' he says, 'I'm gaun to meet my sweetheart.'

She says, 'I know,' she says, 'ye're goin' to meet your sweetheart, but I've been stannin' here,' she says, 'for over a year,
and,' she says, 'I know,' she says, 'that you've been meetin' your
sweetheart all this time,' she says, 'every Sunday night, at half-

past ten, and,' she says, 'your sweetheart's not fair to you,' she says, 'for she's carryin' on with another chap.'

'Oh,' he says, 'I wouldn't believe that.'

'But,' she says, 'all right,' she says, 'you can go up,' she says, 'to meet her, but go up to the bush farther on, and you'll hear for yourself.'

So when he went up to the bush farther on, he heard this sweetheart sayin' to his own sweetheart, 'He's always carryin' on wi' ye.'

'Ah, well, I'll need to hurry on,' she says, 'for that boy frae the top of the glen's comin' doon to meet me, and I dinnae want tae make a fool of him, ye know,' she says, 'kiddin' him on.'

So he staunds, hearin' aa this. So anyway, he left her and cam back to the gate, and here's this lady always standin' at the gate, dressed in white. So she says to him, 'Now you've found out for yourself.'

'Yes,' he says, 'I've found out for myself.'

'Well,' she says, 'now, what are ye goin' to do now?'

'Well,' he says, 'I've nothing to do now but go home again.'

'Well,' she says, 'I know you've been meetin',' she says, 'this girlfriend of yours for over a year,' she says. 'Could you meet me,' she says, 'for a week?'

'Well,' he says, 'I dinnae know, for a week – I dinnae see no harm of meetin' ye for a week,' he says, 'when I could come for over a year meetin' her, always at half-past ten at night. There could be no harm in meetin' ye for a week.'

'Well,' she says, 'I want you to meet me every night for a week, at half-past ten, the same time. Could ye do that?'

'Well,' he says, 'I dinnae see nothing haudin' me back frae daein' that, when I'm happent to meet this girl for over a year.'

'Well,' she says, 'the bargain's made?'

'Yes,' he says, 'the bargain's made.'

Now he's away. He left her again, and promised to meet her next Monday.

So when he was away from home now, he was wonderin', like, aboot the girl, like, false to him all the time, ye see – he went away home – never tellt his mother that she'd been false to him. But next morning he was oot in the field again, for he used to enjoy himsel, whistlin' and singin' to himsel when he was workin'. But Monday mornin', when he went oot, he never sung nor anything, he wudnae eat nothing, so he's aye thinkin' awa to himsel. So his father says, 'Well,' he says, 'there must be something ado wi' the laddie.' 'Ach,' she says. 'There's nothing.'

So he asked the foreman, 'What like is the boy getting on in the field?'

'Well,' he says, 'there's something ado wi' the bodie. He'll no hardly do nae work nor nothing. An,' he says, 'he'll no whistle nor anything.'

So anyway, whenever night's come, he got his supper again, and he's away down now, meetin' his sweetheart again.

So when he was away doon meetin' his sweetheart, the aul' man says, 'Whaur is he awa tae?'

'Och,' she says, 'ye ken what like you and me was when we were young. He's been gaun that lang,' she says, 'that he'll – be gettin' mairrit.'

'Oh,' he says, 'there might be something in that, tae.'

So he's away down, meetin' his sweetheart again, but he cam back again – he's aye gettin' worse and waur, every day and nicht, wi' meetin' her, he's aye gettin' worse. So began this twelve months.

'Well,' he says, 'I dinna like the look of my son, he's been gettin' waur, every day meetin' her – he's aye gettin' worse.'

'Oh,' he says, he says, 'I'll tell the foreman to go doon eftir him aa richt.'

So the next nicht again, when he got up he got his bitie of supper, and he's away doon meetin' his sweetheart again. So when he went away down now, the foreman followed him. So when he was awa aboot a mile and a hauf or two miles doon the road, here he seen the young fella throwin' his airm roon the same as that – a boy throwin' his airm roon a lassie goin' awa doon the road, and then speakin' tae hes-sel an aathing.

'Gode bliss me!' he saud, 'what's adae wi' him?' he says. 'Has he gone off his heid?'

So he was talkin' to him aa the time gaun doon and aathing,

same as a bloke speakin' tae his sweetheart. So he seen this chap gaun in through a gate, and gaun into an auld washbeen, like aa ruins. So he was stannin' back – when he seen this thing he made hame, to tell the auld man.

So the auld man says, 'I dinnae ken what to dae wi' him.'

So anyway, the next nicht again he says, 'The best thing ye can dae,' he says, 'is I think I'll go doon masel,' he says, 'and see whit the laddie is gettin' on.'

So the aul' man next nicht followed them doon. So whenever he seen him there he seen his son throwin' his airms roon this lassie's neck and speakin' awa and aathing, and then he listened for a while, and he heard the lassie speakin' back tae him. So when he heard that, he says, 'Gode bliss me!' he says, 'I hope,' he says, 'he didnae dae the ither lassie in.'

Away he cam hame. So we leave with the aul' man goin' to the young boy and the lady – so he went doon to this old washbeen and doon tae a little room. An' here when he cam doon to the little room here was the table spread and fire burnin' and aathing, and wine and everything on the top of the table. So they dined there tae aboot twelve o'clock. So when they dined there tae twelve o'clock, she lookit at the young fellie; she says, 'Ten meenits to twelve,' she says, 'aboot time,' she says, 'ye're gettin' hame. And,' she says, 'I'll convoy you,' she says, 'on to the [?] haa road, and up to the fairm.'

'Aye,' he says tae hessel, 'well,' he says, 'I've been carryin' on with a girl,' he says, 'for over a year, an',' he says, 'that's a thing that she never said to me, for to convoy me,' he says, 'home.' He says, 'It's always me, it's left to the gentleman to convoy the girl home.' The two of them went away. She says, 'You don't need to stand,' she says, 'and speak,' she says, 'for I'll need all my time.'

So the two of them left. So she cam up to the road turnin' up to the fairm. Well, she's been aboot close on two miles away, from the auld ruins. So she says, 'I'll have to be biddin' ye goodnight,' she says.

So he told her, 'Good-night.'

'Be sure and see me the morn,' she says, 'it's the last night.'

So she was away. So he was goin' up frae the wood, and he

happened to say to hissel, 'Perhaps – I hope,' he says, 'it's not a ghost I'm speakin' to, and not makin' dates with.'

'Oh no,' she says, 'it's not a ghost,' she says. 'I'm always here.'

So anyway, Jeck, he went away now; well he's aye broodin' afore, but he was broodin' twenty times worse now when he went hame an – what he was doin'.

So next mornin' again, it was the last day, so he went away doon this night again, but the whole three of them went down this time – father and mother and son. So the two of them was goin' down the road after the son, when the father and mother seen his hauns goin' round the lady, and the lady speakin' back to him and asked if he had seen nothing but hesself. So the mother thocht that he was goin' off his head, and thought, like, that he'd done his sweetheart in. So she says, 'The best thing I can do,' she says, 'is go up to the farm where the girl's workin' and see if she's always there.'

So the farmer he went up to the farm, 'Oh, yes,' he says, 'the girl's always here – how are ye askin' that?'

'Well,' he says, 'it's the funny things that happen. So,' he says, 'are ye sure,' he says, 'the girl's –'

'Oh yes,' he says, the other farmer, 'the girl's here, for she's jist newly home after milkin'.'

So they cam down and aathing now. An' I'll leave off o' them again, back into John again.

So Jack he went intae the house again where the lady was. So he dined away there again. So, anyway, when – she says, 'This is the last night,' she says, 'it's time,' she says, 'twelve,' she says, 'ye'd better be goin' home.'

When she said that, he went out again and made home again, and –

'Now,' she says, 'it's the last night. Don't come down again here again,' she says. 'I'll come up there tomorrow. I'll come to you,' she says, 'in the mornin'.'

So he was wonderin' now what kind o' a lady he feart to tell his people about – comin' up, and didnae know whit she wis, when she says –

So anyway the morn cam anyway, and Jeck he was sittin' at his breakfast, when a rap cam to the door. So when the rap cam to the door, the mother went ootside and see who was there, and here was the young lady.

So she said, 'Who are ye wantin'?'

'Oh,' she said, 'ye've a young man stayin' here,' she says.

'Yes,' she says, 'I've only one young man, and that's my son.'

'Oh,' she says, 'I'm the lady,' she says, 'he's been walkin' out with.'

So when the son went out, here was the young lady, and she cam and took him inside, and the young lady cam in, the auld man went out, and here when he lookit round here's a great big – where the washbeens, auld ruins wis, wis a castle.

So he asked her, 'What's the idea?' he says, 'of stoppin' doon in that auld ruins? – in aboot the castle, all the time.'

'Oh,' she says, 'this is a long story,' she says. 'A long time back,' she says, 'I was the young lady, jist what I'm now,' she says, 'and my brother was left that place, and he was a jealous brother. I was coortin' a young gentleman,' she says, 'and my brother was jealous, and,' she says, 'he got a witch that stopped at the other side of the hill, to enchant me intae a ghost,' and the first man as could carry on and make love to her for a week would break her enchantment. That's the only way that they could get her enchantment broken.

THE APPARITION OF ARRAN

Source: Cuthbert Bede, *The White Wife*
Narrator: Unknown (Kintyre, 1861–5); Bede's informant learned the story at the
beginning of the nineteenth century from 'a pious old woman, a native of Arran,
who had been intimate with the little woman and her husband'

About a century ago there lived in Arran an old woman named Marie Nic Junraidh, or Mary Henderson, who was exceedingly diminutive, but very courageous and intelligent. She was returning home late, one dark night, and had to cross a bridge which had the reputation of being haunted by something awful, and at which bold strong men had been terrified. But although it was night-time and dark, yet the bold little woman took courage to cross the bridge; and when she came to it, she saw something of an awful appearance standing before her. She would not turn back; so she spake to it, and it spake to her again, and then assumed a human shape, which she readily recognized, and said, '*An tu Fionla?*' ['Art thou Finlay?'] The appearance answered that he was Finlay. She said that she had known him when he was alive, but that he had died some years before. He said it was quite true; and that he was the same Finlay.

'Then what is the reason,' she said, 'that you appear before a frail little woman, and seek thus to alarm me? Why did you not appear before strong men, if you had anything upon your mind that you wished to tell?'

'I did appear several times to strong men,' answered the spirit; 'but they were always frightened, and ran away without speaking to me. You have done well to stay and speak to me, and I can now ease my mind. When I was in the flesh I stole some plough-irons; and I can get no rest until they are restored to their rightful owner. So you will go tomorrow, without fail, to yonder place, and there you will find the plough-irons; and if you will take them and lay them by the wayside, I shall get my rest, and I will not trouble you or any other person after this.'

The little woman then took courage and proposed many questions to the apparition, all of which he readily answered. He told her how long she would live, also her husband and other members of her family. He also told her the state of her departed friends and neighbours; and told her to warn a certain neighbour to give up his evil doings, for that he was in great danger. She promised that she would attend to all his demands; and he then vanished and allowed her to cross the bridge and get safely to her own home. The next morning she went to the spot and found the plough-irons, which she took and left by the wayside, where their previous owner found them; but it was observed that he did not live long after picking them up. She gave the warning to the neighbour, and he received it and repented him of his sins; and both she and her husband died at the time that had been foretold. After her interview with the spirit, the bridge was not haunted by night, nor was anyone troubled by the apparition.

IT

Source: Rev. Biot Edmonson and Jessie M. Saxby, *The Home of a Naturalist*
Narrator: 'Mam Kirsty', the authors' old nurse; collected by Jessie Saxby

Every year, at Yule-time, a house was troubled, and no person could stay in it. At last a bold-hearted fisherman undertook to break the power of evil by remaining in the house during its afflicted period. He sat down in one of the rooms, and lighting a candle, began to read the Bible. Suddenly he heard a noise, as if dead meat were being dropped along the passage. Seizing his Bible in one hand and an axe in the other, he rushed to meet the supernatural foe. 'It went out at the door; he followed. It took the road to the cliffs; he followed hard after. It quickened its speed; he did the same. Just as it was going to jump into the sea from the high cliff, he said a holy word, and slung his axe, which stuck fast in it. Hasting home, the man persuaded some friends to accompany him to the spot. There it was, with the axe sticking in it. The men covered it with earth, and dug a trench around it, so that neither beast nor body could go near it.'

'But what was it like?'

'The men called it a sea-devil, and all the description they could ever give of it was, that it resembled a large lump of grey *slub* (jelly-fish sort of stuff).'

'Had it a face?'

'No; it had no form at all.'

'How could it walk? It must have had *legs*, at least.'

'No; it had no legs nor wings, but it kept the man running, and run what he could, he could not go so fast as it.'

'What *could* it be?'

'That no human can tell. The men never could tell what it was like, but they called it a sea-devil, and they said it was the same thing which came up at the Haaf one day, and told the fishers that they must never go to sea on the fourth day of Yule, else evil would betide them.'

MY GRANDFATHER IS ARISING

Source: J. G. Campbell, *Witchcraft and Second Sight in the Highlands and Islands of Scotland*
Narrator: Unknown, Ross-shire

Among the hills of Ross-shire, an old man, who in his time was not 'canny', died in his son's house, a lonely hut in the hills remote from other houses. He was stretched and adjusted on a board in a closet, and the shepherd, leaving his wife and children in the house, went to the strath for people to come to the wake and funeral. At midnight, one of the children, playing through the house, peeped in at the keyhole of the closet and cried out, 'Mother, mother! my grandfather is rising.' The door of the closet was fast locked, and the dead man, finding he could not open it, began to scrape and dig the earth below it, to make a passage for himself. The children gathered round their mother, and in extremity of terror all listened to the scraping of the unhallowed corpse. At last the head appeared below the door, the corpse increased its exertions, and the terror of the mother and children became intense. The body was half-way through below the door when the cock crew and it fell powerless in the pit it had dug. That pit could never afterwards be kept filled up to the level of the rest of the floor.

FIVE STORIES OF THE EVIL EYE

Source: R. C. Maclagan, *Evil Eye in the Western Highlands*
Narrators: 1, An Argyllshire islander. 2, A native of Uist. 3, A young woman.
4, Unnamed informant from Tarbat, Ross-shire. 5, Unknown

I

Witchcraft is all gone now, and it is well it is, for it was a bad thing. But if that is gone, there is another thing that has not gone yet, and that is Cronachadh [the Evil Eye]. I saw a breeding sow in my own house, and one day a neighbour came in, and she said that that was a splendid sow. I answered that she was very good. Well, the woman went out, and she was no time away when the sow gave such a scream, and going round about she fell on the floor. With this D. Mac A. came in, and he asked who was the last person that had seen the sow. I told him it was such and such a woman. 'Well,' said he, 'it was she that did the harm, but if you have any oil beside you, I believe I shall not be long putting her right.' I got saithe oil for him, and he took the sow between his two legs, and poured a cupful into her mouth. She screamed, and I thought she was mad, but in a minute's time she was all right. Now, wasn't that the bad woman?

2

Indeed, witchery was in it. I myself went one day to a neighbour's house for a young cock, and they had a calf tied behind the door. I was not long in the house till a girl came in. When I got the bird I went away, and I was only a short time away when the calf became unwell. The people of the house sent word to a woman that was there, who had skill of witchery, as people would be saying, asking her to come to look at the calf. The woman came, but if she came, the calf was dead before she came.

As soon as she looked on it, she said to them on the spot, that it was the 'Eye' that caused the death. And more than that, she told them who had done the mischief (wounding). Here is how she said: 'Have you not had two women here sometime today?' and when they answered that there had been, she said: 'One of them was fair and the other dark. There was a grey shawl on the fair one, and it was she that wrought the witchery.' Now that was quite true, for the girl that came in when I was in the house was fair, and there was a grey shawl on her.

3

You have seen my cousin J.'s third boy. He was the finest and nicest looking of all the children. When six months old he was a very pretty child. One day a woman came into the house; the baby was on his mother's arm, and the visitor began to praise the child, and praised it very much. She was hardly away when a man came, and he began to praise the child as the woman had done. After he went away like a shot the baby took ill. They did not know what was the matter with him, or what to do, for he was growing worse. He continued in that way for some days. At last granny said she was sure he had been *air a chronachadh*, and advised the mother to consult a woman who was supposed to have knowledge to cure such cases. J. was not willing to go at first, but granny insisted that it would do no harm at any rate to go and speak to the woman. She went, but did not tell anybody at the time, for of course they would be speaking about it. As soon as she told the woman why she had come, the woman told her that the child had been injured by the Evil Eye, and she described exactly the man and woman who had done the harm, although my cousin had not mentioned man or woman to her. Was it not wonderful how she knew the very ones that had done it?

4

One of my sisters was blighted by a woman who lived beside them. She was well known for her uncanny ways. The way the thing happened was this: The little girl was tied on an elder sister's back, and they were sent out for a walk. They had not gone far when the woman in question came forward, and putting the shawl back from the child's face said, 'What a pretty little girl! which of them is this?' When the children returned their mother found that the young one was very ill, and on questioning the elder girl, she said that they had met this woman and repeated what she had said. Mother at once suspected what was the matter, sent for the woman, and charged her with having hurt her child. She protested that she had not done the child any injury, but the elder girl spoke up and said, 'Yes, you looked at her and said she was pretty, and did not bless her.' The woman admitted this, and that if she had done any harm to the child she was sorry for it, but it could be sorted if wrong had been done. She operated a charm, and the child was soon as brisk as ever.

5

A man ploughing, who thought very well of his horses, said to his master on seeing another he knew approaching, 'Here comes —, and he will ruin both the horses if he can, for he has the Evil Eye.' His master said, 'I'll tell you what you will do, and if you do it he can do the horses no harm. When he begins to praise either or both just begin to run them down, and be sure you say as much against them as he shall say for them.' He of the Evil Eye came up, and commencing with 'What a fine pair of horses you have,' went on to enumerate their good points. The servant objected that they looked better than they were, that their looks were the best of them, and for every point in their favour the other mentioned, the lad said something to counterbalance it. The other began to show signs of impatience, and went on his way not very well pleased with the way his opinions of the horses had been disputed. 'Well done, you have saved the horses,' said his master. 'Did I do it right?' said the lad. 'Yes, indeed, you could not have said more than you have said.'

SECOND-SIGHT STORIES

Source: Lord Archibald Campbell, *Records of Argyll*
Narrators: As described

I

Related by John MacNiven, Barrapul

I was coming from Scarnish a few years ago, and had a horse and cart, and another man, John MacKinnon, Sanndaig, with me. When about a quarter of a mile from Moss Church the dun mare stood, and would not move. After urging her on, I said, 'What can be wrong with her? She never refused to go on before.'

MacKinnon lifted his head and looked out, took hold of the reins, and said, 'Let her stand a little.' After three or four minutes he said, 'Drive her now.'

I said, 'Go on, Ellie.' She started at once. I said, 'I never saw her stand so before.'

MacKinnon said, 'How could she go on and a funeral passing us?'

2

Related by John MacNiven

I was coming from Scarnish one night a few years ago, and a young woman was with me, walking by my side; all at once she took me by the arm, and began to pull me to the side of the road, saying, 'A funeral is coming. I put God between you and me. I will not go a step further with you.' She stepped outside the road, and kept on. Shortly after, she came to the road, and asked if I was struck or hurt – as I went fair through the middle of the funeral. I never noticed anything more than usual.

414

3

Related by Alexander Brown, Balefuil

One early morning I was going to the house of Allan MacDonald, and walking beside a turf wall I fell to the ground. I thought
nothing of this; but a few seconds after, I fell again. I blamed my
want of watchfulness of my steps, rose and went on, and shortly
I fell again. I looked about me, and thought I saw the shadow of
a woman standing at my side, and when I walked again I felt as
if she touched my shoulder, and fell again; this time I walked or
crawled on my knees to the house, the shadow following me,
but never touching me again. Next night I went to the wake of
an old woman who had died on a farm. I was asked to go next
day for strings for the coffin, and I carried the strings in the
pocket which was on the side I was knocked down from. I have
no other explanation to give of the phenomena but that it was
the old woman who died that was walking with me the previous
evening and knocking me down.

4

Related by John MacDonald, Balefuil

I was one night in a house in Balefuil, and a lot more of young
lads were with me. When we were cracking, and all sitting, I saw
the appearance of a dead woman, dressed in her winding-sheet,
coming to the house. I went back a little to let her pass. She
went on in the direction of Hugh Brown, Manal, and went all
over him. Immediately he turned pale and sickish, and rose and
went out. I, understanding what was wrong with him, followed
him. Outside he began to vomit, and latterly went into a
fainting-fit. After he revived he was asked what had come over
him. He said he could not tell, but he had felt a great heaviness
and weight coming all over him suddenly, and he felt sick tired,
and like to faint, and so he thought by going out to the air he
would be better. I told him all I saw some time afterwards.

5

Gathered as facts from different parties

One of the crofters of Balevulin, A. MacDonald, had a few years ago a boat for sale, because he could not get a crew to go out with it to fish. A few of the knowing folks about there noticed two strangers paying visits to the boat when high and dry on the beach, and when diligent search was made for them they always disappeared. They were seen several times coming in this strange way, and none of the seers could make out who they were; others said that strange noises would be heard in the boat when none was near it. An apprehension took hold of the minds of the crew that the boat was destined to drown someone, and the sight-seers confirmed them in their notions; and in this way MacDonald could neither persuade the old crew to go out nor get a new one in their place, and he was obliged to haul up the boat and place it in the market for sale. After lying a considerable time it was purchased by the sons of Neil MacDonald of Balemartin, with the full knowledge of all the rumours that were abroad about it. After they had had the boat in Balemartin for some time, some curious sights and noises were seen and heard about the boat, which made them regret their purchase, and they went to the Balevulin man to have the bargain made void. As he would not hear of it, they consulted Mr Sproat as to whether they could not compel the seller to take it back. Mr S. advised them in the negative, and told them their fears were only superstitious. However, they would not fish in it, and pulled it up, where it lay some time. This last harvest they launched her again; and while fishing for lobsters with two men in it, the purchaser's son being one, the boat got on a rock at Hynish, capsized, and MacDonald's son was drowned.

6

Related by John Hamilton

Two or three years ago a number of people were in our house one winter's night, and among the rest John MacKinnon, Sanndaig, was in. We were talking about things in general, and John said to me, 'You are to be at a funeral very soon.'

'That cannot be,' I said, 'as it will be my uncle that will go to the first one; I was at the last.'

'Both of you will be the same day at a funeral; and as a sign that I am telling the truth, you and I will be below the bier at a certain named place.'

In less than two weeks there were two deaths in Barrapole, and the funerals were on the same day. I went to the one, and my uncle went to the other. I forgot all about John's saying, till just at the place he mentioned. I was one of four below the bier, and looking opposite me there was John, who gave me a wink; and at once it brought his saying of a fortnight before to my memory.

WITCHES AS SHEEP

Source: J. G. Campbell, *Witchcraft and Second Sight in the Highlands and Islands of Scotland*
Narrators: A native of Tiree; Hector M'Lean, Coll
Type: ML3055 'The Witch that was Hurt'

A native of Tiree was on his way home to the west end of the island in the evening with a new gun in his hand. When above the beach called Travay, he observed a black sheep running towards him from across the plain of Reef. Alarmed by the animal's motions, he put a silver sixpence in the gun, and on its coming near enough, took aim. The black sheep instantly became a woman, whom he recognized, with a drugget coat wrapped about her head. The same woman had often persecuted him before, particularly in shape of a cat. She asked him to keep her secret, and he promised to do so, but one day, when drunk in the village to which the woman belonged, he told his adventure and the name of the woman. In less than a fortnight after he was drowned, and the witch (for such the woman was universally reputed to be) was blamed as the cause.

Hector M'Lean, in Coll, according to his own account, was coming in the evening from Arinagour to Breacacha, a distance of four miles along what was then throughout the greater part a mountain track. When halfway, at Airidh-mhic-mharoich, a black sheep came about his feet, and several times threw him down. At last he took out a clasp-knife, and threatened the sheep, if it came near him again, to stick it with the knife. It, however, again and again came and threw him down. In endeavouring to stab it, the knife closed upon his own hand between the finger and thumb, and cut him severely. On coming to the large open drain or stream below Breacacha Garden, he stood afraid to jump across, in case the black sheep should come about his legs, and make him fall in the drain. He was now, however, within hail of his own house, and whistled loudly for his dog. It came, and was fiercely hounded by him at the sheep. Every time the dog made a rush and came too near, the sheep became an old woman, whom Hector recognized as one of his acquaintances, and jumped in the air. She asked him to call off his dog, and he refused. She asked him again, and promised, if he would do so, to befriend him in right and wrong. At last he did call the dog, but it would not obey. He caught it by the back of the neck, and it tried to turn upon himself. He promised to keep his hold till the woman made her escape. The witch became a hare, and Hector called out to her, as she seemed to have such wonderful power, to 'add another leg to her stern, to make her escape the faster.' When she was some distance away, he let go the dog, and went home. The dog did not come home till the following afternoon; it followed the hare, compelled it to take refuge on a shelf of rock, and lay below on the watch, till forced by hunger to go home. The woman upbraided Hector, the first time she met him, for letting go the dog.

Afterwards, when he went as servant-man to Arileod farm in the neighbourhood, the same woman was often seen by him, in the shape of a hare, sucking the cows. His dog, whenever it caught sight of her, gave chase, and compelled her to resume her proper shape. When he left the farm, she was not seen there for some days. He went in search of her, and accused her to her face of having been the party that troubled the farm. She got into a rage, and said she would punish him for raising such a story about her. He answered that the proprietor of the island had offered a reward for the discovery of the guilty person, and if all the women in Coll were gathered on one hillock his speckled dog would pick her out as the offender. To this she made no reply. He asked her to go to Arileod dairy that night, so that people would not have it to say it was for him the evil had arisen. She said this was *Wednesday* night, and it was out of her power to do anything, but the following night she would go, and he would hear of it. On Thursday night she loosened the cows in Arileod byre, let in the calves, and did much mischief.

WITCHES AS HARES

Source: J. G. Campbell, *Witchcraft and Second Sight in the Highlands and Islands of Scotland*
Narrator: Unknown
Type: ML3055 'The Witch that was Hurt'

A young man, in the island of Lismore, was out shooting. When near Balnagown Loch, he started a hare, and fired at it. The animal gave an unearthly scream, and it then for the first time occurred to the young man that there were no hares in Lismore. He threw away his gun in terror, and fled home. Next day he came back for the gun, and heard that a reputed witch of the neighbourhood was laid up with a broken leg. Ever after the figure of this woman encountered him and gave him severe thrashings. This preyed on his mind, and he never came to any good. He proved brooding, idle, and useless.

A Manxman, who was in Tiree a few years ago, told the following story. A party of sportsmen, engaged in coursing, were at a loss for a hare. An old woman told her grandson to go to them, tell them they would get a hare at a certain spot, and get half a crown for himself. The boy went, got his half-crown, and guided the sportsmen to the spot his grandmother had indicated. When the hare started he cried, 'Run, granny, run!' The hare made straight for the old woman's house, the dogs lost sight of it at the back of the house, and the old woman was found sitting at the fireside.

In Wigtonshire a hare ran up the chimney, and a suspected witch near hand was found with burnt feet.

THE BLACKSMITH'S WIFE OF
YARROWFOOT

Source: William Henderson, *Folk-Lore of the Northern Counties*
Narrator: Unknown, probably from the mss. of Thomas Wilkie
Type: ML3057 'The Witch-Ridden Boy'

Some years back, the blacksmith of Yarrowfoot had for apprentices two brothers, both steady lads, and, when bound to
him, fine healthy fellows. After a few months, however, the
younger of the two began to grow pale and lean, lose his
appetite, and show other marks of declining health. His brother,
much concerned, often questioned him as to what ailed him, but
to no purpose. At last, however, the poor lad burst into an
agony of tears, and confessed that he was quite worn out, and
should soon be brought to the grave through the ill-usage of his
mistress, who was in truth a witch, though none suspected it.
'Every night,' he sobbed out, 'she comes to my bedside, puts a
magic bridle on me, and changes me into a horse. Then, seated
on my back, she urges me on for many a mile to the wild moors,
where she and I know not what other vile creatures hold their
hideous feasts. There she keeps me all night, and at early
morning I carry her home. She takes off my bridle, and there I
am, but so weary I can ill stand. And thus I pass my nights while
you are soundly sleeping.'

The elder brother at once declared he would take his chance
of a night among the witches, so he put the younger one in his
own place next the wall, and lay awake himself till the usual time
of the witch-woman's arrival. She came, bridle in hand, and
flinging it over the elder brother's head, up sprang a fine
hunting horse. The lady leaped on his back, and started for the
trysting-place, which on this occasion, as it chanced, was the
cellar of a neighbouring laird.

While she and the rest of the vile crew were regaling themselves with claret and sack, the hunter, who was left in a spare stall of the stable, rubbed and rubbed his head against the wall till he loosened the bridle, and finally got it off, on which he recovered his human form. Holding the bridle firmly in his hand, he concealed himself at the back of the stall till his mistress came within reach, when in an instant he flung the magic bridle over her head, and, behold, a fine grey mare! He mounted her and dashed off, riding through hedge and ditch, till, looking down, he perceived she had lost a shoe from one of her forefeet. He took her to the first smithy that was open, had the shoe replaced, and a new one put on the other forefoot, and then rode her up and down a ploughed field till she was nearly worn out. At last he took her home, and pulled the bridle off just in time for her to creep into bed before her husband awoke, and got up for his day's work.

The honest blacksmith arose, little thinking what had been going on all night; but his wife complained of being very ill, almost dying, and begged him to send for a doctor. He accordingly aroused his apprentices; the elder one went out, and soon returned with one whom he had chanced to meet already abroad. The doctor wished to feel his patient's pulse, but she resolutely hid her hands, and refused to show them. The village Esculapius was perplexed; but the husband, impatient at her obstinacy, pulled off the bedclothes, and found, to his horror, that horseshoes were tightly nailed to both hands! On further examination, her sides appeared galled with kicks, the same that the apprentice had given her during his ride up and down the ploughed field.

The brothers now came forward, and related all that had passed. On the following day the witch was tried by the magistrates of Selkirk, and condemned to be burned to death on a stone at the Bullsheugh, a sentence which was promptly carried into effect. It is added that the younger apprentice was at last restored to health by eating butter made from the milk of cows fed in kirkyards, a sovereign remedy for consumption brought on through being witch-ridden.

SHORT-HOGGERS OF WHITTINGHAME

Source: Robert Chambers, *Popular Rhymes of Scotland*
Narrator: Unknown
Type: ML4025 'The Child Without a Name'

It is supposed to be not yet a century since the good people of Whittinghame got happily quit of a ghost, which, in the shape of an 'unchristened wean', had annoyed them for many years. An unnatural mother having murdered her child at a large tree, not far from the village, the ghost of the deceased was afterwards seen, on dark nights, running in a distracted manner between the said tree and the churchyard, and was occasionally heard crying. The villagers believe that it was obliged thus to take the air, and bewail itself, on account of wanting a name – no anonymous person, it seems, being able to get a proper footing in the other world. Nobody durst speak to the unhappy little spirit, from a superstitious dread of dying immediately after; and, to all appearance, the village of Whittinghame was destined to be haunted till the end of time, for want of an exorcist. At length it fortunately happened that a drunkard, one night on reeling home, encountered the spirit, and, being fearless in the strength of John Barleycorn, did not hesitate to address it in the same familiar style as if it had been one of his own flesh-and-blood fellow-toppers. 'How's a' wi' ye this morning, Short-hoggers?' cried the courageous villager; when the ghost immediately ran away, joyfully exclaiming:

> 'O weel's me noo, I've gotten a name;
> They ca' me Short-hoggers o' Whittinghame!'

And since that time, it has never been either seen or heard of. The name which the drunkard applied to it denotes that the ghost wore short stockings without feet – a probable supposition, considering the long series of years during which it had walked. My informant received this story, with the rhyme, from the lips of an old woman of Whittinghame, who had *seen* the ghost.

THE STORY OF TAM M'KECHAN

Source: Hugh Miller, *Scenes and Legends of the North of Scotland*
Narrator: Unknown
Type: AT1137 'The Ogre Blinded'

The mill of Eathie was a celebrated mill. No one resided near it, nor were there many men in the country who would venture to approach it an hour after sunset; and there were nights when, though deserted by the miller, its wheels would be heard revolving as busily as ever they had done by day, and when one who had courage enough to reconnoitre it from the edge of the dell might see little twinkling lights crossing and recrossing the windows in irregular but hasty succession, as if a busy multitude were employed within. On one occasion the miller, who had remained in it rather later than usual, was surprised to hear outside the neighing and champing of horses and the rattling of carts, and on going to the door he saw a long train of basket-woven vehicles laden with sacks, and drawn by shaggy little ponies of every diversity of form and colour. The attendants were slim unearthly-looking creatures, about three feet in height, attired in grey, with red caps; and the whole seemed to have come out of a square opening in the opposite precipice. Strange to relate, the nearer figures seemed to be as much frightened at seeing the miller as the miller was at seeing them; but, on one of them uttering a shrill scream, the carts moved backwards into the opening, which shut over them like the curtain of a theatre as the last disappeared.

There lived in the adjoining parish of Rosemarkie, when the fame of the mill was at its highest, a wild unsettled fellow, named M'Kechan. Had he been born among the aristocracy of the country, he might have passed for nothing worse than a young man of spirit; and after sowing his wild oats among gentlemen of the turf and of the fancy, he would naturally have settled down into the shrewd political landlord, who, if no builder of churches himself, would be willing enough to exert the privilege of giving clergymen, exclusively of his own choosing, to such churches as had been built already. As a poor man, however, and the son of a poor man, Tam M'Kechan seemed to bid pretty fair for the gallows; nor could he plead ignorance that such was the general opinion. He had been told so when a herd-boy; for it was no unusual matter for his master, a farmer of the parish, to find him stealing peas in the corner of one field, when the whole of his charge were ravaging the crops of another. He had been told so too when a sailor, ere he had broken his indentures and run away, when once caught among the casks and packages in the hold, ascertaining where the Geneva and the sweetmeats were stowed. And now that he was a drover and a horse-jockey, people, though they no longer told him so, for Tam had become dangerous, seemed as certain of the fact as ever. With all his roguery, however, when not much in liquor he was by no means a very disagreeable companion; few could match him at a song or the bagpipe, and though rather noisy in his cups and somewhat quarrelsome, his company was a good deal courted by the bolder spirits of the parish, and among the rest by the miller. Tam had heard of the piebald horses and their ghostly attendants; but without more knowledge than fell to the share of his neighbours, he was a much greater sceptic, and after rallying the miller on his ingenuity and the prettiness of his fancy, he volunteered to spend a night at the mill, with no other companion than his pipes.

Preparatory to the trial the miller invited one of his neighbours, the young farmer of Eathie, that they might pass the early part of the evening with Tam; but when, after an hour's hard drinking, they rose to leave the cottage, the farmer, a kind-hearted lad, who was besides warmly attached to the jockey's only sister, would fain have dissuaded him from the undertaking. 'I've been thinking, Tam,' he said, 'that flyte wi' the miller as ye may, ye would better let the good people alone – or stay, sin' ye are sae bent on playing the fule, I'll e'en play it wi' you; rax me my plaid; we'll trim up the fire in the killogie thegether; an' you will keep me in music.' 'Na, Jock Hossack,' said Tam, 'I maun keep my good music for the good people; it's rather late to flinch now; but come to the burn edge wi' me the night, an' to the mill as early in the morning as ye may; an' hark ye, tak a double caulker wi' you.' He wrapt himself up closely in his plaid, took the pipes under his arm, and, accompanied by Jock and the miller, set out for the dell, into which, however, he insisted on descending alone. Before leaving the bank, his companions could see that he had succeeded in lighting up a fire in the mill, which gleamed through every bore and opening, and could hear the shrill notes of a pibroch mingling with the dash of the cascade.

The sun had risen high enough to look aslant into the dell, when Jock and the miller descended to the mill, and found the door lying wide open. All was silent within; the fire had sunk into a heap of white ashes, though there was a bundle of faggots untouched beside it, and the stool on which Tam had been seated lay overturned in front. But there were no traces of Tam, except that the miller picked up, beside the stool, a little flat-edged instrument, used by the unfortunate jockey in concealing the age of his horses by effacing the marks on their teeth, and that Jock Hossack found one of the drones of his pipes among the extinguished embers. Weeks passed away, and there was still nothing heard of Tam; and as everyone seemed to think it would be in vain to seek for him anywhere but in the place where he had been lost, Jock Hossack, whose marriage was vexatiously delayed in consequence of his strange disappearance, came to the resolution of unravelling the mystery, if possible, by passing a night in the mill.

For the first few hours he found the evening wear heavily away; the only sounds that reached him were the loud monotonous dashings of the cascade, and the duller rush of the stream as it swept past the mill-wheel. He piled up fuel on the fire till the flames rose half-way to the ceiling, and every beam and rafter stood out from the smoke as clearly as by day; and then yawning, as he thought how companionable a thing a good fire is, he longed for something to amuse him. A sudden cry rose from the further gable, accompanied by a flutter of wings, and one of the miller's ducks, a fine plump bird, came swooping down among the live embers. 'Poor bird!' said Jock, 'from the

fox to the fire; I had almost forgotten that I wanted my supper.'
He dashed the duck against the floor – plucked and embowelled
it – and then, suspending the carcase by a string before the fire,
began to twirl it round and round to the heat. The strong
odoriferous fume had begun to fill the apartment, and the
drippings to hiss and sputter among the embers, when a burst of
music rose so suddenly from the green without, that Jock, who
had been so engaged with the thoughts of his supper as almost
to have forgotten the fairies, started half a yard from his seat.
'That maun be Tam's pipes,' he said; and giving a twirl to the
duck he rose to a window. The moon, only a few days in her
wane, was looking aslant into the dell, lighting the huge melancholy cliffs with their birches and hazels, and the white flickering
descent of the cascade. The little level green on the margin of
the stream lay more in the shade; but Jock could see that it was
crowded with figures marvellously diminutive in stature, and
that nearly one half of them were engaged in dancing. It was
enough for him, however, that the music was none of Tam's
making; and, leaving the little creatures to gambol undisturbed,
he returned to the fire.

He had hardly resumed his seat when a low tap was heard at
the door, and shortly after a second and a third. Jock sedulously
turned his duck to the heat, and sat still. He had no wish for
visitors, and determined on admitting none. The door, however,
though firmly bolted, fell open of itself, and there entered one of
the strangest-looking creatures he had ever seen. The figure was
that of a man, but it was little more than three feet in height; and
though the face was as sallow and wrinkled as that of a person of
eighty, the eye had the roguish sparkle and the limbs all the
juvenile activity of fourteen. 'What's your name, man?' said the
little thing coming up to Jock, and peering into his face till its
wild elfish features were within a few inches of his. 'What's your
name?' '*Mysel' an' Mysel'*,' – i.e., myself – said Jock, with a policy
similar to that resorted to by Ulysses in the cave of the giant.
'Ah, *Mysel' an' Mysel'*!' rejoined the creature; '*Mysel' an' Mysel'*!
and what's that you have got there, *Mysel' an' Mysel'*?' touching
the duck as it spoke with the tip of its finger, and then transfer-
ring part of the scalding gravy to the cheek of Jock. Rather an

unwarrantable liberty, thought the poor fellow, for so slight an acquaintance; the creature reiterated the question, and dabbed Jock's other cheek with a larger and still more scalding application of the gravy. 'What is it?' he exclaimed, losing in his anger all thought of consequences, and dashing the bird, with the full swing of his arm, against the face of his visitor, 'It's that!' The little creature, blinded and miserably burnt, screamed out in pain and terror till the roof rung again; the music ceased in a moment, and Jock Hossack had barely time to cover the fire with a fresh heap of fuel, which for a few seconds reduced the apartment to total darkness, when the crowd without came swarming like wasps to every door and window of the mill. 'Who did it, Sanachy – who did it?' was the query of a thousand voices at once. 'Oh, 'twas *Mysel' and Mysel'*,' said the creature; ''twas *Mysel' and Mysel'*,' 'And if it was yoursel' and yoursel', who, poor Sanachy,' replied his companions, 'can help that?' They still, however, clustered round the mill; the flames began to rise in long pointed columns through the smoke, and Jock Hossack had just given himself up for lost, when a cock crew outside the building, and after a sudden breeze had moaned for a few seconds among the cliffs and the bushes, and then sunk in the lower recesses of the dell, he found himself alone. He was married shortly after to the sister of the lost jockey, and never again saw the good people, or, what he regretted nearly as little, his unfortunate brother-in-law. There were some, however, who affirmed, that the latter had returned from fairyland seven years after his mysterious disappearance, and supported the assertion by the fact, that there was one Thomas M'Kechan who suffered at Perth for sheep-stealing a few months after the expiry of the seventh year.

THE HUMBLE-BEE

Source: Hugh Miller, *My Schools and Schoolmasters*
Narrator: Hugh Miller's cousin George
Type: ML4000 'The Soul of a Sleeping Person Wanders on Its Own'

Two young men had been spending the early portion of a warm summer day in exactly such a scene as that in which he communicated the anecdote. There was an ancient ruin beside them, separated, however, from the mossy bank on which they sat, by a slender runnel, across which there lay, immediately over a miniature cascade, a few withered grass stalks. Overcome by the heat of the day, one of the young men fell asleep; his companion watched drowsily beside him; when all at once the watcher was aroused to attention by seeing a little indistinct form, scarce larger than a humble-bee, issue from the mouth of the sleeping man, and, leaping upon the moss, move downwards to the runnel, which it crossed along the withered grass stalks, and then disappeared amid the interstices of the ruin. Alarmed by what he saw, the watcher hastily shook his companion by the shoulder, and awoke him; though, with all his haste, the little cloud-like creature, still more rapid in its movements, issued from the interstice into which it had gone, and, flying across the runnel, instead of creeping along the grass stalks and over the sward, as before, it re-entered the mouth of the sleeper, just as he was in the act of awakening. 'What is the matter with you?' said the watcher, greatly alarmed. 'What ails you?' 'Nothing ails me,' replied the other; 'but you have robbed me of a most delightful dream. I dreamed I was walking through a fine rich country, and came at length to the shores of a noble river; and, just where the clear water went thundering down a precipice, there was a bridge all of silver, which I crossed; and then, entering a noble palace on the opposite side,

I saw great heaps of gold and jewels; and I was just going to load myself with treasure, when you rudely awoke me, and I lost all.'

6: THE SECRET COMMONWEALTH

THE YOUNG MAN IN
THE FAIRY KNOLL

❀

Source: J. G. Campbell, *Superstitions of the Scottish Highlands*
Narrator: Unknown
Type: ML4075 'Visits to Fairyland'

Two young men, coming home after nightfall on Hallowe'en, each with a jar of whisky on his back, heard music by the roadside, and, seeing a dwelling open and illuminated, and dancing and merriment going on within, entered. One of them joined the dancers, without as much as waiting to lay down the burden he was carrying. The other, suspecting the place and company, stuck a needle in the door as he entered, and got away when he liked. That day twelvemonths he came back for his companion, and found him still dancing with the jar of whisky on his back. Though more than half-dead with fatigue, the enchanted dancer begged to be allowed to finish the reel. When brought to the open air he was only skin and bone.

This tale is localized in the Ferintosh district, and at the Slope of Big Stones in Harris. In Argyllshire people say it happened in the north. In the Ferintosh story only one of the young men entered the brugh, and the door immediately closed. The other lay under suspicion of having murdered his companion, but, by advice of an old man, went to the same place on the same night the following year, and by putting steel in the door of the fairy dwelling, which he found open, recovered his companion. In the Harris story, the young men were a bridegroom and his brother-in-law, bringing home whisky for the marriage.

Two young men in Iona were coming in the evening from fishing on the rocks. On their way, when passing, they found the shï-en of that island open, and entered. One of them joined the dancers, without waiting to lay down the string of fish he had in his hand. The other stuck a fish-hook in the door, and when he wished made his escape. He came back for his companion that day twelvemonths, and found him still dancing with the string of fish in his hand. On taking him to the open air the fish dropped from the string, rotten.

Donald, who at one time carried on foot the mails from Tobermory, in Mull, to Grass Point Ferry, where the mail service crosses to the mainland, was a good deal given to drink, and consequently to loitering by the way. He once lay down to have a quiet sleep near a fairy-haunted rock above Drimfin. He saw the rock open, and a flood of light pouring out at the door. A little man came to him and said in English, 'Come in to the ball, Donald,' but Donald fled, and never stopped till he reached the houses at Tobermory, two miles off. He said he heard the whizz and rustling of the fairies after him the whole way. The incident caused a good deal of talk in the neighbourhood, and Donald and his fright were made the subject of some doggerel verse, in which the fairy invitation is thus given:

> 'Rise, rise, rise, Donald,
>   Rise, Donald, was the call,
> Rise up now, Donald,
>   Come in, Donald, to the ball.'

It is well known that Highland fairies who speak English are the most dangerous of any.

A young man was sent for the loan of a sieve, and, mistaking his way, entered a brugh, which was that evening open. He found there two women grinding at a handmill, two women baking, and a mixed party dancing on the floor. He was invited to sit down, 'Farquhar MacNeill, be seated.' He thought he would first have a reel with the dancers. He forgot all about the sieve, and lost all desire to leave the company he was in. One night he accompanied the band among whom he had fallen on one of its expeditions and, after careering through the skies, stuck in the roof of a house. Looking down the chimney, he saw a woman dandling a child, and, struck with the sight, exclaimed, 'God bless you.' Whenever he pronounced the Holy Name he was disenchanted, and tumbled down the chimney! On coming to himself he went in search of his relatives. No one could tell him anything about them. At last he saw, thatching a house, an old man, so grey and thin he took him for a patch of mist resting on the house-top. He went and made inquiries of him. The old man knew nothing of the parties asked for, but said perhaps his father did. Amazed, the young man asked him if his father was alive, and on being told he was, and where to find him, entered the house. He there found a very venerable man sitting in a chair by the fire, twisting a straw rope for the thatching of the house. This man also, on being questioned, said he knew nothing of the people, but perhaps his father did. The father referred to was lying in bed, a little shrunken man, and he in like manner referred to his father. This remote ancestor, being too weak to stand, was found in a purse suspended at the end of the bed. On being taken out and questioned, the wizened creature said, 'I did not know the people myself, but I often heard my father speaking of them.' On hearing this the young man crumbled in pieces, and fell down a bundle of bones.

The incident of the very aged people forms part of some versions of the story, 'How the Great Description (a man's name) was Put to Death'. Another form is that a stranger came to a house, and at the door found an old man crying, because his father had thrashed him. He went in, and asking the father why he had thrashed his aged son, was told it was because the grandfather had been there the day before, and the fellow had not the manners to put his hand in his bonnet to him!

THE FAIRY MIDWIFE

Source: R. H. Cromek, *Remains of Nithsdale and Galloway Song*
Narrator: Unknown
Type: ML5070 'Midwife to the Fairies'

The fairies' love of mortal commerce prompted them to have their children suckled at earthly breasts. The favoured nurse was chosen from healthful, ruddy-complexioned beauty; one every way approved of by mortal eyes. A fine young woman of Nithsdale, when first made a mother, was sitting singing and rocking her child, when a pretty lady came into her cottage, covered with a fairy mantle. She carried a beautiful child in her arms, swaddled in green silk: 'Gie my bonnie thing a suck,' said the fairy. The young woman, conscious to whom the child belonged, took it kindly in her arms, and laid it to her breast. The lady instantly disappeared, saying, 'Nurse kin', an' ne'er want!' The young mother nurtured the two babes, and was astonished whenever she awoke at finding the richest suits of apparel for both children, with meat of most delicious flavour. This food tasted, says tradition, like loaf mixed with wine and honey. It possessed more miraculous properties than the wilderness manna, preserving its relish even over the seventh day.

On the approach of summer the fairy lady came to see her child. It bounded with joy when it beheld her. She was much delighted with its freshness and activity; taking it in her arms, she bade the nurse follow. Passing through some scroggy woods, skirting the side of a beautiful green hill, they walked midway up. On its sunward slope a door opened, disclosing a beauteous porch, which they entered, and the turf closed behind them. The fairy dropped three drops of a precious dew on the nurse's left eyelid, and they entered a land of most pleasant and abundant promise. It was watered with fine looping rivulets, and yellow with corn; the fairest trees enclosed its fields, laden with fruit, which dropped honey. The nurse was rewarded with finest webs of cloth, and food of ever-during substance. Boxes of salves, for restoring mortal health, and curing mortal wounds and infirmities, were bestowed on her, with a promise of never needing. The fairy dropt a green dew over her right eye, and bade her look. She beheld many of her lost friends and acquaintances doing menial drudgery, reaping the corn and gathering the fruits. This, said she, is the punishment of evil deeds! The fairy passed her hand over her eye, and restored its mortal faculties. She was conducted to the porch, but had the address to secure the heavenly salve. She lived, and enjoyed the gift of discerning the earth-visiting spirits, till she was the mother of many children; but happening to meet the fairy lady, who gave her the child, she attempted to shake hands with her. 'What ee d'ye see me wi?' whispered she. 'Wi' them baith,' said the dame. She breathed on her eyes, and even the power of the box failed to restore their gifts again!

THE CHANGELING

Source: Robert Chambers, *Popular Rhymes of Scotland*
Narrator: Written down by Charles K. Sharpe from memories of the narration
of his Nurse Jenny, *c*. 1784
Type: ML5085 'The Changeling'

Nurse Jenny speaks – 'A'body kens there's fairies, but they 're no sae common now as they war lang syne. I never saw ane mysel', but my mother saw them twice – ance they had nearly drooned her, when she fell asleep by the waterside: she wakened wi' them ruggin' at her hair, and saw something howd down the water like a green bunch o' potato shaws.' [Memory has slipped the other story, which was not very interesting.]

'My mother kent a wife that lived near Dunse – they ca'd her Tibbie Dickson: her goodman was a gentleman's gairdner, and muckle frae hame. I didna mind whether they ca'd him Tammas or Sandy – I guess Sandy – for his son's name, and I kent him weel, was Sandy, and he –'

Chorus of Children – 'Oh, never fash about his name, Jenny.'

Nurse – 'Hoot, ye 're aye in sic a haste. Weel, Tibbie had a bairn, a lad bairn, just like ither bairns, and it thrave weel, for it sookit weel, and it,' &c. [Here a great many weels.] 'Noo, Tibbie gaes ae day to the well to fetch water, and leaves the bairn in the house by itsel': she couldna be lang awa', for she had but to gae by the midden, and the peat-stack, and through the kail-yaird, and there stood the well – I ken weel about that, for in that very well I aften weesh my,' &c. [Here another long digression.] 'Aweel, as Tibbie was comin' back wi' her water, she hears a skirl in her house like the stickin' of a gryse, or the singin' of a soo; fast she rins, and flees to the cradle, and there, I wat, she saw a sicht that made her heart scunner. In place o' her ain bonny bairn, she fand a withered wolron, naething but skin

440

and bane, wi' hands like a moudiewort, and a face like a paddock, a mouth frae lug to lug, and twa great glowrin' een.

'When Tibbie saw sic a daft-like bairn, she scarce kent what to do, or whether it was her ain or no. Whiles she thocht it was a fairy; whiles that some ill een had sp'ilt her wean when she was at the well. It wad never sook, but suppit mair parritch in ae day than twa herd callants could do in a week. It was aye yammerin' and greetin', but never mintet to speak a word; and when ither bairns could rin, it couldna stand – sae Tibbie was sair fashed about it, as it lay in its cradle at the fireside like a half-dead hurcheon.

'Tibbie had span some yarn to make a wab, and the wabster lived at Dunse, so she maun gae there; but there was naebody to look after the bairn. Weel, her niest neibour was a tylor; they ca'd him Wullie Grieve; he had a humpit back, but he was a tap tylor for a' that – he cloutit a pair o' breeks for my father when he was a boy, and my father telt me –' [Here a long episode, very tiresome to the audience.]

'So Tibbie goes to the tylor and says: "Wullie, I maun awa' to Dunse about my wab, and I dinna ken what to do wi' the bairn till I come back: ye ken it's but a whingin', screechin', skirlin' wallidreg – but we maun bear wi' dispensations. I wad wuss ye," quo' she, "to tak tent till 't till I come hame – ye sall hae a roosin' ingle, and a blast o' the goodman's tobacco-pipe forbye." Wullie was naething laith, and back they gaed thegither.

'Wullie sits down at the fire, and awa' wi' her yarn gaes the wife; but scarce had she steekit the door, and wan half-way down the close, when the bairn cocks up on its doup in the cradle, and rounds in Wullie's lug: 'Wullie Tylor, an ye winna tell my mither when she comes back, I'se play ye a bonny spring on the bagpipes.'

'I wat Wullie's heart was like to loup the hool – for tylors, ye ken, are aye timorsome – but he thinks to himsel', "Fair fashions are still best," an' "It's better to fleetch fules than to flyte wi' them;" so he rounds again in the bairn's lug: "Play up, my doo, an' I'se tell naebody." Wi' that the fairy ripes amang the cradle strae, and pu's oot a pair o' pipes, sic as tylor Wullie ne'er had seen in a' his days – muntit wi' ivory, and gold, and silver, and dymonts, and what not. I dinna ken what spring the fairy played, but this I ken weel, that Wullie had nae great goo o' his performance; so he sits thinkin' to himsel': "This maun be a deil's get; and I ken weel hoo to treat them; and gin I while the time awa', Auld Waughorn himsel' may come to rock his son's cradle, and play me some foul prank;" so he catches the bairn by the cuff o' the neck, and whupt him into the fire, bagpipes and a'!

'Fuff,' [this pronounced with great emphasis, and a pause].

'Awa' flees the fairy, skirling: "Deil stick the lousie tylor!" a' the way up the lum.'

JOHNNIE IN THE CRADLE

Source: Katharine Briggs, *A Dictionary of British Folk-Tales*
Narrator: Andrew Stewart; collected by Hamish Henderson, School of
Scottish Studies
Type: ML5085 'The Changeling'

A man and his wife were not long married, and they had a
wee kiddie called Johnnie, but he was always crying and
never satisfied. There was a neighbour near, a tailor, and it came
to market day, and Johnnie was aye greeting, and never growing.
And the wife wanted to get a day at the market, so the tailor said
he'd stay and watch wee Johnnie. So he was sitting sewing by
the fire, and a voice said: 'Is ma mother and ma faither awa'?' He
couldn't think it was the baby speaking, so he went and looked
out of the window, but there was nothing, and he heard it again.
'Is ma mother and ma faither awa'?' And there it was, sitting up,
with its wee hands gripping the sides of the cradle. 'There's a
bottle of whisky in the press,' it says. 'Gie's a drink.' Sure
enough, there was one, and they had a drink together. Then wee
Johnnie wanted a blow on the pipes, but there was not a set in
the house, so he told the tailor to go and fetch a round strae
from the byre, and he played the loveliest tune on the pipes
through the strae. They had a good talk together, and the wee
thing said, 'Is ma mother and ma faither coming home?' And
when they came, there he was 'Nya, nya, nya,' in the cradle. By
this time the tailor knew it was a fairy they had there, so he
followed the farmer into the byre, and told him all that had
happened. The farmer just couldn't bring himself to believe it;
so between them they hit on a contrivance. They let on that a lot
of things had not been sold at the market, and there was to be a
second day of it, and the tailor promised to come over again to
sit by the bairn. They made a great stir about packing up, and
then they went through to the barn, and listened through the

443

keek-hole in the wall. 'Is ma mother and ma faither gone?' said the wee thing, and the mother could just hardly believe her ears. But when they heard the piping through the cornstrae, they kent it was a fairy right enough, and the farmer went into the room, and he set the griddle on the fire and heated it red hot, and he fetched in a half-bagful of horse manure, and set it on the griddle, and the wee thing looked at him with wild eyes. When he went to it to grip it, and put it on the griddle, it flew straight up the lum, and as it went it cried out, 'I wish I had a been longer with my mother. I'd a kent her better.'

MAKING A WIFE

Source: R. H. Cromek, *Remains of Nithsdale and Galloway Song*
Narrator: Unknown
Type: ML5087 'The Trows' Bundle'

Alexander Harg, a cottar, in the parish of New Abbey, had courted and married a pretty girl, whom the fairies had long attempted to seduce from this world of love and wedlock. A few nights after his marriage, he was standing with a *halve* net, awaiting the approach of the tide. Two old vessels, stranded on the rocks, were visible at mid-water mark, and were reckoned occasional haunts of the fairies when crossing the mouth of the Nith. In one of these wrecks a loud noise was heard as of carpenters at work; a hollow voice cried from the other, 'Ho, what'r ye doing!' 'I'm making a wyfe to Sandy Harg!' replied a voice, in no mortal accent. The husband, astonished and terrified, throws down his net, hastens home, shuts up every avenue of entrance, and folds his young spouse in his arms. At midnight a gentle rap comes to the door, with a most courteous three times touch. The young dame starts to get up; the husband holds her in forbidden silence, and kindly clasps. A foot is heard to depart, and instantly the cattle low and bellow, ramping as.if pulling up their stakes. He clasps his wife more close to his bosom, regardless of her entreaties. The horses, with most frightful neighs, prance, snort, and bound, as if in the midst of flame. She speaks, cries, entreats, struggles: he will not move, speak, nor quit her. The noise and tumult increases, but with the morning's coming it dies away. The husband leaps up with the dawn, and hurries out to view his premises. A piece of moss oak, fashioned to the shape and size of his wife, meets his eye, reared against his garden dyke, and he burns this devilish effigy.

SANNTRAIGH

Source: J. F. Campbell, *Popular Tales of the West Highlands*
Narrator: Alexander M'Donald, tenant, and others, Barra, July 1859; collected
by J. F. Campbell and Hector MacLean
Type: ML5082 'Fairy Borrowing'

There was a herd's wife in the island of Sanntraigh, and she had a kettle. A woman of peace [fairy] would come every day to seek the kettle. She would not say a word when she came, but she would catch hold of the kettle. When she would catch the kettle, the woman of the house would say,

> 'A smith is able to make
> Cold iron hot with coal.
> The due of a kettle is bones,
> And to bring it back again whole.'

The woman of peace would come back every day with the kettle and flesh and bones in it. On a day that was there, the housewife was for going over the ferry to Baile a Chaisteil, and she said to her man, 'If thou wilt say to the woman of peace as I say, I will go to Baile Castle.' 'Oo! I will say it. Surely it's I that will say it.' He was spinning a heather rope to be set on the house. He saw a woman coming and a shadow from her feet, and he took fear of her. He shut the door. He stopped his work. When she came to the door she did not find the door open, and he did not open it for her. She went above a hole that was in the house. The kettle gave two jumps, and at the third leap it went out at the ridge of the house. The night came, and the kettle came not. The wife came back over the ferry, and she did not see a bit of the kettle within, and she asked, 'Where is the kettle?' 'Well then I don't care where it is,' said the man; 'I never took such a fright as I took at it. I shut the door, and she did not come any more with it.' 'Good-for-nothing wretch, what didst thou do? There are

two that will be ill off – thyself and I.' 'She will come tomorrow
with it.' 'She will not come.'

She hasted herself and she went away. She reached the knoll,
and there was no man within. It was after dinner, and they were
out in the mouth of the night. She went in. She saw the kettle,
and she lifted it with her. It was heavy for her with the remnants
that they left in it. When the old carle that was within saw her
going out, he said,

> 'Silent wife, silent wife,
> That came on us from the land of chase,
> Thou man on the surface of the "Bruth",
> Loose the black, and slip the fierce.'

The two dogs were let loose; and she was not long away when
she heard the clatter of the dogs coming. She kept the remnant
that was in the kettle, so that if she could get it with her, well,
and if the dogs should come that she might throw it at them.
She perceived the dogs coming. She put her hand in the kettle.
She took the board out of it, and she threw at them a quarter of
what was in it. They noticed it there for a while. She perceived
them again, and she threw another piece at them when they
closed upon her. She went away walking as well as she might;
when she came near the farm, she threw the mouth of the pot
downwards, and there she left them all that was in it. The dogs
of the town struck up a barking when they saw the dogs of
peace stopping. The woman of peace never came more to seek
the kettle.

THE GIRL WHO EMPTIED
THE INEXHAUSTIBLE MEAL CHEST
OF THE FAIRIES

Source: Rev. James MacDougall, *Folk Tales and Fairy Lore*
Narrator: Unknown
Type: ML5071 'The Fairy Master'

Once upon a time a young maiden went to drive her father's cattle to the hill. A fairy knoll lay before her in the path she took; and after she came in sight of it, she met a band of fairies, with one taller than the rest at their head. This one seized her and, with the help of the others, took her away with him to the fairy knoll.

As soon as he had got her within the knoll, he put her under an obligation to bake into bread all the meal in the meal chest, before she would receive her wages and permission to go home.

The chest was but small, and so the poor maiden imagined that she would not take a long time in emptying it. But in this she was greatly deceived. For though she began to bake, and kept at it with all her strength day after day, her labour was to all appearance in vain. As she would empty the chest it would fill again. At length she saw that her task, and, therefore, her captivity, would never come to an end. This thought so grieved her that she burst out a-crying.

In the fairy knoll was an old woman who had been carried off by the fairies in her youth, and who had been so long there that she had lost all hope of ever getting out. This woman beheld the plight of the maiden, and on calling to mind her own misery when she was first in the same strait, she took great pity upon her, and told her how she would empty the chest. 'Every time you cease baking, you are making bread of the remaining sprinkling of meal,' she said. 'But, after this, do you put the sprinkling of meal back into the chest, and you will see that it will be emptied of all the meal it contains in a short time.'

The maiden did as the old woman directed her, and the meal came to an end, as she had said. When the girl saw the chest empty, she went joyfully to the chief of the fairies, and asked him to let her go away, because she had finished the task laid upon her. But he did not believe her, till he looked into the meal chest, and saw that it was empty. Then he gave the maiden her wages and leave to depart. And as she was going out, he said: 'My blessing on thee, but my curse on thy teaching mouth.'

MAM KIRSTAN'S STORIES OF
THE TROWS

Source: Rev. Biot Edmonson and Jessie M. Saxby, *The Home of a Naturalist*
Narrator: 'Mam Kirsty', the authors' childhood nurse, Unst; collected
by Jessie Saxby
Type: ML5070 'Midwife to the Fairies'

Mam Kirstan (so tradition saith) was fetched to a Trow's wife, and when she was there she saw them rolling up something to resemble a cow. She contrived to throw her bunch of keys into the heap without the Trows seeing her to do so. When she got home she found her own cow dead, as her husband had omitted to 'sain the byre' [guard the byre by spells] She told him to open the beast, and he would find her keys there. Accordingly he did so, which proved that the cow had been changed. When the Trows take anything they always leave some resemblance of the stolen property in its place.

On another occasion when Kirstan was among the Trows, she had to dress a baby, and one of the grey men brought a box of curious ointment, with which the child was to be anointed. While doing so Kirstan chanced to put up her hand to her eye, and left some of the Trow's ointment on it. From that time her sight became so keen that she could see a boat on the ocean twenty miles away, and could tell the position and features of every man in it. But she had 'taken the virtue from their ointment'. So one day a Trow-man met her on the hill, and says he, 'Ye travel light and brisk for sae auld a wife.' Never suspecting who he was, Kirstan answered, 'It's my gude sight that helps me alang.' 'And which eye do you see best upon, gude wife?' asked the Trow. Kirstan told him readily enough, and he instantly put his little finger to the eye she had indicated, and she was blind on it ever after.

Mam Kirstan said that whenever she was 'fetched' the Trows pressed her to eat, but she would not touch their food. They even marked a cross upon the butter they set before her, thinking to beguile her in that way, but nothing would tempt her to partake, knowing that if she did so she would be in their power, and they would be able to keep her as long as they liked.

At another time, when she was required professionally, the Trow who fetched her took her in his hands and muttered, 'Safe there, safe back,' and Kirstan found herself over the sea in another island. When matters were satisfactorily concluded in the Trow's domestic circle, he told her to follow him, and he brought her back the same way. Her husband never knew that she had been farther than her own kail-yard until he discovered that she was cold and weary, and her clothes damp from the sea spray. 'Kirstan!' he exclaimed, 'gude be aboot de! Whars do been?' Then her tongue was loosed, and she told her adventure.

KATHERINE FORDYCE AND
THE TROWS

Source: Rev. Biot Edmonson and Jessie M. Saxby, *The Home of a Naturalist*
Narrator: 'Mam Kirsty', the authors' childhood nurse, Unst; collected
by Jessie Saxby
Type: ML4077 'Caught in Fairyland'

There was a woman called Katherine Fordyce, and she died
at the birth of her first child – at least, folks thought she
died. A neighbour's wife dreamt shortly after Katherine's death
that she came to her and said, 'I have the milk of your cow that
you could not get, but it shall be made up to you; you shall have
more than that if you will give me what you will know about
soon.' The goodwife would not promise, having no idea what
Katherine meant, but shortly afterwards she understood that it
was a child of her own to which Katherine referred. The child
came, and the mother named it Katherine Fordyce; and after it
was christened the Trow-bound Katherine appeared to the
mother again and told her that all should prosper in her family
while that child remained in it. She told her also that she was
quite comfortable among the Trows, but could not get out
unless somebody chanced to see her and had presence of mind to
call on God's name at the moment. She said her friends had
failed to sain her at the time of her child's birth, and that was
how she fell into the power of the Trows.

Prosperity came like a high tide upon the goodwife's household until her child Katherine married. On the girl's wedding
night a fearful storm came on, 'the like had no' been minded in
the time o' anybody alive'. The Broch was overflowed by great
seas, that rolled over the skerries as if they had been beach-
stones. The bride's father lost a number of his best sheep, for
they were lifted by the waves and carried away, and 'some folk
did say that old men with long white beards were seen stretching

their pale hands out of the surf and taking hold of the creatures'. From that day the goodwife's fortunes changed for the worse. A man called John Nisbet saw that same Katherine Fordyce once. He was walking up a daal near her old home, when it seemed as if a hole opened in the side of the daal. He looked in and saw Katherine sitting in a 'queer-shaped armchair, and she was nursing a baby'. There was a bar of iron stretched in front to keep her a prisoner. She was dressed in a brown poplin gown – which folk knew by John's description to be her wedding-dress. He thought she said, 'O Johnnie! what's sent *de* here?' And he answered, 'And what keeps *you* here?' And she said, 'Well; I am well and happy, but I can't get out, for *I have eaten their food*!' John Nisbet unfortunately did not know, or forgot to say, 'Gude be aboot wis,' and Katherine was unable to give him a hint, and in a moment the whole scene disappeared.

M'ROY'S WIFE

Source: J. Grant, *Legends of the Braes o' Mar*
Narrator: Unknown

A bachelor bold – one of Dalmore's tenants – wandering through the hills after his 'beasties', sat down to rest on a hillock. Around was a small patch, the heather of which had been burnt some years previously, and the stumps now lay, whitening on the ground.

In the good old times, when the 'yewie wi' the crookit horn' flourished, when it was a noble deed to do the Excise, many a goodly black pot has been run primely over these same white cows. Now my bachelor fell a-considering the immense quantities of little black holes, the grotesque bends, the mathematical figures, the twists, the twirls, the oddities and whirlimagigs of these remnants of the burning. All of a blow – he saw with a start – the black holes became an ocean of little eyes looking hard at him; of a blow the ocean of little eyes began to wink very cunningly indeed; of a blow the grotesque bends formed themselves into little legs and feet, arms and hands; of a blow the diagrams, triangles, parallelograms, trapeziums, etc., shaped themselves into sprawling little bodies; and of a blow the twists, the twirls, the oddities and whirlimagigs were nothing more or less than a dance, a boiling, a riot, a tumbling, wheeling, rolling, tumbling fermentation of little folkies – the queerest sight that mortal ever saw. With great presence of mind M'Roy, for so our hero named, seized a pebble, and, rousing himself from fascination of the view, threw it over the spot, exclaiming, 'all that is within be mine, in God's name.'

Presto, a beautiful woman stood before him, with no more clothing to spare than when her mother bare her. But the bachelor bold – his presence of mind did not fail him even here

– threw his plaid over her, and, modestly turning away, waited until she had arrayed herself as well as might be. In fine, he led her home with him, and in finer he led her to the altar also and gave up bachelorship.

Some years after, a drover and his son – a boy about twelve years old – passing to the south through Braemar, asked and got leave to lodge for the night in M'Roy's house.

While the two sat at their brose, the goodwife was busy arranging things for the night. The boy, after a first earnest look at her, could not, it seemed, take his eyes from her. Ever and anon he pulled his father by the sleeve, and whispered, 'How very like mother the housewife is!'

The drover, from the first time his attention was called to the fact, endeavoured to silence the boy, though imitating him in his scrutiny of their hostess. It was impossible for M'Roy not to notice the unusual interest they took in his better half.

'You must see something,' said he, in displeasure, 'very strange about my wife to make you look at her in the way you do.'

'Yes, indeed; for unless I had buried my own wife,' – the drover mentioned the year, day, and hour – 'I would swear that were she.'

Wonderful coincidence! It happened that the time he mentioned to the very hour agreed with the date on which she had been found by the Braemar man. They went earnestly to prove and probe the matter. The woman, who chanced to be milking her kine when the dialogue took place, made her appearance. On the statement of certain facts, as one recollecting the incidents of a dream, the whole of a past life slowly dawned upon her. She recognized the drover for her husband, his boy for her child, and asked after the rest of the family by their names. The longer they sat and talked, the more vividly her former life came back to her memory; till at length every particular of it became as clear as those of our own are to us.

The case was now clear. She had been spirited away by the fairies, and a substitute put in her place. As she sat by the fire between her two husbands, smoothing down the raven curls of her son, whose head lay in her lap, and looked dreamily into the fire, what strange thoughts must have passed through her mind!

'Well,' quoth the drover, breaking a long silence, 'what is to be done?'

'Let her decide,' said M'Roy, 'whether she will stay with me or go with you.'

'Then,' replied she, after a long pause, 'I will go to my bairns.' And M'Roy was once more a bachelor.

THE GOODMAN OF WASTNESS
AND THE SELKIE

Source: G. F. Black, *County Folk-Lore III: Orkney and Shetland Islands*
Narrator: Unknown; collected by W. Traill Dennison
Type: ML4080 'The Seal Woman'

The goodman of Wastness was well-to-do, had his farm well stocked, and was a good-looking and well-favoured man. And though many braw lasses in the island had set their caps at him, he was not to be caught. So the young lasses began to treat him with contempt, regarding him as an old young man who was deliberately committing the unpardonable sin of celibacy. He did not trouble his head much about the lasses, and when urged by his friends to take a wife, he said, 'Women were like many another thing in this weary world, only sent for a trial to man; and I have trials enouch without being tried by a wife. If that ould fool Adam had not been bewitched by his wife, he might have been a happy man in the yard of Edin to this day.' The old wife of Longer, who heard him make this speech, said to him, 'Take doo heed de sell, doo'll may be de sell bewitched some day.' 'Ay,' quoth he, 'that will be when doo walks dry shod frae the Alters o' Seenie to dae Boar of Papa.'

Well, it happened one day that the goodman of Wastness was down on the ebb (that portion of the shore left dry at low water) when he saw at a little distance a number of selkie folk on a flat rock. Some were lying sunning themselves, while others jumped and played about in great glee. They were all naked, and had skins as white as his own. The rock on which they sported had deep water on its seaward side, and on its shore side a shallow pool.

The goodman of Wastness crept unseen till he got to the edge of the shallow pool; he then rose and dashed through the pool to the rock on its other side. The alarmed selkie folk seized their seal-skins, and, in mad haste, jumped into the sea. Quick as they were, the goodman was also quick and he seized one of the skins belonging to an unfortunate damsel, who in terror of flight neglected to clutch it as she sprang into the water.

The selkie folk swam out a little distance, then turning, set up their heads and gazed at the goodman. He noticed that one of them had not the appearance of seals like the rest. He then took the captured skin under his arm, and made for home, but before he got out of the ebb, he heard a most doleful sound of weeping and lamentation behind him. He turned to see a fair woman following him. It was that one of the selkie folk whose seal-skin he had taken. She was a pitiful sight; sobbing in bitter grief, holding out both hands in eager supplication, while the big tears followed each other down her fair face. And ever and anon she cried out, 'O bonnie man! if there's onie mercy i' thee human breast, gae back me skin! I cinno', cinno', cinno', live i' the sea without it. I cinno', cinno', cinno', bide among me ain folk without me ain seal-skin. Oh, pity a peur distressed, forlorn lass, gin doo wad ever hope for mercy theesel'!' The goodman was not too soft-hearted, yet he could not help pitying her in her doleful plight. And with his pity came the softer passion of love. His heart that never loved women before was conquered by the sea-nymph's beauty. So, after a good deal of higgling and plenty of love-making, he wrung from the sea-lass a reluctant consent to live with him as his wife. She chose this as the least of two evils. Without the skin she could not live in the sea, and he absolutely refused to give up the skin.

So the sea-lass went with the goodman and stayed with him for many days, being a thrifty, frugal, and kindly goodwife. She bore her goodman seven children, four boys and three lasses, and there were not bonnier lasses or statelier boys in all the isle. And though the goodwife of Wastness appeared happy, and was sometimes merry, yet there seemed at times to be a weight on her heart; and many a long, longing look did she fix on the sea. She taught her bairns many a strange song, that nobody on earth ever heard before. Albeit she was a thing of the sea, yet the goodman led a happy life with her.

Now it chanced, one fine day, that the goodman of Wastness and his three eldest sons were off in his boat to the fishing. Then the goodwife sent three of the other children to the ebb to gather limpits and wilks. The youngest lass had to stay at home, for she had a beelan foot. The goodwife then began, under the pretence of house-cleaning, a determined search for her long-lost skin. She searched up and she searched down; she searched but and she searched ben; she searched out and she searched in, but never a skin could she find, while the sun wore to the west. The youngest lass sat in a stool with her sore foot on a cringlo. She says to her mother, 'Mam, what are doo leukan for?' 'O bairn, deu no tell,' said her mother, 'but I'm leukan for a bonnie skin tae mak a rivlin that wad ceur thee sare fit.' Says the lass, 'Maybe I ken whar hid is. Ae day, win ye war a' oot, an' ded tought i war sleepan i' the bed, he teuk a bonnie skin doon; he gloured at it a peerie minute, dan folded hid and led hid up under dae aisins abeun dae bed.'

When her mother heard this she rushed to the place, and pulled out her long-concealed skin. 'Farewell, peerie buddo!' said she to the child, and ran out. She rushed to the shore, flung on her skin, and plunged into the sea with a wild cry of joy. A male of the selkie folk there met and greeted her with every token of delight. The goodman was rowing home, and saw them both from his boat. His lost wife uncovered her face, and thus she cried to him: 'Goodman o' Wastness, fareweel tae thee! I liked dee weel, doo war geud tae me; bit I lo'e better me man o' the sea!'

And that was the last he ever saw or heard of his bonnie wife. Often did he wander on the sea-shore, hoping to meet his lost love, but never more saw he her fair face.

WATER-HORSE AND WOMEN

Source: J. G. Campbell, *Superstitions of the Scottish Highlands*
Narrators: Unknown

A young woman herding cattle drove her charge to a seques-
tered part of the hill, and while there a young man came
her way, and reclining his head on her lap fell asleep. On his
stretching himself she observed that he had horse-hoofs, and
lulling him gently managed to get his head rested on the ground.
She then cut out with her scissors the part of her clothes below
his head and made her escape. When the water-horse awoke and
missed her it made a dreadful outcry.

A water-horse in man's shape came to a house in which there
was a woman alone; at the time she was boiling water in a clay
vessel, such as was in use before iron became common. The
water-horse, after looking on for some time, drew himself nearer
to her, and said in a snuffling voice, 'It is time to begin courting,
Sarah, daughter of John, son of Finlay.' 'It is time, it is time,'
she replied, 'when the little pitcher boils.' In a while it repeated
the same words and drew itself nearer. She gave the same answer
drawing out the time as best she could, till the water was boiling
hot. As the snuffling youth was coming too near she threw the
scalding water between his legs, and he ran out of the house
roaring and yelling with pain.

THE LAIRD OF LORNTIE

Source: Robert Chambers, *Popular Rhymes of Scotland*
Narrator: Unknown
Type: ML4070 'The Sea-sprite Haunting the Fishing-boat'

The young laird of Lorntie, in Forfarshire, was one evening returning from a hunting excursion, attended by a single servant and two greyhounds, when, in passing a solitary lake, which lies about three miles south from Lorntie, and was in those times closely surrounded with natural wood, his ears were suddenly assailed by the shrieks of a female apparently drowning. Being of a fearless character, he instantly spurred his horse forward to the side of the lake, and there saw a beautiful female struggling with the water, and, as it seemed to him, just in the act of sinking. 'Help, help, Lorntie!' she exclaimed. 'Help, Lorntie – help, Lor—,' and the waters seemed to choke the last sounds of her voice as they gurgled in her throat. The laird, unable to resist the impulse of humanity, rushed into the lake, and was about to grasp the long yellow locks of the lady, which lay like hanks of gold upon the water, when he was suddenly seized behind, and forced out of the lake by his servant, who, farther-sighted than his master, perceived the whole affair to be the feint of a water-spirit. 'Bide, Lorntie – bide a blink!' cried the faithful creature, as the laird was about to dash him to the earth; 'that wauling madam was nae other, God sauf us! than the mermaid.' Lorntie instantly acknowledged the truth of this asseveration, which, as he was preparing to mount his horse, was confirmed by the mermaid raising herself half out of the water, and exclaiming, in a voice of fiendish disappointment and ferocity:

> 'Lorntie, Lorntie,
> Were it na your man,
> I had gart your heart's bluid
> Skirl in my pan.'

461

THE GLASTIG, OR MAID OF GLEN DUROR

Source: Rev. James MacDougall, *Folk Tales and Fairy Lore*
Narrator: Unknown

There was a Glastig in Glen Duror, whom people called the 'Maiden'. She was an earthly woman at first. Two or three hundred years ago she was a dairymaid between Glen Duror and Glen-a-Chulish; and her name and surname, and even the farm where she was reared, are still remembered.

She was taken away out of child-bed by the fairies, and she returned no more. But according to tradition she was changed into a Banshee, or Glastig, who took shelter in the ravines and clefts of the rocks between the two glens. She frequented, in particular, the Robbers' Ravine on the south side of Ben Vehir, and there she was often seen by the passers-by.

It appears that the liking she formerly had for cows and all kinds of cattle stuck to her as a Glastig. Often she was to be seen in the midst of the cattle, as if she were engaged in counting them; and before markets, and at the time of changing tenants, as if she were separating the outgoing part of the stock, or taking possession of the part newly come in. If she happened to have a greater liking for one of the tenants than for the rest, she was very careful of his cattle; and at the time of flitting, she would place every obstacle between him and the lifting of them off the ground. According to tradition, this happened for the last time about thirty years ago. At any rate, from that day to this, the Glastig has been neither seen nor heard. Perhaps she was chased out of the glen by the screaming of the whistles of steamers passing up and down Loch Linnhe, or by the blasts fired by the quarriers of the quartz-rock at the foot of the Dogs' Ravine. At any rate she has departed, and no one misses her.

Many a tale was told about her, and many a pail of milk was spent on her by the dairymaids at the shielings of the glen. For the night they left the pail full of milk for her, they would find everything right next day; but the night they neglected to do this, the calves would be let out of the fold, and the cows would be sucked dry next morning.

MACDONALD OF THE ISLES'S
BIG PLOUGHMAN AND THE
BLACK CHANTER

Source: Lord Archibald Campbell, *Records of Argyll*
Narrator: Unknown; collected by Hector MacLean in Ballygrant, Islay

When MacDonald of the Isles resided in the palace of Finlagan Isle in Loch Finlagan, he had a ploughman who, from his large stature, was called the Big Ploughman. He was out one day ploughing, and he had a boy with him driving the horses, as was the custom in those days. He was seized with strong hunger, and he said to the boy –

'My good fellow, were it to be got in an ordinary way or magically, I would take food in the meantime, were I to have it.'

After having said these words, he and the boy took another turn with the team to the side of Knockshainta. There was an old grey-haired man by the side of the hill, who had a table covered there with all good eatables. The old man asked them to come up and partake of what was on the table. The ploughman went; but the boy was frightened, and would not go. After the ploughman had partaken enough of the good things before him, the old man gave him a chanter to try. When he put his fingers on it, he, who never played any music before, played as well as any piper that ever was in the island of Islay. A day or two after this, MacDonald heard in his palace on Island Finlagan the Big Ploughman playing the black chanter. He inquired who it was that was playing. They told him that it was the Big Ploughman. When he heard how well the ploughman played, there was nothing but to get for him the big bagpipe of three drones, and he was MacDonald's piper as long as he lived.

MacDonald went on a trip to the Isle of Skye. He took with him thence a young man of the name of MacCrimmon, who was fond of music, and was doing a little at it. He went to the Big Ploughman to learn more music from him than he had already. MacCrimmon and the ploughman's daughter began courting; and in consequence of the fancy that the girl took to MacCrimmon – believing that he would marry her – she took the black chanter, unknown to her father, out of the chest, and gave it to MacCrimmon to try it. When MacCrimmon had tried it, he could then play as well as the Big Ploughman himself. The girl asked the chanter back; but he entreated her to let him have it for a few days until he should practise a little further on it. A few days afterwards MacDonald of the Isles went off to Skye, and MacCrimmon went along with him. He did not give back the chanter, and neither did he come back himself to marry the Big Ploughman's daughter. The people of Islay say that it was in this manner that the music went from Islay to the Isle of Skye.

THE BLACK LAD MACCRIMMON
AND THE BANSHEE

Source: Rev. James MacDougall, *Folk Tales and Fairy Lore*
Narrator: Unknown

It appears that the fairies were excellent musicians, and that their choice of all musical instruments was the bagpipes. Often did the wayfarer hear its sound coming from the fairy knoll, which happened to be in his path, and often did he feel its sweet music tempting him to walk in, and lift his foot in the dance with the fairies.

This art which they possessed they are said to have taught to some men for whom they took a liking, and who are still remembered in tradition. Among these was the Black Lad MacCrimmon.

Up to the Black Lad's time, the MacCrimmons were not better than other good pipers in the Highlands. He was the first of them who rose above all the rest in fame, and who was commonly called 'The King of Pipers'.

He was the youngest of three sons, and the least thought of by his father. When his father would take down from the back of the crooked stick the great bagpipes, which he called the Black Gate, and he himself would play the first tune on it, he would hand it to his eldest son, and when his eldest son had done with it, he would hand it to the second son; but when the second son had done with it, the Black Lad would not get the honour of blowing so much as one blast into the bag. He was also kept down by the rest, and left to do every piece of work that was more slavish than another.

On a certain day, his father and his two brothers went to the fair, and left him alone at home. After they had gone, he got hold of the chanter, and began to play upon it. And in the midst of the playing, who should come upon him but the Banshee from the castle.

'Thou art busy discoursing music, Lad,' said she. He answered that he was. 'Which wouldst thou prefer, skill without success, or success without skill?' said she then. He answered that he would rather have skill without success. She pulled a hair from her head, and asked him to put it round the reed of the chanter. When he had done that, she said to him: 'Place now thy fingers on the holes of the chanter, and I will lay my fingers on thy fingers.' As soon as that was done, she said: 'When I shall lift my finger, lift thou the finger which happens to be under it. Think now of any tune thou pleasest, and play it with me in the way I have told thee.' He did so, and played the tune skilfully. When he had finished the tune, she said: 'Now thou art the King of Pipers. Thine equal was not before thee, and thine equal shall not be after thee.' She then bade him good-day, and departed.

As soon as she had gone, he took down the Black Gate and began playing on it. There was not a tune he could think of which he did not try and which he could not play with ease. Before he ceased his father and brothers had returned from the fair. And when they approached the house, they heard the music, and stood to listen. 'Whoever is playing, it is on the Black Gate,' said the father to his sons. They went on, but the music ceased before they reached the house.

They went in, but none of them let on that they had heard the music till night came. Then the old man took down the great bagpipes, and after he himself and his two eldest sons had played tune about, he asked the Black Lad to take his own spell of it. 'Is it I?' said he. 'I am not worthy of that honour. It is enough for me to be a slave to you all.' 'Take the bagpipes, and thou shalt no longer be asked to do slavish work,' said his father. He took the pipes at last, and struck up the finest music anyone in the house had ever heard. 'The music has left us,' said the father to the other sons. 'None of us will come in the wake of the Black Lad.' He spake truly, for the like of the Black Lad never lived, either in his own time, or since.

MACPHIE'S BLACK DOG

Source: J. G. Campbell, *Superstitions of the Scottish Highlands*
Narrator: Donald Cameron, Ruaig, Tiree, 1863

Mac-vic-Allan of Arasaig, lord of Moidart, went out hunting in his own forest when young and unmarried. He saw a royal stag before him, as beautiful an animal as he had ever seen. He levelled his gun at it, and it became a woman as beautiful as he had ever seen at all. He lowered his gun, and it became a royal stag as before. Every time he raised the gun to his eye, the figure was that of a woman, and every time he let it down to the ground, it was a royal stag. Upon this he raised the gun to his eye and walked up till he was close to the woman's breast. He then sprang and caught her in his arms. 'You will not be separated from me at all,' he said, 'I will never marry any but you.' 'Do not do that, Mac-vic-Allan,' she said, 'you have no business with me, I will not suit you. There will never be a day, while you have me with you, but you will need to kill a cow for me.' 'You will get that,' said the lord of Moidart, 'though you should ask two a day.'

But Mac-vic-Allan's herd began to grow thin. He tried to send her away, but he could not. He then went to an old man, who lived in the townland, and was his counsellor. He said he would be a broken man, and he did not know what plan to take to get rid of her. The honest old man told him, that unless Macphie of Colonsay could send her away, there was not another living who could. A letter was instantly sent off to Macphie. He answered the letter, and came to Arasaig.

'What business is this you have with me,' said Macphie, 'Mac-vic-Allan?'

Mac-vic-Allan told him how the woman had come upon him, and how he could not send her away.

'Go you,' said Macphie, 'and kill a cow for her today as usual; send her dinner to the room as usual; and give me my dinner on the other side of the room.'

Mac-vic-Allan did as he was asked. She commenced her dinner, and Macphie commenced his. When Macphie got his dinner past, he looked over at her.

'What is your news, Elle-maid?' said he.
'What is that to you, Brian Brugh,' said she.
'I saw you, Elle-maid,' said he,
'When you consorted with the Fingalians,
When you went with Dermid o Duvne
And accompanied him from covert to covert.'
'I saw you, Brian Brugh,' she said,
'When you rode on an old black horse,
The lover of the slim fairy woman,
Ever chasing her from brugh to brugh.'

'Dogs and men after the wretch,' cried Macphie, 'long have I known her.'

Every dog and man in Arasaig was called and sent after her. She fled away out to the point of Arasaig, and they did not get a second sight of her.

Upon this Macphie went home to his own Colonsay. One day he was out hunting, and night came on before he got home. He saw a light and made straight for it. He saw a number of men sitting in there, and an old grey-headed man in the midst. The old man spoke and said, 'Macphie, come forward.' Macphie went forward, and what should come in his way but a bitch, as beautiful an animal as he had ever seen, and a litter of pups with it. He saw one pup in particular, black in colour, and he had never seen a pup so black or so beautiful as it.

'This dog will be my own,' said Macphie.

'No,' said the man, 'you will get your choice of the pups, but you will not get that one.'

'I will not take one,' said Macphie, 'but this one.'

'Since you are resolved to have it,' said the old man, 'it will not do you but one day's service, and it will do that well. Come back on such a night and you will get it.'

Macphie reached the place on the night he promised to come.

They gave him the dog, 'and take care of it well,' said the old man, 'for it will never do service for you but the one day.'

The Black Dog began to turn out so handsome a whelp that no one ever saw a dog so large or so beautiful as it. When Macphie went out hunting he called the Black Dog, and the Black Dog came to the door and then turned back and lay where it was before. The gentlemen who visited at Macphie's house used to tell him to kill the Black Dog, it was not worth its food. Macphie would tell them to let the dog alone, that the Black Dog's day would come yet.

At one time a number of gentlemen came across from Islay to visit Macphie and ask him to go with them to Jura to hunt. At that time Jura was a desert, without anyone staying on it, and without its equal anywhere as hunting ground for deer and roe. There was a place there where those who went for sport used to stay, called the Big Cave. A boat was made ready to cross the sound that same day. Macphie rose to go, and the sixteen young gentlemen along with him. Each of them called the Black Dog, and it reached the door, then turned and lay down where it was before. 'Shoot it,' cried the young gentlemen. 'No,' said he, 'the Black Dog's day is not come yet.' They reached the shore, but the wind rose and they did not get across that day.

Next day they made ready to go; the Black Dog was called and reached the door, but returned where it was before. 'Kill it,' said the gentlemen, 'and don't be feeding it any longer.' 'I will not kill it,' said Macphie, 'the Black Dog's day will come yet.' They failed to get across this day also from the violence of the weather and returned. 'The dog has foreknowledge,' said the gentlemen. 'It has foreknowledge,' said Macphie, 'that its own day will come yet.'

On the third day the weather was beautiful. They took their way to the harbour, and did not say a syllable this day to the Black Dog. They launched the boat to go away. One of the gentlemen looked and said the Black Dog was coming, and he never saw a creature like it, because of its fierce look. It sprang, and was the first creature in the boat. 'The Black Dog's day is drawing near us,' said Macphie.

They took with them meat, and provisions, and bedclothes,

and went ashore in Jura. They passed that night in the Big Cave, and next day went to hunt the deer. Late in the evening they came home. They prepared supper. They had a fine fire in the cave and light. There was a big hole in the very roof of the cave through which a man could pass. When they had taken their supper the young gentlemen lay down, Macphie rose, and stood warming the back of his legs to the fire. Each of the young men said he wished his own sweetheart was there that night. 'Well,' said Macphie, 'I prefer that my wife should be in her own house; it is enough for me to be here myself tonight.'

Macphie gave a look from him and saw sixteen women entering the door of the cave. The light went out and there was no light except what the fire gave. The women went over to where the gentlemen were. Macphie could see nothing from the darkness that came over the cave. He was not hearing a sound from the men. The women stood up and one of them looked at Macphie. She stood opposite to him as though she were going to attack him. The Black Dog rose and put on a fierce bristling look and made a spring at her. The women took to the door, and the Black Dog followed them to the mouth of the cave. When they went away the Black Dog returned and lay at Macphie's feet.

In a little while Macphie heard a horrid noise overhead in the top of the cave, so that he thought the cave would fall in about his head. He looked up and saw a man's hand coming down through the hole, and making as if to catch himself and take him out through the hole in the roof of the cave. The Black Dog gave one spring, and between the shoulder and the elbow caught the Hand, and lay upon it with all its might. Now began the play between the Hand and the Black Dog. Before the Black Dog let go its hold, it chewed the arm through till it fell on the floor. The Thing that was on the top of the cave went away, and Macphie thought the cave would fall in about his head. The Black Dog rushed out after the Thing that was outside. This was not the time when Macphie felt himself most at ease, when the Black Dog left him. When the day dawned, behold the Black Dog had returned. It lay down at Macphie's feet, and in a few minutes was dead.

When the light of day appeared Macphie looked, and he had not a single man alive of those who were with him in the cave. He took with him the Hand, and went to the shore to the boat. He went on board and went home to Colonsay, unaccompanied by dog or man. He took the Hand up with him that men might see the horror he had met with, the night he was in the cave. No man in Islay or Colonsay ever at all saw such a hand, nor did they imagine that such existed.

There only remained to send a boat to Jura and take home the bodies that were in the cave. That was the end of the Black Dog's day.

HURRAH FOR KINTAIL!

Source: J. G. Campbell, *Witchcraft and Second Sight in the Highlands and Islands of Scotland*
Narrator: Unknown
Type: ML5005 'A Journey with a Troll'

A shepherd in Kintail, living alone in a bothy, far from other houses, after kindling in the evening a bright cheerful fire, threw himself on a heather bed on the opposite side of the house. About twenty cats entered and sat round the fire, holding up their paws and warming themselves. One went to the window, put a black cap on its head, cried 'Hurrah for London!' and vanished. The other cats, one by one, did the same. The cap of the last fell off, and the shepherd caught it, put it on his own head, cried 'Hurrah for London!' and followed. He reached London in a twinkling, and with his companions went to drink wine in a cellar. He got drunk and fell asleep. In the morning he was caught, taken before a judge, and sentenced to be hanged. At the gallows he entreated to be allowed to wear the cap he had on in the cellar; it was a present from his mother, and he would like to die with it on. When it came the rope was round his neck. He clapped the cap on his head, and cried 'Hurrah for Kintail!' He disappeared with the gallows about his neck, and his friends in Kintail, having by this time missed him, and being assembled in the bothy prior to searching the hills, were much surprised at his strange appearance.

THE FAIRY BAN'

Source: R. de B. Trotter, *Galloway Gossip*
Narrator: Unknown

It's an awfu bit thereawa onywey for folk seein things.

There's a bit burn comes doon frae the Bogue an Ardoch wey, doon by the Holm Mill, an rins inta the Garpel; an there's a brig ower't on the aul' road yt gangs ower the Mulloch tae the Aul' Clachan.

Weel, the doctor's faither wus oot yae munelicht nicht seein some unweel buddy aboot the Hardlan, an he was comin alang naur this brig, whun he met a great ban' o' fairies comin alang in a raw, a' haudin ither's han's an singan.

They wur aboot fowr fit high, an a' dress't in green, an there wus a gey wheen lassie yins amang them.

He didna ken hoo tae wun bye, for the road wus nairra, an he stood up tae the side. Than yin o' them cry't oot – 'Open! an let the honest doctor through;' an wi that they pairtit i'e middle, an stood at the twa sides o' the road till he wun bye.

They had queer hats on, an every yin as he gaed bye pu't it aff an made a gran' boo, an a' the lassie yins made a curtsey.

The doctor pu't his hat aff too, an boo't richt an left till he wun bye them, an than he turn't an bad them 'Gude-nicht,' an they answer't him 'Gude-nicht,' but he could see naething o' them.

It wud be aboot 1797, in the wunter time, an it couldna be an alcoholic vision, for he wus a man yt wudna taste drink o' ony kin. It seems he affen saw fairies, an they wur ey verra civil tae him, though the yins at the Holm Glen got an ill name thereawa.

THE FAIRY FAREWEEL

Source: R. H. Cromek, *Remains of Nithsdale and Galloway Song*
Narrator: Unknown

The 'Fairy Fareweel' is a circumstance that happened about twenty years ago, and is well remembered. The sun was setting on a fine summer's evening, and the peasantry were returning from labour, when, on the side of a green hill, appeared a procession of thousands of apparently little boys, habited in mantles of green, freckled with light. One, taller than the rest, ran before them, and seemed to enter the hill, and again appeared at its summit. This was repeated three times, and all vanished. The peasantry, who beheld it, called it 'The Fareweel o' the Fairies to the Burrow hill'!

FURTHER READING

SOURCES OF STORIES IN THIS BOOK

'Bede, Cuthbert' (i.e., Bradley, Edward)
The White Wife: with other stories, supernatural, romantic and legendary,
London: Sampson Low, Son, and Marston, 1865

Black, G. F.
County Folk-Lore III, Orkney and Shetland Islands, London: The Folk-Lore Society, 1903

Briggs, Katharine M.
A Dictionary of British Folk-Tales in the English Language, incorporating the F. J. Norton Collection, 4 vols., London: Routledge & Kegan Paul, 1970–71

Buchan, Peter
'Ancient Scottish Tales', edited by John A. Fairley in *Transactions of the Buchan Field Club,* vol. 9, Peterhead: Buchan Field Club, 1908

Campbell, Lord Archibald
Records of Argyll: Legends, Traditions, and Recollections of Argyll Highlanders, Edinburgh and London: William Blackwood and Sons, 1885

Campbell, John Francis
Popular Tales of the West Highlands, Paisley and London: Alexander Gardner, 1893 (1st edn, 1862)

Campbell, John Gregorson
Clan Traditions and Popular Tales of the Western Highlands and Islands, London: David Nutt, 1895
Superstitions of the Highlands and Islands of Scotland, Glasgow: James Maclehose & Sons, 1900
Witchcraft and Second Sight in the Highlands and Islands of Scotland, Glasgow: James Maclehose & Sons, 1902

Carrick, John Donald
The Laird of Logan: or, Wit of the West, Glasgow: David Robertson, 1835 (new edition of 1854 contains memoirs of Carrick and his collaborators William Motherwell and Andrew Henderson)

Chambers, Robert
Popular Rhymes of Scotland, London and Edinburgh: W. & R. Chambers, 1870 (1st edn, 1826)

Scottish Jests and Anecdotes, Edinburgh: William Paterson, n.d. (1st edn, 1832)

Cromek, R. H.
Remains of Nithsdale and Galloway Song, with Historical and Traditional Notices Relative to the Manners and Customs of the Peasantry, London: T. Cadell and W. Davies, 1810

Dewar, John
The Dewar Manuscripts, Volume One: Scottish West Highland Folk Tales, translated by Hector Maclean, edited by The Reverend John Mackechnie, Glasgow: William Maclellan, 1963

Dixon, John H.
Gairloch in North-West Ross-shire: its records, traditions, inhabitants and natural history, Edinburgh: Cooperative Printing Company, 1886

Douglas, Sir George
Scottish Fairy and Folk Tales, London: Walter Scott, n.d. (1893)

Edmonson, Biot, see Saxby, Jessie M.

Folk-Lore Society
Folk-Lore Journal, London: The Folk-Lore Society, 1883–89
Folk-Lore Record, London: The Folk-Lore Society, 1878–82

Henderson, William
Notes on the Folk-Lore of the Northern Counties of England and the Borders, London: Longmans, Green & Co., 1866

Grant, J.
Legends of the Braes o' Mar, Aberdeen: Lewis and James Smith, 1861

Jervise, Andrew
The History and Traditions of the Land of the Lindsays in Angus and Mearns, with notices of Alyth and Meigle, Edinburgh: Sutherland and Knox, 1853

MacDougall, James
Folk and Hero Tales: Waifs and Strays of Celtic Tradition, Argyllshire Series, No. III, London: David Nutt, 1891
Folk Tales and Fairy Lore in Gaelic and English, Edinburgh: James Grant, 1910

MacInnes, Duncan
Folk and Hero Tales: Waifs and Strays of Celtic Tradition, Argyllshire Series, No. II, London: David Nutt, 1890

Maclagan, R. C.
Evil Eye in the Western Highlands, London: David Nutt, 1902

Miller, Hugh
Scenes and Legends of the North of Scotland, or, The Traditional History

of Cromarty, London: Johnstone and Hunter, 1850 (1st edn, 1835)
My Schools and Schoolmasters: or, The Story of My Education, Edinburgh: Johnstone and Hunter, 1854

Monteath, John
Dunblane Traditions, Glasgow: John Miller, 1887

Ramsay, Edward Bannerman
Reminiscences of Scottish Life and Character, Edinburgh: Edmonston & Douglas, 1862

Saxby, Jessie M., and Edmonson, Biot
The Home of a Naturalist, London: James Nisbet and Co., 1888

School of Scottish Studies
Scottish Studies, Edinburgh: School of Scottish Studies, 1957–
Tocher: Tales, Songs, Tradition, selected from the Archives of the School of Scottish Studies, Edinburgh: School of Scottish Studies, 1971–

Scott, Sir Walter
Waverley, London: J. M. Dent and Sons, 1969 (containing General Preface of 1829 edition)

Sutherland, George
Folk-Lore Gleanings and Character Sketches from the Far North, Wick: printed at 'John O'Groat Journal' office, 1937

Trotter, Robert de Bruce
Galloway Gossip, or the Southern Albanach 80 Years Ago, Dumfries: Robert G. Mann, The Courier and Herald Press, 1901

GENERAL

Aarne, Antti
The Types of the Folktale: A Classification and Bibliography, translated and enlarged by Stith Thompson, 2nd revision, Helsinki: Suomalainen Tiedeakatemia, Academia Scientiarum Fennica, 1961 (Folklore Fellows Communications, no. 184)

Aitken, Hannah
A Forgotten Heritage: Original Folk Tales of Lowland Scotland, Edinburgh and London: Scottish Academic Press, 1973

Baughmann, Ernest W.
Type and Motif Index of the Folktales of England and North America, The Hague: Mouton & Co., 1966 (Indiana University Folklore Series no. 20)

Bruford, Alan
The Green Man of Knowledge and Other Scots Traditional Tales, Aberdeen: Aberdeen University Press, 1982

Bruford, Alan, and MacDonald, D. A.
Memory in Gaelic Storytelling, Edinburgh: School of Scottish Studies, University of Edinburgh, 1979
Scottish Traditional Tales, Edinburgh: Polygon, 1994

Buchan, David
Scottish Tradition: A Collection of Scottish Folk Literature, London: Routledge & Kegan Paul, 1984

Campbell, John L., and Hall, Trevor H.
Strange Things: The Story of Fr Allan McDonald, Ada Goodrich Freer, and the Society for Psychical Research's Enquiry into Highland Second Sight, London: Routledge & Kegan Paul, 1968

Carmichael, Alexander
Carmina Gadelica: Hymns and Incantations, 6 vols., Edinburgh: Oliver & Boyd, 1900–1971

Chambers, William
Memoir of Robert Chambers with Autobiographic Reminiscences, Edinburgh: W. & R. Chambers, 1872

Christiansen, Reidar Th.
The Migratory Legends: A Proposed List of Types with a Systematic Catalogue of the Norwegian Variants, Helsinki: Suomalainen Tiedeakatemia, Academia Scientiarum Fennica, 1958 (Folklore Fellows Communications, no. 175)

Delargy, J. H.
'Three Men of Islay', in *Scottish Studies*, vol. 4, Edinburgh: Oliver & Boyd for the School of Scottish Studies, 1960

Dorson, Richard M.
The British Folklorists: A History, London: Routledge & Kegan Paul, 1968

Douglas, Sheila
The King o the Black Art and other Folk Tales, Aberdeen: Aberdeen University Press, 1987

Halpert, Herbert
'A Bibliographical Essay on the Folktale in English', in Halpert (ed.), *A Folklore Sampler from the Maritimes*, St John's, Newfoundland: Memorial University of Newfoundland Folklore and Language Publications for the Centre for Canadian Studies, Mount Allison University, 1982

Henderson, Hamish
Alias MacAlias: Writings on Songs, Folk and Literature, Edinburgh: Polygon, 1992

Kirk, Robert
The Secret Commonwealth and A Short Treatise of Charms and Spells,

edited with a commentary by Stewart Sanderson, Cambridge and Totowa, New Jersey: D. S. Brewer Ltd and Rowman & Littlefield for the Folklore Society, 1976

McKay, John G.
More West Highland Tales, 2 vols., Edinburgh and London: Oliver & Boyd for the Scottish Anthropological and Folklore Society, 1940 and 1960

MacLellan, Angus (tr. John Lorne Campbell)
Stories from South Uist, London: Routledge & Kegan Paul, 1961
The Furrow Behind Me: The Autobiography of a Hebridean Crofter, London: Routledge & Kegan Paul, 1962

Nutt, Alfred
'The Campbell of Islay Mss. at the Advocate's Library, Edinburgh', in *Folk-Lore*, vol. 1, London: The Folk-Lore Society, 1890

Ó Súilleabháin, Seán
A Handbook of Irish Folklore, Dublin: Folklore of Ireland Society, 1942; Hatboro, Pennsylvania: Folklore Associates, 1963

Ó Súilleabháin, Seán, and Christiansen, Reidar Th.
The Types of the Irish Folktale, Helsinki: Suomalainen Tiedeakatemia, Academia Scientiarum Fennica, 1963 (Folklore Fellows Communications, no. 188)

Thompson, Stith
The Folktale, New York: Holt, Rinehart & Winston, 1946; reprinted Berkeley, Los Angeles, and London: University of California Press, 1977
Motif-Index of Folk-Literature: A Classification of Narrative Elements in Folktales, Ballads, Myths, Fables, Mediaeval Romances, Exempla, Fabliaux, Jest-Books and Local Legends, revised and enlarged edition, 6 vols., Copenhagen: Rosenkilde & Bagger, 1955-58.

Whyte, Betsy
The Yellow on the Broom: The Early Days of a Traveller Woman, Edinburgh and London: W. & R. Chambers, 1979

Williamson, Duncan
The Broonie, Silkies and Fairies: Travellers' Tales, Edinburgh: Canongate 1985
Don't Look Back, Jack!, Edinburgh: Canongate, 1990
Fireside Tales of the Traveller Children, Edinburgh: Canongate, 1983
The Horsieman: Memories of a Traveller 1928-1958, Edinburgh: Canongate, 1994
Tell Me a Story for Christmas, Edinburgh: Canongate, 1987

Williamson, Duncan and Linda
A Thorn in the King's Foot: Folktales of the Scottish Travelling People, Harmondsworth: Penguin Books, 1987

Williamson, Linda
'What Storytelling Means to a Traveller: An Interview with Duncan Williamson, one of Scotland's Travelling People', in *Arv: Scandinavian Yearbook of Folklore*, vol. 37, Stockholm: Almqvist & Wiksell International for The Royal Gustavus Adolphus Academy, Uppsala

The journals *Scottish Studies* (1957–) and *Tocher* (1971–) published by the School of Scottish Studies, University of Edinburgh, are both full of good things. Particularly important is the feature on 'Storytellers and Storytelling' in *Tocher* 31 (1979).

TALE-TYPE INDEX

Aarne–Thompson Tale-Type Numbers

CHRISTIANSEN *MIGRATORY LEGENDS* NUMBERS

GLOSSARY

abune	above	*cloutit*	sewed
ae	one	*cocks upon*	
aisins	eaves	*its doup*	sits up
amaist	almost	*collop*	slice of meat
aoineadh	steep promontory	*creel*	wicker basket
		cringlo	low stool
bairnie	little child	*crowdie*	oatmeal and cold
bane	bone		water
bannock	oat or barley cake	*cutty*	girl
beelan	sore		
begunkin'	cheating	*dichtin' her*	
bere	barley	*een*	rubbing her eyes
biggit	built	*ding*	strike
birse	bristle	*divots*	turfs
boll	a dry measure of	*dochter*	daughter
	around 140lb	*durk*	knife
	(63.5kg)		
bood	must have been	*eachrais*	
brose	porridge	*ùrlair*	witch
brugh	prehistoric tower	*een*	eyes
buddo	darling		
buskit	dressed	*factor*	agent
		fendin'	living
callants	boys	*fit*	foot
carle	man	*flechs*	fleas
carlin	man	*fleetch*	humour
caulker	glass of whisky	*flit*	move
ceilidh	party	*forbye*	besides
chappit	knocked		
clachan	hamlet		
claes	clothes	*gaads*	fine clothes
clappin'	patting	*gaed*	went
clashes	tales	*gang*	go
cleekit	stole	*gaper*	dart

gaud o' ern	iron bar	*limmers*	villains
gerse	grass	*listed*	enlisted
gin	if	*little-stoup*	punch bowl
glave	sword	*loup*	leap
gomeril	fool	*lowsed*	exhausted
goodman	man, head of household	*lum*	chimney
goodwife	woman, mistress of household	*malison*	curse
		maun	must
graip	fork	*mell*	hammer
greetin'	crying	*mony*	many
gret	cried	*moudiewort*	mole
guidewife	woman	*muckle*	great
guttery	muddy	*muime*	mother-in-law
		muirlag	a basket shaped like an egg
haigh	crag		
hale	whole	*mutch ajee*	cap awry
henwife	witch	*mutch-croon*	cap
hokit	dug	*mutchkin*	a measure of drink, around $\frac{3}{4}$ pint (0.43l)
holm	islet		
houlet	owl		
humph	hunchback		
hurcheon	hedgehog	*neeve*	fist
		nieve	fist
ilk ane	each one		
ilka	each	*onygate*	anyway
		or	ere
kale-		*owre*	over
custocks	cabbage stalks	*oxter*	arm, armpit
keekit	looked		
kemping	working	*pechin'*	panting
ken	know	*pibroch*	bagpipe music
killogie	kiln	*plies*	strands (in a rope)
kist	chest		
knowe	hillock	*plotted*	boiled
		pock	bag
lameter	cripple	*priggit*	begged
lang syne	the old days	*puddick*	frog
lat	let	*puddock*	frog
lauch	laugh	*pyock*	bag
lave	the rest		
leman	lover	*rapes*	ropes

raxed	reached	*steekit*	shut
riddle	coarse sieve	*stend*	leap
ripes	reaches	*stoond*	ache
rowed	rolled	*swerf*	faint
rung	stick		
		taid	toad
sain	protect by ritual	*taigle*	confound
	sign	*tint*	lost
saithe	blessed	*tocher*	dowry
sark	shirt		
sgalag	ploughman	*unco*	very, unusually
sgeulachd	stories		
sguaise	flirt	*wab*	weaving
shackle-		*wal*	well
banes	wrist-bones	*washbeen*	washtub
shearn	dung	*wat thooms*	wet thumbs
shï-en	fairy dwelling	*weasand*	throat
shieling	shepherd's hut	*wedder*	wether (castrated
sicker	hard (of bargain)		ram)
siller	silver	*whilk*	which
skeps	beehives	*whins*	gorse
skerry	islet	*withy*	wicker basket
sliom	sleek	*wolron*	savage
smalls	wrists, ankles and	*woodie*	rope of twigs and
	knees		bark
smoored	smothered	*wuss*	wish
spotch	seek	*wydit*	waded
spouss	seek		
stane	stone	*yett*	gate
stapple	stem	*yill*	ale

READ MORE IN PENGUIN

In every corner of the world, on every subject under the sun, Penguin represents quality and variety – the very best in publishing today.

For complete information about books available from Penguin – including Puffins, Penguin Classics and Arkana – and how to order them, write to us at the appropriate address below. Please note that for copyright reasons the selection of books varies from country to country.

In the United Kingdom: Please write to *Dept. JC, Penguin Books Ltd, FREEPOST, West Drayton, Middlesex UB7 OBR.*

If you have any difficulty in obtaining a title, please send your order with the correct money, plus ten per cent for postage and packaging, to *PO Box No. 11, West Drayton, Middlesex UB7 OBR*

In the United States: Please write to *Consumer Sales, Penguin USA, P.O. Box 999, Dept. 17109, Bergenfield, New Jersey 07621-0120.* VISA and MasterCard holders call 1-800-253-6476 to order all Penguin titles

In Canada: Please write to *Penguin Books Canada Ltd, 10 Alcorn Avenue, Suite 300, Toronto, Ontario M4V 3B2*

In Australia: Please write to *Penguin Books Australia Ltd, P.O. Box 257, Ringwood, Victoria 3134*

In New Zealand: Please write to *Penguin Books (NZ) Ltd, Private Bag 102902, North Shore Mail Centre, Auckland 10*

In India: Please write to *Penguin Books India Pvt Ltd, 706 Eros Apartments, 56 Nehru Place, New Delhi 110 019*

In the Netherlands: Please write to *Penguin Books Netherlands bv, Postbus 3507, NL-1001 AH Amsterdam*

In Germany: Please write to *Penguin Books Deutschland GmbH, Metzlerstrasse 26, 60594 Frankfurt am Main*

In Spain: Please write to *Penguin Books S. A., Bravo Murillo 19, 1° B, 28015 Madrid*

In Italy: Please write to *Penguin Italia s.r.l., Via Felice Casati 20, I–20124 Milano*

In France: Please write to *Penguin France S. A., 17 rue Lejeune, F–31000 Toulouse*

In Japan: Please write to *Penguin Books Japan, Ishikiribashi Building, 2–5–4, Suido, Bunkyo-ku, Tokyo 112*

In Greece: Please write to *Penguin Hellas Ltd, Dimocritou 3, GR–106 71 Athens*

In South Africa: Please write to *Longman Penguin Southern Africa (Pty) Ltd, Private Bag X08, Bertsham 2013*

READ MORE IN PENGUIN

A SELECTION OF FICTION AND NON-FICTION

The Inn at the Edge of the World Alice Thomas Ellis

Five fugitives from Christmas are lured by an advertisement to a remote Scottish island. 'With her warm, acerbic wit, Alice Thomas Ellis has the audacious gift of moving us by her manner of poking fun at human misery. She edges the supernatural with sensible restraint and conjures forth a story full of pleasure' – *Mail on Sunday*

Notes of a Native Son James Baldwin

Richard Wright's *Native Son*, Hollywood's *Carmen Jones*, boyhood in Harlem, the death of his father, recovery and self-discovery as a black American in Paris – these are some of the themes of James Baldwin's early essays, which established him as among the greatest prose stylists of the century.

Florence: The Biography of a City Christopher Hibbert

A celebration of an extraordinary metropolis, *Florence* explores the art, literature, archaeology and social history that have shaped Italy's famous city across the ages, and is also an indispensable guide through the streets of Florence today.

Shelley and His World Claire Tomalin

'A vivid, amusing yet heartbreaking picture of Shelley emerges: poetry, politics, travel, friendships, love affairs, scandals, mysteries, children, visions – all gracefully combined' – *London Review of Books*

The Penguin Guide to Jazz on CD, LP and Cassette
Richard Cook and Brian Morton

'An incisive account of available recordings which cuts across the artificial boundaries by which jazz has been divided ... each page has a revelation; everybody will find their own' – *The Times*

READ MORE IN PENGUIN

A SELECTION OF FICTION AND NON-FICTION

Some Irish Loving   Edna O'Brien

The Irish approach to love is a many-splendoured and ripened refinement of the senses, which includes the barbed cosiness of friendship, the fleetingness of sex and the drama of woe. Edna O'Brien reflects these varieties in her selection of poems, letters, plays and story excerpts.

Memories of the Ford Administration   John Updike

'Updike is surely the finest chronicler of post-war American life, and what a sad, if sadly beautiful, chronicle he has made. At the centre of all is loss, loss of love, of opportunity, of time itself . . . one of the best things you are likely to read this year' – *Irish Times*

Cider With Rosie   Laurie Lee

In telling the story of his early life in a remote Cotswold village, Laurie Lee gives us a loving and intimate portrait of a country childhood and an unforgettable record of an era and a community that have disappeared.

Visiting Mrs Nabokov   Martin Amis

'Amis is as talented a journalist as he is a novelist, but these essays all manifest an unusual extra quality, one that is not unlike friendship. He makes an effort; he makes readers feel that they are the only person there' – *The Times*

Acts of Defiance   Jack Ashley

Devastated when a minor operation in 1968 resulted in the total loss of his hearing, the Labour backbencher Jack Ashley, now Lord Ashley, had even announced his resignation to the press. What he went on to achieve is shown here in both a remarkable autobiography and a classic essay on the arts of politics and the possible.

Famous Trials Volumes 1–9

From matricide to mutilation, poisoning and cold-blooded murder, this classic series, now reissued in Penguin, contains nine volumes of gripping criminal investigations that made headlines in their day.

READ MORE IN PENGUIN

A SELECTION OF FICTION AND NON-FICTION

A Damsel in Distress   P. G. Wodehouse

There are some rather unusual things going on at Belpher Castle. For one thing, the Earl's sister is set on pairing off her stepson, Reggie, and niece, Lady Patricia. But the latter has her sights set elsewhere . . . Love, anarchy, Machiavellian plots, silly asses – perfect Wodehouse reading!

The Rapstone Chronicles   John Mortimer

The rise and rise of the odious arch-Tory Leslie Titmuss is charted here, from his days as an unpopular schoolboy to his success as the pragmatic and self-seeking Secretary of State. 'Beautifully written, witty and often very, very funny' – *Spectator*

Leonardo   Serge Bramly

'Bramly makes it possible for us better to understand Leonardo's greatness. He does this by fixing him in his time, and interpreting his life and work with an unfailing intelligence and sympathy. This is a very fine book' – *Daily Telegraph*

Romancing Vietnam   Justin Wintle

'Mr Wintle has written what may be the best account so far of life in post-war Vietnam' – *Economist*. 'An excellent traveller. Wintle is inquisitive, is not burdened by self-consciousness – and things happen to him' – *Daily Telegraph*

Travelling the World   Paul Theroux

Now, for the first time, Paul Theroux has authorized a book of his favourite travel writing, containing photographs taken by those who have followed in his footsteps. The exquisite pictures here brilliantly complement and illuminate the provocative, wry, witty commentaries of one of the world's greatest travellers.

READ MORE IN PENGUIN

A SELECTION OF FICTION AND NON-FICTION

My Secret Planet Denis Healey

An anthology of the prose and poetry that has provided pleasure and inspiration to Denis Healey throughout his life. 'His boyhood, days at Oxford, the war, politics, the arts, death and the spiritual life ... these are all pieces to be relished' – *Sunday Times*

Genie Russ Rymer

A compelling and searching history of Genie who, at thirteen, had spent her entire childhood in one room, caged in a cot or strapped to a chair. Almost mute, without linguistic or social skills, Genie aroused great excitement among the scientists who took over her life. 'Moving and terrifying ... opens windows some might prefer kept shut on man's inhumanity' – Ruth Rendell

Falling in Love Jacky Fleming

Brilliant, bawdy and irreverent cartoons about falling in love ... 'I couldn't put it down. My advice to anyone thinking of falling in love, about to fall in love or already in love is – Stop! Buy this book, a pound of chocolates and go home by yourself for the evening. You'll have a much better time' – Sandi Toksvig

A Place of Greater Safety Hilary Mantel

Hilary Mantel's award-winning fictional history of the French Revolution. 'She has soaked herself in the history of the period ... and a striking picture emerges of the exhilaration, dynamic energy and stark horror of those fearful days' – *Daily Telegraph*

The New Spaniards John Hooper

Few of the millions of visitors Spain receives each year see beyond the hotels and resorts of its coastline. In this completely revised edition, there are chapters on, among other things, Spain under Socialism, women's changing role, bullfighting, and what John Hooper calls 'the cult of excess'.

READ MORE IN PENGUIN

A SELECTION OF OMNIBUSES

The Cornish Trilogy Robertson Davies

'He has created a rich oeuvre of densely plotted, highly symbolic novels that not only function as superbly funny entertainments but also give the reader, in his character's words, a deeper kind of pleasure – delight, awe, religious intimations, "a fine sense of the past, and of the boundless depth and variety of life"' – *The New York Times*

A Dalgliesh Trilogy P. D. James

Three classics of detective fiction featuring the assiduous Adam Dalgliesh. In *A Shroud for a Nightingale*, *The Black Tower* and *Death of an Expert Witness*, Dalgliesh, with his depth and intelligence, provides the solutions to seemingly unfathomable intrigues.

The Pop Larkin Chronicles H. E. Bates

'Tastes ambrosially of childhood. Never were skies so cornflower blue or beds so swansbottom ... Life not as it is or was, but as it should be' – *Guardian*. 'Pop is as sexy, genial, generous and boozy as ever, Ma is a worthy match for him in these qualities' – *The Times*

The Penguin Book of Modern British Short Stories
Edited by Malcolm Bradbury

This anthology is in many ways a 'best of the best', containing gems from thirty-four of Britain's outstanding contemporary writers. It is a book to dip into, to read from cover to cover, to lend to friends and read again.

Lucia Victrix E. F. Benson

Mapp and Lucia, *Lucia's Progress*, *Trouble for Lucia* – now together in one volume, these three chronicles of English country life will delight a new generation of readers with their wry observation and delicious satire.

READ MORE IN PENGUIN

A SELECTION OF OMNIBUSES

The Penguin Book of Modern Women's Short Stories
Edited by Susan Hill

'They move the reader to give a cry of recognition and understanding time and time again' – Susan Hill in the Introduction. 'These stories are excellent. They are moving, wise, and finely conceived ... a selection of stories that anyone should be pleased to own' – *Glasgow Herald*

Great Law and Order Stories
Edited and Introduced by John Mortimer

Each of these stories conjures suspense with consummate artistry. Together they demonstrate how the greatest mystery stories enthrall not as mere puzzles but as gripping insights into the human condition.

V. I. Warshawski   Sara Paretsky

In *Indemnity Only*, *Deadlock* and *Killing Orders*, Sara Paretsky demonstrates the skill that makes tough female private eye Warshawski one of the most witty, slick and imaginative sleuths on the street today.

A David Lodge Trilogy   David Lodge

His three brilliant comic novels revolving around the University of Rummidge and the eventful lives of its role-swapping academics. Collected here are: *Changing Places*, *Small World* and *Nice Work.*

The Rabbit Novels   John Updike

'One of the finest literary achievements to have come out of the US since the war ... It is in their particularity, in the way they capture the minutiae of the world ... that [the Rabbit] books are most lovable' – *Irish Times*

READ MORE IN PENGUIN

A SELECTION OF OMNIBUSES

Zuckerman Bound Philip Roth

The Zuckerman trilogy – *The Ghost Writer*, *Zuckerman Unbound* and *The Anatomy Lesson* – and the novella-length epilogue, *The Prague Orgy* are here collected in a single volume. Brilliantly diverse and intricately designed, together they form a wholly original and richly comic investigation into the unforeseen consequences of art.

The Collected Stories of Colette Colette

The hundred short stories collected here include such masterpieces as 'Bella-Vista', 'The Tender Shoot' and 'Le Képi', Colette's subtle and ruthless rendering of a woman's belated sexual awakening. 'A perfectionist in her every word' – *Spectator*

Collected Stories Beryl Bainbridge

This volume, which represents the complete short stories of Beryl Bainbridge, also contains the novella, *Filthy Lucre*, written when the author was thirteen. They will delight the many admirers of Beryl Bainbridge's exceptional art.

The Complete Saki

Macabre, acid and very funny, Saki's work drives a knife into the upper crust of English Edwardian life. Here are the effete and dashing heroes, the tea on the lawn, the smell of gunshot, the half-felt menace of disturbing undercurrents ... all in this magnificent omnibus.

The Best of Modern Horror
Edited by Edward L. Ferman and Anne Jordan

Encounter the macabre, the grotesque and the bizarre in this chilling collection of horror stories representing the cream of the infamous *Magazine of Fantasy and Science Fiction*.

READ MORE IN PENGUIN

A SELECTION OF OMNIBUSES

Italian Folktales Italo Calvino

Greeted with overwhelming enthusiasm and praise, Calvino's anthology is already a classic. These tales have been gathered from every region of Italy and retold in Calvino's own inspired and sensuous language. 'A magic book' – *Time*

The Penguin Book of Lesbian Short Stories
Edited by Margaret Reynolds

'Its historical sweep is its joy, a century's worth of polymorphous protagonists, from lady companions and *salonières* to pathological inverts and victims of sexology; from butch-femme stereotypes to nineties bad girls' – *Guardian*

The World of Mrs Harris Paul Gallico

Here, together in one volume, are the complete adventures of Ada Harris, spirited, game-for-anything charlady of Willis Road, Battersea. Carrying with her a magical ability to put things right, a sympathetic twinkle in her eye and an unswerving faith in 'Im Above, Mrs Harris is one of Paul Gallico's most delightful and uplifting creations.

Collected Short Stories Graham Greene

The thirty-seven stories in this immensely entertaining volume reveal Graham Greene in a range of moods: sometimes cynical, flippant and witty, sometimes searching and philosophical. Each one confirms V. S. Pritchett's statement that Greene is 'a master of storytelling'.

The Collected Stories William Trevor

'His prose is various and subtle. His plots adroitly bring whole lives into the view through the keyhole of the story ... He writes about adolescent misfits and unattractive women, about the drab, shaming pain of not being loved ... a masterly short-story writer' – *Sunday Times*